Trap

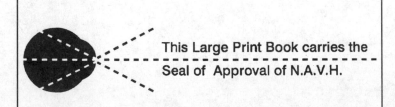

This Large Print Book carries the
Seal of Approval of N.A.V.H.

TRAP

ROBERT K. TANENBAUM

THORNDIKE PRESS

A part of Gale, Cengage Learning

GALE
CENGAGE Learning·

Farmington Hills, Mich • San Francisco • New York • Waterville, Maine
Meriden, Conn • Mason, Ohio • Chicago

GALE
CENGAGE Learning®

LIBRARY OF CONGRESS CATALOGING-IN-PUBLICATION DATA

Tanenbaum, Robert.
  Trap / by Robert K. Tanenbaum. — Large Print edition.
    pages cm. — (Thorndike Press Large Print Thriller)
  ISBN 978-1-4104-8273-0 (hardback) — ISBN 1-4104-8273-1 (hardcover)
  1. Karp, Butch (Fictitious character)—Fiction. 2. Ciampi, Marlene (Fictitious character)—Fiction. 3. Legal stories. 4. Suspense fiction. 5. Large type books.
  I. Title.
PS3570.A52T74 2015b
813'.54—dc23   2015027626

Published in 2015 by arrangement with Gallery Books, an imprint of Simon & Schuster, Inc.

Printed in the United States of America
1 2 3 4 5 6 7 19 18 17 16 15

To those blessings in my life:
Patti, Rachael, Roger, Billy,
and my brother, Bill;
and
To the loving Memory of
Reina Tanenbaum
My sister, truly an angel

ACKNOWLEDGMENTS

To my legendary mentors, District Attorney Frank S. Hogan and Henry Robbins, both of whom were larger in life than in their well-deserved and hard-earned legends, everlasting gratitude and respect; to my special friends and brilliant tutors at the Manhattan DAO, Bob Lehner, Mel Glass, and John Keenan, three of the best who ever served and whose passion for justice was unequaled and uncompromising, my heartfelt appreciation, respect, and gratitude; to Professor Robert Cole and Professor Jesse Choper, who at Boalt Hall challenged, stimulated, and focused the passions of my mind to problem-solve and to do justice; to Steve Jackson, an extraordinarily talented and gifted scrivener whose genius flows throughout the manuscript and whose contribution to it cannot be overstated, a dear friend for whom I have the utmost respect; to Louise Burke, my publisher, whose enthusiastic support, savvy, and encyclopedic smarts qualify her as my first pick in a b-ball game of three-on-three in the Avenue P park in Brooklyn; to Wendy Walker, my talented, highly skilled, and insightful editor, many thanks for all that you do; to Natasha Simons and Sarah Wright, the inimitable twosome whose adult supervision, oversight, brilliant copyediting, and rapid responses are invaluable and profoundly appreciated; to my agents, Mike Hamilburg and Bob Diforio, who in exemplary fashion have always represented my best interests; to Coach Paul Ryan, who personified "American Exceptionalism" and mentored me in its finest virtues; to my esteemed special friend and confidant Richard A. Sprague, who has always challenged, debated, and inspired me in the pursuit of fulfilling the reality of "American Exceptionalism"; and to Rene Herrerias, who believed in me early on and in so doing changed my life, truly a divine intervention.

PROLOGUE

Zak Karp flexed against the ropes that bound his wrists to the arms of the wooden chair. It did no good. He kicked his legs, grunted, and gasped; the veins in his muscular forearms and one in his forehead bulged from the exertion. With a curse he gave up, his breath coming out in white clouds of condensation in the frigid air.

Sitting in the chair next to him with his eyes closed, Zak's twin brother, Giancarlo, let his breath out slowly. "Quit fighting it," he said quietly, and then opened his eyes. "The more you struggle, the tighter the knots get. I think if I can just relax enough, I might be able to slip out of mine. But I can't concentrate with you thrashing around like a fish out of water."

"Well, you better hurry before our 'friend' gets back, oh great Yoda," Zak replied. "I'm too young to die . . . I've never even been past third base with a girl or pitched for the

Yankees. And, I was about to become bar mitzvah with every obnoxious, pimple-faced thirteen-year-old Jewish kid on the Upper East Side."

Giancarlo couldn't help chuckling at his twin's dark humor despite their predicament. But then he frowned. "I thought you gave up on that," he said. "You didn't want to identify as being a Jew anymore."

As Giancarlo spoke he studied his "older" brother's handsome face with its strong Italian features and coloring of their mother, Marlene Ciampi. He knew there was some bruising on the other side of his face from blows he'd received from their abductor, but Zak was a tough guy and not about to acknowledge that it hurt. He was Giancarlo's elder only by a few minutes but all of their lives he'd been first in many ways. Bigger, stronger, faster — the better, more natural athlete. He'd also been born with the fiery temperament of the Mediterranean side of their family, which sometimes worked to his advantage — such as making quick decisions and following through without hesitation — but had also landed them in hot water on occasion. *Such as now,* Giancarlo thought.

Giancarlo had the more delicate visage — still leaning more toward their mother's

10

Sicilian ancestry than their father's Slavic roots, but more refined and paler than his brother. Although an average, if determined, athlete, he also played a half-dozen instruments from the violin to the accordion, and schoolwork came easily for him. Zak was no slouch when it came to brains, even if he sometimes acted before thinking, but Giancarlo was decidedly the more cerebral, and cautious, of the two.

"Yeah, well, maybe this Nazi son of a bitch changed my mind for me," Zak retorted, and then twisted violently against the restraints for what little good it did. He bellowed with helplessness.

They both knew that no one would hear him. The old tenement building was as solid as the Manhattan bedrock on which it stood. Rust-colored brick walls, thick subflooring, and massive beams that comprised the loft seemed to absorb sound into the shadows. They could hear the outside world through the missing panes of glass in some of the windows. But other than the loud clomping of their heavy-booted captor's comings and goings, they'd not heard any other sounds of habitation from the floors below them.

The loft itself appeared to be in the midst of a renovation project that had ground to a halt. Several sawhorses and odd bits of lumber and drywall, as well as the bench, were scattered around the largely empty open space. But no workmen had been by in the two days since their abduction, and the teens had surmised that they were sitting in the detritus of yet another New York City developer who'd run out of money in mid-construction.

The building itself was near the East River, and they could clearly hear the frequent sounds of water traffic, especially the clarion whistles of the tugboats, which seemed to be both plentiful and close by. Most of the windows in the loft were boarded up or covered with sheets, but by craning their necks, they could see through two large picture windows behind them that weren't covered. Across a short distance they observed another former tenement that had been converted to condominiums with lots of windows and a new façade partly covering the old bricks.

"I hope that's because you've had a change of heart about what it means to be a Jew, not because you're afraid of what might happen," Giancarlo said. "Because if that's the case, you'd be better off committing to Mom's Catholic side of the family. That way you can ask for forgiveness and *poof* when

12

you die you go straight to paradise. Judaism's a little nebulous on whether there's any such thing as heaven."

"Up yours," Zak retorted. "I'm serious. This guy's an example of what Jews have always had to put up with. If I have to die, like Mrs. Lubinsky said, I'll choose to do it as a Jew; I'm just saying I'd like to get through my bar mitzvah first."

Giancarlo bit off the sarcastic remark he was going to make and nodded. "Sorry I doubted you."

"Yeah, it's okay," Zak replied. "I would have doubted me, too. But enough of all this talk about dying; I'm not ready. So start meditating or whatever it is you do and make like Houdini and escape before the Storm Trooper gets back."

Giancarlo's response was interrupted by a moan from their right. They looked over to where an old woman lay on a filthy mattress that had been placed on the floor.

"I don't think Goldie's doing so good," Zak observed. "She hasn't opened her eyes since we got here."

Giancarlo shook his head, then suddenly shrieked.

"Jesus! What's the matter with you?" Zak demanded in anger and alarm.

"A rat! A rat just crawled up on my

shoulder!"

"Where is it now?"

"I don't know; it jumped down when I shouted!"

"You mean when you screamed like a twelve-year-old girl at a Justin Bieber concert. I thought it was something serious."

"I don't like rats."

"You and our pal," Zak said. "You see the way he freaks when he sees a rat? Anyway, it's gone now so go back to being calm and get us out of here."

Giancarlo had just closed his eyes again when they heard someone stomping up the stairs and knew that their abductor had returned. The door opened, revealing a tall young man in his midtwenties with a shaved, bullet-shaped head and the sculpted body of a weight lifter. His thin lips turned down in a perpetual frown, and his dark eyes had a feral intelligence to them. But his notable features were the "Sieg Heil" that had been tattooed in black letters two-inches high across his forehead, and the swastikas inked onto the temples on either side of his head.

The young man trudged into the room and stopped next to the workbench. "Looks like the old Jew bitch isn't long for this world anyway, *ja mein kleiner Juden*?"

14

"Give me a break with the lousy German," Zak scoffed. "You're just a muscle freak from Brooklyn, and you sound like a bad Arnold Schwarzenegger movie."

The young man's face flushed dark red as he stormed over to where the twins sat. "Great, now you've done it again," Giancarlo said dryly. This wasn't the first time his brother had antagonized their abductor, hence the bruising.

However, just as the young man raised his hand to hit him, Zak yelled, "Hey creep, you see the rat?"

The young man stopped in his tracks and his eyes grew round with fear. He whirled in the direction Zak was nodding. In the shadows over by the wall, a large gray rat sat on its haunches watching them. Looking around wildly, the young man picked up a piece of wood from the floor and flung it at the rodent. The rat easily dodged the missile and scampered back through a hole in the wall of one corner of the room.

Turning back toward the twins, the young man sneered. "I'm not afraid of a fucking rat."

"Yeah, sure you're not. That's why you're shaking like a leaf."

This time the young man backhanded Zak across his face. The teen absorbed the blow without a sound, except to spit blood out from his now-split lips. He glared up at his assailant. "You'll regret that."

The young man raised his hand again but hesitated when their eyes met. He quavered ever so slightly and lowered his hand. "We'll see who has regrets here in a minute when you're begging for your life," he laughed. He held up a cell phone as he typed in a number. There was a pause as he listened to the line ringing.

"You there, Karp?" he snarled. "I'm putting you on speakerphone."

"I'm here," a voice replied. "Let the boys and the woman go; they had nothing to do with what happened to your mother."

The young man laughed derisively. He picked a gun up off of the table, an older model Luger, and walked toward the twins. "Are you listening, Karp?" he shouted. "I want you to hear me shoot your sons."

"They didn't do anything to you," Karp replied evenly.

"No, but you did," the young man repeated. "My mom's dead because I wasn't there to save her. And you know why, Karp? Because you and your nigger cop had me locked up."

"You were arrested for refusing a lawful command."

16

"I was arrested because I'm white, and I was exercising my right to free speech," the young man retorted. "And then you kept me in jail because you think I planted that bomb."

"I was asking you questions," Karp said. "That's my job. Look, I know you didn't plant that bomb."

"You're lying; all Jews lie," the young man yelled into the phone. "You're trying to trick me. Besides, it is too late and you and I both know it. But you made me do it, Karp. I told you my mom needed me, but you wouldn't listen. Instead, you decided I was guilty and went after my mom."

"What do you mean?"

"I mean you fucking burned my mom's apartment while I was in jail!"

"That's not true. She was smoking in bed and her cigarette started a fire."

The young man's face contorted in rage. "More lies! I'm not listening to any more lies. So I'm going to give you a choice, Karp, which kid gets it first?"

"Please, as a father I'm asking you not to do this . . ."

"Dad?" Giancarlo said.

"It's okay. It's going to be okay."

"See, you'll even lie to your kids," the young man said. "It's not going to be okay.

17

But I am going to give you a choice, Karp, which one do I shoot first?"

"Me, shoot me." The old woman's voice surprised them all. Goldie Sobelman was standing unsteadily on her feet, her hands bound at the wrist in front of her. "I'm old. Shoot me if you must kill someone for your mother."

The young man pointed the gun at her.

"No, me," Giancarlo said. "I'm not afraid of you, you Nazi son of a bitch."

The young man's eyes blazed with rage as he swung the gun back toward Giancarlo. "Well, you should be," he snarled.

"Hey, asshole!" Zak yelled.

"WHAT?" the young man shouted back.

"Catch."

1

Brooklyn, weeks earlier

The large man in the Brooks Brothers suit sitting in the back of the bar on Jay Street in Brooklyn nudged the nicely dressed younger man next to him. "There's the bitch now." He then rose from his seat and lifted his hand as the slightly stooped, elderly, gray-haired woman bundled against the cold in a long wool coat walked in the door.

She spotted him and grimaced as if she'd just smelled something rotten before she noticed the young man. A look of pain and sorrow crossed her face, but when he couldn't look her in the eyes, she took a deep breath and let it out with the shake of her head. Her mouth was set in a firm, hard line as she navigated through the other patrons to their table.

When she arrived, the older of the two men stuck out his hand, but she ignored it and turned toward his younger companion. "I can't say I approve of the company you keep these days, Micah, but it is nice to see you," she said as she sat down.

"It's good to see you, too, Rose," Micah Gallo replied quietly.

A waitress strolled over and Rose Lubinsky asked for a glass of water. Shrugging, the older man tapped the rim of his highball glass to indicate that he wanted another Old Forester bourbon. Pricey stuff, but the president of the largest teachers union in New York State, with his quarter-of-a-million-dollar salary and under-the-table perks, could afford it.

Despite his expensive tastes in clothes, cars, women, and bourbon, Thomas "Tommy" Monroe came from the old Irish-Italian neighborhood of Bensonhurst, the son of a schoolteacher mom and a truck-driving father. A big guy, he'd played football for a second-tier college team until he got kicked off the squad for fighting with his teammates and coaches, and then walking out on an "anger management" class he'd been ordered to attend if he wanted to stay. Following an "incident" in which he'd been accused of raping a coed at a fraternity party, he'd then been invited to leave the college altogether and had to finish his degree and get his teacher's certificate at a small liberal arts college in New Jersey that didn't care about his character as long as he paid his tuition.

After graduation, he took a job as a PE teacher and wrestling coach at Public School 238 in Brooklyn but found his true calling working for the Greater New York Teachers Federation. Like all other public school teachers, he'd had to sign up with the union when he first got hired — there was no choice in the matter and dues were automatically taken out of his paycheck. But as the son of a teamster and a proud member of the teachers union, he'd been fine with it and soon found out that his penchant for cracking heads and kicking asses on behalf of the GNYTF was useful to the hierarchy. He could turn on the macho charm when necessary, but it was his ruthlessness and street smarts that helped him climb the union power ladder and eventually got him elected president.

That had been twenty years ago and now in his early sixties, the former athlete had gone to seed. His ruddy Irish face and red nose belied his affection for booze and the good life, as did the beer belly that hung over the top of his expensive, tailored pants. And he'd long since lost his sense of duty to union members, except as pawns to manipulate in order to stay in power and fund his lifestyle.

"Whatever works" was his motto when dealing with opponents, both those inside the union — including reform-minded individuals — and those on the outside. One of the most tenacious of the latter, and the reason for this meeting with Rose Lubinsky, were the proponents of charter schools. The charter school movement in New York got its start in 1998, and after being held in check — mainly due to union lobbying — for ten years, had been expanding ever since thanks in large part to Lubinsky, the president of the New York Charter Schools Association and the heart and soul of the movement. Limited to a hundred schools in that first decade, there were four times that number now and a serious threat to the union and thus to Monroe.

The reasons were simple. First of all, the charter schools, although public and taxpayer-funded, were nonunion. This diluted the power of the traditional large teachers unions like the GNYTF to control education in New York State. And every one of those nonunion teachers represented a loss in union dues. Fewer bucks meant losing political clout by curtailing lobbying, or outright buying of, politicians and the leaders of the union-funded, anti-charter parent groups. It also meant less money for the union president's salary and bonuses, as well as the hidden slush fund available for his "expenses."

For the first time in years, Monroe felt his position as union president was being threatened by increasingly unhappy members. Every student sitting in a charter schoolroom instead of the union-dominated public school rolls meant less money from the state and federal governments which based their financial support on enrollment. Losing funding affected raises and bonuses for union teachers, too. However, the members' dissatisfaction was as much about working conditions as it was money. Public school classes were overcrowded, filled with indifferent and even hostile students, and lacked any support from most of the parents.

Charter schools were a different story with a combination of better or equal pay, safer working conditions, students who wanted to learn, and administrations that by and large saw themselves as partners with their faculty. The best teachers, as well as the more dedicated students, were leaving the public schools as fast as they could find an opening with a charter school. Only the limited number of positions available kept the desertions from becoming an all-out stampede.

Meanwhile, union members were openly questioning if Monroe was losing his grip. Meetings were becoming increasingly contentious, and his spies reported teachers grumbling about his ostentatious lifestyle; his reform-minded union opponents were gaining ground.

Since the beginning, Monroe had fought the charter school movement tooth and nail. Fear had been a major tactic, telling teachers that charter schools were a threat to the union, and without the union to protect them, all the benefits like pensions, health coverage, and wages they'd won over the years would be lost. Using a public relations firm, and aided by a compliant media, he mislabeled charter schools "elitist," especially in black and Hispanic neighborhoods, claiming that they were a conservative white man's conspiracy to remove the best and brightest from the " 'hood" and leave everyone else to suffer. It didn't matter to his public relations spiel that charter school enrollment was predominantly from minority neighborhoods. "Divide and conquer" was the purpose behind "racist" charter schools, he claimed, and that played well with his core constituency.

If words and fear didn't work, he fell back on payoffs and intimidation, including physical attacks and character assassination. A few years earlier, he'd employed such against one particularly difficult opponent, the man now sitting next to him, Micah Gallo, at the time a young, energetic Hispanic who had started the first charter school in Brooklyn for low-income, disadvantaged children.

Gallo had grown up in that neighborhood, had even been the leader of a gang. But he survived the public schools and after graduating from a teachers college had quickly signed on with Lubinsky and the charter school association, which helped him launch the Bedford-Stuyvesant Charter School. The school had been a resounding success. Although its teachers were initially paid less than union teachers in the public schools, their working conditions were far superior, even though they'd had to share space with a public school, and soon the students' test scores outstripped their public school counterparts by large margins.

Monroe felt the tide turning against him and the union when *The New York Times* published a big feature story on Gallo and his school, comparing it favorably to the public schools in the five boroughs. When the story came out, and then was picked up by local television stations, Monroe took a lot of heat from union teachers and parents. It had made them look bad, they said, and they wanted to know why he'd been unable to counter. This time they weren't so accepting of his promises to quash the charter school movement, and his attempts to get his pals in the media to back him met with shrugs and noncommittal responses.

Monroe decided that it was time to eliminate the competition and started by trying to buy Gallo. He offered him the position of assistant superintendent of the Greater New York school system at a salary many times what he made at the charter school with broad hints of there being more where that came from. The young man turned him down and threatened to go to the press if he tried to bribe him again.

So he reverted to his more base nature. He arranged for die-hard union supporters to try to intimidate Gallo by lurking outside the school and following him home. They punctured his tires and scratched the paint on his car. When that didn't work, a "specialist" was called in; in the dead of night, Gallo's car was firebombed.

Instead of chasing Gallo off, however, the bombing backfired. Charter school parents started escorting him to and from work and watched his neighborhood. An even more in-depth article appeared in a weekly alternative newspaper, *The West Village Spectator,* written by investigative journalist Ariadne Stupenagel. The article and citizen complaints put the pressure on the police to step up patrols and get serious about trying to catch his antagonists. Even Monroe's ties to the police union reps did him no good; in fact, he was warned that if something bad happened to Gallo all bets were off.

Gallo weathered the storm, though not without damage. Monroe's spies reported that he didn't appear to be sleeping well and dark circles had appeared below his eyes. "He seems tense, like another good shove and he might break," one said. But he refused to give in, and Monroe looked for the proverbial last straw. Alas, Olivia Stone, his longtime partner in crime, provided it.

Stone, the former attorney for the teachers union, had high aspirations. With the financial and "get the vote out" backing of the union, Stone had campaigned for and been elected district attorney of Kings County, which encompassed all of the two million–plus residents of Brooklyn. She was unqualified for the job, having spent a few years in the Legal Aid Society Office before following the money to the teachers union. However, the incumbent district attorney's campaign had been torpedoed by scandal — an alleged affair with a stripper from the Brighton Beach section of Brooklyn — two weeks before the election. Of course, Monroe's political operatives created and disseminated the faux rumored affair. By the time the incumbent had dispelled the false allegations, the smear tactic had worked; he was out of office and Stone was in.

It was real handy to have the DA of Kings County to help deal with problems, such as Micah Gallo. They'd concocted a plan to finish the job that Monroe had started. When one of Monroe's spies told him that Gallo sometimes took his school laptop computer home with him, they knew they had what they needed.

Gallo's school was actually located in a portion of one of Brooklyn's shuttered public high schools. As charter schools were still tax-supported and the equipment inside the schools was owned by the public, techni- cally, taking the laptop to his residence — even if for work purposes — was illegally removing school property.

A cooperative police detective took an anonymous complaint from a "concerned source" that school equipment had been disappearing and that Gallo was suspected of selling it off and lining his own pockets with the proceeds. Stone secured a search warrant from a union-supported judge and the police raided Gallo's home where not only was the "stolen school property" laptop located but also several other pieces of equipment.

Of course, it was all a big setup. Teachers and administrators routinely took work-related material and equipment home. The additional "public school equipment" was planted. Gallo was arrested.

This time Monroe's lackeys in the press were only too happy to jump all over the story. The former gangbanger-turned-heroic-educator's fall from grace was just too good a scandal. A little bird had even tipped off a photographer for the *New York Post* so that there was a perp photo on page three of Gallo being led from his home in handcuffs.

Monroe at first declined to comment on "the unfortunate situation." But when pressed for a quote, he "reluctantly" acknowledged that "the lack of oversight and supervision" at charter schools was one

of the "major drawbacks. They sort of operate under their own rules even with taxpayer
money."

Gallo still had his supporters in the media,
including Stupenagel, who wrote a scathing
piece about the "politically motivated attack
on charter schools by drumming up a
ridiculous charge against one of the charter
schools movement's bright young stars."
The reporter noted the connection between
Monroe and Stone and accused the two of
"colluding in order to preserve the union's
power and influence."

Monroe denied any involvement in Gallo's
troubles. However, Stone shot back at the
critics in media interviews by noting "we
don't make the laws; we are charged with
enforcing them and prosecuting those who
break them. We believe, and the grand jury
agreed, that there is sufficient evidence
indicating that Mr. Gallo broke the law,
stole equipment owned by the taxpayers,
and needs to answer for that. However, we
will try this case in court, not the media."

Gallo had his other supporters, too, chief
among them Rose Lubinsky. She had taken
the fight to the media, some of which
questioned the motives behind Stone's
prosecution of Gallo. The district attorney
took a lot of heat, but she didn't cave. She

knew the power and money she craved relied on the support from the teachers union. Stone and Monroe were determined to create a chilling effect on other charter supporters by prosecuting and breaking Gallo.

Besides, Monroe thought, *if Stone backed off, Gallo would have become the darling of the media and Stone would have taken a major political hit.* By sticking to her "we don't make the laws" mantra and going forward with the charges against Gallo she could attack the charter school system and argue that she had no choice but to follow up on the case presented to her by the police.

Unfortunately for Gallo, neither he nor the charter system was insured for this sort of legal battle. Determined to save his freedom and reputation against the false charges, he spent his life savings and mortgaged his home. The school was forced to close.

Told that Gallo was desperate, Monroe arranged a meeting. He told the young man that not only could he make the charges go away, but "I like your spunk, kid" and that he would hire him as his personal aide. It was a lifeline thrown by the devil, but Gallo grabbed it.

In the few years since, Gallo had sealed the deal by becoming the union's chief anti-charter school advocate. Of course, he knew where the warts were in the charter system and how best to attack the public's perception of its schools. He'd become such a vocal opponent of "elitist, racist" charter schools that Monroe sometimes wondered if the young man truly believed what he was saying.

Broken psychologically, financially, and physically, Gallo had taken to the hefty union salary and "perks" like a newborn to his mother's breast. The young man with the cool car, tailored suits, and a 3,000-square-foot condo in Brooklyn Heights looking out over the East River at the Manhattan skyline seemed a different character altogether from the fiery crusader for education reform and charter schools.

However, Monroe's strategic conversion of Gallo had not destroyed the charter school movement. Indeed, those in the association had circled the wagons and then led by Rose Lubinsky had become even more cohesive and determined. Also a leader in the New York City Jewish community, Lubinsky was beyond reproach and there was not going to be any going after her on trumped-up charges. Not in Manhattan where New York County DA Roger "Butch" Karp was impervious to outside pressure.

Lubinsky rightfully blamed Monroe and Stone for her protégé's downfall. A brilliant strategist, she had built her political, financial, and academic bona fides upon the charter schools' quantified academic success. Their statewide reading and math test scores embarrassingly overwhelmed its failing public school counterparts. Her efforts were about to finally culminate in a bill currently before the New York legislature that would not only increase state funding for charter schools but also increase its numbers, as well as implement a voucher system allowing school parents to place their children in success-driven schools and avoid dangerous and underperforming public schools.

Under Monroe's direction, the union and its backers had attacked the proposed legislation, throwing money at politicians, advertising agencies, and "pay-as-you-go" protesters who assembled outside Albany's capitol building to wave their signs and shout slogans that Monroe's hired public relations firm dreamed up. However, his lobbyists had just that morning told him that public sentiment in favor of charter schools and vouchers was running at such a high level that even the greediest of Albany's corrupt public servants were running scared.

Demonstrators in favor of the charter school legislation were petitioning Albany's legislators in overwhelming numbers. Already, there were in excess of fifty thousand students on charter school waiting lists. Guided by Lubinsky, the New York Charter Schools Association had launched an adroit advertising campaign that was long on the facts reflecting academic achievement and devoid of contentious mudslinging. Several of the charter school ads struck a note of conciliation in an effort to appeal to the reform-minded members of the union as "partners in our children's education." And that alone, according to Monroe's political advisers, was enough to cause a seismic shift beneath the power-structure of the union and his position in it.

Something had to be done and that was why Rose Lubinsky was sitting across from him at the Jay Street Bar and why he'd brought Gallo along hoping that the young man might appeal to her emotionally. But in body language and tone she obviously didn't want to be there.

"Need another beer, Micah?" he asked.

"No, I'm good, thanks," Gallo replied, still not looking at his former mentor.

"Suit yourself," Monroe said before turning his attention back to Lubinsky. "I hear congratulations are in order . . . you have a book coming out about your life?"

"That's right, but I'm not here to socialize, Monroe," Lubinsky said, her voice hard and clipped, which brought out the slight accent of her native Poland.

Monroe smiled though he personally loathed and feared the woman. He spread his hands. "I was hoping we might reach an accommodation on the assembly bill," he said.

"The New York Charter School Fairness in Education Act you mean," Lubinsky said without humor.

"Yeah, that one."

"Accommodation," Lubinsky snorted derisively. "You mean you're going down in flames and trying to save your bacon."

Monroe's smile disappeared. "It's going to be a hard fight either way, and in the meantime a lot of money is being tossed around that would be better off spent on students and teachers' salaries."

This time, Lubinsky laughed so hard that tears sprang to her eyes. "Tommy Monroe, that's a rich one," she said when she was

35

able to pull herself together. "As if that has ever been your priority." She leaned across the table and glared. "Public schools in the five boroughs are all but war zones, Monroe. Even metal detectors don't deter the violence and threats. Teachers and students who want an education are caught in the crossfire, and what have you done about it, except line your pockets with union dues."

Lubinsky glanced over at Gallo, who blinked twice and looked away. "When I started as a schoolteacher," she continued, "I was all for the union. Someone needed to stand up for better wages and working conditions. We needed tenure to make sure the politicos weren't firing teachers or censoring those who didn't agree with them. But somewhere along the line, the union lost its way. Guys like you took over and created your own little fiefdoms and dropped the ball for the students and the good teachers. Now you can't get rid of bad teachers, not without a lot of money and time; even if you can get them out of the classroom, they're put into your 'rubber rooms,' where they hang out on the computer and run their own businesses or chat on Facebook, all on the taxpayer's dime. But just for another good laugh, tell

me about this 'accommodation' you're of-
fering."

All semblance of friendliness left Monroe's
face. He sat back in his chair and drained
the remaining bourbon left in his glass. He
then waved for the waitress to bring him
another shot.

"You get the bill withdrawn," he said, "and
we both announce a joint committee to
study how the public school system and
charter schools can work together toward a
mutual goal of providing a good education
to all children. We meet and hammer out a
compromise we can all live with, and next
year, the union won't oppose the legislation; hell, we might even cosponsor it with
you. It would be a win-win all the way
around, isn't that right, Micah."

At the mention of his name, Gallo picked
up his head and looked Lubinsky in the eyes
for the first time. "Everybody can't go to
charter schools, Rose," he said quietly. "If
this bill goes through, it will hurt all those
kids who attend public schools."

Looking at her former protégé Lubinsky
shook her head. "So keep the status quo,
Micah? The system you had to fight and
claw your way out of?" She tilted her head
and smiled tightly. "So that fat cats like this
man you've allied yourself with can live the

37

good life while public schools swirl down the drain, taking all those kids with them? We offer a chance for the kids to capture the dream and, yes, hope, Micah, and the possibility of change. I can't believe I'm hearing this from you of all people."

Lubinsky turned back to Monroe. "Perhaps if you'd suggested this compromise years ago instead of protecting your little fiefdom, and ruining lives and careers along the way, I might have trusted you," she said. "Even now I'd possibly consider it for the sake of the children if I had any reason to believe that you'd honor your word. But I don't. You're a bully and as far as I'm concerned a criminal; now you're just trying to stall this legislation and hope it goes away. You've failed the kids, you've failed their parents, and you've failed the teachers. I don't want anything to do with you and your accommodations."

Monroe scowled, then leaned forward and spoke in a low voice. "I don't like you and you don't like me, but I'm sure we can still work this out. And I'm sure I can find a way to sweeten the pot; we'll call it a . . ."

"A bribe, Monroe?" Lubinsky finished the sentence. "I expected as much. It's why there's a section in the bill calling for an independent audit of the Greater New York

School District and the union. We'd like to know where all of that money has been going before we start a new budget process, and that probably concerns you more than anything, doesn't it?"

The waitress arrived with the bourbon, and Monroe downed half of it in a single gulp before slamming the glass back down on the table. "I got nothing to hide," he snarled, then pointed a finger at her face. "But you're fucking with the wrong guy."

Lubinsky's mouth twisted. "It didn't take long for the wolf to drop the sheepskin disguise," she said, then sighed. "But I could not give in to your bribes or your threats, Monroe. The guilt I would feel abandoning all those children to the sort of education you and your ilk provide would be too much." She paused to look at Gallo. "I learned a long time ago that guilt is a cancer that eats at your soul."

Monroe started to say something back but Lubinsky held up her hand as she stood. "Don't bother; this conversation's over." She smiled at Gallo. "Micah, you will always be welcome to return to us, but I think you need to look inside yourself before it is too late." With that she turned and walked away without looking back.

Watching her go, Monroe's face turned

beet red with anger. He finished the rest of his drink and waved at the waitress for yet another. He glanced at Micah, who sat staring at his beer. "Don't let her bother you, kid," he said. "Fucking Jews are always acting like they are above it all. It's nice when you get to pick and choose students for their precious little elitist schools, but what about the other million kids?"

Gallo nodded but didn't say anything. Monroe scowled and picked his cell phone off the table and punched in a speed dial number.

"She's not going for it," he said into the receiver. He listened for a moment and turned slightly away from Gallo. "Goddamn it. We can't risk this bill passing." He listened some more. "Yeah, well, both of our asses will be on the line if they ever start looking at the books."

2

Karp smiled when a knock on the door of his office and the subsequent opening of it revealed the large, muscular frame of Detective Clay Fulton. "Good afternoon, Clay, what brings you to my inner sanctum?" he asked.

Fulton, the head of the squad of New York Police Department detectives assigned to assist the district attorney of New York County with investigations, didn't return the smile. "Hey Butch. Got a minute?"

"Yeah, sure," Karp replied. "I was about to head out of here to meet up with the boys. A friend is giving a talk at the Third Avenue synagogue this evening that we wanted to catch, but I got time. What's up?"

He and Fulton had known each other since Karp was a wet-behind-the-ears assistant district attorney working for the legendary New York DA Francis Garrahy and Fulton was a rookie cop. In a sense,

they'd grown up in the system together —
by-the-book prosecutor and hard-nosed
detective — and when Karp won the election as district attorney years after Garrahy's death and two successors' tenure, one
of his first acts was to ask his friend to run
the elite DAO detective squad. There was
not a more honest or dedicated crime
fighter in Gotham than the former college
football All-American. Karp could tell by
the look on his face that this was not a social
call.

"We got another one," Fulton said as he
walked across the wood-paneled office and
placed a copy of the evening *New York Post*
on Karp's desk. "Seen this?"

Screaming off the top of the front page in
the paper's typical tabloid style was the
headline: Skinheads Rampage in Central
Park! A triple-stacked, sub-headline followed beneath with: Elderly Jewish Couple
Hospitalized. 7th Hate Crime This Winter.
Cops Apparently Clueless.

Karp felt the old competitive zeal that
tended to well up inside of him when evil
reared its ugly head in his jurisdiction. The
investigation into the surge in hate crimes
by young neo-Nazi skinheads and the apprehension of the perpetrators was the
responsibility of the New York Police

Department. But it would be his office that would prosecute them when they were caught, and he intended — if the evidence indicated — to demonstrate in court that these were not isolated incidents, but part of a larger, organized conspiracy.

He'd asked Fulton to track the cases and keep him apprised. So far the thugs had set fire to a synagogue, badly burning a rabbi who tried to put the fire out; assaulted Jews; and several months earlier in November gone on a rampage in the predominantly Jewish Diamond District, shattering windows before moving on to other Jewish-owned businesses they'd identified in different parts of the city. They'd chosen the date carefully, as it fell on the anniversary of Kristallnacht, or Night of Broken Glass, when in November 1938 paramilitary forces and non-Jewish civilians in Nazi Germany and Austria ransacked Jewish-owned stores and synagogues. Shards of glass from the smashed windows had littered the streets, giving rise to the name. As German authorities looked on, without attempting to stop it, hundreds of Jews died, thousands more were severely injured, and more than thirty thousand were arrested and sent to death camps, never to be heard from again.

Seventy-plus years later, the neo-Nazis in

New York had accomplished their mission, and most had faded back into the shadows from whence they came. There'd been a few arrests, but the suspects had sullenly refused to talk, and the evidence against them had mostly resulted in a few misdemeanor assault and destruction of private property charges.

The New York version of Kristallnacht had struck a particularly troubling note with Karp. Several years earlier, his twin sons had come to him and their mother, Marlene Ciampi, and announced that they had decided to pursue going through with the bar mitzvah. As Marlene had been raised in a strict Roman-Catholic family, but hadn't brought up the boys as such, and Karp was Jewish more by spiritual and moral adherence than obeisance to strict religious practices, the decision surprised them. Their daughter, Lucy, was a decidedly devout Catholic and, in fact, claimed to speak to and receive guidance from a martyred saint from the sixteenth century. But the twins had never shown any religious inclinations.

Although initially Karp had wondered how long the quest would last, he'd been pleased that the boys had stuck to it even though the road to their bar mitzvah had been more challenging than most. He'd even agreed to teach classes dealing with Old Testament morality tales at the synagogue when asked by the rabbi, and enjoyed both the challenge of reaching out to young minds and the extra time with his sons. But of late Zak had been wavering on his commitment to go through with the ceremony, and Karp wondered if the neo-Nazi rampages and the media aftermath had anything to do with that.

The New York Kristallnacht had another personal impact on Karp. His friends, Moishe and Goldie Sobelman, owned Il Buon Pane, a small bakery on the corner of Third Avenue and 29th Street, that the thugs had targeted. The Sobelmans were both survivors of the Nazi death camps, and Karp rushed right over when he heard they had been victimized again. He found Moishe outside on the sidewalk, sweeping up the glass from the shattered windows of his shop.

"Moishe, I'm so sorry," Karp had said, hugging his friend.

The old man had smiled and patted him on the back. "At least neither of us were hurt," he had replied, then sighed and stood quietly for a moment, leaning on his broom and looking at the pile of glass in front of him. "The more things change, the more

45

they stay the same, eh, my friend?"

Not knowing quite what to say, Karp had remained silent with his hand on Sobelman's shoulder. Then the baker looked up at him, his eyes wet with tears. "Stop them, Butch," he had said quietly. "Stop them before this goes any further. It started like this all those years ago, and before it was over millions of people were dead."

Karp had promised that he would do everything in his power to bring the perpetrators to justice. But looking at the newspaper headline now in his office, the words seemed hollow.

"It's only a matter of time before someone gets killed," Fulton stated aloud.

"Any suspects?" Karp asked.

"The usual head cases, that's it."

Karp knew what he meant by that. The "usual head cases" were getting bold, at least when they weren't breaking the law, and holding demonstrations in various city parks and outside the Museum of Jewish Heritage, otherwise known as the New York City Holocaust Museum, in Battery Park, as well as on the sidewalks next to the Israeli consulate. They were loud, aggressive, and offensive but other than the usual misdemeanor assaults, failures to follow lawful orders from police officers to allow

46

people to walk past them, and lack of permits for their demonstrations, they avoided committing any felonies. They'd also grown more sophisticated than in years past, using the publicity to get their message into the media and draw other misguided citizens to their cause.

Karp thought about it for a moment, then rapped his knuckles on the newspaper. "Stay on it, Clay," he said as he stood up. "Sooner or later, they'll make a mistake and we'll go after them."

He walked around the desk as the detective rose to meet him. Fulton was stockier, with broader shoulders, but Karp, a former star college basketball player, was half a head taller at six-foot-five. "I've got to run, the car's waiting for me. Let me know if anything breaks."

Fulton left the way he came in, but Karp went through a side door of his office to a small anteroom where he took a private elevator reserved for the district attorney and judges down to the Leonard Street side entrance of the Criminal Courts Building. The massive, squat edifice at 100 Centre Street housed the criminal courts — notably the Supreme Courts where felonies were tried — the judges' robing rooms and chambers, criminal court records, grand jury

47

rooms, and the offices of the New York County district attorney. At its northern end it was connected by an enclosed walkway, the "Bridge of Sighs," to the Manhattan Detention Complex, popularly referred to as The Tombs.

The Criminal Courts Building had been Karp's "home away from home." Waiting for him now outside its doors was a large, dark bulletproof sedan driven by police officer Eddie Ewin.

"Where to, Mr. Karp?" the young officer asked when he got in.

"The Third Avenue synagogue off 67th Street."

The winter light was already starting to fade, the street lights illuminating the snow that had been falling all day, when the car pulled to the curb in front of the synagogue. Karp saw Isaac and Giancarlo standing on the snow-covered steps leading into the building with Goldie and Moishe Sobelman. Zak stood with his head down while Giancarlo and Moishe appeared to be talking to him. Goldie was at Zak's side with her hand on his shoulder.

He took a moment to study his boys. They'd grown up so fast, and it was hard to believe that the tiny twin babies he'd held were now young men, and it wouldn't be long before they'd be out of the house.

When Zak and Giancarlo began their quest, they were already a little older than the traditional age of thirteen when most Jewish boys go through the bar mitzvah, the rite of passage from the innocence of youth to the responsibilities of manhood. Then the process had taken even longer due to a life that didn't follow the normal pattern of two young men growing up in America. As the district attorney of New York, Karp was a magnet for sociopaths, terrorists, and other violent criminals of all makes and models. Marlene, who'd once headed the Sex Crimes Bureau at the DAO as an assistant DA, had left the office to become a private investigator/attorney now specializing in advocating for and protecting women from miscreant abusers, also attracted the dark side at an unusual rate. Their children had not been immune to the dangers inherent in their parents' careers, and in fact had been under siege from dangerous felons and maniacs most of their lives, disrupting normal childhood and youth pursuits. As such, the road to Jewish manhood had been a long one, but at last the boys were in the final stages of their studies needed to achieve their goal.

However, Zak was having misgivings. In

fact, just the previous evening, he and his father had a conversation in which the boy said he didn't see the point of going through with a ceremony marking his entry to manhood at seventeen years old when he'd already confronted more adult world issues than most people dealt with in a lifetime.

"I'm not trying to talk you into anything, Zak," Karp responded. "But I'm sure you know that the bar mitzvah is more than just a symbolic 'rite of passage.' "

"I know, I know," Zak said with a sigh. "It also means I'm now accountable for my actions. But haven't I been accountable enough? I mean, how many other kids have been kidnapped, shot at, bombed, and chased like me and Giancarlo? And now with these neo-Nazi jerks running around, maybe I'm tired of having a target on my back."

Zak said it lightly, but the truth of it went right to Karp's heart. "I'm not going to argue with you about that," he'd agreed. "You, your brother, sister, and mom have all had to take on more of this world's dark aspects than you should have. I was just pointing out that going through with your bar mitzvah is saying more than one day you're a boy and the next you're a man."

"I get it," Zak replied. He was quiet for a

moment and then looked sideways at his father. "Will you be disappointed with me if I don't go through with it?"

Karp put his arm around the shoulders of his son. "Zak, I've been proud of you from the moment I laid my eyes on you," he said. "And I'm even prouder of you now. I understand you're dealing with an internal dilemma, and I can respect that. This decision is yours and yours alone to make, and whatever you decide I will think just as highly of you."

"Thanks, Dad," Zak said with a smile but then frowned again. "Even if I wanted to go through with it, I still don't know what I'm going to do. It's not just the whole idea of whether I'm done with the whole 'becoming a man thing.' You know that Rabbi Hamilburg is asking everyone to come up with something special for the ceremony. Some of the younger guys are putting on a skit, or doing a research paper on Jewish history that they have to present to the parents. And my genius bro, Giancarlo, is outdoing everybody by singing that dumb song; I don't have anything compared to that."

Karp laughed. That "dumb song" was "Va, pensiero," also known as the "Chorus of the Hebrew Slaves," from the third act of

51

Giuseppe Verdi's opera *Nabucco*. Inspired by Psalm 137, it told the story of Jewish exiles in Babylon after the loss of the First Temple in Jerusalem: a fitting project for a young man's bar mitzvah.

He'd heard Giancarlo, who had a lovely Irish tenor, practicing with his voice coach, and the beauty of it, and his son's talent, had brought tears to his eyes. It would be a hard act to follow, especially for an uber-competitive brother.

"I don't think the rabbi is asking that every one of these projects be on the same level, just so long as it's from the heart," Karp said.

"But that's just it," Zak replied. "I don't have anything that would come from the heart."

They'd dropped that aspect of the conversation and moved on to the topic of this evening's talk by Rose Lubinsky. When Moishe told him about what she would discuss, he thought it was something his sons should hear. Although they were more inclined to spend the time with their video games, or playing pickup basketball at the local "Y," they'd agreed to meet him at the synagogue and listen to Lubinsky.

Karp thanked Officer Ewin for the lift. "We'll catch a cab home." He then got out of the car and walked over to where his sons and the Sobelmans were standing. "Good evening, Moishe and Goldie, I hope this riffraff wasn't bothering you."

Goldie laughed but didn't speak. In fact, she'd rarely spoken since being freed from a Nazi death camp after the war, choosing instead to use sign language as she did now while Moishe translated, "Not these two beautiful boys. They are perfect in every way."

"Oh, I could tell you some stories," Karp said with a smile, "but in general, I think you're right. And thank you."

"I was just asking the boys if they're going in to hear tonight's speaker," Moishe said, pointing up the steps to the synagogue's entrance.

"And their reply?"

Moishe looked down at Zak, who'd ducked his head. "I believe Giancarlo is, but Zak seems to be weighing his options."

"I don't know," Zak added. "I was thinking I might just go home."

Moishe nodded slightly. "Are you ill?"

"No, I'm okay."

The old man pursed his lips. "Butch, would you and Giancarlo be so kind as to escort Goldie in so that she can get a good seat? I think I'll stay here with Zak for a

53

moment, and I'll be in shortly."

Karp glanced over at Giancarlo and nodded up the stairs. "Sure. Goldie, you ready to go in?"

The old woman smiled and presented her elbow to Giancarlo to escort her. The three then left her husband and Zak alone on the steps.

3

The long gray rat crept suspiciously through the snow around a classic rat trap, a metal cage that contained the object of his desire. He wanted the fat, juicy piece of meat within the wire mesh that surrounded it on all but one side. Sniffing, he could just catch the scent of man on the cage, as well as on the still warm flesh inside, a scent that urged caution. He lightly grabbed a piece of the cage with a paw and stood to peer over the top and ascertain that there was no opening there either.

Intelligent and genetically predisposed to survival, he and his kind were the most successful mammals on the planet outside of man; they'd found their way to every continent except Antarctica, and lived anywhere the presence of man made life easy pickings. He hadn't lived three years — a long time for *Rattus norvegicus* on the dangerous streets of New York City — *or* grown nearly two feet long from the whiskers on his nose to the tip of his hairless tail by being careless.

Still, these were the days of hunger and desperation, even for a rat, as the city was locked in one of its coldest winters in fifty years. Protein was hard to come by. He needed to eat.

Nearly a foot of fresh snow had fallen since morning and he felt exposed in the dim glow of the street lights illuminating the street beyond the alley entrance. Instinct told him to run back into the shadows beyond the reach of the light. Still, he hesitated, then reached a paw through the mesh on the side closest to the meat. But the prize remained just beyond the range of an outstretched claw.

Frustrated, the rat pulled its foreleg out and then scratched absentmindedly behind his ear. Sitting back on his haunches, he licked his front paws and smoothed his whiskers like some ancient Chinese philosopher contemplating a philosophical question. But there was only one answer: he couldn't reach the meat from any point outside of the cage; if he wanted it, he'd have to go inside.

The risk was too great. The rat turned away, then stopped. Wasn't he the winner of a thousand territorial fights and another thousand to determine who would have the right to mate and pass his DNA on to countless other generations of urban rats? He wanted that meat, and by God he was going to get it.

The rat stalked toward the entrance of the cage. He stepped gingerly inside, jumpy with the smell of metal and man all around him, but his hunger was now insatiable. His stomach gurgled and he salivated. He was only inches to salvation from starvation in winter and the possibility of living for one more glorious summer.

Then he was standing above the metal plate on which the meat rested. The smell of the morsel filled his nostrils and removed all fear. He placed a paw on the metal and then reached forward with the other.

The metal plate shifted, and he knew in that moment that he was caught. Still, he abandoned his prize and flung himself backward in an attempt to escape. He almost made it, too. Instinctively, he stuck his paw beneath the spring-loaded door as it slammed into place and yanked up. But the lock had already set and his effort was in vain.

However, there wasn't time to think through his predicament. He whirled at the sound of another animal in the alley. The shadow of a man fell over the cage and trapped animal. The man reached down for the handle but reflexively pulled his hand back when the rat leaped, snarling and with bared fangs.

The man chuckled. "Oh, you're a nasty one," he said, smiling as he leaned over to study the rat. "Ooooh, and big. It's going to be fun to do you."

The rat backed away from the face of the man. He showed his long, yellow incisors and held his front paws up like a grappler, ready to escape if he could or fight if he must.

The man wasn't going to allow either. He picked up the cage, grunting slightly in surprise at the unexpected weight of the creature. Chortling, he placed the cage on top of a Dumpster, very pleased with his catch. Sometimes he got an alley cat, which were always fun, or the occasional squirrel when he pursued his "hobby" in Central Park. But there was nothing like a good rat. They were so smart and knew what was coming, yet even afraid they were ferocious and that added to his excitement.

With the cage on top of the Dumpster, the man was face-to-face with the rodent. They looked for a moment in each other's eyes — the dark brown of the man, the red of the rat. Then the rat hissed and flung himself at the man's face, causing him to flinch again.

The man was so preoccupied that he almost missed the soft voices and footfalls in the snow from the alley's entrance thirty feet away. He shrank back behind the Dumpster and peeked around the corner as two New York cops walked past, their breath escaping in clouds from their mouths into the frigid air.

The man's heart pounded. He liked to think of himself as tough, but in reality he was a coward. That's what made him dangerous — to rats and anyone else — a type of cowardice that made him angry with self-loathing and hatred for anyone he perceived as "looking down" on him. He shivered with fear and cold and set the cage back down in the snow behind the Dumpster, so he couldn't be seen from the street if the cops came back. It was early evening, though already dark, and so cold that the sidewalks in that part of East Harlem were nearly deserted as people hunkered down.

He stamped his feet to warm them up. The shoes he wore weren't the best for snow. He loved cherry red, high-top Chuck

Taylor "old school" basketball shoes; loved them so much that he had nearly a dozen pairs so that if one pair wore out, he always had a new pair to replace them. Red, always red, like the anger that burned inside of him. Red like fire.

The man pulled a plastic water bottle from the backpack he'd stashed next to the Dumpster, opened the valve, and pointed it at the rat. He squeezed and a stream of liquid shot from the opening and doused the rat, which responded with outraged squeals. Backing as far into a corner of the cage as possible, the rat shook itself and wiped at the noxious liquid with its paws. But the man continued to spray him until he was soaking wet.

When the bottle was empty, the man stood and placed it in the Dumpster. He looked down at the rodent, which was panting in fear and quivering with rage as it watched him. "You think you're so tough," the man sneered. He pulled out a box of wooden matches and carefully removed one before squatting in front of the case. Showing the rat the match, he then lit it, the smell of sulfur momentarily replacing the stench of gasoline. "Let's see how you handle this."

Sensing the approach of death, the rat rushed at the man, knowing that he'd never achieve his goal. As such he made it even easier for the tossed match to reach him and ignite the fuel that soaked his fur. The rat shrieked as he exploded into a ball of fire and began leaping about the cage, screeching almost human-like and rolling over to try to reach the snow.

The pain grew so great that at first he didn't see the man get down on his hands and knees to watch the suffering. When the rat noticed, he rushed up to the side of the cage, extending his paws as if trying to reach the man while biting savagely and futilely at the wire.

"Yesssss," the man hissed with pleasure. "Burn, baby, burn! Oh, it hurts so good." He felt the urge in his loins as each moment of the rodent's torment increased his sexual enjoyment of the spectacle.

The rat died like that, pressed against the side of the cage; still trying to get at his tormentor. Sighing with regret that it was over so soon, the man chuckled to himself. *Good show,* he thought. It was even better than that puppy he'd taken from a little girl one evening last summer and then set on fire in the park. *Rats are always good. Only one thing better.*

The last thought brought a pleasant shiver that coursed its way through his body like a stimulant. He gasped as he recalled each exquisite moment of horror he'd inflicted. The terror on people's faces. The screams. The cries for help. And before that . . . the fear in the intended victim's eyes when she realized what was about to happen. Sighing, he shook his head sadly. *Such a rare treat.* And only under orders, so he had to settle for animals in between "missions."

Pulling his thoughts away from the reverie, the man picked up the cage and tripped the lever to open the door. He shook the cage until the black, still smoldering carcass fell out onto the snow. Stepping around the dead rodent so as to avoid getting any smudges on his red high-tops, the man then walked quickly to the alley entrance. There he looked both ways before stepping out on the sidewalk and scurrying away, the cage dangling from his hand.

"Hey you!" a man's voice called out from the shadows across the street.

He froze. He'd been careless. He'd looked both ways up and down the sidewalk, but he hadn't noticed the two cops had crossed and were standing on the other side behind a parked car.

The man considered running, but he'd never been much of an athlete and knew that they'd catch him. *Besides,* he reminded himself, *you've rehearsed this a thousand times . . . just in case.*

"Yes, sir?" he called out to the cops who were walking across the street toward him. His voice quavered and he hoped they would think it was just the cold. "What can I do for you?"

"Cold night to be out," said one of the uniformed officers, a large man with a scarf wrapped around his face.

"Yes, sir," the man replied. He held up the cage. "We have rats in my mother's apartment," he said. "Borrowed a cage from a friend."

"Got rats in my place, too," the other cop, a short man, said. "But they eventually wise up about the cage and won't go near it. Get a cat."

"I like cats," the young man replied, "but Mother's allergic to cat hair. So I can't have one."

"Well, hope you get 'em with your cage," the second cop said. "Have a good night."

"Thank you. I'm sure I will . . . get them, I mean."

As the cops turned away and began walking off in the direction they'd come earlier, the man heard the big one snicker. " 'We have rats in Mother's house,' " he said, mimicking him. "And Jesus, Joseph, and

Mary . . . you see his face?"

"Yeah, what a freak. And wearing cherry red Chuck Taylors in weather like this; his feet had to be freezing," he heard the shorter cop reply before their voices faded.

The young man stood still for a moment, clenching his fists. Even the fucking cops thought they were better than him. It's part of what made him want to burn things. He imagined running up to the cops and squirting them with gasoline like he had the rat. *Then it would be burn baby burn,* he thought happily.

However, he was powerless to act on his fantasy, so he walked off in the opposite direction. Because of the cold he hadn't gone too far from his home that night and arrived outside the run-down East Harlem walk-up where he and his mother had moved after leaving Brooklyn several years earlier. He looked up at the second floor, to the window of his mother's bedroom, and was disappointed to see that a light was still on. She's up. *She's going to want to talk. I don't want to talk to her.* He considered waiting until she went to sleep, but as the cop had noted to his partner, his high-tops were soaked and he couldn't feel his feet anymore they were so cold.

He climbed the steps to the landing and

pulled four keys on a ring from his pants pocket. There was a strong piece of string attached to the ring and the other end tied to a belt loop so that he wouldn't lose them. One of the keys he inserted into the door lock and another he used to turn the dead-bolt to let himself into the building.

The other two keys were for the locks leading to their rooms on the second floor. He unlocked those and turning the knob as quietly as he could he entered the apart-ment. Muffled voices from down the hallway meant his mother was watching television. Removing his coat and hanging it on a peg next to the door, he crept toward his bedroom, hoping she might not hear him.

"Son?" his mother's voice called out. "Is that you? Come see your mother."

The young man hung his head. There was no escaping it. As he walked down the hallway to her room, he hoped that she was watching something she liked so that the conversation would be short.

"To the moon, Alice," the fat man on the television screen bellowed just as he opened the door to her room. *Good,* he thought, *she loves old reruns of* The Honeymooners. *She won't want to talk long.*

His mother was propped up on pillows on her bed. She smiled when he entered the room, and stubbed out her cigarette butt in an overflowing ashtray. She held out her arms. "There's my sweet boy," she cooed. "Come give your mother a hug."

Dutifully he walked over and submitted to her embrace and the kiss on his cheek. "How come you're not asleep, Mother?" he asked.

"I was waiting for my baby boy to come home. You know I can't rest when you're out there. There's bad people out there; it's not safe."

"I was out applying for a job," he said. "But you go to sleep now. I'm cold and going to go change my clothes."

"Did you get a job? No? That's okay, you'll find something when the time is right. But you go on and change; you're going to catch your death out there in those basketball shoes; we need to get you some winter boots. And baby, there's a chicken pot pie for you in the oven."

"Thanks, I'm hungry," he said and leaned over to kiss her cheek. "You need to stop smoking in bed."

The young man left the room and went out to the kitchen, where he located the pot pie, which he took to his room. He walked over to his desk — actually an old wooden door set across cinder blocks — and sat down to remove his wet shoes and socks. Standing, he took the shoes over to where a half-dozen other pairs of cherry red Chuck Taylor basketball shoes were lined up at the foot of his twin bed according to the age and condition of each pair — oldest to newest. He placed the wet pair in their proper spot and then returned to his desk, wondering if he could talk his mother into a new pair as the oldest was looking a bit frayed.

Thinking about his mother, he wondered if other people felt the same way about theirs. On one hand, she was one of the few people who ever treated him nicely and never acted like she was better than him. That was saying a lot as he didn't really have any friends, and his one sexual relationship was all about physical release and domination and nothing to do with love or tenderness. On the other hand, he didn't really feel love or tenderness toward his mother either — or anybody else for that matter — and thought of her more as a possession, someone whose attentions he tolerated because it made his life easier.

The young man then turned to the one possession he treasured as much as his collection of shoes — his laptop computer. Reaching for and moving the mouse, he smiled slightly as the computer hummed and the screen sprang to life with the photograph of a burning building from a newspaper article.

Time to do a little trolling, he thought happily as he signed onto Facebook from one of his many aliases — a pretty young woman named Brenda with a photograph he'd downloaded from another internet site — and began searching for a post to comment on. He solicited social media "friends" the way some people collected baseball memorabilia, though not for social purposes. What he enjoyed was causing pain and suffering by inserting himself into the lives of strangers in ways they did not expect.

After a minute, he located a comment from a young woman in Georgia who was describing the events of her bridal shower. He smiled and began to type. "Honey, I hate to be the one to tell you this, but your fiancé is cheating on you."

A few moments passed when there was a reply. "Who is this? Why are you saying this?"

The young man giggled. "You don't know me, but your fiancé does. Let's just say I know what I'm talking about."

"You're lying," the other woman replied. "He's right here and says he's never seen you before."

"Of course he would," the young man typed back. "Ask him about the fraternity party last fall." He'd, of course, looked at his victim's photographs and noticed they included her with a young man standing outside a University of Georgia fraternity house.

A couple of minutes passed this time and the young man laughed, thinking about the conversation the woman and her fiancé were having. He decided to add fuel to the fire. "Don't worry about it, sweetie. I don't want him back. He's okay in bed but nothing special."

The reply came quickly. "This is Tom. I don't know who you are or why you're doing this, but if I find you, I'll kick your ass."

"You mean instead of spanking it when you're calling me 'baby'? I don't think so, lover," the young man typed. "You two have a good night and enjoy your honeymoon. But I do hope you get that little 'medical issue' cleared up before then; all it takes is a shot of penicillin."

Laughing, the young man signed out of that Facebook alias and was about to sign on to another when the computer notified him that he had a new email message. He didn't get many messages, so he quickly

69

switched over to his email. What he saw made him even happier than tormenting a young engaged couple.

There was no name to indicate who it was from, just "No-Reply" and a computer-generated number. The subject line gave a date and time, and said "Meet me at the usual place." He knew there would be no other message in the body of the email, so he didn't bother to look. *So the boss wants to see me.* The thought made him happy. That meant there was a job, and he did enjoy his work.

4

"You don't have to wait for me," Zak said to Moishe as the others disappeared into the synagogue.

"I'm not ready to go in," the old man said. "And it's been a long time since we've talked."

"I saw you Sunday at the bakery," Zak reminded him.

"Ah yes, your father and his passion for my cherry cheese coffeecake."

"He says it's the best in the five boroughs and that means the whole world."

Moishe laughed. "He is too kind. But it was a busy morning; you and I had no chance to catch up." They were both silent for a moment, then the old man cleared his throat as he looked up at the golden reflection of the setting sun on the windows of Midtown skyscrapers. "So your father tells me that you're thinking that you might not go through with your bar mitzvah."

Zak tensed at the question but then quickly relaxed. He'd known the old man since childhood and he was more like a favorite uncle than just a family friend. "I don't see the point." He shrugged. "I'm seventeen. If I was going to do it I should have done it years ago."

"I've known old men who bar mitzvah," Moishe said with a shrug. "I didn't go through with it until I was in my twenties and after I had immigrated to America."

Zak looked over with interest. He'd heard some of the stories about Moishe — the escape from the Sobibor death camp, his time fighting the Germans as a partisan living in the woods. Those were his kind of stories. "I didn't know that," he said. "Why did you wait?"

Moishe sighed and shook his head. "At first, I had no choice," he said. "The Germans had invaded the Netherlands, where I was from, and were rounding up Jews to send to the death camps. We went into hiding, and it was too dangerous to have a bar mitzvah when I turned thirteen. After my family and I were sent to Sobibor it was not possible; most rabbis never made it past the first day of their arrival."

The old man bowed his head. "Even if it had been possible, to be honest, I wanted no part of God or being Jewish in a religious sense. After all, look where being Jewish got my family and six million others. Persecuted. Murdered. Simply because of who we were."

"So why did you eventually go through with it?" Zak asked.

Moishe turned to study the boy's face with his clear blue eyes. "That's a very good question," he said. "In that camp I lost my family, my friends, and my faith in God. I believed that we had been forsaken, that God had abandoned his supposedly 'chosen people.' As you know, when a young man is bar mitzvah he makes a pact with God to follow the commandments and behave ethically according to Jewish law, and yet where was God when 'His' people were forced from their homes onto cattle cars to be taken to camps set up specifically for the purpose of murder. Then upon arrival to be herded into gas chambers or lined up and shot; their bodies thrown into pits or burned to ash in the crematoria. It did not seem to me that God was holding up his end of the deal. I was angry with God; I cursed him."

"I've wondered that myself about the Holocaust," Zak said.

"Well, you should because the answer lies at the very heart of Judaism," Moishe replied. "Only after I came to America and the horror and sadness of the preceding years faded somewhat was I able to reflect on it. Only then was I able to look at the evil men who had persecuted us and compared them to the many good men and women and children who were their victims. It was then I realized that those men were gone, defeated, banished, and reviled as the monsters they had been, and yet we were still here — God's chosen people. Those others tried to exterminate us, subjected us to unspeakable horrors, but we survived, not them. Suddenly, I was proud to be a Jew: not just a Jewish partisan fighting in the forest, but part of a heritage that for thousands of years has stayed faithful to the concept of one God, one law, one people, and that no matter what cruel fates history and other people had thrown at us, we had outlasted all of them with our identity intact. That's when I decided to seek my bar mitzvah and seal my end of that pact with God and our people."

Zak thought about what Moishe said before replying. "I understand how you would make that decision after everything you had been through. But I don't feel that same connection; I guess I just don't feel Jewish."

Moishe turned his face away from a cold, stiff breeze that found its way down Third Avenue. "No one can, or should, force you to 'feel Jewish,' or go forward with the bar mitzvah," Moishe said. "I think all of our young men should ask themselves before their bar mitzvah if they 'feel Jewish' instead of just going through the motions because that's what their parents expect." He patted Zak on his shoulder. "You know, I'm glad you are giving this so much thought; you're not like all those thirteen-year-olds who are mostly looking forward to the party and getting money from their relatives and friends of their parents. If you don't feel Jewish in your heart and soul, then you should not go through with it."

Zak smiled slightly and nodded. "Thanks, Moishe. I knew you'd understand. I just don't want to disappoint my dad. When Giancarlo and I first talked about it, he wondered why we were doing it. But then he started teaching classes at the synagogue and I think it got him to think more about being Jewish. I think he got into the whole thing, maybe more than me and Giancarlo."

"Your father wants what's best for you," Moishe assured him. "He is a good man who, perhaps, has grown in his own relationship with God by examining his subjects —

really, discussions about ethics and morality — for the classes he taught. I think you will have to trust that whatever decision you reach, he will stand with you. Now, I need to go in before my friend Rose begins her talk. You're a good man, too. Now, walk with me to the synagogue."

When they reached the door, Zak opened it and let Moishe walk through. But he hesitated to come in. "Maybe I'll just wait for my dad and brother out here."

"It is too cold," Moishe replied. "And I think the speaker is someone you should hear. It's not going to be the rabbi talking your ear off; she is the wife of my oldest and dearest friend, Simon Lubinsky. Humor an old man and sit with me to listen to her story. I think you might get something out of it that could help you with your decision."

Zak tilted his head and laughed. "You're very clever, Moishe. But okay, I think I owe you that much."

The pair entered the synagogue and made their way to where males were seated and took their places next to Karp and Giancarlo. "There's Simon," Moishe said, pointing to another old man sitting in the front row.

Zak spotted Goldie seated in the front row

of the women's section next to his mother, Marlene, and a gray-haired woman. He knew she was Rose Lubinsky not because of her connection to the Jewish community but from photographs of her in the newspaper and stories about her work with charter schools.

All conversations stopped when Rabbi Michael Hamilburg, a much-loved spiritual leader known for his kindness and the gentle way he had of dealing with his flock, walked to the front and greeted them. "Shalom, welcome, friends. We are gathered here on this cold evening to listen to a message I think we will all find moving and thought-provoking. We all know Simon and Rose Lubinsky as fellow worshippers, but tonight I've asked Rose to share her story with you, although it is a difficult one for her to tell. As you all know, she has written a book about her life called *The Lost Children of the Holocaust.* Without further ado, Rose Lubinsky."

With all eyes on her, the gray-haired woman bowed her head and appeared as if she was unsure of what she was about to do. Then Goldie stood and offered her hand, which her friend took and allowed herself to be led to stand in front of the congregation. Goldie kissed her hand and

77

made the sign language symbol of encouragement, then took her seat.

Rose's face was pale but then she cleared her throat and began. "Shalom, my friends, and thank you for coming," she said, her voice quiet, uncertain. "I've asked to speak tonight as a step in a long road toward unburdening myself of the guilt that I have carried for many years and to help me keep a promise."

Many in the crowd frowned, or looked confused. They had known her for many years and could not imagine that she carried some dark secret. "Like any long road, this one starts with a first step, so I will begin like this. I am originally from Lublin, Poland, where my people had lived since the seventeenth century. My father, Shmuel Kuratowski, was a bookkeeper for a gentile farming cooperative outside the city, and a *gabbai* who assisted the rabbi at our local synagogue. I can hardly picture his face before the war, but I remember like it was yesterday his deep, rich voice reading the Torah. My mother, Zofia, was a good woman, who took great care of her husband and her children, and loved God . . . or so I was told. I have no memories of my siblings — I was the youngest of six — and precious few of my mother and father."

As she spoke, Rose's voice began to grow stronger, though all who heard her realized that tears were welling just beneath the surface. "I was five years old in 1939 when the war in Europe broke out. And seven in 1941, when the Germans created the Lublin Ghetto where Jews and many Roma, whom we call gypsies, were forced to live. In 1942, our oppressors began herding the inhabitants of the Lublin Ghetto onto cattle cars to be taken to the death camps to be exterminated, my family among them."

Rose's voice caught and she struggled for a moment before going on. "Although I have few recollections of this, and most of what I know was later told to me by others, my father had somehow managed to save quite a bit of money. When rumors began to fly that we were going to be sent to the camps, my father was able to persuade one of the gentile farmers, Piotr Stanislaw, and his wife, Anka, with whom he'd had a good relationship, to spirit me out of the ghetto. He gave the Stanislaws every cent he had, but there wasn't enough money for my brothers and sister, just me."

Rose took a deep breath and wiped at a tear that trickled down one cheek. "One of my only memories of my mother is the face of a woman crying as she held me one last time. I remember her saying it will be okay. *'We will find you again someday.'* Then my father pried me away from her and handed me to Piotr. *'Remember who you are, Rose; remember your family,'* he said. *'Tak, ojciec,'* yes, Papa, I promised. And then they were gone."

More than seventy years later, Rose bowed her head at the memory. "Simple enough instructions. Remember who you are. Remember your family." She looked up at the faces of her listeners, many of whom had tears in their eyes. "I failed at both, but I was just a little girl, and so perhaps can be forgiven for that at least."

Rose continued with her story about how the Stanislaws took her in, telling their neighbors that she was the child of Piotr's brother who'd served in the Polish army and died during the Nazi invasion. "I was lucky to be blond-haired and blue-eyed, and I did not 'look Jewish.' "

The Stanislaws, she said, did everything to allay any suspicion that their "adopted daughter" was a Jew. They hung a gold cross around her neck, had her baptized, and took her to Catholic mass. "They even gave me a new name, Krystiana, 'follower of Christ,' and forbade me ever using my real name, 'Rose,' even in the privacy of their home."

Rose paused for a moment. "The Stanislaws saved my life," she said. "They fed me, gave me a warm place to sleep, and risked their lives to protect me from the Germans, and they later hid me from the Russians. They helped me escape to America. They showed me love, and for that I am forever grateful." Then her voice grew hard. "But I was stripped of who I was, what I was. My family, my real family, was taken from me and murdered; I was stripped of my culture, my heritage, and my identity. All because we were Jews. In fact, I learned to despise Jews."

Growing angry, Rose began to pace in front of her audience. "The transformation didn't happen overnight. My memories are hazy, but I had loved our Jewish traditions — my father blowing the shofar, and eating apples and honey for Rosh Hashanah; my mother reading the Book of Ruth for *Shavuot,* lighting the menorah for Chanukah. But the Stanislaws told me that it was for my own protection that I had to forget my family and my culture. They didn't have to say much more than that; I was already deathly afraid of the German soldiers who treated people so cruelly on the streets and whom my parents had obviously feared. But it was more than that. I came to view Christians, like the Stanislaws, as my protectors, while Jews were weak and shameful."

The Stanislaws carried the makeover of Rose Kuratowski into Krystiana even further. "Perhaps to protect me, or maybe because they believed it, my parents, as I came to think of them, like most of their neighbors, voiced no objections to what they knew was going on in the death camps. The Polish curse *brudny Zid,* 'dirty Jew' seemed to come too easily from their lips to be wholly a ruse to fit in. But even more shamefully, I used it, too."

Slowly, the memory of her real family faded. "I know they were transported to Sobibor, and though I have no record of what happened to them, I can surmise their fate was the same as three hundred thousand other people who were sent there. Arriving at the depot, they were relieved of their possessions and separated: men and boys capable of labor in one group; women, children, and the infirm in another. The women were forced to strip naked and had their hair shorn; then they were made to run through an enclosure called The Tube and into a building where, they were told, they would take showers. Once they were inside, the doors were locked while soldiers on the outside started an engine and pumped carbon monoxide fumes into the death chamber. When all were dead, the doors on the opposite end were opened and the *Sonderkommandos* — prisoners forced to do this horrific job — removed the bodies and threw them into a pit for burial."

Rose's voice faltered. Then she looked over at her husband who nodded to encourage her. "There are those here who know much more than I about the horrors of Sobibor so I won't go into more detail. But I do know that the Germans kept excellent records, so that I was able to learn the day that my mother and siblings arrived in hell and died. My father was a *Sonderkommando,* and most of them were killed, but he escaped Sobibor and survived the war."

This time when Rose tried to continue, her voice came out as a whisper and she began to cry. However, as Simon began to rise to go to her side, she raised her hand for him to stop. "I'm okay, my dear husband. This is my journey." She took another deep breath. "The war ended; the camps were liberated, and the horror of the German 'Final Solution' became known to the world. The Jews who survived began returning to their homes, or at least they tried to, only to run into the antagonism of their former neighbors who didn't want to give up the property they'd stolen in their absence. What's more, the Jews were a reminder that they had done nothing, said nothing, when their fellow citizens were shipped away to be murdered. In some places, such as Poland, nationalists were no more kind to Jews than the Nazis had been. Even Jewish partisans who had fought the Germans, such as my husband and Moishe Sobelman, were hunted by their former comrades. Jews had to flee again, some to Palestine and the hope of a Jewish state, others to America."

Rose took a deep breath and let it out as a sigh. "But what of the children who were given into the safekeeping of others by their parents? Most would never see their families again, if they even remembered them or knew their true identities. The parents, relatives, and communities who could have supplied a link to their past and to their heritage were gone. We were the lost children of the Holocaust.

"We identified with our new families. Those 'other' people had abandoned us, and worse, they were Jews. We, the children of the lost, had grown up in communities in which Jews were despised, or had deserved what happened to them. The curse 'brudny Zid' did not disappear from Polish lips just because the Nazis were gone.

"I was twelve or thirteen years old and had just finished feeding the chickens in the yard when a strange man appeared on the long drive leading to our home. He looked like a scarecrow. A filthy, skinny, haunted scarecrow with his sunken eyes and hollow cheeks; what little hair remained on his head reminded me of a mangy dog. I stood there watching him approach and suddenly wanted to flee, but I was joined by Piotr Stanislaw and then Anka. He stopped a few feet from me and knelt down. Then he smiled . . . a horrible smile without teeth . . . and called me by a name I had all but forgotten. *'Rose,'* he said.

"I ran behind Piotr's back and begged him to tell the man to go away. The stranger stood up and I could see the pain on his face, but he tried again, stretching out his hands to me. *'Rose, I am your father.'* "

As she spoke, Rose held her arms out in memory of a gesture from long ago. "I remember screaming out of fear and because, I think, I knew that what he said was true."

The child had looked at the man and woman with whom she had lived for the past four years and Piotr nodded. "He said it was true, the dirty scarecrow was my

85

ojciec, my father. My reaction was to scream, *'But he's a brudny Zid, a filthy Jew!'* "

Rose shook her head sadly. "I refused to let him near me. At one point he got down on his knees and begged me to let him hold me. *'You are all I have left,'* he begged. But when Piotr brought me over to him, I spit in his face."

At last the scarecrow who was her father stopped trying and covered his face with his hands. "He let out a sob that was the saddest and loneliest sound I have ever heard. For a moment, I felt sorry for him, but not enough to go to him. And finally Piotr told him, *'Maybe you should leave, and you can try again some other day.'* And so my father, Shmuel Kuratowski, the man who made me my first and only dreidel, who saved every last cent he could so that he and my mother could buy my safety, turned and walked away. . . . I would never see him again."

Rose stopped speaking, too overcome for the moment, and looked out at her audience. Everywhere heads were bowed and tears streamed down cheeks; there were sniffles and coughs and sobs, but no one moved or spoke. However, she was not through with her story.

"If anything after that encounter I became even more anti-Semitic," she said. "I joined

Polish nationalist youth groups where Jews were not welcome and indeed, reviled. I hid my secret ethnicity with such fervor that no one hated Jews as much as I did."

Rose stopped for a moment and looked up at the ceiling of the synagogue. "I turned my back on the God of Israel and threw myself into Catholicism. But the more I rejected my Jewishness, the more the guilt grew in me like a cancer. I could rail against Jews during the day, but in my sleep I saw the devastated face of my father and heard him say, *'You are all I have left.'* Then one day, I was attending a youth rally in the town park when a young Jewish couple and their daughter had the unfortunate luck of wandering into our midst. They were Orthodox and easy to recognize; he in the broad-brimmed black hat and full beard, her in a modest dress with a floral print. The fascists who were in control of our group set upon them, beating the man senseless and tearing the clothes off of his wife and knocking her to the ground."

Closing her eyes as she remembered the scene, Rose shook her head. "At first I did nothing. After all, these were *brudny Zid.* They deserved whatever they got. They'd killed Christ. They were responsible for Godless communism. They made human sacrifices of Christian infants. Nothing was too outlandish to lay at their feet. But then I saw the little girl. She had been standing off to the side crying until her mother was knocked to the ground. That's when she ran forward and threw herself on that poor woman. I realized that she couldn't have been much older than I was when my parents, my real parents, gave me to the Stanislaws for safekeeping. One of the thugs grabbed her by her hair and pulled her up; I thought he was going to strike her or worse. Then something snapped in me. I ran forward and slapped him as hard as I could. Surprised, he dropped the little girl.

"He yelled at me, *'Why did you do that? Are you a Jew lover?'* "

Rose smiled slightly at the old memory. "To this day I don't know why exactly I responded as I did, though I think that guilt, that psychological cancer that had been growing in me since I spit on my father, finally took over. I screamed in his face, *'No. I AM a Jew.'*

"The others in the group stood there stunned. Then one at a time, they turned their backs on me until only the man I had slapped and the terrified family was left. He said, *'I should have known. I could smell it in you. If I were you, I'd leave this place. You have lied to us and we won't forget it.' "*

Rose had gone home to the Stanislaws and told them what she had done. They decided that it was not safe for her to continue living there. "In truth, it wasn't safe for them for me to continue living there," she told the congregation. "I was a reminder that they had been lying to their neighbors and a reminder of the not-too-distant past when they'd looked the other way when my real family and so many others were murdered. They bribed some government official to let me leave the country on a student visa and sent me to New York."

Smiling, she added, "It was the best thing that ever happened to me." She'd been living in the city several years after her arrival when she read a notice in the newspaper that there was to be a reunion of Sobibor survivors.

"I was now a young woman and had never forgotten the look on my father's face, or the sound of his voice, when I rejected him and called him a dirty Jew," she said. "So I went to the reunion hoping against hope that he would turn up there. I imagined a joyous reunion where I would tell him how sorry I was for my words as a child, and how grateful I was for the sacrifices he and my mother made that kept me alive. And he would forgive me and we would be a family."

Shmuel Kuratowski did not appear that day. "However, I met someone who had known my father at Sobibor. His name was Simon Lubinsky, the kindest, gentlest, wisest man I have ever known."

Rose said she'd never told anybody about how she'd treated her father out of shame. "But I felt I could confide in Simon," she said. "So I told him the story I just told all of you and waited for him to pass judgment. It was the longest few seconds of my life, and you know what he said?" She stopped to look lovingly at her husband. "He said, *'You were one of God's angels whom he assigned to bear witness to this colossal outrage. God gave you the strength that someday you would remind us all of the tyranny that exists when people lack virtue and absent themselves from God.'* Six months later, he proposed to me and I was thrilled to say yes."

The couple had returned to Poland in 1980 and located the Stanislaw farm only to find out that Piotr had died. But Anka was still alive and sharp despite her years, filling in some of the gaps of Rose's knowledge about her childhood.

"She said they never heard from my father

90

again after that day but suggested we go to Lublin to see if anyone would remember a man named Shmuel Kuratowski," Rose said. "We succeeded in finding one man, Stefan, who had been a child when my father returned from the camps and rented a small flat in the attic of his family's home.

"Apparently, my father lived by doing odd jobs but seemed to Stefan to be a sad and lonely man who never remarried. Nor did he talk much about his family from before the war, except to say that he had a beautiful daughter who had survived the Nazis and then moved to America, where she lived like a princess in a fairy tale.

"Stefan said that he asked him once why he did not go to America to live with his beautiful daughter, and my father replied, 'What? Me? A *brudny Zid*? Whatever would she do with me in America?' They never spoke of me again."

The Lubinskys learned that her father had died in the early 1960s and had been buried "with no one to read the Kaddish or observe shiva. There was not even a headstone until my generous Simon paid to have one made."

Rose was drawing to the end of her talk and suddenly sounded tired. "This is the first time I have told my story publicly, or to more than my closest friends, though more people will now know because of my book. I feel that the cancer is shrinking, so I want to thank you tonight for helping me keep a promise I once made as a little girl: that I not forget my family, or who I am." She lifted her head and stood up straighter. "I am Rose Kuratowski-Lubinsky, the daughter of a simple bookkeeper and of a mother who loved me so much they gave me to others for safekeeping. Because of them, I am alive today. I am proud to be a *brudny Zid,* and blessed to count so many of you as my friends. Thank you."

As Rose left the front of the synagogue to take her seat next to Goldie and Marlene, who both wept, one at a time members of the audience rose and began clapping. Simon was also standing and took his wife into his arms and held her as her shoulders shook and her tears soaked the tallith he wore around his neck.

5

The young man stood gazing down at the naked, sleeping woman he'd tied to the bed before sexually assaulting her. He imagined dousing her with gasoline and setting her on fire, then watching her writhe in pain and listening with pleasure to her screams. Just the thought made him want to take her again, but instead he took a photograph with his cell phone.

Then she groaned. Only it was not the sound of a victim but of a woman whose appetite for kinky sex was satiated for the moment. He found it amusing that she was driven by the excitement of knowing that he was dangerous — that the role of master and slave could change from erotic role-playing to fatal reality.

The woman looked up at him and saw the renewed lust in his eyes. But she shook her head. "No time. Untie me," she commanded. "I have to get back to the office."

His violent fantasy faded and he did as he was told. Quickly untying the knots, he handed her the lacy black lingerie and conservative gray business suit she'd worn to their assignation at the Seahorse Motel, a run-down, by-the-hour flophouse outside of Atlantic City, New Jersey.

He wasn't sure how he felt about the woman. Love wasn't part of the equation: not for her, and certainly not for him. It was just a word. He wasn't even sure he liked this woman, though they'd been having sex since soon after his fourteenth birthday and she'd been in her late twenties.

Love and like weren't really part of his vocabulary when it came to other people. As far as he was concerned there were three kinds of human beings. Those who could help him get, or do, what he wanted, such as his mother and the woman who was hurriedly getting dressed in the half-light of this dirtbag motel. Next were those people who meant nothing to him except, perhaps, as potential victims, and the social misfits he hung out with in the rare moments when he sought social contact. And last were those people who were dangerous to him, especially the police.

Hate he understood. He hated almost

everybody, including those who fell into the first group, the people who helped him. He enjoyed fantasizing about hurting and killing all of them, particularly with fire. Even his mother fell into that category when she'd make him angry. He hated this woman, too, who pulled his strings like a puppeteer whether for her sexual pleasure or her "projects," but didn't really care about what happened to him. *That's okay,* he thought as she walked into the bathroom to fix her hair and makeup. *I have a few strings to pull, too, and I could give a shit what happens to her.*

Although he didn't think a lot about it, he supposed his predilections started at an early age, even before his dad abandoned him and his mother when he was five. He didn't remember or know much about the man, just that he used to burn him with cigarettes for "being bad" and beat his mother, called her a "whore," and burned her, too. The old man was the first person he could remember hating, but rather than feeling any empathy for his mother, he mostly felt contempt. She was weak. She was incapable of protecting herself or him from the man. He discovered early on that he enjoyed hearing her scream and that was the only thing he missed when his dad left one day and didn't come back.

He knew he wasn't what other people considered "normal," not that he really cared. Never had. In school, the other kids made fun of the way he looked — what his mother called his "affliction" — and the burn marks on his hands and arms, even if he was able to hide those on his chest and back beneath his shirt. He got pushed, hit, spit on, and teased mercilessly, but he just bided his time, held grudges, and looked for his moment to strike back. In the meantime, he was content to stay to himself on the playground and sit alone at lunch.

The odd little boy was mostly ignored by his teachers. He didn't cause problems, and they had their hands full with plenty of others who did in the overcrowded public school classrooms of the Bedford-Stuyvesant neighborhood where he grew up. Oh, there were signs early on: he liked to play with fire and once set his mother's apartment on fire and later tossed a lit match in a waste-paper basket at school. But no one put together the incidents of small animals being maimed and sometimes covered with lighter fluid and ignited with the quiet middle-school boy.

However, adolescence changed that; all of that biding his time, carrying grudges, the seething anger began to boil over. It started with a bullying episode in the sixth grade when he stabbed an older boy who'd been calling him names in the neck with a pencil. It escalated the next year when a pretty black girl in his homeroom class told on him after he'd grabbed one of her budding breasts and squeezed so hard she'd screamed in pain. That had earned him a trip to the principal's office and a series of meetings with the school psychologist, who talked to him about "inappropriate behavior" and "needing to find more responsible ways to interact with your peers."

He promised to behave, but he didn't really mean it. The next day, he'd walked up behind the girl and sprayed the back of her curly black hair with lighter fluid. She didn't notice anything was wrong until he lit a match and tossed it at her head. Even then her reaction was delayed when the eyes of her friends grew suddenly wide a few moments before she felt the searing pain from the flames.

The look on her face and those of her friends brought a wide smile to his face, and their screams made him laugh. He didn't even think about running away before the male teacher grabbed him roughly and held him until the police arrived.

This time they took him to a hospital mental ward to be evaluated by a psychologist, who concluded that he was one of the youngest examples of an advanced antisocial personality disorder the doctor had come across in all of his years in practice. His mother had been upset and cried when he was committed to juvenile detention for eighteen months. But he'd beamed with pride sitting at the defense table in the courtroom and listening to the psychologist on the witness stand warn the judge that the defendant was "a budding sociopath who needs intensive treatment and even then will probably remain a danger to others upon his release."

When he got out, he was worse. His earlier crimes had merely been preliminary flashes of anger and an indifference to the pain or suffering of others, except as a means of entertainment for himself. But by the time he was released back into the custody of his mother, who'd moved to a different neighborhood in Brooklyn, he was seething. Very little made him happy: burning things, especially living things, though sometimes torching a building was exciting, too; cherry red Chuck Taylor basketball shoes; red like fire, red like pain, red like the anger in his head; and his laptop computer.

Family pets began to go missing in the new neighborhood, then their charred bodies would show up in alleys and parks. A few vacant warehouses and old tenements went up in flames. But no one got terribly alarmed until a teenaged black couple out on a date in Coney Island narrowly escaped death when their car exploded in a ball of fire. They'd been fortunate that the crude timer set to ignite an incendiary device taped onto the gas tank had been the work of an overly ambitious amateur; they'd already exited the car and were walking away when the delayed charge went off. They'd escaped with minor cuts and burns, and a frightening story to tell the newspapers.

No suspect claimed responsibility or was found. But some of the neighbors began to whisper among themselves about the strange teenager who lived with his mother in a dilapidated townhome in the Brighton Beach area. Rumor said he'd been in juvie, something about setting another classmate's hair on fire.

The rumors proved true, of course, and were corroborated after he threw a Molotov cocktail into the basement of an elderly Jewish couple in the neighborhood. The couple were badly burned and nearly died from smoke inhalation, but were saved by a man who rushed into the burning home and carried them out. A tip was phoned in to the police from someone who claimed to have seen the young man near the home. Whether that was true or not, or just someone acting on a hunch, the detectives who responded surprised him and found two more bombs in the shed behind the townhome; both bottles matched the make of the bottle used in the bombing and, after obtaining a warrant, further investigation of his computer revealed numerous searches for bomb-making instructions, including for Molotov cocktails.

After his arrest, he was appointed a young, female attorney from the Legal Aid Society, the New York version of a public defender's office, and that's how he met the woman who was walking out of the bathroom adjusting a brunette wig and putting on sunglasses. "You have money for the bus?" she asked.

"Why can't you give me a ride?" he asked sullenly.

"You know why," she replied. "We can't be seen together."

"You could drop me off on some corner in Manhattan."

The woman shook her head. "Can't risk it. Especially with our new project."

A familiar hot anger threatened to flare up. *You can still overpower her. Tie her up. Set the room on fire,* a voice whispered in his head. *But then there'd go your meal ticket,* another voice warned.

As his Legal Aid attorney, given the heavy caseload, incompetence, and corruption at the Kings County DAO, the woman persuaded the lame prosecutor to plea bargain the attempted murder charge to assault. He'd spent his fifteenth birthday back in juvenile detention. She tried to convince the psychologists that their efforts to "reach" him were succeeding. But his relationship with the woman had gone far beyond attorney-client privileges. Something about him seemed to turn her on, and during one of their meetings at the juvie center's private attorney-client makeshift meeting room she'd reached under the table and touched him where previously he'd been touched in *that* way only by himself.

Even back then he realized that her erotic attraction had more to do with his "personality" than his looks. But he recognized that she was one of those people who could do something for him, both sexually and legally, so after he got out of detention he played along with her game and let her set the rules. No kissing; this wasn't about affection, just "the act." No being seen together. No calling — she'd contact him via email, but no message other than time, date, and where, which most often was "the usual place," aka the Seahorse Motel. He was to reply with a blank email if he couldn't make it, or nothing at all if he could; he always made it.

The sexual relationship had gone on for years, even after she left the Legal Aid Society. They also had a "business relationship," what she called her "projects," which meant paying him to terrorize, hurt, and, on two occasions, kill people she considered to be in the way of her goals. He'd at first been surprised to learn that they had so much in common; her conscience was no more troubled by what she asked him to do than his was in doing it. He thought that probably had a lot to do with her attraction to him — like two vicious, singular animals coming together only to mate.

It was all fine with him, but he was getting tired of the long bus ride to Atlantic City, which was several hours from Manhattan. "Then I want more money," he said. "I'm through riding that fucking bus. I want to buy a car."

The woman regarded him coolly for a moment with her green eyes before nodding. "Do this right, and I'll see about a bonus."

"Better be a big bonus, and don't fuck with me."

"Are you threatening me?"

"Take it any way you want."

The woman laughed. "I already took it the way I wanted. But finish our little project and you'll get your car." She paused. "In the meantime, there's someone I want you to meet. Come to my office tomorrow night."

"I thought we couldn't be seen together," he replied.

She ignored the sarcasm in his voice. "Come to the side entrance. The security guard will let you in. He'll keep his mouth shut."

"What time?"

"Seven. Do you have an idea on when you're going to do it?"

"Yeah, I read about some book signing. I'll do it then."

6

Moishe Sobelman woke up from his nap in a cold sweat. In his dream, the German officer, Hans Schultz, the man who'd torn him from the arms of his father, knelt in the road, crying and begging for his life: *"I only did what I was told."* But Moishe ordered him to laugh like he'd laughed listening to desperate people dying in the Sobibor gas chamber. Then with the coward giggling hysterically in terror, the sweat beading on his face, his eyes starting in fear, Moishe dropped the garrote over his head and yanked it tight . . .

He supposed the dreams were tied to Rose Lubinsky's talk at the synagogue a week earlier. Although he'd heard the story before, listening to her tell it in front of the congregation had been overwhelmingly powerful. *The Lost Children of the Holocaust.* He'd thought over and over about the title of her book and its significance. He wondered if those children who, unlike Rose, did not know, or remember, their past felt some absence, some truth that was hidden from them. Not knowing their true identities, unaware of their heritage, having forgotten those who brought them into the world and loved them.

Lubinsky's message had clearly touched many others, judging from the response. Moishe had stolen a quick glance at Zak Karp and noted the tears in his eyes. The boy felt him looking and turned his head and gave him a quick smile before wiping at his tears, embarrassed like any macho kid to have been caught crying. But there had not been time to talk to him alone again after Lubinsky's presentation before Butch, Zak, and his twin brother, Giancarlo, left for home. He hoped that before too long he might get a chance to discuss the effect of her talk on a youngster searching for his own identity.

Moishe sat up and experienced a moment of dizziness. He'd started taking naps after closing the bakery for the day so that he could stay awake a little longer at night. It was the only time he had to read anymore; but if he didn't rest before dinner, he'd only make it a few pages in whatever book he had before he'd be snoring. He was a voracious reader, as if making up for the lost time stolen from his youth. Afraid that time would run out before he could finish, he'd devoted himself to the classics. Just that year he'd finished *Moby-Dick, The Sun Also Rises, Heart of Darkness, How Green Was My Valley,* and *Anna Karenina.* Currently he was working on *David Copperfield.*

However, there was another reason to rest up this afternoon. Rose Lubinsky had asked if he and Goldie would sponsor a book signing at Il Buon Pane that night. "Mostly friends and supporters, including some of my colleagues at the New York Charter Schools Association," she said. He had, of course, quickly agreed. "We'd consider it an honor."

Based on Rose's estimate, they had expected maybe twenty people. However, they had not counted on a review of Rose's book appearing in the Sunday *New York Times,* describing it as a "powerful memoir of loss, courage, sacrifice, and salvation" and "a little known, and heart-rending, story from the Holocaust that has been nearly lost with the passage of time." The article had mentioned that there would be a signing at the bakery.

"I didn't mean for them to put that in the article," Rose had apologized. "I hope you

106

don't mind."

"Mind?" Moishe replied. "Me mind free advertising? Between the front room and the back, we can seat maybe sixty people in a pinch."

Moishe could hear Goldie puttering about in the kitchen of their apartment above the bakery, a two-story brick building built at the turn of the twentieth century, preparing *holishkes,* one of his favorites. His wife liked falling asleep next to him as he read. She avoided naps, per se; to be honest, she had more energy than he did. *She'll probably outlive me, too,* he thought, *which is good because I would not want to ever be without her.*

Goldie still had nightmares about her time in the death camps. But even though he always asked if she wanted to talk about them, she always responded that she was not going to "ruin a moment of sunshine or destroy a day of love" by letting the nightmares take up any part of her waking life. "It is my way of getting back at the Nazis," she signed to him the first time he asked. "They are gone — no more than ashes in the ground and the shades of nightmares. But I am alive. I laugh, I love, I enjoy every moment I spend on this earth with my beloved husband. I won, they lost;

that's all that needs to be said."

Moishe did not have nightmares often, but his tended to stay with him longer. Transported with his family to Sobibor from the Netherlands, he was the only surviving member. His mother and sister had died in the gas chamber within the first few hours; his father had later died of typhus.

It was shortly after that he met Simon Lubinsky and his father, Shlomo, a jeweler. They'd been deported from the village of Wieniawa near the city of Lublin; the women and younger children in the family, plus Simon's grandparents, consigned to the same cruel fate in the gas chamber. Thin and bookish, Simon had immediately attached himself to Moishe, already a hardened survivor of the camp. The younger boy's dependence grew when Simon's father was executed with a garrote by a cruel Ukrainian guard named Demyan Voloshyn.

In late spring 1943, new inmates arrived at Sobibor with disturbing news. They were part of a work party assigned to dismantle the death camp at Belzec and hide every trace that it had ever existed. Those prisoners still at Belzec were lined up and shot, and only the new arrivals had been kept alive due to their expertise in hiding the evidence of mass murder. Inmates like Moishe began to talk with those they trusted about revolting. "We're all going to die," he told Simon. *"But I would rather die fighting these bastards than waiting to be butchered like sheep."*

However, the conspirators lacked any military training and leadership beyond a teenaged boy. Then in September, a different sort of prisoner arrived at the camp: Soviet-Jewish prisoners of war led by Polish-Jewish prisoner Leon Feldhendler and Soviet-Jewish POW Alexander Pechersky. These were not shopkeepers and craftsmen, at least not anymore; they were battle-hardened veterans who had no intention of dying without a fight, and began to form a plan for an uprising. They trusted few of the other prisoners, who they knew might turn them in for some bit of food or another day avoiding the gas chamber and firing squads. But they did confide in a few who seemed to have some fight left in them, such as Moishe Sobelman, who insisted that his friend, Simon, be included.

By that fall only six hundred prisoners were left in the camp and it was evident that the Germans were planning something. On October 14, Feldhendler and Pechersky decided they couldn't wait any longer. The plan was to kill all the guards and walk out of the main gate of the camp. They began by covertly killing eleven German SS officers and several guards. But they were discovered and had to break into the armory to battle the remaining Ukrainian guards.

When prisoners who were not part of the uprising plan realized what was happening, some joined in but others were too frightened and cowed and remained in place. Meanwhile, three hundred prisoners rushed through the gate and under the fence only to face a minefield surrounding the camp. Many died in that rush to freedom, cut down by bullets or explosions.

Moishe chose to cross the minefield, being careful to try to step where others had until reaching a spot where the man in front of him had died in a blast. After that he was on his own. "Stay back," he ordered Simon, "and then follow in my footsteps." Somehow they both reached the forest.

Of the three hundred escapees, half were either cut down by bullets and bombs or rounded up and executed in the days that followed. Less than half who survived would not live out the war — they were killed by either Germans or native Poles. Some, like Moishe and Simon, were able to find and join partisan fighters and for a time were welcomed.

In late 1944, their band encountered a group of armed Ukrainians, former prison camp guards, trying to make their way east to the advancing Red Army. The two friends had heard that after the uprising, the remaining prisoners had been executed and the Germans rapidly demolished the Sobibor camp and plowed it under to make it appear as if the land was only a farm. Now the Germans were retreating, and their Ukrainian henchmen were trying to rejoin their former comrades.

The two groups might not have fought except that suddenly Simon stood up from where he'd been kneeling behind a tree. "It's Voloshyn," he shouted at Moishe, and then without saying anything else began advancing on the Ukrainians, firing as he went.

Moishe stood and began to attack as well, pulling the other partisans into the fight. The Ukrainians tried to fight back but outnumbered and outgunned, they were driven back. Not even bothering to take cover or deviate from a straight path, Simon ignored the bullets whistling around him and continued shooting at the largest of the enemy fighters.

Moishe looked up just as a bullet struck

Voloshyn. He saw the impact that spun the man around before he fell to the ground.

Seventy years later, Moishe remembered the moment in vivid detail. But when they were still a hundred yards from the body of their tormentor, new shots rang out. Red Army troops, drawn by the sound of the guns, had appeared from the forest on the other side of the Ukrainians, who called out in Russian that they were being attacked by Jews. The tide of the battle turned and the partisans were forced to retreat.

After the defeat of Germany in 1945, Simon hoped to return to his former home in Lublin. "You can join me," he said to Moishe. "We'll find wives, have families together, and remain friends forever."

However, like many Jews who tried to return to their homes, Simon learned that he was no more welcome than he had been when the Germans invaded. In fact, Polish nationalists took up where the Germans left off in blaming Jews for their troubles. It became dangerous to remain in Poland as the Soviet Union seized the Eastern bloc countries.

"I'm going to try to go to America," Moishe told his friend one day. "I want you to come with me."

Simon would not meet Rose for several

more years, after he'd come to the States with Moishe and Goldie Sobelman. One day he'd returned from a reunion at the New York Holocaust Museum for Sobibor escape survivors and breathlessly told Moishe that he'd just met "the most beautiful woman in the world and my future wife."

Some people had looked at the lovely, lively Rose Kuratowski — she'd taken her family name back — and the skinny, rather plain Simon with his Orthodox dress and wondered how long such an odd couple would last. But Moishe and Goldie knew that Rose was smitten with her "kind, gentle, wise" husband and that he in turn adored her above all else. Even more tragedy had not destroyed them when their only child, a son named for his grandfather Shlomo, died in Vietnam serving in the U.S. Marine Corps.

As Simon had predicted, he and Moishe had remained friends, serving as each other's best man at their weddings and even gone through the bar mitzvah together as "old men" in their twenties. As the years passed, both had done quite well in America — Moishe with his bakery and Simon as a diamond merchant. Shortly before meeting Rose, Simon had gravitated toward a more Orthodox brand of Judaism and took to wearing the Orthodox style of broad-brimmed black hat, black suitcoat, starched white shirt, and black pants. "I want to look Jewish in memory of my family," he explained to Moishe.

Many years had passed and life in America had done much to keep the ghosts of the horrific past at bay, but it had all come back with the force of a hurricane the previous November, when neo-Nazis had rampaged in New York on the anniversary of *Kristallnacht*. The young fascists had broken the windows in his shop and ransacked the interior while he and Goldie stayed in their apartment above the store. He stood by the door with a meat cleaver in his hands, determined to defend his wife with his life, until the sound of approaching police sirens had chased the bastards away. But the fear remained, dredging up old memories that troubled his sleep.

The attack had thrown him into a deep depression as he was reminded that the ghosts of the past lived on in the hateful minds of the living. The joy he found in running the bakery left him, as did the genial way he usually greeted his guests. Instead he found himself wondering which of them secretly harbored anti-Semitic feelings.

As usual, it was Goldie who coaxed him

out of it. One morning as he was dragging his way through the routine, snapping at his employees and hardly saying a word to his customers, she grabbed him by the elbow and propelled him to the door leading to their upstairs apartment.

"What's the matter with you?" she signed, her hands flying the way they did when she was angry.

"What do you mean?" he asked, though he knew what she was getting at.

"You're acting like all the life has been sucked out of you," she signed. "Why? Is it those half-wits who broke our windows? After all we've been through you're going to let a few Nazis ruin the years we have left? The years we've earned?"

Moishe's shoulders slumped. "We can't escape the past."

Anything else he was going to say left his mind when Goldie grabbed both sides of his face. "Only if you let it catch up to you," she said, speaking aloud for one of the rare times, which generally only happened when she was really angry or really happy. "And if you do that, then they've won. After all these years, they've won."

She reminded him of the note he'd written to her that had changed her mind after she'd rejected his initial proposals of mar-

115

riage when they were still in Europe. He'd started by handing her a note saying he wanted to marry her and have children. But she'd scolded him in a message she wrote back. *How can you talk about love and marriage and bringing children into a world as evil as this one? Stupid man.*

However, he'd persisted, asking her the same question day after day until one day he walked up and said goodbye. Although she'd pretended that she didn't care, she asked nonchalantly why he was going. He told her he was going back to Sobibor to lie down and die there.

"But why?" she'd signed.

"If they can stop us from falling in love, marrying, and having children," he'd replied, "if they can convince us that there's no more room in this world for love, then they've won anyway. Why not give them my bones, too, to mix with those of my sister, mother, and father and so many of my friends."

In that moment, Goldie's heart had melted. She'd agreed to marry him, and they'd kissed for the first time. And many years later, she'd reminded him of what he'd written to her. "That's the man I married. That's my fine Jewish warrior. That's the good and decent man who stood up to the darkness and vanquished it."

Looking in her merry blue eyes, Moishe felt the burden drop from his shoulders. He laughed. "Your fine Jewish warrior? I hadn't heard that one. . . . Sooo, what should a fine Jewish warrior expect from his lovely Jewish wife when he returns from the wars?" He'd wiggled his eyebrows suggestively until the anger left her face and she giggled.

"We'll see if he's truly returned or if he's putting on an act hoping to get lucky," she said, and then laughed as she sidestepped his attempt to grab her.

With the dream fading into the blackness from which it had come, Moishe got to his feet and shuffled out to the kitchen as he rubbed the sleep from his eyes. He spotted the *holishkes* cooling on the counter. Goldie was preoccupied with something else so he snuck over and was preparing to grab a bite when he heard his wife clear her throat behind him. He froze and turned.

Goldie was looking at him with one eyebrow raised. "What do you think you're doing?" she signed.

"Nothing."

"You old liar. You were trying to steal a *holishke.*"

Moishe pretended to be chagrined. "I was just trying to ensure that the quality was up to your usual standards."

"I can assure you it is," Goldie replied with a laugh. "But dinner's not quite ready. There will be no *holishkes* for you until you go downstairs and make sure everything is ready for the book signing. It starts at eight, which gives us less than two hours."

"Fine," Moishe pouted. "Slave driver."

Moishe returned to the bedroom and got dressed. He then walked down the stairs and through the door leading to the bakery, where he navigated in the soft illumination of the street lights coming in through the newly replaced windows.

When he first purchased Il Buon Pane from its original owner, the man who'd given him his start in the business, the bakery was comprised of the building on the corner. However, due to its growing popularity, when the store next door became available he purchased it and opened a large sitting area for his customers to relax, enjoy their coffees and baked goods, catch up on the latest news, and meet with friends. That afternoon the sitting area had been transformed into a small auditorium, with rows of folding chairs provided by the charter schools association and set up by the Karp boys after they got out of school, facing toward a podium where the guest of honor would speak.

Moishe went back into the bakery kitchen, turned on the light, and looked with satisfaction at the trays of strudel, cinnamon rolls, and cherry and blueberry cheese coffeecake he would be serving at the book signing. He then turned on the industrial-sized coffee urns before wandering back out into the front of the store.

Walking over to the door, he was about to turn on the lights when he looked across the street and froze. Lurking in the shadows, he could see four or five figures of men with bald heads talking together in a group. But that wasn't what sent a chill up his spine. It was the red armbands with the white circle on which the black swastika was imprinted.

Moishe left the lights off and hurried upstairs. He told Goldie about the men across the street.

Goldie thought about it for a moment. "If they're trying to intimidate us into canceling the book signing, it's not going to happen," she signed. "But we have to be mindful of our guests' safety. Call Butch; he'll know what to do. Then call Rose and Simon and warn them. After that we'll have our dinner."

So it was that an hour later as people began arriving for the book signing, the

119

guests found a strong police presence standing in front of a small group of neo-Nazis protesting using bullhorns and signs with slogans like The Holocaust Is a Jew Lie! and Don't Believe the Zionist Lies of Lubinsky. The police set up barriers across the street from the bakery and told the men, mostly young, to remain behind them or face arrest. Meanwhile, a group of counterprotesters, many of them minorities and charter school supporters, had formed kitty-corner from the bakery and across from the Nazis, so the police had stationed several more officers between the two groups.

When Butch Karp arrived with his wife and sons, he sought out Moishe and Goldie in the crowd. "Sorry you have to put up with those idiots," he said, indicating the skinheads.

"All part of living in America," Moishe said with a shrug. "Even Nazis have the right of free speech. I'm good with it, but thank you for arranging the police help, and it looks like Rose has a few supporters in the other crowd."

"Thank Detective Clay Fulton," Karp replied. "I told him about it and he got right on it. He's outside now making sure no one does anything stupid. Ah, it looks like your guest of honor is arriving."

Moishe turned to see Rose Lubinsky enter the bakery. Simon was already there, having come from his job while his wife had been attending a political rally for the charter school bill. She hesitated at the door and glanced over her shoulder at the Nazis across the street. Her face was ashen when she turned back and walked swiftly over to the Sobelmans.

"I am so sorry," she cried. "I've brought this upon you."

Hugging his friend, Moishe stepped back and patted her shoulders. "Nonsense. I wouldn't have it any other way," he said. "We have to stand up to the darkness and vanquish it."

"Well, you are very brave and gracious," Lubinsky said.

Moishe looked over at Goldie and winked. "Think nothing of it; it's just how a fine Jewish warrior rolls."

7

Like everyone else at Il Buon Pane, Karp stood and applauded when Rose Lubinsky finished her talk and concluded with a question and answer format that could have gone on for another hour. Then he and Marlene got in line, waiting to approach the table where the author had taken a seat to sign books.

When they reached the front, Rose was trying to peer around them with a perplexed look on her face. Karp turned to see what she was looking at, but all he saw was a room full of chatting people, most with *The Lost Children of the Holocaust* clutched in one hand while the other held a cup of coffee or a pastry.

"You looking for someone?" he asked.

As though startled from a dream, Lubinsky looked up at him but then smiled. "I thought for a moment I saw an old friend, but I guess I was mistaken," she replied. "I wouldn't have expected him to show up — just wishful thinking, I guess."

"Maybe the next signing," Karp said. "I don't think Moishe could have squeezed one more body in here."

"I know. I'm a little embarrassed about that," Lubinsky admitted. "Apparently, the publisher told the *Times* book reviewer that I'd be here, but I'd intended this to be a small gathering for friends and the people I work with at the charter school association."

"Speaking of which," Marlene chimed in, "how's that going?"

"I'm scheduled to speak to the assembly's Education Committee next week," Lubinsky said. "If the bill comes out of committee with bipartisan support, I think it will pass the state assembly. So I'm going to nudge them along."

"What's the opposition like?" Karp asked.

"Running scared," Lubinsky replied. "A lot of hand-wringing and union, partisan attempts to persuade the public — i.e., the politicians umbilically tied to the union and those who watch the polls — that it will be the end of public school education as we know it."

"Maybe that's a good thing," Marlene said.

"Well, we're not trying to destroy the

public school system," Lubinsky said. "We're trying to improve it and offer students who truly want an exceptional public education a choice. We are public after all."

"I take it the teachers union doesn't see it the same way?"

Lubinsky thought about it for a moment before she spoke. "I don't know about the teachers, particularly the young ones — I think there's some unrest. But the union leadership isn't happy; we're a threat to their power, finances, and perks. They want to protect their golden goose."

"What are they doing about it?"

The old woman shrugged. "You mean besides the usual 'lobbying' — and by that I mean bribing — politicians and the media? There's been some attempts to intimidate me and my colleagues — the usual anonymous phone calls at three a.m., nasty notes left on the windshields of cars . . . that sort of thing. A few weeks ago, the union president Tommy Monroe asked me to meet with him so he could propose a 'compromise' if I'd get the bill pulled."

"You turned him down?" Karp asked.

"Yes, the time for compromise is over," Lubinsky replied. "We would have been happy to work something out years ago, but they've fought us every step of the way — bought politicians, lied about the purpose of charter schools and the makeup of the student body, and then painted us as racists and elitists. But the worst thing was they did it knowing they were hurting children."

Karp looked over Marlene's shoulder at the line of people still waiting, some of them with "hurry up and get on with it" looks on their faces. "Well, good luck," he said. "I think you're on the right track. I'd like to hear more about it, but we don't want to hold everybody up."

An hour later, Karp and his family were talking to Moishe and Goldie Sobelman when he spotted another familiar face approaching. "Well, Alejandro Garcia," he said with genuine affection. "I heard from the boys that you were working with the charter school association."

The young Latino flashed a toothy smile. Alejandro "Boom" Garcia had once been a notorious gang member in Spanish Harlem by the time he was fourteen. He'd earned his nickname for his willingness to use a gun to protect his home turf and friends from larger gangs. But after a short stint in juvie, he'd turned his life around with the intercession of one of Marlene's friends, a

Jesuit priest named Mike Dugan, as well as discovering a latent talent as a rapper.

Although mistrustful of police and even Karp as the New York district attorney, Garcia had several times saved the day — as well as members of the Karp-Ciampi family — against myriad bad guys. He was smart, tough, loyal, and fearless.

Karp and Marlene had been surprised when the twins told them a few months earlier that Garcia had gone to school to get his teaching certificate. After all, he'd been signed to a lucrative recording contract. "He's still recording," Giancarlo had assured them. "But he wants to give something back, especially to kids in Spanish Harlem. He got a job right out of school with the Nuevo Día Charter School and uses some of his music money to sponsor scholarships. He's also real involved with the bill to change charter school legislation with Mrs. Lubinsky."

"*Buenas noches,* Mr. Karp," Garcia said, and turned to Marlene, "and you, too, Ms. Ciampi. I see you're still hangin' with The Man."

"Someone's got to keep him real," Marlene replied with a laugh while Karp grinned.

"Yeah, I 'spose." Garcia smiled. "But you

ever get tired of him, give me a call."

"Well, Alejandro," Marlene giggled. "I'm old enough to be . . . to be . . . your older sister."

"Yeah, but you still fine, *bella dama.*"

"So what brings you to Il Buon Pane, other than to flirt with my wife?" Karp asked. "Just to support Rose?"

"That and somebody to watch her back," Garcia said. "Things are getting pretty hot with this legislation." He nodded toward the front door of the shop. "And you never know what sort of *pendejos* will show up."

Karp nodded. "You're right there. But I think Detective Clay Fulton and his men have things under control. Speak of the devil . . ."

The others turned to look where Karp indicated in time to see Fulton open the door and walk into the shop. He walked over stomping his feet and waving his arms to get warm. "Man, it's cold out there," he said.

"Come, my friend," Moishe exclaimed. "Let me get you something warm to eat and drink. I'll send one of the waitresses outside with coffee and something to eat for your officers; most of our guests have left, and there's no sense letting it go to waste."

"Thanks, Mr. Sobelman," Fulton replied.

"I'm sure they'll appreciate that."

"What about our 'friends' across the street?" Karp asked.

"Mostly dispersed, though there's a few die-hards hanging in. This isn't their neighborhood and they got what they wanted — face time on the ten o'clock news. Meanwhile, the neighborhood turned out in force. The Sobelmans have a lot of friends."

"Any arrests?" Karp asked.

"Yeah, a thug named Lars Forsling," Fulton responded.

Karp frowned. "The name sounds familiar."

"He's got a mouth on him and gets in the paper a lot," Fulton said. "He was arrested last summer for spray painting Nazi crap on the wall of the Third Avenue synagogue. We also suspect he was involved in the rampage in November but haven't been able to prove anything. A real piece of work."

"Oh yeah, now I remember," Karp said. "What did he do this time to get arrested?"

"Well, I hate to say it, but he slipped away from the area where we had them barricaded. Next thing we know, he's over on the side of this building where some of the guests, including Mrs. Lubinsky, were parked. An officer spotted him and told him to move along, but he gave him some lip about the sidewalks being a public place and having a right to be there. So we tossed him in a squad car for disobeying a lawful order. We still got him in a car until I can spare someone to take him downtown. I'm sure he'll enjoy spending the night in The Tombs, though it won't be his first time."

Fulton gratefully accepted a cup of coffee from Goldie, which he drank hurriedly. "Well, I want to get back out there. Maybe I can take a few of those to-go cups, Moishe, and help your girl out."

When the big detective left with the waitress, Karp walked over with Marlene and Garcia to where Rose was being helped into her long wool coat by her husband, Simon. "Are you two ready to leave?" he asked.

"I am," Rose Lubinsky replied. "My ride needs to get going; she lives in Queens and we have an important strategy meeting tomorrow regarding the charter school bill. But my Simon is staying behind to help the Sobelmans clean up. Actually, I think he just wants to shoot the breeze with his friend; those two are like glue and paper — once you put them together, it's impossible to tear them apart."

"I assure you, my love," Simon Lubinsky

objected, "I will be along by taxi as soon as I have helped our friends. I wasn't planning on going to the office until noon tomorrow and can sleep in. But you are the one who needs to sleep."

"Simon Lubinsky! Are you trying to tell me that I need my beauty sleep?"

Simon placed his hands over his heart. "Never! From the moment I first saw you, I knew I was looking at the most beautiful woman in the world, and my opinion has grown only stronger since."

Rose Lubinsky laughed. A surprisingly young sound, as though from a girl. "You old flatterer. If that is your opinion, then tomorrow we must take you to the eye doctor for stronger glasses. But tonight I will accept your sweet lie." She stepped forward and kissed him. "I love you, Simon, nothing will ever change that."

With that Rose Lubinsky turned toward two young women standing behind her and then nodded at Garcia. "You ready?"

"Yes, señora, your driver awaits," the young man replied gallantly.

Karp and the others watched the four leave. As she drew near the door, Rose hesitated and looked back at her husband. She smiled and then raised her hand to blow him a kiss. Simon reached up as if to pluck it from the air and touched his fingers to his lips. He then looked up at Karp and blushed slightly. "An old habit," he said.

"Nothing wrong with it," Karp said with a smile. He then turned and began to walk toward Marlene and his sons, who were chatting with Goldie near the pastry counter.

Suddenly, there was a flash of light outside that illuminated the streets as though the sun had jumped out from behind a cloud. Everything beyond the windows seemed to have been frozen in place like a photograph — police officers standing near their cars or by the barricade, a few demonstrators and a television crew huddled by the back door of their van.

Then with an enormous roar and shattering of glass, the windows on the side of the bakery blew in. The world went black as Karp was knocked to the ground.

It took a moment for Karp to realize what had happened. *A bomb.* His next thought was of Marlene and the twins. He pressed himself up, feeling the broken glass beneath his hands, though pain didn't register.

Immediately, he spotted his family. Marlene was wiping something off Giancarlo's face. *Blood.* Zak was helping Goldie to her feet.

Sounds seemed to be muted, and he wondered if he'd lost his hearing in the blast. But then it came back as if someone had turned up the dial on the radio. He heard screams and shouts. Car horns were going off outside, and there was another noise that didn't register, then he knew, it was the sound of fire.

"You okay?" he shouted at Marlene.

"Yes, go!" she replied, pointing toward the door.

Karp ran, the glass and debris crunching beneath his feet. The front of the store was virtually untouched and nothing seemed out of place except the orange glow illuminating the streets. He burst out of the door and ran around the corner.

Half a block away a car was engulfed in flames. He saw a short, barrel-chested man hurl himself at the front passenger side door, seemingly oblivious to the fire. Silhouetted by the blaze, and with what appeared to be superhuman strength, he tore the door open and nearly off its hinges.

Karp suddenly realized that the man was Alejandro Garcia. He reached inside the burning car and grabbed whoever was sitting there and then threw himself backward. He landed on the sidewalk; the arms of his coat were on fire as was the woman he held in his arms.

Running toward the young man, Karp pulled off his own suit jacket. Reaching the pair, he used the jacket to swat out the flames, aware of the intense heat at his back.

Other men appeared, police officers and locals, shouting though he was too wrapped up in trying to help the two victims to understand. They grabbed Garcia and the woman to pull them away from the car. More hands pulled at his arms and pushed him to safety as well.

Time seemed to stand still. A fire truck and a paramedic van arrived. Garcia and the woman, Rose Lubinsky, were hustled aboard. Karp watched them speed away but had no concept of how much time had passed since the explosion.

Someone — Marlene — pushed a cup of coffee into his hands and wrapped a blanket around his shoulders. Finally, the shock began to wear off, and as it did, he was filled with anger. He walked to the front of Il Buon Pane and looked across the street at the police cruiser where Lars Forsling had been placed following his arrest.

Forsling was looking back at him. His white, tattooed face was illuminated by the street lights and the crime scene lights that had been brought to the scene. Their eyes met and then the young man smirked. He mouthed a word.

Karp couldn't hear him but he knew without a doubt what Forsling had said. *Jew.*

In that moment, Karp saw himself crossing the street and dragging the thug out of the cruiser, then beating him with his fists. Breaking his nose. Blacking his eyes. Beating the smirk off his face. But the moment passed.

Instead, he pointed at the police cruiser. "Take that son of a bitch down to Centre Street and lodge him in The Tombs," he told the sergeant standing next to him. "I'll be in my office in an hour. Stay with him until I get to you."

8

"What took you so long, Gallo?" Tommy Monroe looked at his watch. "I thought I told you to be here by eight at the latest. It's almost nine."

Micah Gallo shrugged. "I had a few errands to run and traffic coming over the Queensboro was stacked up."

Monroe frowned and took a sip from the highball glass. "What were you doing in Manhattan?"

Gallo felt his face flush. "Just some shopping and met a friend for late lunch."

The big Irishman narrowed his eyes and studied his "protégé," then grinned and shook a sausage-sized finger at the younger man. "You was off getting laid," he said, smirking. "A little afternoon nooky. Am I right? I am, aren't I?"

Gallo used the excuse to hide his slip about his previous whereabouts. He smiled and looked sheepishly around the Jay Street

Bar as though caught in the act. "Yeah, an old flame. It was just supposed to be lunch."

Monroe belly-laughed. "Yeah right, 'lunch,' and I'm drinking Coca-Cola."

"What's the big deal about being here by eight, anyway? We meeting somebody?"

"Nah," Monroe said, shaking his head. "Just got some shit to go over regarding the legislature for next week."

Monroe glanced up at the television that was hanging on the wall opposite the table where they sat and motioned for the waitress. When she came over, he held up his empty glass. "I'll take another and whatever my young friend here wants. And see if you can get the tube switched over to the news."

"What's on the news that you're so interested in?"

Monroe glanced sideways at him. "Nothing in particular. I just like keeping up with current events, you know. And maybe there'll be some news about Yankee spring training."

Gallo shook his head. "Too cold outside for me to even be thinking baseball already."

"Yeah, but rookies report in a few weeks," Monroe pointed out. "Then the pitchers and catchers. They're all down in Florida while we're freezing our nuts off up here.

Lucky stiffs."

Gallo nodded. "Yeah, lucky." He was glad to have the conversation turn to something other than where he'd been. He wasn't meeting a friend for a late lunch. He wasn't shopping or getting laid. He'd gone to Il Buon Pane to listen to Rose Lubinsky talk about her book . . . and to tell her that he was sorry. That he wished he had her courage; that he wished he hadn't given in to the bullying and threats and wanted to be forgiven and be there at her side when she spoke to the politicians about a bill that would change the course of charter schools for the betterment of the children of New York forever.

But even before he got out of the cab outside of the bakery, he knew that it was too late for him. That he'd been bought and corrupted and didn't have the inner strength to go up against Monroe and the union. He just hoped that he might get a moment to speak to her outside of anyone else's hearing to say he was sorry, wish her luck, and then leave to meet his master.

Except you didn't even have the balls to do that, he thought. He'd walked in the door shortly before Lubinsky began her talk and stayed in the front part of the store while other people filtered in and moved forward to take seats. He'd stayed back in the shadows as she went to the podium but then he heard a familiar voice behind him.

"Well, Micah Gallo, what brings a *pendejo* like you to a nice place like this."

Gallo immediately recognized the sing-song, Latin-accented words as belonging to an angry Alejandro Garcia. He'd turned around and found himself looking down into the short, broad-shouldered young man's smoldering eyes.

Caught off guard, Gallo didn't know what to say. All the things he'd considered saying to Rose Lubinsky weren't intended for anyone else. "I was just . . ."

"Just what, *panocha*? Spying for your punk boss?"

Deep in his gut, Gallo felt a sudden warming of the old anger and temper that had been a part of him back when he and Garcia were both leaders of their respective Latino gangs. Garcia in Spanish Harlem; Gallo in Bedford-Stuyvesant. Back then, they'd been a lot alike in many ways. Both had grown up on the hard streets where they'd had to learn to be a man when most boys their ages were still playing kid games and were curious about girls. They'd both also exhibited the kind of leadership and decision-making skills that had earned them the respect and leadership among older teens.

Although separated by the East River and with little opportunity for contact, Gallo and Garcia had been aware of each other but not rivals. For one thing, they weren't with the big, drug-dealing inner city gangs; theirs were more the old-fashioned neighborhood gangs, as much a collection of friends as anything else. They could be violent if pushed or defending their "turf," but mostly they avoided trouble and just wanted to be left alone.

Back in the day, a challenge like Garcia's would have been fighting words. But not anymore, so he just shook his head. "I don't want any trouble, Alejandro. I just saw that she was having a book signing, and I wanted to wish her luck."

Garcia had glanced at the front of the room. Rose Lubinsky was looking over the crowd, smiling and nodding at friends. Then she'd looked up and spotted the two of them and her smile faltered.

Gallo blinked to clear his eyes of the tears that had suddenly sprung into them. But Lubinsky had turned to say something to the small man who had escorted her to the stage.

"I think you better leave," Garcia said. "She doesn't need your kind of luck. You're free to go back and report that you followed her here and did your job. Otherwise, we'll see all of you union *pendejos* in Albany next week."

. Again the old anger flared for a moment but it faded just as quickly. He might have once been a hard-nosed street gangster who had clawed his way out of the 'hood and put himself through college. He may have overcome enormous odds to go on and get his teaching license by working two jobs and avoiding the people and circumstances of his past life. He may have once been so fired up about the charter school movement — so committed to helping kids like himself — that he'd taken out enormous loans, put his house up for collateral, and sunk every cent he had in the Bedford-Stuyvesant Charter School. That brave, altruistic young man was gone; he'd first lost everything, and then been replaced by a spineless "yes man" addicted to fast cars, loose women, nice clothes, a luxurious condo, and . . . *la vida fácil,* the easy life.

So Gallo turned and left without responding to Garcia or looking back to see if Rose Lubinsky was watching anymore. Outside, he shivered both from the cold and his warring emotions. The lighting was weak and everyone was bundled against the cold but for a moment one face some twenty-five feet away from him looked familiar. But the young man disappeared back into the crowd and he wasn't sure.

"Yo, Micah, you going to order something?"

Monroe's gruff voice brought him out of the memory. His boss and the waitress, a bottle blonde wearing too much makeup, were both looking at him, waiting for him to order. "You'll have to forgive him," Monroe said with a wink, "he spent the afternoon getting busy, if you know what I mean."

Gallo blushed as the waitress laughed. "Yeah, I'll have a beer."

"What kind, honey?" the waitress replied sweetly, obviously taken with his dark good looks.

"Uh, Schaefer."

Monroe made a face. "You still drinking that swill? At least order a microbrew or something decent."

Gallo shrugged. "It's what I grew up with, and I like it. Just a Schaefer, please."

When the waitress left, Gallo turned back to Monroe. "So what's so important?"

"Stopping this fucking bill is what's important," Monroe replied. For the next half hour, he went over the strategy for the next week: who needed to have his or her arm twisted; places and hands where some cash might do some good; favors that needed to be called in.

"To be honest, it wasn't going to be enough."

"Wasn't?"

"Isn't," Monroe corrected himself. "It isn't going to be enough. You know what I meant."

The way he said it — all worried and angry — made Gallo wonder if the man was cracking. "Maybe we're pushing back too hard," he suggested. "Maybe we can still reach a compromise. It would take some adjustments, but maybe we can figure out a way to work with the charter schools, and still keep the union strong."

Monroe looked at him for a moment like he was nuts, then laughed, or more accurately, snorted. "Adjustments? What adjustments? Adjusting to being out of a job? Adjusting to a prison cell? Or have you forgotten that part of the bill means someone will be poking around in the books? We tried to compromise with that bitch, she wasn't budging. We'll all hang if she gets her way."

"I haven't done anything wrong."

Monroe gave him a funny look. "No?

Where do you think all the money for your playboy lifestyle comes from?"

"My salary," Gallo replied. "And bonuses."

"Yeah, and where do you think those bonuses come from," Monroe shot back. "We're not I-fucking-BM and you're not a shareholder. Bonuses, Christ, don't make me laugh." He leaned across the table and pointed his finger in Gallo's face. "Listen to me, buddy boy, I've been taking care of your ass, but you better remember who buttered the bread. You're in this up to your eyeballs. I go down, you go down; we all go down together, which means, we do whatever it takes to make sure this bill doesn't pass."

Gallo hung his head. *It doesn't get any more clear than that,* he thought. *The asshole not only bought you, he made sure that if you ever did grow a set of balls, and tried to do anything about it, he'd cut them right off.*

"Well, I'll be damned," Monroe said suddenly.

Looking up to see what the Irishman was talking about, Gallo followed his eyes to the television. It took him a moment to realize what he was looking at beyond the words "News Alert!" flashing on the bottom of the screen. A car was burning and people were rushing about.

"Hey Julie," Monroe bellowed. "Turn up the tube, would ya?"

Standing next to the bar, Julie the waitress pointed and pressed the TV remote and a newscaster's voice broke through the background noise of the pub: "*. . . where an apparent car bomb has exploded outside this Midtown bakery where charter schools association president and author, Rose Lubinsky, talked about her new book . . .*"

Slowly Gallo rose to his feet, his eyes wide with horror, his jaw slack. The newscaster continued: "*. . . gang of neo-Nazi skinheads earlier clashed with neighborhood residents and supporters of Mrs. Lubinsky . . . early reports are one dead, two in critical condition, numerous injuries . . . District Attorney Butch Karp is at the scene . . . reports of one arrest . . .*"

Gallo turned toward Monroe. "Did you do this?" he asked, his throat suddenly bone dry and his voice coming out as a croak.

Monroe sat back in his seat and laced his fingers together behind his head as he studied Gallo. Then he shook his head. "Fuck no," he said. "It was probably those Nazi assholes. They didn't like her 'cause she was a Jew. Hope they all fry in hell."

"I got to go," Gallo said, grabbing his coat off the back of the chair.

"Yeah, sure," Monroe said. "This is upsetting news. But Micah . . ."

"What?"

"Who butters your bread?"

"You do, Tommy."

"Attaboy, you just remember that and you'll be fine."

9

Karp looked through the one-way glass into the interview room at The Tombs as the muscular young man in the gray jail jumpsuit slouched in a chair on the other side as if he didn't have a care in the world. In fact, he was humming, a slight smirk on his tattooed face.

"What's that song?" asked Fulton, who was standing next to him looking at Lars Forsling with disdain etched into his big dark face. "I've heard it before."

"The 'Horst-Wessel-Lied,' sort of a national anthem for the Nazis in World War II," Karp replied. "Just in case we couldn't figure out his political leanings."

There was a knock on the door and in walked Assistant District Attorney Ray Guma, a longtime friend and colleague of Karp. Once an athletic, ruggedly handsome man with curly dark hair, Guma had been reduced by cancer to a shell of his former self. His face was much thinner, his cheekbones pronounced and the dark brown eyes deep in their sockets. The hair was still curly, though thinner and nearly snow white, and he was so thin, his body seemed barely able to support the suit he wore.

However, the old fire that had defined him as a college baseball player and tenacious prosecutor still burned, and even though he only worked part-time, he was still one of the best at the DAO. Driving back to 100 Centre after the bombing, and deciding how to proceed, Karp had thought immediately of the former "Italian Stallion" to assist him with the case.

"What's the word, Goom?" Karp asked, dreading the answer.

A look of pain and anger crossed Guma's face as he glanced at the skinhead in the next room. "As you know, one dead at the scene, a Miss Mary Calebras, an elementary school teacher at The New Hope Charter School in Yonkers," Guma replied. "Unfortunately, I was just informed that a second young woman, Tawanna Moham-mad, also a schoolteacher in Queens, died in the ER a few minutes ago."

"What about Rose Lubinsky and Alejandro Garcia?"

"Alejandro will be okay. Second degree

burns on his hands and arms, a little on his face, but he was wearing gloves and a leather coat. It could have been much worse. Brave kid though."

Karp nodded. "Yeah, he's never lacked for courage. And Rose . . . ?"

Guma sighed and shook his head. "Doesn't look good," he said. "Severe burns over eighty percent of her body, and that's tough on anybody, but especially somebody her age. They got her in Intensive Care and are trying to make her comfortable — she's in and out of consciousness — but the prognosis isn't very hopeful." He looked again at Forsling. "Son of a bitch."

Karp looked back at Forsling and nodded. "Yes, he is, now let's go see if he's also guilty."

The three men went out into the hallway, where a stenographer carrying a small black box waited. Karp nodded to her and turned to Guma. "If you don't mind," he said. "I know the cops were going to round up some of our boy's Nazi pals, and I'd like you to handle the interrogations. Maybe one of them heard Forsling say something about this before it happened."

Guma turned and left. Then Karp, the steno, and Fulton entered the room where Forsling sat behind a table. He looked up and sneered but didn't say anything.

Karp paused for a moment and looked at his opponent, noted the "Sieg Heil" tattooed on his forehead. As if showing off, Forsling turned his head to the side so that the prosecutor could see the swastikas on the side of his face.

"Good evening, Mr. Forsling," Karp began.

"I got nothing to say to you, Jew," Forsling snarled.

Again Karp waited before answering. He could still see the burning car and the bodies inside. He'd watched as the paramedics loaded Rose Lubinsky into an ambulance and heard her husband, Simon, crying out in anguish as he climbed in after her. The shocked, horrified faces of his own sons threatened to blind him, and then there was the image of the smirking face of Lars Forsling in the window of the police cruiser mouthing one word: *Jew.*

And yet he felt neither rage nor a need to revenge his friends and family. Nearly all of his adult life he'd dealt with the worst of the city's worst examples of human beings — the homicidal maniacs, the cold-blooded sociopaths, the child killers, and the violent rapists, the brutal and the vicious. But he'd learned to put his feelings aside so that he could do his job, and his job was to get at the truth; personal revulsion and rage aimed at a suspect could get in the way of that if he let it. Oh, at trial he might call forth righteous indignation or anger for the jury at the precise moment it was needed, but that was all part of his disciplined trial preparation.

Sitting down across from Forsling, Karp indicated that the steno should take her place at the end of the table. The woman did so, placing the black box in front of her and opening the case to reveal a stenographer's machine. Meanwhile Fulton stood against a wall where he could watch his boss and the suspect.

"Mr. Lars Forsling, I'm District Attorney Roger Karp . . . ," he began.

"I know who you are, Jew . . ."

The hatred in the young man's voice was palpable but he didn't let it deter him. ". . . and I'd like to ask you a few questions regarding the fatal car bombing this evening at Third Avenue and 29th Street in New York County. Also present are Carole Mason, a stenographer in my office, and Detective Clay Fulton, who is in charge of the district attorney's detectives squad. You have a right to remain silent. Do you understand?"

"The cops already read me my rights."

"Humor me," Karp replied evenly. "Do you understand you have the right to remain silent?"

"Jawohl."

"I believe you answered 'yes' in German," Karp said. "However, I need you to answer in English, please."

"Yes, I understand."

"Anything you say may be used against you in court, do you understand?"

"Yes."

"You also have the right to have an attorney present during questioning. If you can't afford an attorney, one will be provided for you. Do you understand this?"

Forsling didn't say anything but nodded.

"You've indicated that you understand by nodding. However, Carole Mason needs to hear an answer."

"Yes, Karp, I understand English. Get on with it."

"Now, having been advised of your rights, are you willing to make a statement without your lawyer being present?"

"White men don't have rights in this country anymore."

Karp looked at Forsling for a moment, then continued. "Are you willing to answer any of my questions now?"

"Am I under arrest for the bomb?" Forsling interrupted.

"You were arrested for disobeying the lawful command of a police officer," Karp answered. "And again, are you willing to answer my questions?"

Forsling jabbed a thumb over at Fulton. "And if I'm not, you'll have your house nigger beat me up."

Karp looked over at Fulton, who smiled and shrugged his shoulders. He'd heard it all, too, and it wasn't the first time a suspect had used a racial slur on him.

"That's not the way we do things here. Whatever you think of me, or Detective Fulton, we're after the truth, period. Will you answer my questions?"

Forsling laughed bitterly. "Why should I, Karp? You and your nig . . . your cop . . . think I did it, and that's all that matters. The white man can't get a break, especially if he's a white man who dares open his mouth in the defense of his race. For all I know, you planted that bomb so you'd have a reason to go after us for murder."

Karp drummed his fingers on the table. "I don't care about your politics, Lars. And I haven't decided any such thing, that's why I want to ask you questions. What I do know is that you were present. That you had

152

targeted the meeting where the victims were going to be for your demonstration. And that you were arrested near the car that exploded."

"So that makes me guilty, right?" Forsling scoffed. "A bunch of niggers riot, burn stores, and kill whites, and they're just 'venting.' A few white men voice their opinion and they're 'racists and bombers,' ain't that right?"

"It makes you a person of interest; it doesn't make you guilty," Karp replied calmly. "I also know that you were sitting in the police car when the bomb went off and had a view of Mrs. Lubinsky's car. And *that* makes you a potential witness."

Forsling tilted his head to the side. "If I answer your questions, can I leave?"

"I'm afraid you're going to have to wait and go before a judge in the morning on the failure to obey a lawful command."

"I can't; I have to get out." Forsling's voice changed; instead of pugnacious, he sounded a little desperate.

"Maybe you should have thought about that before you disobeyed the police officer. This won't be the first time you've spent the night in The Tombs . . ."

"My mom's home alone," Forsling inter-

153

rupted. "She's an invalid and needs help at night."

"I can't do anything until the judge sets bail," Karp said. "But I can ask that NYPD do a welfare check, make sure she's okay. Or you can make a call and see if a friend or neighbor can watch out for her."

Forsling scowled and shook his head. "She'd freak if some nigger or spic cop showed up. And we don't have any neighbors who'd help; they're all a bunch of fucking illegal immigrants, spics and hebes."

"That's the best I can do," Karp said. "Now, are you willing to answer my questions?"

Forsling sighed and shook his head. "Not that it will do any good, but yeah, okay, let's talk. I know you won't do anything with it, but what about the funny-looking nigger who was there?"

"What about this individual?"

"I saw him over by the car," Forsling said. "He was out in the street and leaned over when he was walking past, like he was tying his shoe or something."

"When was this?"

"After I got arrested. Of course, nobody cares if a nigger is wandering around. But I go for a stroll and it's a fuckin' federal offense."

Karp ignored the racial slurs. "So you said this individual was 'funny-looking.' What do you mean by that?"

Forsling shrugged. "You know, like his face was like half-black, half-white . . . like he had that thing that Michael Jackson had."

"Vitiligo," Fulton interjected. "It causes a decrease in skin pigmentation."

"Yeah, whatever," Forsling said. "He looked like a fuckin' mutant, or like he was trying to be white; like they all want to be white."

"Anything else about this individual other than he was walking past the vehicle that was bombed and had this skin condition?" Karp asked.

"Yeah, two things," Forsling said. "First was that right before the bomb went off, I saw him walk away from the other jokers in that crowd. Then he took out his cell phone and punched in some numbers."

"So what?" Karp said. "Maybe he was placing a call or texting."

"Yeah, maybe," Forsling said. "But he wasn't talking into the phone or even looking at it when that Jew bitch and her friends got in the car. He was watching them and then BOOM!"

Karp and Fulton exchanged looks. "You said there were two things; what was the second?"

"Yeah, his shoes."

"What about his shoes?"

"Bright red high-tops," Forsling said with disdain. "It's cold as shit outside, snow on the ground, and Casper the friendly half-nigger ghost is wearing cherry red canvas high tops. . . . Now that's all I'm going to say; we'll see what you do with it, Karp. I think I want that lawyer now."

A few minutes later, after Forsling had been led back to a holding cell, Karp leaned back in the chair and looked up at Fulton. "What do you think?"

"About him or what he said about the case?"

Karp laughed. "Well, let's hear both."

"Well, he's a piece of shit racist son of a bitch," Fulton said. "I still like him for this, but I admit my judgment might be a little clouded. The guy with the red shoes sounds a little far-fetched, and even if there was a guy like that, Forsling might just be tossing that out there, hoping we'll bite."

"In other words, we've got to run this to the ground," Karp said. "Something about Forsling doesn't feel right . . . it's too easy. I'm sure NYPD is already on it and will check the dash cams on the patrol cars and be looking for any security cameras that might have something. But let's get a set of eyes on those recordings, too, see if you can spot this guy in the red shoes. Also, the television crews were out in force — maybe they got something."

Fulton grimaced. "Getting the media to cooperate in a police investigation is worse than pulling teeth," he said.

"Yeah, but we have two people murdered, and Rose is in critical condition. While they're on the scene, maybe they'll do the right thing," Karp said. "It can't hurt to ask."

"Not as long as you're doing the asking," Fulton replied with a grin.

Karp smiled back. "That's what I got Guma for; we'll see if he's got any of that old Italian charm left."

10

Micah Gallo hesitated outside the main entrance of Bellevue Hospital like a man on the edge of a bad dream knowing that if he moves forward something terrible will happen. And yet he is unable to turn and walk away, aware that the nightmare was of his own making, and therefore he had to confront what waited beyond the doors or it would haunt him the rest of his life.

He hadn't intended to go to the hospital. After leaving Monroe at the Jay Street Bar, he'd headed for his apartment, intending to numb his concerns about what had just happened to Rose Lubinsky with marijuana and beer. Monroe said he'd had nothing to do with the bomb, and that the skinheads were probably to blame. He wanted to believe it. But with doubt roiling around in the pit of his stomach like a restless snake, he'd suddenly flipped around and taken the exit back over the Williamsburg Bridge into

Manhattan.

Heading north on FDR Drive, he berated himself for lacking the courage to approach Lubinsky at the book signing to apologize. *And now it might be too late,* he thought, and pounded the wheel. He wondered if deep inside something in him had wanted to warn her that she was pushing powerful people toward desperate measures.

Yeah, the trouble with that is you knew it days ago, and again tonight before the bomb even went off, said one voice in his head.

It doesn't prove anything, said its counterpart. *It might not have been the same guy.*

You're trying, Micah, but you're not fooling yourself, came the reply. *Think about it.*

Pulling into the Bellevue parking lot, Gallo knew what the voice was talking about. It began several nights earlier when Monroe asked him to go with him to the Kings County District Attorney's Office on Jay Street. *"Our friend District Attorney Olivia Stone has some ideas about how to stop this charter school bill."* They were met at a side door by an overweight, balding security guard who'd been told to watch for them. The guard seemed to know Monroe and let them in without comment as though it was nothing out of the ordinary.

They took the elevator and then walked into the reception area through an unlocked glass door. Monroe led the way across the room to another wooden door and knocked. There was the sound of scrambling and voices from behind the door. Monroe gave him an odd look and shrugged.

A woman's voice then shouted for them to enter. Monroe opened the door and looked in. The same woman snapped, "You're early." She sounded peeved.

"Traffic was light," Monroe answered. He then glanced over his shoulder at Gallo, who'd hung back. "Take a seat out here for a few minutes. I'll come get you."

Monroe walked into the room, but before he closed the door, Gallo caught a glimpse of another man in the room. It was just for an instant, yet one he would never forget. The stranger was a black man and appeared to have some sort of disfigurement on one side of his face, as though he'd been burned or had a skin disease that had caused his dark skin to turn white.

A few minutes later, Monroe opened the door again and motioned for him to come in. The black man was nowhere to be seen inside the room. Micah noted a side door and presumed he'd gone out that way and thought it odd that they were obviously trying to keep him from being seen. But at the time he'd thought no more about it and soon had other issues to deal with as Monroe pointed to a couch for him to sit and sat down next to him.

They were seated across a glass-and-steel table from Olivia Stone, an attractive woman in her late forties with short blond hair, green eyes, and the figure of a woman who spent a lot of time in the gym. Gallo had seen her before and she'd always been immaculately coiffed to the point of rigidity; however, that night she appeared to have forgotten to fix her hair, and her lipstick looked like it had been applied hurriedly.

I wonder if the black guy had anything to do with that, Gallo mused as he glanced around the room. He seemed to get an answer when he looked back at Stone, who was regarding him with a slight, knowing smile on her face as if she'd guessed what he was thinking . . . and found it amusing to let him know it was true.

However, the conversation had quickly turned to the charter school bill. Gallo was aware that in large part she owed her position to the financial and voter support of the teachers union. *As well as the property on Long Island, Miami, and the Caribbean that Monroe's told me about,* he thought. So he wasn't surprised when it turned out that she was willing to resort to illegal measures to make sure that the status quo was maintained for Monroe and the teachers union.

Stone smiled again, not coyly this time but wolfishly. "So, Micah, what have we — I mean, you — got on Rose Lubinsky that we can use?"

A chill ran down Gallo's spine. "What do you mean?" he said, though he knew exactly what she was talking about because he'd lived through it.

"Any bad habits? Maybe an affair? Anything from her past that she might not want made public," Monroe said.

"Maybe she takes school equipment home with her," Stone added with a grin.

Stone's pointed comment felt like a slap to his face. He wanted to get up and walk out. He knew where this conversation was heading and wanted no part of it. But instead he sat there, his face burning and his pride nowhere to be found.

Monroe shot Stone a "back off" look, but she ignored him. "Come on, Micah, quit acting like you don't know how this game is played. What do you got on the bitch?"

Gallo shook his head. "Nothing."

"What?" Stone said. "I don't think I heard

you correctly."

"I don't have anything," Gallo replied. "She's about the cleanest, most blameless person I've ever known."

"Come on," Stone said, rolling her eyes. "Nobody's perfect. You worked with her. Ate dinner with her. You were friends. Surely there's something, even if it was completely innocent, that we can find a way to use."

"What do you want me to fucking say?" Gallo shot back, finally finding some measure of courage. "Her family was wiped out in the Holocaust; she lived because they gave her to a Christian couple to raise. At some point she was anti-Semitic because of her upbringing, but she wrote a book about it so she's already 'outed' herself. Other than that she's dedicated to her husband, who is just as faithful to her. She doesn't smoke. She doesn't drink. She doesn't do drugs. And even if she ever borrowed a pencil from the school, after what you did to me, she's doubly careful."

Gallo turned to look at Monroe. "The kids in these schools mean everything to her. I think it's her way of paying back what she thinks she owes the past. I don't know if you ever felt that way about our students, Tommy. I know I did once, but somewhere along the line we sold out. But she hasn't."

Monroe scowled. "The union's done a lot for the kids and the teachers."

"Maybe, but 'done' is the operative word," Gallo said. "It's still not too late. We can work something out with the charter schools. I'll talk to Rose. Maybe she'd back off on going through the books — call it water under the bridge."

"You saw how she reacted to my offer," Monroe pointed out.

Anything else Gallo was going to say was interrupted by a derisive laugh from Stone, who got up, walked around the table, and then sat on the edge of the couch next to Gallo. "That's all very sweet about the kids and losing your way, worthy of a Tony Award if you ask me. But the time for negotiating and compromising is over. Like Tommy said, she's not reasonable."

Stone leaned closer to Gallo, pressing one of her legs up against his. "If you care for this woman, you need to help us find a way to stop her," she said, leaning toward him as if Monroe wasn't even in the room. "I'm not about to let some old crusader ruin my plans, and I've got big plans, pretty boy."

Gallo moved his leg away from hers. "Even if I could come up with some piece-of-crap offense like you used against me, she's tougher than I am. I know her; she'd die before she backed down or let herself be bought off by you."

Stone and Monroe had given each other a look when he said that, which at the time he took to be one of anger or frustration. But as he got out of his car to walk over to the hospital, he wasn't so sure. It was definitely a case of 20/20 hindsight and conjecture, but now he thought the look was between two people who had reached some sort of decision.

He realized what that was outside of Il Buon Pane that night. Leaving Stone's office, the black man's disfigurement was the only thing that had stood out to Gallo. However, at the bakery another memory lurched back into his conscious mind. He recalled that in the moment Monroe swung the door shut, he'd noticed the man's shoes. Cherry red high-tops. And he remembered that because he'd seen that face and those shoes in the crowd of counterdemonstrators across the street from the Nazis. It was only a glimpse before the man disappeared in the crowd, and at the moment he had not associated it with Stone and Monroe and the look they'd shared. Not until he was sitting in the Jay Street Bar with Monroe, staring in disbelief up at a television screen.

You don't know for sure, he warned himself as he stood in front of the hospital, watching as what seemed to be a flood of injured, sick, and mentally ill humanity limped, staggered, and were carried in and out of the doors. He looked up at the tall, gray, square box of a hospital and thought about Rose Lubinsky lying in one of the rooms in pain, possibly dying. *Yet she would have cared more for every one of these people than for herself,* he thought.

He took a step toward the doors before Monroe's voice echoed down the corridors of his mind. *"Who butters your bread, Micah?"* Nausea threatened to overcome him as he also recalled his answer. *"You do, Tommy."* *And if they go down, you go down,* said the voice of self-interest.

Gallo started to turn back toward his car and almost bumped into a family rushing toward the entrance. A young man carried an obviously pregnant young woman in his arms, struggling as she cried out in labor. Straggling along behind him were two children — a girl of about five or six, crying as she held the hand of an uncooperative toddler. The young man turned back and spoke to them urgently. *"Date prisa, los niños!"*

Hurry up, children, Gallo translated. He

166

held out his hands to the children as he spoke to the young man. "I'll help you with them."

The young man looked troubled about leaving his children to be brought along by a stranger. But then his wife screamed and he turned without saying another word and hurried toward the entrance.

Gallo walked more slowly behind with the trusting children holding his hands. By the time they reached the lobby of the hospital, a swarm of nurses had the pregnant woman in a wheelchair and were taking her away. The young man turned to Gallo and smiled. *"Gracias, amigo."*

"De nada. Tenga cuidado de sus hijos y buena suerte con el nuevo bebé."

"Thank you, I will," the young man said, taking his hand. "You are a good man to help a stranger and his children."

Gallo didn't know what to say as his eyes filled with tears, so he just shook the other man's hand and turned to walk up to the information desk. "I'm here to see Rose Lubinsky," he said to the large black woman behind the desk.

The woman typed the name into her computer and then frowned. "She's in the Intensive Care unit," she said. "No one but immediate family are allowed to see her."

"I'm her son," Gallo said.

The woman frowned again. "I don't see a son listed, only a husband."

"That would be my dad, Simon Lubinsky. They must have been in a hurry and forgot to include me."

The woman gave him a suspicious glance. "I'll see if I can get ahold of someone on ICU. It might take a few minutes, so go have a seat in the waiting room, and I'll come get you."

Gallo did as he was told, sitting in the only seat available, next to a man holding a bloody rag against his stomach as he moaned and spoke what sounded like Russian. Across from them a woman shivered and sweated, crying out in delirium as her anxious boyfriend or husband patted her shoulder and looked around desperately. He stood up and walked around the corner and peeked out at the woman behind the information desk. She was arguing with a police officer who was holding on to a handcuffed man as he vomited on the floor.

Gallo turned and made his way across the room to the double swinging doors that he'd seen patients and doctors going in and out of and walked through. He found himself walking rapidly along a crowded, bustling hallway filled with doctors, gurneys, nurses, paramedics, and patients. He approached a man in green surgeon's scrubs who stood looking down at a clipboard.

"Which way to Intensive Care?" he asked.

Without looking up from the clipboard, the doctor pointed to a sign on a wall that read "ICU" in big bold letters and had an arrow pointing down another hallway. By following arrows, he found an elevator that carried him to a floor that had another ICU sign pointing to the left. He turned a corner and realized he had reached his destination, not because of the sign hanging above more swinging doors but the people who stood and sat outside them.

Standing in the center of them was Alejandro Garcia, dressed in a hospital gown with his hands bandaged. The stocky young man saw him coming and moved to get in his way. "Second time tonight . . . what the fuck you doing here, *pendejo,*" he swore.

It had been a long, trying night. Gallo's anger finally boiled to the surface as he came chest to chest with his former rival. "Call me that one more time and . . ."

". . . and what?" Garcia spat. "You got no business here. These people are Rose's friends, people who love her. They stick by

169

her, thick and thin. That doesn't include you."

The situation was about to get out of hand when Simon Lubinsky pushed through the doors from the Intensive Care unit. He looked sad and worn out, then confused when he saw Gallo. But then he nodded. "Let him by, Alejandro . . ."

Garcia frowned. "But . . ."

Lubinsky held up his hand. "Please, now is not the time for this, Rose wants to see him."

"But how does she know he's here?" Garcia asked.

"I don't know," Lubinsky replied, "but somehow she knew he would come. So let him pass."

Garcia glared at Gallo one more time but then stepped aside. As he approached the old man, Gallo said, "Simon, I'm so . . ."

"I know, Micah, I know, but there's no time to waste. You must hurry."

Simon escorted him back past the nurses' station to a room and told him to go in. "I'll wait out here," he said.

Gallo entered the dark room and waited for a moment for his eyes to adjust to the gloom. As they did, he saw Rose lying in the bed, covered nearly head to foot in bandages. Only one arm and hand that had somehow escaped the flames lay on top of the sheet.

"Rose?" he said as he approached her bedside.

Rose Lubinsky responded by raising her unbandaged hand for him to hold. He grabbed it tenderly and bent over to kiss her fingers, but she pulled him closer and whispered. "You know."

"I don't understand, Rose. Know what?" he replied.

"Who did this?" She turned her head slightly so that she could look at him with the one eye not covered by gauze.

"The Nazis."

The eye glittered. "You know better than that."

"I don't . . . not for sure."

"Micah, my son, for your sake," she said, her breath laboring from the pain, "don't try to live with the guilt. It will eat you."

"Oh, Rose," he cried out quietly. "I'm not brave like you. I'm as bad as they are."

"No," she said. "You are lost, but you are good. They must be stopped . . . for the children. Promise me . . ."

Gallo wanted to stand up and turn away from her. *Who butters your bread, Micah?* But instead he nodded. "I'll try."

Rose Lubinsky seemed to relax and

171

squeezed his fingers. "Goodbye, Micah. I have always loved you. Now, please, send Simon . . . then wait for him."

Tears streaming from his eyes, Gallo left the room and saw Simon standing across the hallway. "She wants you," he said.

Simon nodded and then walked slowly back to the room where his wife waited as though by his pace he could delay the inevitable. Gallo watched him enter the room and close the door, then left the ICU. He didn't join the others and avoided looking at them.

A few minutes later, whether five or twenty-five Gallo in his grief didn't know, Simon Lubinsky returned carrying a manila envelope. "She . . . she . . . ," he tried to say, but choked on the words. "My love is gone." He seemed to stumble a bit then and Garcia rushed up to support him.

After a moment, Simon patted the young man on his broad shoulders and straightened up and looked at Gallo. He held out the manila envelope. "She asked me to give this to you," he said. "She said you would know what to do with it."

Gallo took the envelope, opened it, and pulled out a document. He read it briefly, his brow furrowing. "I don't understand. When did she give this to you?"

"There are many things in God's world that we aren't meant to understand," Lubinsky said. "But she gave it to me earlier tonight, after the book signing. She said she saw you come in and leave, and had hoped to speak to you." He shook his head. "Rose was always intuitive, but even I had no idea what she meant when she said that if anything happened to her, I should give you this."

Gallo bowed his head as a sob escaped his lips. The old man reached out and stroked his hair. Then with a sigh, the young man raised his head and turned toward Garcia.

"You have no reason to trust me," he said. "But I could use your help."

"What are you planning to do?" Garcia asked, his eyes wet but his face grim.

"Get even."

"Then let's ride, hombre."

11

By the time Lars Forsling saw a judge and walked out of The Tombs it was noon. He was tired, angrier than ever, and panicked about his mother. After he told Karp he wanted a lawyer, the conversation had ended and he was turned over to a sleepy Legal Aid attorney, who basically told him not to talk to the prosecutors anymore and that he'd have to wait until morning to get out on bail.

He was allowed to make a phone call but his mother didn't pick up. That in itself wasn't alarming; often as not she'd been drinking heavily and was asleep — or passed out — by eight. However, he couldn't reach her after he was released either because the jail had not returned his cell phone. "Take it up with the DA," he was told, "they're onto it right now."

So he'd hurried to the Canal Street subway station, jumped the turnstile, and took the green line north to 116th. Along the way he kept to himself and avoided the hard glares of a group of young blacks. His night in The Tombs had been sleepless, as he was locked up in a cell next to an immense dark Jamaican who kept telling him what he was going to do "to your cracker ass if'n I get a chance." But then and on the trip north, he was in no position to say or do anything, except quietly hate.

As the train rattled and rolled, sliding to each stop to let passengers on and off, Forsling grew more impatient and agitated. He imagined his mother's panic. He'd spent the night out before, of course, but never without telling her, and he'd always had his phone to check up on her. Sometimes that meant having to go home sooner than he'd wanted as she complained bitterly about having to spend a night alone with her real and imagined dangers. *"What if some negro breaks in and rapes me,"* she'd cry. *"You know they're just looking for a chance. Then you'll be sorry."*

It was hard for him to imagine anyone wanting to have sex with his mother. As she told him at least several times a week, she'd once been a great beauty — a long-legged dancer who'd arrived in New York from Wisconsin to try out for the Rockettes at Radio City Music Hall. That hadn't worked out the way she'd hoped *"because those other girls were jealous of my looks and talent. They were sleeping with the bosses so they made sure I didn't get the job and upstage them."*

Greta Forsling had survived, like so many other young women who came to Gotham seeking fame on the Great White Way, as a waitress. However, she'd managed to get some bit parts in the chorus or as a walk-on for off-Broadway shows. One of those was to be her ticket to stardom until she'd been seduced and impregnated with Lars by the show's producer. *"He said he was Italian, but I know he was a Jew,"* she'd told her son since childhood. *"He lied to me, and then after I got pregnant, he wanted me to have an abortion. But I wouldn't, so he left me for some whore. I gave up being a star so that you could live."*

When young Lars asked about his father all she'd add was that *"he was like all the other Jews and the negroes and spics who see a beautiful blond woman. There's just one thing on their filthy minds."*

Greta told her son that she was related to Swedish nobility and that was the only thing that might save him from the taint of his *"half-Jewish blood."* He would have to listen to her, and obey her without question, if he wanted to *"burn"* the accident of his birth out of his body. *"We must be vigilant and make sure that the evil never gets a chance to take over,"* she warned him. *"But you're lucky you have me as your mother. I love you, and I'll save you from yourself."*

After Lars's birth, they'd moved to Brooklyn, where she'd found more work in diners, working for men who invariably fell into the category of "niggers, Jews, and spics," and all of whom seemed to spend most of their time trying to get her into bed. Not that she resisted all of them. Ever since Lars could remember there'd been a steady stream of men of all types and colors going into her bedroom at night and not coming out until morning. They'd look down at the boy sleeping on the couch — some would smirk, others would pat him on the head and even give him the change from their pockets, but few ever came back for seconds.

Whatever beauty Greta Forsling once had faded into a frowsy, overweight, bottle-blonde with veins in her cheeks from too much cheap vodka, and deep lines around her eyes and mouth from chain-smoking cigarettes. And she'd gone downhill from there.

She never seemed to keep a job for long — blaming it on "sexual harassment" and other women's jealousies — which meant they never lived anywhere for any length of time either. Lars got used to coming home from school to find an eviction notice on the door and his mother gone. Sometimes she scribbled a note on the notice to tell him where to look for her; other times she just left him to figure it out himself or wait for her to come looking for him.

The constant moving, his embarrassment over the tattered clothes he wore, and his overbearing, usually drunk mother meant that he'd had few friends. Any time it looked like he might have found one, his mother would discourage it. The neighborhoods where they could afford to live were all poor and mixed race, and she didn't want him *"hanging out with mud people,"* warning that close associations with other races and ethnicities might *"bring out the Jew in you."*

It wouldn't have mattered if he'd found a friend. Sooner or later he'd go home and there'd be a new eviction notice and he'd be off to a new part of the city and a new school.

The closest he ever came to having peers was in high school, where for a time he'd hung out with other "alternative" kids who didn't fit into the social strata. They wore black clothing, dyed their hair and eyebrows the color of coal, and used dark eye shadow while working to maintain perfectly pasty complexions. They'd gather behind the gym, smoke cigarettes, and talk about how "fucked up" the world was, but they weren't really friends. Mostly just a collection of outcasts drawn together by their antisocial attitudes.

Another eviction notice had arrived during his junior year in high school. It was something of a miracle that he'd made it that far, but he wasn't stupid and something inside of him had made him cling to the hope of someday bettering his situation. However, this time he never went back.

They'd moved over to Manhattan and a run-down, two-story walk-up on the Upper East Side. But not *that* Upper East Side, the one with all the rich, well-dressed people, who drove expensive cars and lived in nice, clean buildings with doormen and security guards. No, their neighborhood, though technically the Upper East Side, was only a few blocks south of East Harlem. A land of crime-ridden, crumbling tenements, and more closely resembling the economic conditions and cultural makeup of the latter than the former.

By this time his mother had given up even pretending to look for work. She'd become so obese, which had contributed to her diabetes, that she qualified for disability checks and spent most of her days and nights propped up beneath stained, threadbare silk sheets in a worn-out king-sized bed eating junk food, reading romance novels, smoking cigarette after cigarette until the ashtrays were overrun with butts, and drinking her vodka with 7Up.

Sometimes she'd go for a month or more without leaving the apartment; Lars cashed her disability checks for her and bought whatever it would cover. It was all she could do to waddle to the toilet and back to her bed. She rarely bathed, preferring to cover up any bodily odors with a cheap perfume.

And yet, despite all of that, Lars Forsling loved his mother. When she wasn't warning him about the "Jewish poison" coursing through his veins, or berating him for forgetting her cigarettes or vodka, or reminding him that she'd "given up everything" so that he could live and that he was "cruel" to leave her alone, she was the only person who'd ever said she loved him. He was "the smartest boy in your school . . . the best-looking . . . the nicest." Whatever the danger of his father's diseased blood, he had pure

Nordic DNA that would "burn it out of your body so long as you listen to your mother."

He knew that their relationship was dysfunctional and that his dependence on her was unhealthy. From time to time he'd dreamed of moving to Idaho, where he'd be welcomed into one of the white supremacist camps. But whenever he brought it up, his mother would scream at him for being ungrateful for all she'd sacrificed and then weep hysterically and threaten to kill herself. So he'd resign himself to the life he had, at least while his mother was still alive.

Although indoctrinated in racism since childhood, Lars had not acted on his beliefs until his midtwenties, when on a whim he decided to attend an American Nazi Party meeting he'd seen advertised on a flyer taped to a street light pole. Held in the basement of The Storm Trooper, a dive bar in Hell's Kitchen, the meeting had been attended by only a dozen or so brown-shirted young- to mid-forties-aged men sporting red-black-and-white Nazi armbands. A small, dumpy man in a black SS shirt with a Hitler-style mustache named Bob Mencke had led the meeting, starting with a loud, off-key and poorly pronounced singing of "Horst-Wessel-Lied," followed by a lengthy diatribe essentially blaming all the woes of the poor, white males in America on blacks, "fags," and Jews.

Mencke had finished his speech with an admonition to prepare for the coming race war, and a plea to members to pay their association dues "so that our good works can continue," as well as to purchase his monthly newsletter, *The New York Der Stürmer.* He concluded the meeting by asking "all new recruits" — Lars was the only one — to introduce themselves.

Uncomfortable and embarrassed, Forsling had stood and stammered out his name and that he was of pure Nordic blood. "And all of my life, I've been told about the bad things that are being done to the white race." Not knowing what else to say, he'd started to sit down but stopped when, led by Mencke, the other members began to applaud. It was the first time in his life he'd heard that sound applied to him, and so was the warm welcome he received when the meeting adjourned and the members went upstairs to drink beer.

Forsling was hooked. He realized that most of the members were what larger society would label "losers." Some of them were simply socially inept in more mainstream groups, others lacked intelligence and so were easily led, and some just plain violent, angry young white males looking for justification to vent. Smart if undereducated, Forsling soon stood out among the losers as a leader. He immersed himself in Nazi culture and education, reading *Mein Kampf* and tracts by European and American Nazis so thoroughly that Mencke began asking him to speak at meetings.

It was from his studies that he'd learned about the "Aryan mecca," in parts of Idaho, where he dreamed that the sort of acceptance he'd received from the New York members would be greatly magnified. He might even find a good Aryan wife and live his life among pure white people in the pristine mountains. *But not while Mom's alive.*

In preparation for the race war and to make himself appear more formidable, he bought himself an old set of weights and worked out incessantly in his bedroom. He'd followed that up by getting "Sieg Heil" tattooed across his forehead, and when that was met with words of respect and admiration from his peers, as well as seeing the intimidation it generated among the general population, he'd added the swastikas on his temples. No one minded when he began affecting a slight German accent, and when one of the other members noticed, he'd said he got it from his mother "who comes from Swedish nobility."

Forsling liked to be thought of as tough and ready to fight. But beneath the tattoos and leather coats he was still a frightened boy growing up in tough neighborhoods without a father and with a slovenly, abusive drunk of a mother. He got in a few scrapes when he had other, rougher members of the gang with him to do most of the fighting, but he left the truly violent work to those who enjoyed it, like Jimmy Gerlach, who worked as a bouncer at The Storm Trooper. According to his admirers in the club, Gerlach had served time in Attica for manslaughter after he punched a black man who died after he fell and hit his head.

There was one thing Forsling feared more than anything else: rats. Ever since he could remember he'd been terrified of them. His mother attributed it to a time when he was still an infant and she'd heard him crying. *"I went to check on you in your crib and there was this enormous rat biting your face,"* she said. *"That was another time I saved you."* But whatever the cause, even the sight of one could be enough to cause him to panic.

Forsling's role as a leader in the group had changed dramatically when he suggested the group participate in Kristallnacht USA. He'd read that the Nazi party and other white supremacist groups were going to commemorate the German event by attacking Jewish businesses and homes on the anniversary.

Mencke, who as it turned out was always more talk than action, had argued against it. "The time isn't right," he said. "We need to continue to grow and marshal our forces."

However, most of the rest of the group had been persuaded by Forsling's enthusiasm and voted to participate. It marked the change in leadership of the group, though Mencke remained *Oberkommando.* Still, Forsling was in charge and led the planning for Kristallnacht.

Although the group caused quite a bit of damage to Jewish businesses and defaced the doors and walls at the Holocaust Museum in Battery Park, Forsling was disappointed when only half the members reported for duty. He was even more disappointed when the national commemoration fizzled out. He'd been arrested outside the museum and charged with vandalism, which got him his first night in The Tombs, though he'd been able to get one of the girls who hung around the group to look in on his

185

mom so the next day's lecture would be mild. That arrest, and his subsequent dressing-down of the absent members, vaulted him to the top of the group's hierarchy, with even Mencke addressing him as an equal.

High on the praise of his social group, Forsling had looked for another venue in which to make a name for himself and found it when he was looking through the Sunday *New York Times* book section and saw the announcement about Rose Lubinsky's book signing at Il Buon Pane. He hadn't intended on getting arrested that night and had actually snuck away from the protest to find a tree to pee behind when he got caught walking back on the street next to the bakery.

He was actually proud of how he'd stood up to Karp and the black detective. But he knew that his mother was going to be an angry, weeping mess when he got back home.

Forsling was working on his explanation to his mother when he rounded the corner and saw the fire truck and crowd of onlookers halfway down the block in front of the walk-up where he lived. He walked faster. *Has to be that family of spics next door using the stove to heat their apartment again,* he told himself and began to run.

Only it wasn't the family next door. He arrived in front of his home and stared up at the second floor, with its shattered windows and the smoke damage evident on the outside. The top of the building was virtually gone, the roof having caved in before the firefighters could put the blaze out. He ducked under the yellow tape that had been wrapped around the outside of the walk-up.

"Hey, buddy, get outta there," a man in a firefighter officer's uniform yelled at him.

"This is my house," Forsling explained. "I live here with my mom."

The officer, who was standing near the truck, gave the other man a look and walked over. He held out his hand but Forsling ignored it as he looked back at the building. "Son, I'm Captain Bo Loselle of the New York Fire Department. I'm afraid I have some bad news."

Forsling looked at him wildly "What bad news? What do you mean? Where's my mom?"

"There was a fire. It appears to have started in your mother's bedroom."

"So what hospital is she in?"

Loselle shook his head. "I'm sorry. She

187

didn't make it. She's at the city medical examiner's office. I can have one of my men give you a ride . . ."

Forsling stared at Loselle as if he didn't comprehend what the other man was saying. His eyes began to water, then grew wide as his face contorted into a mask of rage. "The fucking Jew did this."

Loselle frowned. "It looks like she fell asleep smoking in bed. We've only done a preliminary search, but there doesn't appear to have been any accelerants used that would indicate arson."

Forsling backed away from the fire captain. "Of course not. You'd lie for the fucking Jew. You're probably one yourself."

"Son, I know this is a shock," Loselle said. "Let one of my guys take you to the hospital, get you something for your nerves so you can calm down."

"Calm down?" Forsling shouted. "My mom was just murdered by a fucking Jew and his nigger cop, and you want me to calm down? I'll show that bastard Karp that two can play this game."

"Karp?" Loselle asked. "You mean the DA?"

However, Forsling didn't answer. He just turned and ran back the way he'd come, planning how to get even. And then get away to Idaho.

12

The intercom on Karp's desk buzzed, which was followed by the voice of his longtime receptionist Darla Milquetost. Judging by her tone, he knew that she didn't particularly like the person she was passing along to him, so he wasn't surprised when she said it was his wife, Marlene, on the phone. The widow Milquetost ran a tight ship and had her "rules" about access to her boss, which Marlene tended to ignore most times just to antagonize — he was sure — his employee.

"Thank you, Darla," he said, and then punched a button. "Hi, baby, what's up?" he said, looking over at where Clay Fulton was leaning against the bookshelf. He held up a finger to indicate that he'd only be a minute. "Sorry to bother you, Butch," Marlene said. "I was just trying to get a handle on when you thought you might be home. Giancarlo's singing at his school concert tonight, and I have a few errands to run."

Karp winced. "Thanks for the reminder," he said. "I'll know better pretty soon."

"Okay, I'll call you back in a bit," Marlene replied.

In all the excitement, he'd forgotten that Giancarlo was singing the Hebrew Slaves Chorus from *Nabucco* for the first time in public. There hadn't been much of a chance to talk to Marlene after the bombing. He'd gone straight to his office and she'd driven Goldie and Moishe to the hospital to be with Simon and Rose Lubinsky. Then Marlene had called to say that Rose had died from her injuries and she'd be home after she made sure the Sobelmans and Simon Lubinsky were cared for.

When he heard her come in that night, he looked at the clock: 3 a.m. "You okay?" he'd asked but she didn't answer, except to slide into bed, put her head on his chest, and then cry herself to sleep.

After she fell quiet, he lay in the dark, thinking about Rose's story and about Simon meeting "the most beautiful woman in the world" after all he'd been through, only to have it end this way. He listened to Marlene's quiet breathing and felt the beating of her heart against his chest and thought about what it would be like to lose her. He'd come close before — Marlene was every bit the magnet for trouble that he'd been, maybe more so as she sometimes sought it out — but "close" wasn't the same as the finality of Rose Lubinsky's death. He just knew that he would be devastated beyond words.

Away from the office, removed from the world of indictments and trial preparation, Karp allowed himself to feel the anger about what had happened to Rose and the two young women who'd also died. Just because he had to compartmentalize his emotions in order to do his job correctly, it didn't mean he was some automaton who could ignore his friends' pain or not feel grief himself over the loss of a friend when time and circumstance allowed. He was still thinking about Rose when he quietly got up in the morning so as not to wake Marlene, dressed, and then walked outside of their loft building on Crosby Street.

"Ready to go, Mr. Karp?" asked Officer Eddie Ewin, who was standing by the sedan.

"You go ahead, Eddie," he replied. "I think I'm going to walk this morning. I can use the fresh air."

By the time he arrived at 100 Centre Street, Karp had stowed his emotions and had shifted gears to thinking about his interrogation of Lars Forsling. He was greeted by the little man with the pointed nose who ran the newsstand in front of the building. "Morning, Butch . . . asshole whoop," said "Dirty Warren" Bennett, who had Tourette's syndrome and was known for his physical tics and profanity. He handed Karp a morning copy of *The New York Times*, which of course led with a photo and story about the bombing; there was a sidebar story with a headline about possible neo-Nazi suspects. "Sorry to hear . . . oh boy oh boy nuts shit . . . your friend."

"Yeah, me, too," Karp replied. "Thanks, Warren."

"I hear it was the Nazi . . . bastards bitches balls whoop oh boy . . . that did it."

Karp shrugged. "I don't know, Warren; we're still trying to figure it out."

Dirty Warren peered up at him through his thick, smudged glasses with his weak blue eyes. "Hey got one for you . . . whoop?"

Karp sighed and shook his head. He and Bennett had been playing a movie trivia game for years and the little man had yet to stump him. "I don't know if I'm in the mood, Warren."

"Yeah, well, this one . . . son of a bitch whoop whoop fuck me . . . won't take long, it's about a reporter who gets it wrong and . . . oh boy ohhhh boy . . . an innocent man goes to prison for murder."

Karp furrowed his brow. Sometimes Dirty Warren seemed to know more about what went on in his office than some of his assistant district attorneys. "You wouldn't be talking about *Stranger on the Third Floor,* circa 1940. Peter Lorre's the killer, and John McGuire is the reporter who testifies against the wrong man, Elisha Cook Jr., and gets him sent to prison." He smiled. "You trying to tell me something, Warren?"

The news vendor grinned. "Nah, I ain't the one with the . . . fuck this oh boy tits . . . law degree. But sometimes the obvious guy . . . whoop whoop . . . ain't the guilty guy, am I right?"

Karp had looked sideways at him. "You sure you aren't a Harvard Law grad?"

"Nah, why would I . . . fuck you whoop oh boy asswipe whoop whoop . . . want to waste my money at Harvard?"

"Good point," Karp had said, and he had left the news vendor laughing and cursing.

The morning had been consumed by the usual activities of the district attorney of New York County, which encompassed the island of Manhattan, and meant dealing with some four hundred homicides, fifteen hundred rapes, seventeen thousand robberies, twenty thousand felony assaults, sixteen thousand burglaries, and forty thousand grand larceny cases every year. And that didn't include many times that number of misdemeanors. Under his supervision were six trial bureaus and a number of specialized bureaus encompassing rackets, frauds, appeals, and homicide, all with their bureau chiefs, assistant chiefs, and some five hundred assistant district attorneys, plus their support staff.

During the lunch break, Karp decided to head uptown to see how Moishe and Goldie Sobelman were holding up at Il Buon Pane. He found Moishe inside sweeping up glass as workmen installed plywood to cover up the shattered window spaces. He noted blood on some of the glass in the pile his friend had created.

Moishe stopped his sweeping and leaned on his broom. He looked at the pile of glass. "It seems that we Jews are always sweeping up glass and wiping up blood," he said quietly. "And then burying our dead."

The old man's head had dipped and his shoulders began to shake. Karp realized he was crying and walked over to put a hand on his shoulder. "I'm so tired of this, Butch, sometimes I just want to give up, quit fighting."

Karp patted him on the back. "I know you're tired. You've had to put up with broken glass and blood far more than most can even imagine. But if you give up, they win, and you can't allow that, not after everything you've been through. Rose wouldn't want that."

"Now you sound like my wife," Moishe said with a small chuckle as he wiped at his eyes. "And she says she is only mimicking what the man she married told her."

"A wise woman, that Goldie."

"Yes," Moishe replied. He shook his head. "I just can't believe that Rose is gone. I've known her for most of my adult life. I always knew that her past as one of the lost children haunted her. Now, just as she was purging herself of the guilt with her book, this happens. It seems so unfair."

"How's Simon?"

"Devastated, of course. He told me at the hospital that Rose had a premonition yesterday that something bad was going to happen. Now he blames himself for not protecting her."

"Obviously there's nothing he could have done," Karp said. "You can't act on premonitions. But when you see him, tell him we're going to do everything we can to get the person, or persons, who did this."

"Do you think it was that Nazi son of a bitch?"

Karp had hesitated, not sure how to answer, still mulling his conversation with Forsling and questions that had been boiling around in his head all morning. "He's a suspect," he replied after a moment, "but there may be other suspects as well. I can't talk about it right now because you may be called as a witness at a future trial."

Moishe had, of course, understood, and Karp had gone back to work after checking in on Goldie who was upstairs, quietly mourning her murdered friend. The afternoon was getting late when Fulton dropped by to update him on the Lubinsky murder investigation.

"I just got off the phone with the bomb squad guys," he said. "It was a fairly sophisticated device triggered by a cell phone call that set it off."

"Military?"

Fulton shrugged. "Maybe. But while it was not your run-of-the-mill Molotov cocktail, anyone with a computer who knows how to find such things could have put it together. No, the tough part was the bomb material: C-4 plastic explosive. Not easy stuff to get, though not impossible either. It was in a small container — probably no bigger than four inches by six inches — and attached to the gas tank."

"Any way of telling how long it had been there?"

Fulton shook his head. "Not really. The container had strong magnets — one was still attached to a piece of the tank — and it could have been placed earlier in the day, or when it was parked outside the bakery."

Karp sat for a moment tapping a pencil on a yellow legal pad he'd been making notes on all day. He furrowed his brow as he looked at the list of items on the pad, including what his lead investigator had just told him.

"All right, boss, what gives?" Fulton asked, and settled into the leather chair across the desk from Karp.

Looking up at his longtime friend and colleague, Karp tapped the pad one more time. "A friend reminded me this morning that the obvious suspect isn't necessarily the best one," he said. "Forsling's a racist son of a bitch, but something tells me he's the wrong guy for this."

"Not disagreeing, but why do you say that?"

"Well, for one thing, he was in custody and didn't have his cell phone when the bomb went off."

The big detective shrugged again. "Could have been one of his pals," he said. "He was arrested walking down the street where the car was parked. It wouldn't have taken but a few seconds for him to reach down and slap the bomb up under the gas tank."

"Why take a chance on doing it there?" Karp countered. "Take a chance on getting caught?"

"These guys aren't rocket scientists. Besides, they like getting in the news; it's all about the publicity and their egos."

"Maybe most of them aren't the brightest bulbs," Karp said. "But Forsling isn't stupid, and I don't think he was looking for publicity or he'd have taken credit. He doesn't have much of a record either. A few disorderly conducts, a vandalism-criminal mischief misdemeanor from November. It's quite a jump from there to planting a 'somewhat sophisticated' bomb that kills three people."

"They all get started somewhere."

Karp looked back down at his pad. "Yeah, maybe," he said. "I know some bombers like to stick around and watch. They enjoy seeing the suffering and fear. But they usually blend in with the crowd and don't draw attention to themselves. Not like some guy with Nazi facial tattoos, wearing a swastika

199

armband, and leading a noisy group of protesters. He might as well have rented a spotlight and stood under it. Something just doesn't add up."

Fulton nodded. "Again, I'm not disagreeing, but we're running it to the ground either way. In fact, Guma was on his way to check out some bar over in Hell's Kitchen that's a hangout for the white supremacist crowd, see if anybody there has anything to say or knows Forsling."

"Not likely to talk much," Karp noted.

"No, but part of crossing T's and dotting I's," Fulton replied. "Might help us eliminate him. Or maybe turn up somebody who would blow up a car and kill three women. So you got anybody else in mind?"

"What about the guy Forsling told us about?"

"The dude with the skin condition and red shoes," Fulton said. "There was nothing on the dash cams of the police cruisers, but Guma was going to check in with some woman he knows at one of the television stations that was there and see if they'll cooperate. He was going to go to the bar after that."

"You saw the guy?"

"Yeah, I saw somebody who fit the description," Fulton acknowledged. "But maybe Forsling picked him out of the crowd and tossed him out there like a red-shoed herring. No one saw him over by the car, except Forsling . . . allegedly. Besides, what's his motivation?"

Karp drew a line around a series of words on his pad. "Nazis weren't the only people who weren't fond of Rose," he said.

Fulton raised an eyebrow. "The charter school bill? The union? That's pretty drastic politics."

"Agreed," Karp said. "But tempers are pretty hot about the topic right now."

"So some union teacher with a mental problem goes off the deep end."

"Maybe. Or maybe, like the bomb, it's more sophisticated than that."

"The union brass?" Fulton whistled. "That would take some brass. Blowing up the opposition to defeat a bill. Why not just pay a few politicians?"

Before Karp could answer, his intercom buzzed. Darla Milquetost, sounding only slightly annoyed, announced, "There's a Detective Parker here who says he needs to speak to Mr. Fulton."

Fulton got up from the chair. "Parker's one of the guys assigned to this case," he said, walking across the room and opening the door. A young man appeared on the other side and said something to Fulton, who cast a worried look back over his shoulder at Karp. "Let's find out where he went," Fulton said, and then shut the door.

Karp could tell by the look on his big brown craggy face that the news wasn't good. "There was a fire early this morning up in East Harlem. One fatality."

"And?"

"The deceased was one Ms. Greta Forsling."

"The mother," Karp said, a feeling of disquiet growing in the pit of his stomach.

"Yeah," Fulton replied. "Apparently, Lars Forsling showed up this afternoon after the fire was out and the victim's body had been removed. He spoke to a fire department captain, Bo Loselle — good guy, I've known him almost as long as I've known you. Apparently, Lars thinks we had something to do with the fire."

"Us?"

"Yeah, mentioned you by name and your nigger cop sidekick, me," Fulton said. "Said he was going to get even."

"We know where he went?"

"Nope. He took off before Loselle could do anything about it."

Again whatever Karp was about to say was interrupted by the intercom buzzer and

Darla Milquetost announcing that Marlene was on the telephone line again. "Butch, I'm going to head over to Il Buon Pane to pick up the boys. Anything new on the case?"

He quickly told Marlene about Forsling and the threats. "I don't know what this guy's going to do. I've got some more work to do, and I'm waiting to hear from Guma, who is trying to find some of Forsling's associates."

"Good to know," Marlene answered. "I just spoke to Alejandro. He's planning to stop by your office with another guy named Micah Gallo, who works for the teachers union but used to be one of Rose's favorites. 'Jandro wouldn't say much on the phone and doesn't trust cops — as we know — but says you'll be interested in what they have to say. So am I, so take good notes."

Hanging up with his wife, Karp looked over at Fulton, who said, "Think I'll go make a few calls and see if we can't find Forsling before he does something stupid. And I better get in touch with Guma and tell him to keep an eye out in case our favorite Nazi decides to drown his sorrows at that bar."

13

"So what did you want to see me about?"

District Attorney Olivia Stone sat back in her chair and waited for Tommy Monroe to tell her why he'd called in a panic, saying they needed to talk "immediately." She'd never liked him much, found him to be crude and unattractive, with a bad habit of fixating on her cleavage when they talked. Early on in their relationship, when she was an underpaid Legal Aid attorney trying to get a cushy job with the union, she'd used her physical assets to her advantage. But after she got the position, and established herself as more valuable in their mutual quest for power and money, she'd made it clear that he needed to keep his hands and eyes to himself.

A few months after she was hired, they'd gone on a trip to Las Vegas for a convention of teachers unions, and after buying her numerous drinks had tried putting the moves on her. That's when she'd spelled it out. "It's not part of the deal." She'd expected him to respond with anger, but instead he'd laughed and said, "That's okay, sweet cheeks, I can get sex anytime; finding a smart, crooked lawyer is a little tougher."

Every once in a while he'd say something to let her know that he was still entertaining amorous thoughts. But as district attorney, she'd been even more unambiguous that the power dynamic had changed; she was the power now.

Yet, it wasn't just his oafish leers or suggestive remarks that formed her low opinion of him. While he could be clever in his dishonesty, and certainly knew how to wield power to achieve their shared goals, the years of being the top dog of a politically powerful organization had made him arrogant and careless. As she continued to set her aspirations at ever higher levels, such as a seat on the federal bench, or even governor, she'd worried that he was becoming a liability. However, she still needed the backing of his union, and so for the time being their fates were tied together.

Monroe leaned forward in his seat across from her and tossed a computer flash drive onto her desk. "This," he said.

"What is it?"

"A copy of the video taken by security cameras at headquarters about three a.m. There was a break-in."

"A break-in? Who breaks into a teachers union office?"

Monroe pointed to the flash drive. "Take a look."

Frowning, Stone picked up the flash drive and inserted it into the USB port on her computer. Grainy video feeds from four security cameras popped up in the quadrants on her screen. At first there was nothing; then two men appeared in the upper left-hand quadrant that showed the glass front doors of the building. They were all wearing black balaclava masks and gloves, except for one of the men, who appeared to have something white around one of his hands.

The men knew what they were doing, quickly gaining entry and then disappearing from that camera's view. They showed up again in the next frame, racing through a semi-dark hallway; then in a third in front of a door Stone knew led to Monroe's office. Again the lock wasn't an obstacle.

This time, however, when the men entered the office, one of them pulled out a can of spray paint and used it on the security camera lens. "What's that on his hand?"

Stone asked as the screen turned black.

"Looks like a bandage," Monroe said.

The recording stopped. "That's it?" Stone asked.

"Got 'em leaving, too, about five minutes later, but basically that's it."

"So what were they doing? You keep a lot of cash around?"

Monroe shook his head. "There was some petty cash in a drawer, but they left it," he said, then hesitated.

"Well?"

"Well, it looks like they were after my computer."

"They stole your computer?" Stone asked incredulously.

"No, they didn't steal it," Monroe replied. "I think they were looking for information."

Stone felt her stomach contract and the muscles of her face tighten. This was not going well. "What were they looking for?"

"I can't be sure."

"Why not?"

"They wiped the history for everything after I shut it off when I left the office yesterday."

Stone eyed the dagger-like letter opener on her desk and imagined sticking it in Monroe's throat. "Well, what *might* they have been after?" she asked, her voice icy and her anger barely under control.

Monroe licked his lips nervously. "I don't think they could have got into my computer. But there are some records on there . . ."

"What records?"

The big man tilted his head to the side. He let out a long breath. "There's one folder in there with some account information and real estate documents that, uh, we'd rather not go anywhere else."

"We'd?" Stone glanced at the letter opener again. "What do you mean 'we'd rather not go anywhere else'? What in the hell did you have on that computer?"

Monroe squirmed in the chair. "Pretty much everything."

"What!" Stone's response wasn't loud but it was hard as a brick to the head. "You fucking idiot."

"Your name's not on any of it," Monroe said. "At least not your real name. It's mostly dummy corporations and surrogates on the leases and documents, and all of it's encrypted."

"Yeah? And in the wrong hands how long do you figure it might take someone to break the code and track some of that down? Maybe lead them back to us? I can't believe you're so stupid."

This time Monroe frowned as his face

flushed with anger. "Don't tell me you don't have 'records' that could incriminate me stashed away somewhere."

Stone's eyes blazed. "Not anywhere anyone else could find." She glared at her partner in crime a moment longer, then took a deep breath and let it out. She'd always believed that she was smarter than everyone around her — that she deserved whatever she wanted because of her superiority — and she hadn't made it this far by panicking when things weren't going right.

"So who do you think was behind this?" she said as she pulled the flash drive out of her computer and put it in the middle drawer of her desk. "The charter school association?"

Monroe looked thoughtful. "Could be. Maybe somebody with his nuts in a twist because of that stupid car bomb."

Stone got the jab. He'd been uncomfortable with the assassination plan even though she'd argued that the timing would be perfect because of threats Rose Lubinsky had been getting from neo-Nazis. Then the thugs had cooperated by showing up to demonstrate. "But don't they have a suspect in custody?"

Monroe shrugged. "My sources in the

NYPD don't know much. And I have no ins at the New York District Attorney's Office."

When Monroe hesitated again, Stone knew more bad news was on the way. "What is it? You got somebody in mind?"

The union president nodded. "I don't know who the shorter guy with the bandaged hand is, but I think the other one is Micah Gallo."

"Well, that's just fucking great," Stone exclaimed. "We should have destroyed him and left it that way."

"I believe you were the one who said, 'Keep your friends close and your enemies closer,' " Monroe pointed out. "You thought it would be useful to corrupt him and use him against the charter schools."

"I believe Sun Tzu said that, but it doesn't matter now. If it's him, what's his game? Blackmail?"

"Could be. Maybe he's been playing us all along, waiting for a chance," Monroe said. "Or maybe revenge?"

"Revenge. He's up to his eyeballs in our little side business. He takes us down, he goes with us."

Monroe shook his head. "I'm not talking about revenge for what we did to him."

"What then?"

"This car bomb stunt," Monroe replied. "He was close to Lubinsky. It might have pushed him over the edge."

"What makes you think that? I mean, with those Nazis there, what connects us?"

"Well, he was supposed to show up at the Jay Street Bar precisely at eight," Monroe explained, "but he was closer to nine. Said he'd been in the city, meeting an old friend. But he was pretty nervous about it. Then when the news came on about what happened, he was real shook up. Took off about as soon as he could get out of there."

Stone didn't answer right away so Monroe used the gap in the conversation to get in another dig. "It was a mistake to have your 'friend' in your office the other night."

"You were early."

"Yeah, early enough to hear all the bumping and grinding. What the hell are you doing fucking that guy anyway? Talk about playing with dynamite."

Stone shot up from her seat and grabbed the letter opener. "How dare you!" she yelled.

Monroe snorted. "What? You going to stab me now because you're playing hide the monkey with a sociopath? That will look good in the papers."

The letter opener clattered to the top of

the desk as Stone sat down with a groan. She was quiet for a moment, then looked up at Monroe. "Do you know for sure if they were able to get into that file folder?"

Monroe shook his head. "No. They wouldn't have known what to look for either. It's named 'Family Album' and I've never showed it to Gallo. And like I said, even if they got into it, it would have just been a bunch of symbols. I've got a computer forensics guy looking at my machine to see if he can tell what they accessed and maybe the history they erased."

"Good. Have you tried to reach him?"

"Who? Gallo? Yeah, I've called him a couple of times, but all I get is his answering machine. I haven't said anything about the break-in."

"What about the police? Did you report it?"

"Are you kidding me? Last thing I need is the cops nosing around."

Stone nodded. "Okay, maybe it won't matter."

"What do you want to do?"

"Don't know yet," she replied. "Think about it. Let me know what your computer guy finds out and if you hear from Gallo. Now I've got to get back to work."

After Monroe left her office, Stone sat

thinking for a few minutes before calling up her email account and opening a new message. In the subject line she typed: "Need to meet asap. Coney Island. Two jobs." She then hit the Send button.

The next five minutes seemed to take forever. Then a message popped into her inbox. "One hour" was all it said. After reading it, she erased both her message and the answer before pressing the intercom button.

"Tony, I've had something come up and need to go out," she said to her office administrator. "Cancel my appointments and send any calls through to the answering service. I'll see you in the morning."

14

Lars Forsling walked through the door leading into The Storm Trooper and paused for a moment to let his eyes adjust to the dimly lit interior. The only windows looking out onto the sidewalk had been painted over to prevent the detractors and the curious from looking in and so the only light came from a few yellow bulbs set in the walls or behind the bar.

The dingy brick interior was decorated with photographs of famous Nazis and of the German Army, as well as the front pages of German newspapers heralding great victories from World War II. Nazi flags and decorative daggers were hung on the walls and from the ceiling, including a particularly large one behind the bar next to a life-sized portrait of Hitler. The whole place smelled of spilled beer, sweaty bodies, and cigarettes — despite New York's ban on smoking in public establishments.

Sitting at the bar were the bouncer, Jimmy Gerlach, and Bob Mencke. Otherwise the dive was empty of patrons and anyone else except for an unshaven, middle-aged barkeep, wearing an old black SS uniform shirt too small for his beer belly, which he left open, exposing his wife-beater undershirt. He looked up and smiled. "Well, if it ain't the man of the hour," he said. "Good work, Lars. I'm surprised they let you out."

"Right on, Lars," Gerlach agreed. "I was there, man, ka-boom, one Jew and two Jew lovers toast."

"I couldn't make it to the rally," Mencke said. "But I knew you were planning something big; I could see it in your eyes, Herr Forsling."

"It wasn't me," Forsling replied.

"Yeah, yeah, sure, I understand," said the bartender, whose name was Frankie LaFontaine. "Mum's the word, but you're among friends; let me buy you a beer, just because . . . wink, wink."

Then LaFontaine saw the look on Forsling's face, and his smile disappeared. "What's up?"

"That fucking Jew district attorney and his nigger cop," Forsling snarled, fighting not to break down. "They killed my mom when I was in lockup. They think I did the car bomb so they burned her out."

"That's fucked up," Gerlach said.

"All part of the Zionist Occupation Government," Mencke added. "They want to shut up anybody who's on to their scheming."

"Damn right. What can we do to help?" LaFontaine asked.

Forsling looked around wildly, shaking his head and breathing heavily. "You still have that Luger?" he asked.

The bartender's eyes widened. "Yeah . . . what are you planning to do?"

"Better if you don't know. That way they can't say you helped me, but if I don't make it, you'll know the truth."

"Where you going to go after you do it?" Gerlach asked.

"Idaho," Forsling replied. "I'll disappear. No one will ever find me. But keep that to yourselves."

LaFontaine looked at the others, who nodded solemnly. He then reached under the bar and brought out something wrapped in cloth; he removed the rags to reveal a vintage German Luger pistol. "I don't know if it even works," he said. "It's an old model. It's loaded, though. . . . Just remember, you didn't get it from me."

"Don't worry, Frankie, I ain't no snitch," Forsling said. "One more thing, I need the van."

LaFontaine shook his head. "The cops can't trace the gun back to me," he said, "but the van is registered in my name. Besides, I need it to get back and forth from my place in Queens. I can't let you have it."

Forsling glared at LaFontaine. Then he picked up the gun and pointed it at the bartender. "I fucking need the van," he said. "You can say I stole it from you."

Several things happened at once. With a growl, Gerlach scooted his bar stool back and started to charge Forsling, who swung the gun in his direction and pulled the trigger. The sound of the gun firing and the sight of the top of Gerlach's head disappearing in a spray of blood and bone seemed to stun everyone for a moment.

Then Gerlach's heavy body collapsed to the floor as Mencke let out a high-pitched scream that seemed to wake the others up. It might have ended badly for Forsling otherwise, but he turned in time to notice LaFontaine make a sudden move for something he had under the bar. He was able to turn the gun toward the bartender just as the other man brought a sawed-off, double-barreled shotgun up.

217

Forsling fired twice more, both bullets striking LaFontaine in the belly. The bartender fell back against the counter, bringing a dozen bottles crashing to the floor.

In the meantime, Mencke just kept screaming until Forsling pointed the gun at the *Oberkommando* of the New York City Nazi Party, who backed up against the wall. "No, don't," the man squeaked just before another bullet struck him in the chest. He slid down the wall with a look of surprise as he gazed down at the growing bloodstain on his shirt.

Forsling stood for a moment as if stunned by his own actions. He couldn't seem to hear, but wasn't sure if that was because of the gunshots or the pounding of his heart in his ears. His breath came in short pants as his mind raced through the past few minutes. *They made me do it,* he thought, the Jew Karp and the nigger cop. *They killed my mom. They pushed me over the edge. It's their fault my mom and my friends are dead.*

All at once, Forsling's mind cleared. He still had a mission to complete. He hurried over to the front door and locked it. He then walked back to the restroom and checked to make sure there was nobody in there. Then returned to the front and slipped behind the bar.

LaFontaine was still alive, holding his hands against his belly. "You son of a bitch," he gasped weakly.

Forsling aimed at the man's head and was going to finish him but then reconsidered. *If you're lucky, nobody heard the first shots,* he thought. The bar was in a warehouse section of Hell's Kitchen and there wasn't a lot of foot traffic. But he didn't want to risk someone hearing more shots.

"You should have given me the van," Forsling said to the wounded man, who didn't reply except to writhe and grunt in pain. He looked under the register and found a box of shells for the Luger. He thought about taking the shotgun but decided against lugging it around. Instead he opened the cash register and took the money before roughly rolling LaFontaine over on his belly and removing the man's wallet and keys.

Someone knocked on the front door. Forsling quickly stepped over the pool of LaFontaine's blood and walked toward the back of the bar. Opening the door and walking out into the alley, he spotted the beat-up, older model Ford Econoline van. It had once belonged to a welder and the faded sign for Eric Woodbury & Sons Metalworks could still be seen on the side. He'd thought about the van on his subway ride over from East Harlem to Hell's Kitchen, and it had helped formulate his plan for revenge.

Forsling got in the van and saw a New York Yankees ball cap on the passenger seat, which he put on to hide his shaved head and tattooed forehead. Starting the van, he drove fast down the alley, nearly striking a white-haired man in a business suit at the entrance. He then pulled into traffic, headed for Third Avenue and 29th Street and Il Buon Pane.

Arriving at the bakery, he noticed workmen for a glass company packing up their truck. He waited and then pulled into the spot next to the side of the bakery, just behind an area of blackened snow where the car had burned the night before.

Pulling the ball cap down and sticking the Luger in the pocket of his black leather coat, he got out of the van and quickly walked to the front of the store. Opening the door, he walked inside and saw two teenaged boys at the counter saying something to the old woman on the other side.

The old woman smiled and made a welcoming sign with her hands though she didn't speak. The boys looked at him curiously. "Sorry, but we're closed," one of them said.

"Oh, uh, I'm with Woodbury and Sons Metalworks. I was told to stop by and see if there was anything the owners needed," Forsling replied, looking past the boys at the room beyond. He'd expected to find the old couple who fit into his plan to get even with Karp. But things had worked out better than he'd hoped.

Forsling had recognized the teens. He'd seen Karp talking to them the night before from the backseat in the police cruiser. But that wasn't all. The district attorney had photos of his family on the wall of his office where he'd been brought. One of them showed Karp with the young men he was looking at.

"Metalworks?" the other, bigger teen asked. "I didn't know someone called for a welder. Who are you?"

The teen's attitude and question irritated Forsling. He pulled the pistol out of his coat pocket. "I'm the guy with the gun, jerk-off," he said. "Now you're all coming with me."

"Like hell we are," both boys said at the same time.

Forsling pointed the gun at the old woman. "Then you can watch her die first," he said.

"All right," the smaller teen replied, and grabbed his brother's shoulder. "Just everybody stay cool."

"That's smart, Jewboy," Forsling sneered. "Let's go."

Forsling made the boys go out the door first. "The old bitch is going to be in front of me," he warned. "So if one of you says something or makes a run for it, I shoot her first."

They got in the van without encountering anyone else. Forsling made the teens sit in the front two seats while he sat in back with the old woman.

"Where we going?" asked the bigger teen, who was driving.

"East Harlem. I'll tell you where once we're rolling."

As the van pulled away from the curb and started to turn right onto Third Avenue, a black truck turned onto 29th Street. The teen hit the brakes and honked.

"What the hell are you doing?" Forsling yelled. "I'll shoot the old bitch and your brother right now."

"Take it easy, man," the teen yelled back. "I'm not used to driving and that guy freaked me out."

"Just drive," Forsling demanded. "But any more crap and somebody's going to die."

15

After Fulton left Karp's office to make his phone calls, everything seemed to happen in bang-bang fashion, like tumblers on a bank vault clicking into place. First, Mrs. Milquetost announced with some trepidation that "a Mr. Garcia and a Mr. Gallo are here to see you. They said you're expecting them?"

"Yes, send them in."

As the pair entered the office and took seats across from his desk, Karp looked them over. They were both Hispanic, blessed with Latin good looks, though one was tall and slender and the other short and built like a fire hydrant. He'd known Garcia for years, but thought Gallo would be new to him except what Marlene had just said. However, when he saw his face, he remembered the news stories several years earlier about the ambitious charter school founder in Brooklyn who'd run afoul of the law.

Back then he was surprised that such a big deal was being made of what seemed to be a minor transgression, and suspected that politics between the charter schools and the teachers union had something to do with it. The young educator had disappeared from sight, and Karp had forgotten about him until now.

He nodded at Garcia. "How are your hands? That doesn't look good." He pointed to the bandages on the young man's right hand, where a spot of bright red blood had appeared.

"Sore, but I'll be okay. A hell of a lot better than the three people I drove there with."

Karp nodded. "Rose was a wonderful woman and a dear friend, and the other victims didn't deserve what happened to them either. All I can say is that we're working to get to the bottom of it." He paused, but only for a moment. "Marlene said you needed to talk to me, but she didn't give me a lot of details."

"We didn't tell her any so she wouldn't be involved in what we had to do," Garcia said. "But we wanted to talk to you about something that we think involves the people who killed Rose and the others."

"Did you try talking to the police who are looking into this?" Karp asked. "Maybe I should call my lead investigator, I think you know him, Clay Fulton, to join us."

"Fulton's all right for a cop," Garcia replied. "But we're not ready to talk to the po-po about this; everything that goes to the cops seems to get back to the wrong people, if you know what I mean. So for now, this is between you and us . . . and actually mostly between you and *mi hermano* here, Micah."

At the introduction, the tall young man leaned across to shake Karp's hand. "I wish I was meeting you under other circumstances — Rose spoke highly of you and your wife. I also wish I didn't have to say what I'm about to . . . or pay the consequences, but I do."

"I think we all wish circumstances were different," Karp replied. "But if you don't mind, let's get down to business. Alejandro, you said this has something to do with the murder of Rose Lubinsky, Mary Calebras, and Tawanna Mohammad?"

Garcia looked at Gallo, who swallowed hard. "I should probably answer that," he said. "You know who I am, right?"

"I remembered when I saw you come in and put two and two together with what

Marlene told me," Karp agreed.

Gallo nodded, and then dug into his coat pocket and produced a flash drive, which he tossed onto Karp's desk. "The information on this is encoded, but I don't expect it's going to be much of an obstacle for your people."

Picking up the flash drive, Karp looked from Gallo to Garcia and back. "Want to tell me what's on it?"

"Mostly documents — secret bank accounts, real estate transactions, dummy corporation paperwork," Gallo replied. "It will lead you to some people who can lead you to some other people, or sometimes directly to them, who own these accounts and property."

"And the significance of that?"

"The money in those accounts rightfully belongs to the Greater New York Teachers Federation," Gallo replied.

"Who do these accounts and the real estate belong to?" Karp asked.

Gallo bit his lip, then responded. "Three people. One of them is me."

"You? You are admitting to the theft of union funds?"

"Yes. Another person is my boss, union president Tommy Monroe."

"And the third?"

"Do you know who used to be the chief counsel for the union?"

The room fell silent as the two young men waited for Karp's answer. There had been other times in his career when there'd be a prescient moment, like that first clap of thunder, when he knew a storm was coming. This was one of those times.

"Olivia Stone," he said quietly. "The current district attorney of Kings County, Brooklyn."

No one spoke for a moment. They didn't have to until Karp cleared his throat and asked, "I take it there's a reason you're coming forward now with this information, and that you believe it's connected to last night's murders. You want to explain?"

"You're aware of the charter school bill that Rose crafted and lobbied for at the state assembly. The one that's opposed by the union."

"Yes."

"Do you know why Monroe and Stone are particularly opposed to this bill?"

"I know it would put nonunion charter schools on a more level playing field for funding and resources with public schools," Karp said.

"That's part of it," Gallo agreed. "But what they're really worried about is that part of the bill that calls for an audit of the union going back ten years. That was one of the things Rose was really pushing for — accountability — to determine whether fees paid by union members, as well as funds provided by taxpayers, were used appropriately. That's what they're afraid of."

Karp held up the flash drive. "And it's all on here?"

"*Sí,* yes," Gallo replied.

"How did you get it?"

Garcia started to say something but Gallo interrupted him. "I took it off of Monroe's office computer early this morning. You'll see that it's date/time stamped. I also sent a copy to a secure location via email."

"Does Monroe know you did this?"

Gallo shrugged. "There are security cameras all over the building and in his office. I was wearing a mask, but I'm sure he'll figure out who was in his office. I wiped what we . . . I mean . . . I was doing on his computer, so he won't know exactly, at least not right away; I'm sure his tech guys will be able to figure it out."

"You realize that what you did was probably breaking the law," Karp said. "Even if you have authority to enter the building, I doubt you were authorized to take this information."

"I realize that," Gallo said. "I will point out that some of the information on the flash drive relates to me."

"And then there's that," Karp went on. "If you're implicating yourself in these crimes — the theft of union funds, grand larceny — I can't look the other way. You'll be charged along with anyone else."

"I understand."

Karp sat back in his seat and studied the young men. Garcia leaned forward with his head down, but Gallo was sitting up, looking him straight in the eye. "It's a brave thing you're doing, the right thing."

Gallo shook his head at the compliment. "I should have done it a long time ago, maybe Rose would still be alive . . . and I wouldn't be looking at time in prison."

"I think I read somewhere once that you never go so far down a path that you can't turn around and take a step back," Karp replied. "You've taken that step. Now before we go any further, and you explain why you think what you've said so far about why this relates to last night's murders, I'd like to know if you'll give a formal statement. If so, I'll call a stenographer in, as well as Detective Clay Fulton. Alejandro may have told you, but he's a New York City police detective who heads a special investigations unit working for my office; he's keeping me apprised of this case, and I think he needs to hear this."

"I'm ready."

"And before we start, I'll be informing you of your rights, including your right to remain silent and your right not to incriminate yourself," Karp warned. "And the right to have an attorney present during questioning."

For the first time, Gallo smiled. "Mr. Karp, you don't know much about my 'formative years,' but I've heard my Miranda warnings before. I'm waiving my rights and will do so again when the stenographer shows up."

Twenty minutes later, sitting in a conference room off of Karp's main office, Gallo told his story, a narrative of union abuse, breach of fiduciary trust, and grand larceny. Karp mostly listened except to ask questions to clarify and expand on what he was hearing. The young man had just started talking about a meeting at Stone's office, when Fulton's cell phone buzzed.

Fulton looked at the caller ID and then back at Karp with a frown. "It's Guma," he said as he stood and walked over to a corner of the room to answer.

Karp could tell by the way his friend's

broad shoulders suddenly tensed that something was wrong. Fulton turned back to him and asked, "Can I speak to you privately?"

With the detective leading the way, Karp followed him outside of the office. "What's up? Guma okay?"

"Yeah, he's fine," Fulton said. "But apparently two patrons at The Storm Trooper bar aren't. We got two dead and a third being transported to the hospital with gunshot wounds. Sounds like Guma missed the fireworks by a few minutes. He thinks he spotted the suspect driving away in a white van with some sort of sign on the side."

"He identify the suspect?"

Fulton shook his head. "Said he didn't get a good look, but he was able to get a few words out of the surviving victim . . ."

"And?"

"Apparently our favorite neo-Nazi may have taken that leap from vandal to killer."

"I don't get it," Karp said. "I didn't see that in him."

"Maybe he just snapped," Fulton replied. "The guy was obviously paranoid. His mom died, so he goes off the deep end and starts blaming you and me."

"But why kill these guys?"

"Who knows? A falling-out. Maybe to get

rid of witnesses. Or somebody said something wrong. But one thing is sure, if he's our guy, he's a cold-blooded killer. Marlene said she was going to Il Buon Pane?"

"Yeah, she was going to pick up the boys."

"I think I'll scramble a couple of squad cars to go over, just in case the Sobelmans and anyone else there is on his revenge list." Fulton nodded at the conference room door. "What about them? What this Gallo guy is saying sounds pretty legit."

"I think it's legit, too. I think we're dealing with two different, unrelated murder cases. I can handle the rest of the interview after I reach Marlene and give her a heads-up. Then I want to get back in there and finish up before anyone gets cold feet."

Karp returned to the conference room and his interrogation of Gallo. He was questioning the young man about meeting Monroe at the Jay Street Bar before the explosion when Mrs. Milquetost knocked on the door. "Marlene is trying to reach you," she said. "It's another emergency."

Excusing himself, Karp called his wife. He'd barely said hello before she interrupted him.

"Butch, I think something's wrong with the boys," she said, the worry in her voice palpable. "I just arrived at the bakery, but the boys are gone and so is Goldie."

"Any idea where they went? What about Moishe?"

"He was upstairs taking a nap," Marlene replied. "He thought Goldie was downstairs. The strangest thing is I think I saw them leaving; Zak was driving."

"Zak was driving?" Karp repeated. "That's crazy — he doesn't even have a license."

"I know," she said. "I didn't get a good look until someone honked at me like maybe he was trying to get my attention. When I looked up, I was sure it was Zak, and maybe Giancarlo in the passenger seat."

Karp felt his stomach tighten. This was another one of those moments before the storm. "What kind of vehicle?"

"A van . . . a white van."

16

For a moment, Karp felt as if someone had knocked the wind out of him. *A white van.* He knew who his sons were with and that they were in mortal danger. Forsling had stepped over that moral line most humans come by naturally that prevents them from taking another's life. The next time it would be easier for him.

A feeling of helplessness washed over him. Once again the necessity of doing his job was affecting the lives of his family. But then the internal focus that he always relied on in times of duress, whether in court or dealing with this sort of threat, took over, and his mind grew clear and voice remained calm. "Where are you now?" he asked his wife.

"Driving north on Third with Moishe. I saw them turn this direction," Marlene said. "Butch, what's going on? Moishe found Goldie's wedding ring on the cash register, and he says she hasn't taken it off in seventy years. He thinks she was letting him know they're in trouble. Does this have something to do with Forsling?"

"I'm afraid so," Karp replied. "Stay after him. I'm going to get Clay to send squad cars to the area; a couple were already en route to Il Buon Pane and should be close. Did this van have writing on the side?"

"Yeah, it was some sort of father-and-sons company van, but the sign was faded so it might not be anymore," Marlene replied. She was quiet for a moment. "How bad is it?"

Karp thought for a moment about how to answer her. He could tell that she was struggling with her fears. But that was how Marlene operated in an emergency — on adrenaline and emotion — and it worked for her. She'd faced plenty of tough, life-threatening situations and had always come out on top. She was not the sort to panic or make a mistake because of stress. Still, this wasn't just dealing with some lunatic with a gun; this lunatic had just killed two people, abducted her sons, and sworn he'd get revenge on Karp. And yet in the final analysis, there would be no fooling her regarding the situation; she'd hear it in his voice.

"Forsling is the chief suspect in a double homicide at a bar in Hell's Kitchen," he said. "Apparently, he shot three of his associates — wounding one of them — before driving to the bakery in that van."

There was another moment of silence while Marlene digested the information. "Okay. We know what we're dealing with."

"Marlene, I'm not going to try to sugarcoat this," he said. "Find our sons. Do what you have to do."

"I will."

"I'm going to let you go so I can reach Fulton and get my guys alerted to find the boys and Goldie."

"Yeah, that would be good . . . Butch, I love you."

"I love you, too."

Karp hung up and poked his head back into the conference room. "I'm sorry but we're going to have to resume this later," he said. "We have an emergency situation I have to deal with. If you'd like to come back to my office and wait with Alejandro, you're welcome to, or you're free to go."

Without waiting for Gallo's reply, Karp turned and went back to his office. Alejandro was standing near the bookshelf, looking at some of the titles, and turned toward him as he walked in. But Karp held up his hand. "Sorry, need to make a call," he said, and pressed a button on the intercom. "Clay, I need you here now."

"On my way. What's up, boss?"

"Forsling has Zak, Giancarlo, and Goldie Sobelman," Karp replied. "Marlene saw the white van from the shooting leaving the bakery and heading north on Third Avenue. She thinks Zak was driving and Giancarlo may have been in the front passenger seat. That would mean Forsling's in back telling them what to do. Marlene's in pursuit but she's at least a few minutes behind them and doesn't know where they're going."

"I might have an idea about that," Fulton said. "I just got off the phone with Guma. He rode to the hospital with the shooting victim, who told him that Forsling has some sort of job as a night watchman at a tenement renovation project over on the East Side."

"He have an address?"

"No, but apparently walking distance from where he lived with his mother. The builder ran out of money so it's just fenced off and he throws Forsling some cash to check on it so that nobody steals the wiring. Otherwise it's an abandoned building, and my guess is it's a good place for us to look. I'll get some patrol cars moving in that direction."

"Okay, thanks, Clay. I'm going to pass that along to Marlene. Get our team ready and I'll see you in my office asap."

"I'll be there soon as I get off the phone," Fulton said, then hesitated. "We'll find them, Butch."

Karp heard the empathy and concern in his friend's voice. Fulton had known the boys since birth and had treated them like sons ever since. "There is no other option," he said, and hung up just as Micah entered the room. He waved the young man to a seat over where Garcia was standing with a look of concern.

"What's going on?" Garcia asked Karp.

Karp normally wouldn't have involved "civilians" in his business or, for that matter, have had them remain in his office. But he was trying to stay focused, and besides, Alejandro had befriended the boys and protected them in the past. Something prompted him to quickly explain even as he was calling Marlene back.

When she answered, her voice was tense. "There's a chance he's headed for an abandoned tenement building that's undergoing renovation over near where he lived with his mom," he told her. "He may be looking for a place to hole up or . . ."

"Or shoot our sons," Marlene finished the

sentence for him.

Karp let the comment pass, though he couldn't ignore the lump in his throat. "Apparently this place may have a fence around it," he said with difficulty.

"There're a lot of old buildings under construction around here."

"That's all I've got," he said, but his intercom buzzed insistently before Marlene answered. Mrs. Milquetost sounded in a near panic, "Mr. Karp, there's a man on line two who says he's going to kill your sons!"

Karp then spoke in the phone. "Marlene, Forsling's calling. I'll put you on speakerphone so you can hear." He then punched the button for Line 2. "This is District Attorney Karp."

"Is that you, Karp, you fucking Jew bastard?"

"I'm here, Lars."

"I've got your kids."

"I'm aware of that," Karp said, trying to sound calmer than he felt. "I'm asking you to let them and the woman go before this escalates."

"Too late, Karp, it's . . ." Whatever Forsling said after that was obscured by background sound.

"I didn't hear what you said."

239

"I said it's too late; it escalated when my mom died. And it's all your . . ." Again, Forsling's sentence was cut off by the sounds. Karp looked up and noted Garcia's furrowed brow but didn't have time to ask about it.

"Did you hear me, Karp?" Forsling asked. A vehicle door slammed and there was the sound of an engine starting.

Stalling for time, Karp asked him to repeat himself.

"I said I'm going to shoot your fucking kids," Forsling said. "I'm especially going to enjoy killing the smart-assed one."

"Lars, this isn't going to solve anything or bring your mother back," Karp said. "Let me send someone there to negotiate with you so that everybody gets out of this safely."

"Safely?" Forsling laughed harshly. "Yeah, right. Like I can trust a fucking Jew. I can see tomorrow's headlines, *Cops Forced to Shoot Mad Dog Nazi.* I'm not falling for your tricks or your lies, Karp." The young man's voice broke. "Besides, I don't give a shit anymore, and I'm not going to prison with a bunch of niggers waiting to jump me."

Wherever Forsling was driving, it wasn't far. The engine stopped and there was the sound of him getting out and closing the door again. "Well, I think we've said everything there is to say," he told Karp. There was the sound of the metal gate being pushed shut and then of him walking across gravel. "But I'll call you back in a minute so that you can listen when I shoot your little Jew boys and that old bitch."

"Forsling!" Karp shouted into the phone but the line went dead.

"He's over near the river," Garcia blurted out.

"What?"

"That's my turf," Garcia replied. "I've been listening to those sounds all of my life. They're tugboat whistles; a bunch of them and they're close. I'm guessing the garbage transfer station at East 91st Street where they load up the barges and then shove them out to the ocean to dump."

Karp nodded and picked up his phone. "Marlene, did you get that? Alejandro thinks he's over near the garbage transfer station on the East River at 91st."

"Already on my way," Marlene replied. "I'm only a few blocks west of there."

After a tense minute, she shouted. "I see the van. It's parked on a side street. And that must be the tenement. There's a padlock on the gate. I think I can squeeze through. . . . I got to run. Butch?"

"Yes."

"When he calls back, stall him as long as you can."

"I will. And Marlene?"

"Yeah?"

"Be careful." But there was no reply.

17

Lars Forsling stopped at the bottom of the stairs leading up to the top floor where his unfinished business waited. He looked down at his Doc Martens boots, and tears fell from his eyes as he contemplated the changes twenty-four hours had brought to his life. The only person who ever really cared for him was dead. And he'd murdered two, or three, of the only friends he'd ever had.

Now he was about to climb fourteen flights of stairs and shoot two teenaged boys and an old woman. *Not your fault,* said that little voice in his head. *They made you do it. They have been against you all of your life. The Jews. The niggers. The kids whose dads hadn't walked out on them. The whole fucking world.*

He thought back about the last time he'd seen his mother. She'd begged him not to go out. "These friends of yours are trouble," she'd said. "What do you do with all that time you spend together?"

"Just hang out," he'd said with a shrug. "Talk."

"Why don't you stay home and talk to your mother tonight?" she'd whined. "I won't be here much longer, you know. I think the Jew doctors are poisoning me. I can hardly get out of bed to go to the bathroom."

Forsling had looked at her and tried not to be repulsed by the pasty swollen face or the partly exposed obese body. "Maybe you should get more exercise, Mom."

That, of course, only set her off. He didn't understand. The medicine the Jew doctors claimed was for her heart actually was killing her, making her too weak to even get out of bed. "I might die tonight, you know, then you'll be sorry you left me home alone."

Forsling almost gave in. But he was the one who'd called for the protest outside of the bakery. "Someone has to stand up to the lies about the 'Holocaust' and the threat of Zionism," he'd told the other drunks at The Storm Trooper bar the night before. If he didn't show up, he'd lose face.

"I got to go," he'd said. "We're having an important meeting. Promise me you won't smoke in bed." But his mother shifted her bulk and turned away from him without saying anything.

"I'll see you later, Mother," he'd said. "I'll check in with you when I get home."

There was still no reply, so he'd left without saying anything else. As usual, he felt guilty leaving her; then again it was no different than any other time he tried to do anything on his own. She even complained when he got the job checking out the tenement construction site, shining a flashlight around a couple times a night to make it look like there was regular security. He didn't like going over there at night — there were a lot of spics and niggers in that neighborhood — but he didn't have a lot of employment options, and he was trying to save up for his move to Idaho.

Looks like I'll be moving sooner than expected, he thought as he began climbing the stairs to the top of the building. He'd saved a few hundred dollars and there'd been roughly another hundred in the till at The Storm Trooper. Enough to get out there, he figured, and once there, he'd drop some hints that he'd been responsible for the car bombing they might have heard about in New York. He imagined the admiring acceptance he'd receive once among the white supremacist militias; he'd assume a fake name and identity and blend in.

Thinking about his new life was followed by a pang of guilt. His mother was lying in a morgue, her skin charred, her lips curled in some ghastly grimace of pain. He imagined the dark figures who'd crept into their home and up the stairs in the dark, dousing her with gasoline as she slept and then lighting the match. She would have woken from her drunken stupor as the flames engulfed her and pain began. And there was no one to protect her. No one to save her. She'd died alone as predicted.

The thought made him angry, and he climbed the stairs faster. He was going to get his revenge and then he'd be on his way to the Promised Land. He'd explained it all to the teenagers and the old woman as they drove north on Third Avenue. "Blame your old man for what's going to happen," he said. "He's trying to frame me for setting off that car bomb . . . him and that nigger cop of his. That's the way you Jews operate. Figure out who needs to be removed so that you can get away with your lies, then get the mud people to do your dirty work."

"My dad wouldn't frame anybody. You didn't plant the bomb?" the skinnier of the teens asked.

Forsling scoffed. "No. I had nothing to do with it, though I could not care less that there's one less Jew in the world. I was there to stand up to the lies about the Holocaust. But I didn't kill anybody. I was sitting in a cop car when the bomb went off. But they hauled my ass to jail, and then burned my mom out, so now you got to pay."

He looked over at the old woman expecting to see fear in her eyes. Instead, she smiled at him then leaned over and patted his knee. "If God wills us to die tonight, so be it," she said, though there was a strange quality to her voice as if she didn't use it much.

When they reached the entrance to the fence around the tenement, Forsling handed a key to the teen in the passenger seat to unlock the padlock and remove the chain so they could drive in. "If you try to run away I'll shoot the old woman and your brother."

Giancarlo had done as he was told and then got back in the van. He'd then instructed the driver to pull up as close to a side door leading into the building as he could and made the passenger get out and unlock the door. With the boys in the lead and the old woman walking in front of him with the gun pointed at her back, they started ascending the stairs.

Reaching the tenth floor, the old woman, who had been struggling, suddenly collapsed. "Carry her," he'd instructed the larger teen, who picked her up and brought her to the loft. He'd then placed her on an old mattress that had been left by workmen.

"You sit," Forsling had told the bigger teen, pointing the gun at an old wooden chair. "And you grab that rope and tie his wrists to the arms of the chair. . . . Now wrap it a few times around his waist."

Once that was done, Forsling had tied the other teen down in a similar fashion though it was with some difficulty with one hand still holding the gun. "Try anything, and I'll make sure the old woman dies first," he'd warned.

Satisfied that both teens were secure, he'd just turned around when he was surprised by a large rat that scurried across the floor ten feet away. He screamed and backed away, almost losing his balance.

"Wow, some tough Nazi you are," said the larger of the two teens. "You peed in your pants?"

Forsling felt shame flood to his face at the kid's comments. He walked up to the mouthy teen and backhanded him across the face.

"Why don't you untie me and see if you

dare doing that again," the teenager snarled.

Forsling struck him again. It felt good. He felt powerful. "Yeah, you're talking big now," he said. "Let's see what you say when I stick this gun in your mouth before I pull the trigger. I've already killed three guys today, and they were my friends. Shooting you will be even easier."

With that he'd stormed out of the loft and down the stairs. He was worried that someone would see the van parked inside the gates and call the cops. But first he placed a call to Karp. He wanted the man to suffer. Negotiate for my safety, yeah right, he thought, like I'm going to fall for that Jew trick.

Karp thought he was stupid, but he had a plan. First he'd get his revenge while Karp listened to his kids die. Then he'd drive the van to Newark, where he'd ditch it and catch a bus to Idaho. There among the green mountains and clear rivers, he'd live among like-minded supremacists, away from the mud people and Jews. Maybe even find a good Aryan woman for a wife.

The daydreaming had been put on hold when he reached the loft and got ready to exact his righteous revenge. At first seeing the rat again had thrown him off, but backhanding the teen had put him back in the mood. He'd loved hearing Karp pleading with him to not kill his sons. "Which one should I shoot first?"

"Me, shoot me." The old woman's voice surprised them all. She was standing unsteadily on her feet, her hands bound at the wrist in front of her. "I'm old. Shoot me if you must kill someone for your mother."

Forsling pointed the gun at her. But looking in her clear, calm eyes, he couldn't pull the trigger.

"No, me," the thinner of the teens said. "I'm not afraid of you, you Nazi son of a bitch."

Anger took over Forsling's brain. He aimed the gun at the teen. "Well, you should be," he snarled, intending to pull the trigger.

"Hey, asshole!" the other teen yelled.

"WHAT?" The kid was really getting on his nerves.

"Catch."

The comment was so unexpected that at first he didn't recognize the large gray object the teen lifted off the floor with the toe of his shoe and flung up at him. Not until the rat landed on the arm he held outstretched with the gun in his hand. Even then the rodent had scampered onto his shoulder and bit him on the ear before he reacted.

First, he screamed so high and so loud that some part of his brain registered surprise that the sound had come from him. Then he shook his arm so violently that the gun flew from his hand and clattered across the floor. Next he reached up with the other hand and grabbed the rat, which bit him again, causing him to howl in pain and fear as he flung the rodent across the room.

At the same time, the larger of the two teens, though still bound by his wrists and waist to the chair, bellowed with rage and propelled himself at Forsling. He struck him so hard he was propelled backward, with the teen landing hard on him.

"Get her out of here," the youth yelled at his brother. Forsling turned and saw that the other teen had slipped his bonds and was helping the old woman toward the door. Then the teen on top butted him in the head.

Hurt and suddenly afraid, at first all he could think about was disentangling himself from the battling youth and fleeing. But all of that weight lifting hadn't been a waste and as he fought back, he discovered his strength, especially against an adversary who was at such a disadvantage. He balled his fist and struck the boy and then struck him again.

Grabbing the teen's neck, he tried to strangle him, but the youth was too strong and struggled, using his knees to strike at Forsling. Getting desperate, he pushed the youth off him and sprung to his feet while his adversary struggled to rise with the chair still attached.

Forsling ran to where the Luger had landed and grabbed it with a yell of triumph. He turned, intending to shoot them all. However, instead he found himself looking at a petite woman who was pointing a gun at him.

For a moment time seemed to stand still. He saw the larger teen still on the floor. The other teen and the old woman were off to the side. "Drop your gun," the woman demanded.

There was a brief moment when he considered doing what she said. But he thought about the past twenty-four hours and then about what the rest of his life would be like. No Idaho, only prison. He raised the weapon and felt something kick him in the chest, and at the same time there was a loud shot that seemed to fill the entire loft. Then something kicked him again and he fell backward to the floor.

Life seemed to play out in slow motion after that. The woman approached, still aiming the gun at him. Her face was a mask of rage, but then it softened as she looked down at him and he wondered if her expression was one of sorrow. Then another face appeared; the old woman, who knelt beside him and held his hand.

One part of him wanted to accept the sorrow and the kindness. But the larger part of him grew angry. Idaho was gone. His mother was dead. He was dying and it was all Karp's fault. But there was still a way to get even, still a way to be a hero to the Aryans in the West.

He tried to speak but it was difficult because of the blood in his mouth. "I did it," he managed to blurt out, raising his head. "It was my bomb that blew up the car. I killed the Jew bitch."

Then it was too much of an effort to speak anymore. His head felt so heavy and he lay it back down. Everything was fading, and the last image was of a mountain stream before the lights went out.

18

Tommy Monroe entered the Jay Street Bar and looked around suspiciously. It was a Tuesday evening and the crowd was light, just a few regulars and a couple of people he didn't know. These he looked over carefully.

One was a young Hispanic guy sitting at the bar, dressed in a long wool coat and beanie cap with a New York Knicks logo, and drinking a beer. He glanced at Monroe and went back to minding his own business. A large black man in a leather coat and black beret sat at a back table with his eyes closed, nodding his head to whatever music was playing into the earplugs he wore as he sipped a glass of wine. Across the room a youngish couple cozied up with their heads together; the man's hand was beneath the table and he appeared to be stroking her leg, from her giggles and mild protest noises.

He nodded to a big, rough-looking guy in

a Yankees letterman's jacket slouching on one of the seats at the bar. The guy wasn't a regular; he was a New York City cop on Brooklyn DA Olivia Stone's payroll who'd been sent on ahead to look out for any traps and provide muscle if needed. His unconcerned facial expression comforted Monroe.

The person he'd come to meet was sitting at the back table where Monroe usually sat. Micah Gallo spotted him and raised his chin to acknowledge he'd been seen, but didn't bother to get up or shake his hand when Monroe approached the table, carrying a briefcase and a laptop. He set the device on the table and the briefcase on the floor, then took a seat.

"Micah."

"Tommy."

"New glasses?" Monroe said, pointing to Gallo's face. "They look good. Sort of Clark Kent, only stylish. Must have cost a bundle."

"Quit with the small talk, Tommy; you could give a shit about my glasses or how I look. Is that my money?" Gallo said, nodding toward where Monroe set the briefcase.

They both fell silent as a buxom, middle-aged waitress approached. "What can I get for you?" she asked with a heavy Brooklyn accent.

"You're new," Monroe said to her, turning on the charm while his eyes flicked to her chest. "Where's Julie?"

"Yeah, honey, just started tonight," the waitress replied, making sure he got a good look at her assets. "Julie's off till tomorrow. The name's Gail. Can I get you anything?"

"I'm sure you could, baby, but in the meantime I'll settle for an Old Forester, make it a double," Monroe said.

"Be right back with that, sweetie."

Monroe watched her sashay away with a smile. But his frown returned. "Your money? You're blackmailing us, you little son of a bitch, and you're calling it your money?"

Gallo shrugged. "Turnabout is fair play. You're a fine one to talk; you ruined my career; bought me off, and you're calling me a son of a bitch?"

Monroe sneered. "It wasn't that hard, pretty boy. Don't tell me you don't like the fancy cars, the nice digs, and the pricey girlfriends."

"I'm not denying that," Gallo said. "But I didn't sign up for killing anybody."

Monroe's face hardened. "I don't know what you're talking about."

"Rose Lubinsky. The other two women. I didn't sign up for that shit, and I want out."

"I still don't know what you're implying,"

Monroe said. He looked around again. Nobody seemed to be paying attention to them. "Let's go have a little talk in my office."

"Your office?"

"The restroom. You go first, I'll follow."

Gallo smirked. "Didn't know you got freaky, Tommy."

"Shut the fuck up. I'm going to check you for a wire."

"A wire? You've been watching too many gangster movies, but okay."

Gallo got up and walked off toward the men's room. Monroe stood. The dirty cop was watching and got up, too. They both followed the younger man.

"Who's your friend?" Gallo said when the other man entered.

"None of your business, pal. Turn around," the cop said as he quickly made sure no one was in the stalls. He looked at Monroe. "Stand against the door so no one comes in."

No sooner did Monroe do as he was told but someone tried to enter the restroom. "Hey, what the fuck," a Spanish-accented voice said from the other side. "You *pendejos* can play with your dicks some other time, I got to take a pee."

"Go away, asshole," the cop yelled. "Official NYPD business."

"Fuck off," Gallo added, then turned around as ordered.

The cop shoved him roughly against the wall and began patting him down. He then removed Gallo's belt and took a pen from his shirt pocket and the cell phone from his pants. The cop walked into one of the stalls and dumped it all in a toilet.

"Hey, what the fuck!" Gallo yelled. "That's my phone, you son of a bitch."

"Can't take any chances that someone is listening in on your cell," Monroe replied with a smile. "You've also heard of pen microphones, and I'm assuming there's the same concern with your belt. Don't worry, you'll be able to buy a new phone with 'your money' later."

"Give me your shoes," the cop demanded.

"You're not going to flush them!" Gallo said with alarm, though he removed the shoes. "They're five-hundred-dollar Guccis."

"Nah," the cop replied. Instead he whipped out a butterfly knife that he opened with a flourish and then pried the heels off the shoes. He looked them over and then at Monroe. "He's clean," he said, and handed the shoes back to Gallo.

"Damn right I am, you fucks," Gallo said

angrily as he put the ruined shoes back on his feet. "I should make you give me an extra thousand for wrecking my shit."

"Cost of doing business," Monroe replied. "Besides, there's a hundred grand in the briefcase. And I already saw that you transferred your money from your 'school' accounts. Way I figure it, you're worth two million easy and that's a lot of phones and shoes. Let's go back to our seats."

As the men left the restroom, the young Hispanic who Monroe had noticed at the bar shoved his way past them. "You girls done powdering your noses?" he said.

The cop continued back over to his place at the bar while the other two returned to their seats. As they sat down, the young Hispanic man exited the restroom, and when he passed by their table, he reached down and placed a flash drive in front of Gallo. "I got your stuff out of the toilet," he said quietly, then continued on his way and left the bar.

Monroe noticed the bandage on the young man's hand. "Your partner in crime," he said to Gallo. "That was a pretty bold move on your part, but I knew it was you on the security tapes."

"I wanted you to know it was me," Gallo retorted. "Otherwise you might have gone to the cops about a 'break-in' and fucked the whole thing up."

Monroe nodded. "I thought maybe that was what you were doing with that," he said, pointing at the flash drive.

"What? And spend the next eight years, at least, in the pen for stealing union funds?" Gallo said. "I may be a coward, but I'm not stupid. I'm also not going to hang around and get indicted for murder. That was fucking stupid to kill Lubinsky."

Monroe's lips twisted. "Look," he said, leaning forward, "it wasn't my idea either. But we were all going down if that charter school bill goes through with the audit clause. You don't want to go to the joint and neither do I. She's crazy, but I went along with her shit because there was no other way out. Lubinsky couldn't be bought and the bill was going to pass. She had to go."

"I hear you," Gallo said. "But it's over the top to me, and I'm getting out. Give me my money."

"Not so fast," Monroe said, turning on the laptop. "I want to make sure I'm getting what I'm paying for."

"No problem," Gallo replied, shoving the flash drive across the table.

Monroe inserted the drive into the laptop

and pressed a few buttons. He looked at the screen and nodded. "How do I know this is the only copy?" hc asked.

"You don't," Gallo said. He nodded at the cop who was sitting at the bar watching them. "But you got the Kings County district attorney in your back pocket and at least one crooked NYPD cop, so I'm sure if you want, you can make lifc very difficult, if not impossible, for me. Like I said, I'm out of here and you'll never hear from me again."

"Yeah, where you heading? Your place in the Keys?"

Gallo laughed. "Sold it. And you think I'm going to tell you? Nah, farther south, Costa Rica, maybe Ecuador, but I won't be sending you a postcard. Two million plus will buy me a ncw name and a lot of fun. So adios, Munroe."

Monroe took a large sip from his bourbon as he watched Gallo walk out the door. He was taking a second sip when there was a sudden flash, followed by a muffled explosion. Car alarms began going off as people inside the bar yelled and ran for the door.

Except not everybody did. The large black man who'd been listening to his music stood and drew a gun from beneath his leather coat. He pointed to the lovey-dovey couple, who were also cops and had jumped to their feet, guns pulled. "I got this. Move!" he yelled.

As the couple ran for the door, the crooked cop at the bar at first seemed confused. Then he began to reach for his gun until Gail, the waitress, who'd been standing behind him, pressed her service revolver against his head. "Drop the gun, scumbag, and don't move," she hissed. "NYPD, and you're under arrest."

"What the —" Monroe exclaimed as he started to panic.

"On the floor," the large black man demanded.

"Who are you?"

"NYPD Detective Clay Fulton. You're under arrest for murder, and you better pray to God you didn't just add to the body count."

"I don't know what you're talking about."

"No? Well, let's go have a little chat with my boss and see about that."

"Who?"

"My boss, Butch Karp, the district attorney of New York County. Let's not keep him waiting. Now put your hands behind your back while I read you your rights."

19

Nine months later . . .

"Oyez, oyez, oyez, all those having business in Supreme Court Part 42, draw near and ye shall be heard," the rotund chief administrative court clerk James Farley intoned. "Put down that newspaper in the back, and all cell phones must be turned off, if not they will be surrendered. The Honorable Supreme Court Justice Peter Rainsford presiding."

As the judge swept into Part 42, otherwise known outside of New York as a courtroom, Karp glanced over at the defense table, where attorney Irving Mendelbaum stood next to his client, the defendant Olivia Stone. It was the morning of the second day of her murder trial, and his former Kings County counterpart looked angry and defiant.

Just the way I want her, Karp thought as his eyes shifted back to Mendelbaum, who gave him a wink. Karp winked back and returned his attention to the judge, who settled into his chair on the dais and urged the attorneys and spectators alike to take their seats.

Tall, thin, and balding with pale blue eyes that could sparkle with merriment over a good joke or blaze with anger for a breach of court decorum, Judge Rainsford had been the perfect choice for this case as far as Karp was concerned. He was not known for being partisan in any way, which had probably hurt his chances over the years for an appointment to a higher state court or federal bench, but it had also earned him a reputation for fairness on both sides of the aisle and with the media. And in a high-profile, politically charged case like this, Karp was grateful not to have a judge intent on grandstanding to score points with voters or party hacks.

Karp respected and liked this judge. Over a good, full-bodied red wine, Rainsford would confess to a penchant for reading crime thrillers and courtroom procedurals but only if they "adhered to reality rather than some legal fantasy that comes out of left field." He also had a son in the Army Rangers who'd served three tours of duty in Afghanistan before returning home alive and unharmed to his grateful parents.

The last time Karp had talked to Rainsford on a social level was at a courthouse Christmas party. The judge was looking forward to retirement, at which point he was going to sell his home in Mount Vernon and move to a farm in Pennsylvania that he and his wife, Fran, had bought years before. "I'd like to be done with all the madness, Butch, and we'll be content to be just simple country folk."

This morning, however, Rainsford was clearly irritated as evidenced by the way he glared at the gallery, which was packed mostly with media types. "It was brought to my attention this morning that someone in the press attempted to contact one or more of the jurors in this case *despite* my admonition to refrain from any such behavior," he said tersely.

Karp glanced back at the spectators in the rows, who were squirming whether they were guilty or not and looking at each other as if it had to be somebody else who had invoked the judge's ire. He imagined the terror the real guilty party must be feeling at that moment.

"Would Phil Manzano stand up," Rainsford demanded.

Several members of the media sniggered

and covered their mouths to hide smiles as one of their competitors, a muckraker for one of the weekly newspapers in Brooklyn, was singled out. It was immediately evident where he sat, as those closest to him slid to either side as though to avoid becoming collateral damage. A small, insipid-looking man with a scraggly mustache rose slowly from his seat.

"Are you Mr. Manzano?"

The little man nodded.

"What's that? I didn't hear you," the judge said.

"Yes, your honor, I'm Phil Manzano," he squeaked.

Rainsford pointed a long finger at the guilty party. "Court security, remove that man and toss him in a cell until I have time to deal with him at the end of the day."

"No, please, I won't do it again," Manzano squealed in terror.

"I know you won't because you won't be allowed back in this courthouse for the duration of this trial," the judge said. He then cast his eyes over the others in the gallery. "And that goes for the rest of you. I will not tolerate anyone interfering with the sanctity of these proceedings, which includes any attempts to contact a member of the jury. Am I clear?"

Karp was amused to watch the rest of the crowd bobbing their heads in unison like a classroom full of kindergartners scolded for refusing to be quiet during naptime.

After Manzano was escorted, still protesting, from the courtroom, Rainsford's glare disappeared and he smiled. "Good morning, counselors, Mrs. Stone. Are we ready to bring in the jury? Good. Mr. Farley, let's get on with it then."

When the jurors were seated, Rainsford turned to Karp. "Are you ready, Mr. Karp?"

"Yes, your honor," Karp said, rising from his seat.

During his opening, Karp had explained that the People's case would actually be comprised of two separate parts "though ultimately we will demonstrate how together they create the whole." The first part, he'd said, would be to dispel what was likely to be the defense contention that Lars Forsling was the murderer.

What he didn't say to the jury was that it was his strategy to "steal the defense's thunder" by essentially presenting their case and then systematically dismantling it.

The second part of the People's case would be to prove that Stone, in concert with teachers union president Tommy Monroe, and her "lover and hired assassin"

267

Yusef Salaam, "also known as Henry Burns," schemed for and then with intent caused the death of Rose Lubinsky, Mary Calebras, and Tawanna Mohammad.

Stone's motivation, as well as Monroe's, he had told the jurors, was to prevent passage of a bill "written by the deceased, Rose Lubinsky, that was before the state assembly last winter.

"This bill would have curtailed the power of the teachers union, whom the defendant counted on for financial and political support," Karp said. "But there was another motive, an even more venal motive. Monroe and the defendant, Olivia Stone, were afraid of a clause in that bill that would have triggered an audit of the union's accounts that would have uncovered years of skimming and the theft of millions of dollars. And the only way they thought they could stop or delay this bill to give them time to cover up their misdeeds was to remove its champion. And so Salaam was dispatched to set a bomb beneath the deceased's car while she was giving a talk about a book she'd written. That bomb would take her life, as well as the lives of two young women who died only because they were friends of Rose Lubinsky and in the wrong place at the wrong time. For no other reason, they would suffer horrible deaths because of the pernicious and evil scheming of the defendant."

As he spoke, Karp had walked toward the defense table and then lifted his arm and pointed at Stone. Already red-faced after his remark about her "lover and hired assassin" Salaam, the former district attorney of Kings County had glared up at him, not bothering to disguise the hatred she felt. Her husband had filed for divorce following her indictment when some of the more tawdry accusations were reported in the press.

As expected, following Karp's remarks, Mendelbaum's opening statement had contended that Forsling, "a murderous, psychotic individual motivated by vile anti-Semitism, as well as a desire to make a name for himself among his fellow Nazis," had planted the bomb beneath the car of a "prominent Jewish author outside of Il Buon Pane, a bakery owned by a Jewish couple, Moishe and Goldie Sobelman, who had survived the death camps of World War II.

"This mad-dog killer then sought to eliminate witnesses by gunning down his own comrades at The Storm Trooper saloon. Then, aware that the law was closing in, he took Goldie Sobelman, as well as my esteemed colleague the district attorney's own children, hostage in order to escape his just punishment. He is not sitting in this seat next to me today, ladies and gentlemen of the jury, because he died at the hands of Mr. Karp's wife."

Mendelbaum had suggested that Karp's prosecution of his client was politically motivated, as well as "a nod to the old boys club, or I should say, 'the old white boys club' at the male-dominated New York District Attorney's Office who felt threatened by the rising star of Olivia Stone. While I personally have great respect for my esteemed colleague Mr. Karp, I would be remiss in my duty to you good people if I did not point out that he is used to being the big man when it comes to law enforcement in the five boroughs, and his name is often discussed in political circles as having aspirations to a higher office. Might those aspirations not suffer a significant blow if a bright young woman, such as my client, were to seek the same higher office?"

However, he had said, Karp's enmity for Stone didn't end at political aspirations. He had noted that Karp and his family were "close personal friends of Rose and Simon Lubinsky, as well as outspoken proponents of the charter school system with all of its elitist and, dare I say it, racist overtones. His own sons attend elitist private schools. Meanwhile, Olivia Stone has been a champion of the public school system — a system, I might add, that helped make this country great — once serving as its chief counsel because she believed it was the best hope for all of our children, not just the chosen few."

Mendelbaum, a great courtroom actor, had placed his hand over his heart and shook his head sadly. "It pains me greatly to suggest that my friend Butch Karp would seize the opportunity once the real killer, Lars Forsling, was dead to eliminate someone he considered a political threat and who represented a different view of what is best for New York's schoolchildren. It is a sad day, indeed."

Karp had listened to the defense opening stone-faced, but internally he'd reacted with a mixture of admiration and humor. The truth was that Irving Mendelbaum was one of his favorite attorneys in the city. Pushing eighty, stooped and rheumy-eyed, Irving looked like somebody's grandfather in his rumpled old suits, but he was no pushover. In fact, he was the unofficial dean emeritus of the New York City defense bar and one of the best trial lawyers in Manhattan.

Wily, prepared, and with the energy of a much younger man, he loved battling prosecutors and did so with zeal and aplomb. But unlike some on his side of the aisle, he also did it ethically and without rancor — a man who truly believed that it was his duty to his client to put the People to the test and make them work to prove their cases beyond a reasonable doubt.

Karp wouldn't have had it any other way. As he often lectured younger assistant district attorneys in his office, the system was tilted in favor of the prosecution "and anybody can win a case against a bad defense attorney." But someone like Irving Mendelbaum would beat them if they weren't prepared and if they did not have the legally admissible evidence to prove their cases "not just beyond a reasonable doubt, but beyond any and all doubt." A great attorney like Mendelbaum would force them to be better prosecutors or they'd lose and be embarrassed in the process.

Mendelbaum was beloved throughout the courthouse, and not just because of his kindly disposition and cheerful attitude toward all who came across his path. He also carried a large Redwell file, which he kept full of candy that he liberally distributed to one and all: court clerks, fellow attorneys, judges, security personnel, and even young ADAs.

It wasn't uncommon to see him surrounded by children, witnesses, the media, and lawyers in the halls of the courthouse, all waiting for a sweet handout. In fact, when Karp arrived in court that morning, he discovered his co-counsel Kenny Katz, a young assistant district attorney, enjoying a Tootsie Pop.

"I see that Mr. Mendelbaum is in the building," Karp had said to his colleague, with an arched eyebrow.

Katz had turned red and quickly removed the sucker. "Uh, sorry, I couldn't resist."

Laughing, Karp had told Katz not to worry about it. "You're not the first ADA who has succumbed to Mr. Mendelbaum's bribes. I may have accepted a treat or two myself from time to time."

Karp didn't mention that one of those times was during the lunch break on the first day of the trial. He'd grabbed a quick hotdog from the vendor across Centre Street, wolfed it down with a can of orange soda chaser, and then, eschewing the lovely early summer day, hurried back to the courtroom to study his notes. But as he'd passed the witness waiting room, he'd looked through the glass and saw with alarm Irving Mendelbaum sprawled on his back on top of the wooden table inside.

Rushing into the room, he shook the old man's arm. "You okay, Irving?" he had asked.

With a snort, Mendelbaum woke and then sat up with a groan. "Why, if it isn't young Mr. Karp, my favorite boychick district attorney," he said with a grin that had charmed juries since before Karp got out of law school.

Karp smiled and shook his head. "That was some opening, counselor. I was about ready to tar, feather, and ride myself out of town on a rail."

Mendelbaum's grin grew even wider as he chuckled. "But then where would I find a worthy adversary? These kids coming out of law school nowadays, hardly worth my time," he said. "Surely you don't expect me to just roll over and play dead. In fact, I intend to kick your heinie on this one."

"I wouldn't put it past you."

Mendelbaum looked at him sideways. "Don't try to soften me up either, you *momzer*," he said. "But I don't suppose you want to level the playing field by telling me your plans?"

"Don't you worry, my friend, you'll find

out soon enough." Karp smiled and turned to go.

"Hey, Butch."

Looking back at the old man, Karp stopped and laughed. Mendelbaum was holding open his Redwell file with its sugary treasures.

"Can I interest you in something sweet?"

"Got any Snickers or Hershey's with nuts in there?"

"Of course I do," Mendelbaum replied.

Karp had enjoyed the banter with his old friend. But when court went back in session and for the next three days, the gloves had come off and Mendelbaum had lived up to his reputation for zealously representing his client.

The first day had been dominated by the prosecution witnesses who would lay the groundwork for the rest of the case. One such witness was Gail Manning, an assistant medical examiner, who had described the fatal injuries. However, Karp had refrained from showing the jury any photographs of either of the two women who'd died in the car or of Rose Lubinsky. Another prosecutor in another jurisdiction might have tried to get such gruesome photographs into evidence. But Karp saw that sort of thing as just a low appeal to the jurors' emotions but unnecessary to the case. Manning's description of the two younger women's fiery deaths and Lubinsky's injuries had been enough.

Other witnesses had included crime scene investigators and photographers to help Karp describe for the jurors the physical layout of the scene. He'd set up an easel on which a large map of the crime scene had been laid. Then as photographs taken at the scene were introduced into evidence, he tacked them to the map where they belonged and drew arrows to indicate the direction of the view. He also had the witnesses draw circles and label them for such details as to where the Nazi demonstrators and the counterdemonstrators had been standing, as well as where Forsling had been arrested and then detained in the back of the police car.

As he built this foundation, he'd ask questions that at the time might have seemed innocuous or unimportant to the jurors. Such as asking the arresting police officer if Forsling would have had a clear line of sight of the counterprotesters, as well as Lubinsky's car, and if he'd confiscated Forsling's cell phone when he placed him in the police car.

Meanwhile, Mendelbaum carefully chose

when and where to pick his fights during his cross-examinations. For instance, he declined to cross-examine Manning or refute most of the details on the easel. However, when it was his turn to question the police officer who arrested Forsling, he challenged the officer's testimony to Karp that Forsling "was nowhere near the car."

"If you weren't even aware that the leader of the Nazi protesters had slipped away from your sight," Mendelbaum said, "how do you know what he was doing before you saw him?"

"I didn't know what he was doing before he was taken into custody," the officer responded. "I meant he wasn't near the car when he was apprehended."

"So you don't know if he planted the bomb?" Mendelbaum pursued.

"I only know that Forsling didn't detonate it because he was in the squad car and had no cell phone," the officer countered.

Although made in bits and pieces, Mendelbaum's points, Karp knew, would be noted by the jurors. However, as he told Katz during a break, "We're not worried about details taken out of context, we're concentrating on the whole that the details create when put together. Our friend Irving doesn't have much to work with so he's trying to plant a seed in some juror's mind that he hopes will sprout into reasonable doubt."

With Mendelbaum sniping where he could like a guerrilla fighter trying to pick off stragglers, Karp continued to relentlessly build his case brick by brick. Now, on the morning of the second day, he was ready to add to that foundation.

"The People call Sergeant Mike Cordova," he said.

Short and broad-shouldered, with a thick graying mustache and pewter hair, Sergeant Mike Cordova was the leader of the NYPD bomb squad assigned to the case. After establishing his credentials and the overall impact of the bomb on the car and its inhabitants, Karp asked him about the C-4 plastic explosive used to detonate the gas tank of the car. "Is it possible to determine whether two different pieces of C-4 came from the same batch?" he asked, turning toward the defense table. He was gratified to see Stone's eyes widen for a moment and Mendelbaum frown, though he wouldn't tie this line of questioning in until later.

"Let me put it this way, it's easier to rule out using chemical analysis that they weren't from the same manufacturer or even batch than it is to say a hundred percent that they are," Cordova said.

"Sergeant, how was the C-4 detonated?" Karp asked.

"It was remote detonated," the sergeant explained.

"Could you explain to the jury what you mean by 'remote detonated' in this particular case?"

"Sure. The bomb consisted of a component from a cellular telephone. Someone then called that number from another cellular phone, which then closed a circuit that caused the bomb to explode."

Karp asked Sergeant Cordova to explain how the process worked. "There's a vibrating mechanism in a cell phone speaker. When the phone is called, it activates the mechanism, which vibrates and completes the connection and detonates the explosives."

"Were you able to locate the cell phone used to detonate the bomb?"

"Most of it was destroyed. So we know the make but very little else."

"What sort of make was it?"

"An NY-Mobile . . . one of those cheap prepaid cell phones you can buy at various stores. You use up the minutes and then toss it."

"So if the phone was destroyed, were you

able to determine where the call came from?"

"Yeah, another NY-Mobile."

"How do you know that?"

"It was located in a Dumpster in an alley between 28th and 29th Streets off of Third Avenue, just a block or so away from the scene."

"And you were able to determine that it was the phone from which the call was made that detonated the bomb?"

"Yeah, we know precisely what time the bomb went off because it was recorded on one of the squad car's dash cams," Sergeant Cordova said. "A call was placed from the phone found in the Dumpster to a number associated with another NY-Mobile phone."

Karp had walked over to the diagram and pointed to the alley between 28th and 29th Streets off of Third Avenue. "Would this be the location of that Dumpster?"

"Yes."

"And is that location closer to the circle marked on the diagram as 'counterdemonstrators' or 'Nazis?' "

"The counterdemonstrators."

Karp looked over at the defense table where Stone sat with her brow furrowed as if confused by his questioning. But Mendelbaum had a slight smile on his face.

"Sergeant Cordova, would you say that this bomb was a fairly sophisticated device? I mean, it's not like someone lit a fuse and tossed a stick of dynamite," Karp inquired.

"No, though they might both have the same effect. But I'd say this was a fairly sophisticated bomb."

"And Sergeant Cordova, approximately a week after this incident, were you called out on another car bombing?"

"Yes, I was."

"And there was the death of another individual associated with this bombing?"

"Yes, a young male died as a result of the blast."

"Were the circumstances of this bombing similar, and by that I mean, was a similar mechanism used to detonate the bomb?"

"Pretty much exactly the same," Cordova replied. "Two NY-Mobile phones, one of them attached to C-4 explosive; the other to make the call."

"Did you do a chemical analysis of the C-4 used in this second bomb?"

"Yes."

"And were you able to compare it to the C-4 used in the first bomb, the one used to murder the deceased in this case?"

"Yes."

"If so, could you explain to the jury the

results of that comparison?"

Cordova nodded and faced the jury. "Chemical analysis indicated that for all intents and purposes they were exactly the same makeup. Like I said earlier, I can't one hundred percent say they were from the exact same batch, but it's pretty damn probable."

"Objection," Mendelbaum said. He rose stiffly from his seat. "Your honor, 'pretty damn probable' is hardly something to ask a jury to base their opinion on."

"Sustained," the judge said. "Mr. Karp, would you like to rephrase your question?"

"Yes, your honor," Karp replied, and turned back to the witness. "Sergeant Cordova, is it your opinion that the two samples of C-4 obtained from these two separate bombings are chemically identical as a result of scientific analysis?"

"Yes, we have a great laboratory — highest rated in the country."

"And Sergeant Cordova, I believe that you told the jury you have worked as a bomb squad detective for more than twenty years and dealt with thousands of cases involving explosives, including C-4?"

"That's correct."

"And is it therefore your expert opinion to a reasonable degree of certainty that the two samples of C-4 you just testified about are likely to have come from the same place?"

"It is."

"No further questions, your honor."

Rainsford looked over at Mendelbaum, who had remained standing after his objection. "Would you care to cross-examine this witness?"

"With pleasure, your honor," Mendelbaum said as he walked quickly over toward the witness stand. "Good morning, sergeant."

"Good morning, Mr. Mendelbaum," the sergeant replied with a smile. Even the cops liked the old gentleman.

"I only have a few questions," Mendelbaum said. "I don't remember Mr. Karp asking if there were any fingerprints found on any of these NY-Mobile cell phones."

"There weren't any."

"And so no one saw somebody use one of these cell phones to detonate either bomb?" Mendelbaum asked with a self-assured smirk.

Cordova then looked over at Karp and smiled. "I know from the investigation that Lars Forsling saw an individual using a cell phone at the moment of the explosion and that we believe that individual was Yusef

Salaam, one of the co-conspirators in this case."

During witness preparation, Sergeant Cordova had been prepared for this line of questioning. Karp laid the trap and Mendelbaum walked right into it.

Mendelbaum suddenly realized that he took the bait. Alarmed, he addressed Judge Rainsford, "Your honor, I ask that the answer be stricken. Neither Forsling nor Salaam will testify."

"Mr. Karp, your response?" Rainsford asked.

"Your honor, Mr. Mendelbaum asked a very broad, open-ended question," Karp said. "Sergeant Cordova properly responded."

"Yes," Rainsford said. "Mr. Mendelbaum . . . Mr. Karp and the court are aware that when you, Mr. Mendelbaum, open a door, it may very well be shut abruptly as this witness just did. You're right, Mr. Karp. Be more careful, Mr. Mendelbaum, your motion is denied. Please proceed."

"Very well, your honor," Mendelbaum said as he turned back to the witness stand. "Sergeant, you told the jurors that you believe that these bombs were sophisticated devices, but isn't it true that anybody with a computer can find out how to make them from the internet?"

Sitting in his seat, Karp made a note on his legal pad. Mendelbaum was somewhat unsettled by the last foray with the witness, and this was an atypical mistake on Mendelbaum's part that Karp would exploit later.

"Yes, you can find almost anything of this nature on the internet," Cordova acknowledged. "We arrested several individuals this past year who had a blueprint for making a viable nuclear weapon they'd found on the internet. They lacked only the radioactive material necessary but were working on getting it."

"Thank God you were able to stop them," Mendelbaum responded. "You and your men are to be commended. But as you said, you can find almost anything on the internet these days. No further questions."

Rainsford looked at Karp. "Redirect?"

"Just a couple questions, your honor. Sergeant Cordova, were you able to link any of these NY-Mobile phones together in any way?"

Karp smiled slightly when he noticed Mendelbaum take sudden notice. *Got ya,* he thought.

"Yes, the two NY-Mobile phones we were able to recover were bought from the same store though on two different occasions."

"Obviously these purchases were made before the bombings?"

"Yes, the day before in each case."

"Are there any other links to the bombings?"

"Well, of course each phone has its own number, and these numbers are sequential to the phone purchased before and after it. And they have to be activated at the store."

"And what's the significance of that?"

"First, the folks at NY-Mobile were able to tell us which store sold the phones," Cordova said. "Then we were able to determine from store records that each of the phones purchased was bought with a second phone with sequential phone numbers. These were the last numbers dialed by the phones we were able to recover."

"And, if you would please tell the jury what that means to you?"

"That the second phones were destroyed in the blasts."

After Rainsford adjourned for lunch, Karp saw Mendelbaum in the hall. "So, boychick, you're killing me in there," the old man complained. "That stuff with the phones. Of course, you know I'm going to have to go for the second blast was a setup to take the blame off Forsling . . . evil charter

286

school types trying to get even. No disrespect to you."

"I think it's time for you to start writing novels, Irving. The evil charter school types? You've got to be kidding me," Karp said.

Ending the banter, Mendelbaum said, "You know I'm calling Marlene to the stand?"

"You do what you need to do, Irving. But be careful, my friend, she's much more clever than I."

After lunch Karp called Captain Bo Loselle of the New York Fire Department to the stand to describe the circumstances surrounding the fire that killed Forsling's mother and subsequent investigation into its cause.

"The call came in about 3 a.m.," explained Loselle, a big man with a thick salt-and-pepper mustache. "By the time the crews arrived, the top floor was engulfed."

"Were you aware that someone was trapped upstairs?"

Loselle nodded. "My men heard a woman screaming for help," he said. "One of my guys, Firefighter Kevin Gilbert, tried to reach her but couldn't because the roof collapsed. He was a real hero — suffered burns and a significant back injury."

"Were you able to determine the cause of

the fire?"

"Yes. The investigation concluded that there were no accelerants used, which is the first clue you look for in arson. But we were able to determine that the victim had been smoking in bed and apparently fell asleep. The cigarette ignited trash on the floor and it spread pretty quickly from there."

"Later that afternoon were you still at the scene when you were contacted by a young male?"

"Yes, we were just wrapping up when we had to stop a young man from entering the domicile. He subsequently identified himself as an occupant of the house. He said he lived there with his mother."

"What, if anything, did you tell him at that point?"

"I informed him that his mother was deceased."

"And what was his reaction?"

"He became distraught," Loselle said. "And angry."

"Did he blame anyone for his mother's death?"

"Yes, excuse my language," Loselle apologized to the jury, "he blamed a 'fucking Jew and his nigger cop.' Then he said, 'I'll show that bastard Karp that two can play this game.' "

"What was your response?"

"I asked him if he meant you. But he took off."

Karp handed Loselle a photograph. "Captain, I'm giving you a photograph, People's Exhibit 21 in evidence. Do you recognize the individual in the photograph?"

Loselle looked at the photograph and nodded. "Yes, that's him."

"Your honor," Karp said, "the record will reflect that the witness identified a photograph previously identified as Lars Forsling. I have no further questions."

Mendelbaum was on his feet and had positioned himself in front of the jury before Rainsford finished asking if he wanted to cross-examine the witness. "Captain Loselle, did this individual, Mr. Forsling, seem rational to you?"

"No, he didn't."

"Did he threaten to get even with a, and I quote, 'fucking Jew and his nigger cop'?"

"Yes, he did."

"And Captain Loselle, did he strike you as the sort of individual who might plant a bomb to kill Jews?"

"Objection," Karp protested, rising to his feet.

"I'll withdraw the question," Mendelbaum said with a smile. "And I have no more questions."

After Loselle left the stand, the judge adjourned early, saying he had some other docket matters to attend to. "See you all tomorrow morning?"

20

"The People call Detective Clay Fulton."

As soon as Fulton, who'd been sitting in the first row behind the prosecution table as the trial resumed the next morning, stood up, Mendelbaum jumped to his feet. "Your honor, the defense objects to this witness being allowed to testify. The defense believes that my esteemed colleague, Mr. Karp, will be attempting to elicit testimony that will be based on hearsay.

"The witness will be asked to testify about the interrogation of one Lars Forsling, who as you know we contend should be the defendant in this case, not Mrs. Stone. As you also are aware, Mr. Forsling is dead, and therefore he can't be cross-examined as to his statements, nor as to the veracity of Detective Fulton's recollection of those events."

The judge looked at Karp, who had remained on his feet, waiting for Fulton.

"Mr. Karp?"

"First, your honor, it is important to note that I, the prosecution, turned over to the defense the dying declaration made by Forsling; such a statement is an exception to the hearsay rules of evidence."

Karp continued, "The defense wants to persuade the jury that Forsling is the bomber who murdered the deceaseds in this case. Hearsay is an out-of-court statement made by the declarant and offered for the truth of the matter asserted. However, in order for the jury to decide if the Forsling dying declaration is trustworthy, all the facts and circumstances must be known to the jury so that the dying declaration can be scrutinized with all the other evidence in context. The chief of the District Attorney's Office detective squad will assist the jury by providing that context. I ask the court to admit this testimony, subject to connection on this crucial evidentiary issue."

Looking over at Mendelbaum, who regarded him with arched eyebrows like one of his former law school professors looking for a weakness in his arguments, Karp smiled and shook his head. "One last point, your honor, Mr. Mendelbaum is trying to have his cake and eat it, too. He wants Forsling's 'dying dec' introduced as an

292

exception to the hearsay rule, but wants to exclude other statements made by Forsling to Detective Fulton, our office steno, Mrs. Carole Mason, and me."

"Ah, but those statements were not made with the Grim Reaper and all of eternity looming over Mr. Forsling's tattooed head, and therefore under the law are considered inherently untrustworthy, and do not carry the same weight as those of a man who knows that the moment of judgment is at hand," Mendelbaum replied.

"The evidence in this case will demonstrate, your honor, that Forsling from his own statements and actions was obsessed with seeking vengeance against Detective Fulton and me because of his delusional, wrong-headed, far-fetched belief that we were responsible for the death of his mother," Karp countered. "That's why he kidnapped my two sons, and Mrs. Goldie Sobelman, and made clear he did it to seek vengeance. In furtherance of that delusional belief, he was in the process of trying to kill all three of them. We will learn from the evidence that his dying dec was nothing more than his last-gasp effort to get back at me."

Rainsford looked from one attorney to the other and nodded. "I'm going to allow

Detective Fulton to testify with the caveat that you prove, Mr. Karp, all that you just said. Mr. Karp, you may now proceed."

Mendelbaum, as he passed Karp on the way back to the defense table, whispered, "Sometimes you have to throw the matzo balls against the wall to see what sticks."

Shaking his head, Karp smiled. Fulton, who'd waited calmly for the lawyers to argue, now stepped up onto the witness stand. A seasoned pro at testifying, he stood tall as he was sworn in by chief court clerk James Farley. He then settled his large frame into the seat and turned toward the judge.

"One moment, Mr. Karp, before you question the witness I want to take a moment with the jury," Rainsford said. "Ladies and gentlemen, generally these legal type arguments are heard at sidebar on the record, outside the hearing of the jury. However, since Mr. Mendelbaum objected to the witness testifying and initiated his legal argument in front of you, the jury, I permitted the legal argument to be fully aired for all of you to hear and I'm sure to understand. I determine the admissibility of evidence, and if it is trustworthy, I permit you to decide whether or not you will accept it in your final determination in this case. In making that determination you should take into account the demeanor of witnesses and the context in which evidence is offered. You may now proceed, Mr. Karp."

Karp then quickly walked the detective through his career with the NYPD up to his current position as the head of the special unit of NYPD detectives assigned to work for the district attorney as investigators. He then brought him to the night of Rose Lubinsky's book signing at Il Buon Pane. "Was there a reason why you and other police officers were at this particular event?"

"Yes, we'd been informed that a crowd of protesters were gathering across the street from the bakery," Fulton replied. "Officers were dispatched for crowd control, and I was present in a supervisory capacity."

"Can you describe the composition of this group of protesters?"

"Yes, they were mostly comprised of what the NYPD Gang Unit describes as white supremacists and/or neo-Nazis, sometimes referred to in the media as 'skinheads,' though that is a misnomer."

"And why would using the term 'skinhead' be inaccurate?" Karp asked.

"Well, the so-called 'skinhead movement,' or group, started in England as a working-class youth subculture comprised of whites and blacks," Fulton explained. "They were identifiable by some of their dress, such as Doc Martens boots, as well as shaving their scalps, thus the term 'skinheads.' However, it wasn't until this subculture arrived in the United States that it took an offshoot lean toward white supremacist ideology. They've kept the clothing and the bald heads, but 'real' skinheads both here and in England actually resent the racism and fascist ideology. The two groups will even clash if they encounter one another."

"So even though the media might refer to that group demonstrating across the street from Il Buon Pane as 'skinheads,' it is more accurate to identify them as Nazis and racists?"

"That's correct."

"Who or what were they protesting?"

"The who would be one of the deceased, Rose Lubinsky, and the what would be a book she wrote describing her experiences during World War II as a young Jewish girl in Poland," Fulton said. "She was given by her parents to a Christian couple to save her from being deported to the Nazi death camps, where her parents and siblings perished. These neo-Nazis deny that the Holocaust occurred and were protesting the book as promoting what they call the 'lies' about what happened to Jews, as well as other minorities, during World War II in Nazi-controlled areas."

"Are these neo-Nazis sometimes known for unprovoked violence against minorities and ethnic groups, including blacks and Jews?"

"Yes. They are frequently involved in assaults on both property and people, including some fatalities. These incidents often are prosecuted under 'hate crime' statutes."

"You testified about the presence of NYPD officers and yourself for crowd control. Were these neo-Nazis the only protesters present?"

"No. After word got out that the Nazis were there, a crowd of what you might call counterprotesters assembled."

"Can you describe the composition of this group?"

"It was somewhat mixed," Fulton responded. "Mostly locals, I'd say, who didn't appreciate the presence of neo-Nazis and racists in their neighborhood, which is mixed as far as race and ethnicity. There were also people who had come to support Rose Lubinsky."

"Detective Fulton, you've described the deceased, Rose Lubinsky, as an author and survivor of the Holocaust. As it relates to this homicide investigation, are you aware of her having any other occupations or causes that she was involved in?" Karp asked.

"Yes. After a long career as a teacher in the New York public school system, Mrs. Lubinsky had been involved for many years in the charter school movement," Fulton said. "At the time of her death, she was the president of the New York Charter Schools Association."

"And was there something in particular regarding her position as the president of the charter schools association that became of interest during the homicide investigation?"

"Yes," Fulton said. "She was the author of a bill that had been introduced to the New York State Assembly."

"In general, what was the purpose of this bill such as you understand it?"

"Basically, it would have put charter schools on a more equal footing with public schools for government funding, as well as removing impediments to the growth of the charter school system and access for students interested in attending charter schools," Fulton said.

"Were there any other particular provisions of this bill that were of note to the investigation?" Karp said as he casually walked over toward the defense table, drawing the jurors' eyes.

"Actually, two," Fulton said. "In general, the bill would have been a potentially serious blow to public schools and public school teachers unions because it would have impacted them financially. But there was also a provision that called for an audit of the Greater New York Teachers Federation that came to our attention during the investigation."

"Did the Greater New York Teachers Federation oppose this legislation?"

"Yes, the federation was on record as opposing the legislation," Fulton replied.

"And who was the president of the Greater New York Teachers Federation at the time?"

"Thomas 'Tommy' Monroe."

Karp turned toward the defense table and stared down at the defendant Olivia Stone, who glared back up at him before looking away. "And what, if anything, was the defendant's affiliation, past or present, with the teachers union?"

"At one time she was chief counsel for the union and reported to Monroe."

"After she left that position, did she have any other association with the union?"

"Yes, the teachers union supported her

election for DA of Kings County, Brooklyn."

"What became of the charter school legislation after the death of Rose Lubinsky?"

"That was nine months ago, but it's my understanding that it was tabled for the time being."

"So the death of Mrs. Lubinsky achieved the union's goal of at least delaying the state assembly vote on this bill?"

"Objection!" Mendelbaum shouted.

"Sustained," Rainsford said. "Mr. Karp, please let's not assume facts not in evidence."

Walking over to the jury box, Karp looked up at Fulton. "Returning to the night of the murders, would it be safe to assume that the objective of the police officers present for crowd control was to protect those attending the book signing, as well as keep the two opposing groups of demonstrators apart?"

"That's correct."

Karp pointed at the diagram. "Detective Fulton, would you please look at People's 1 in evidence."

Fulton reached into the interior pocket of his suitcoat and carefully removed a pair of dark-rimmed glasses that he placed on his broad brown face. "I can now," he said with a smile.

Karp smiled back; his friend resisted wearing glasses unless absolutely necessary. "They make me look old, just like the gray hairs on my temples," he'd complained that morning in Karp's office.

"You can see the circles representing where the two opposing groups were assembled, marked 'Nazis' and 'Locals,' as well as the area marked 'bakery,' a circle marked 'Lubinsky car,' and another circle marked 'police car'?"

"Yes, quite clearly."

"Would you say the diagram fairly and accurately represents the location of these various items as they were on the night of the murders?"

"Yes."

"Did you see Lars Forsling that night in the circle marked 'Nazis'?"

"At that time, I didn't know what his name was," Fulton said. "However, I did see a young man, who I later learned was Mr. Forsling."

"Was there anything about him that caused you to notice him?"

"He was hard to miss," Fulton replied. "For one thing, he had tattoos on his face. But he was also apparently the leader of that group and the most vociferous."

"Was there something else that happened that night that brought Mr. Forsling to your attention? And if so, would you explain the circumstances?"

"Yes. The crowd control officers did their best to contain the groups in specified areas and away from each other and the bakery," Fulton said. "However, the protesters were welcome to leave so long as they didn't try to circumvent the ground rules. In fact, it was a very cold night, and many of the protesters on both sides didn't last long. At some point, Mr. Forsling walked away from the area designated for his group, but instead of leaving, he circled around and was apprehended on the street near the area designated on the diagram as Mrs. Lubinsky's car."

"You said 'apprehended.' So he was arrested?"

"Yes, he'd been told to remain out of that area, and he was placed under arrest for disobeying a lawful command by a police officer."

"What happened to him at that point?"

"He was placed in a squad car — marked 'police car' on the diagram — until we could spare the manpower to take him to The Tombs."

"The Tombs, by which you mean the jail in lower Manhattan, located at 100 Centre Street inside this courthouse building?"

"Yes. It sits at the northern end of this building complex."

"Was it at this point that you learned his name?"

"Yes . . . though not immediately . . . the arresting officer was black and Mr. Forsling initially refused to give his name and had no other identification on him. However, he gave his name to a white officer, who then told me."

"Was Mr. Forsling eventually transported downtown?"

"Yes."

"What happened between his arrest and being taken downtown?"

"The bomb was detonated."

"At that time killing Miss Calebras and Miss Mohammad, and mortally wounding Rose Lubinsky."

"Yes."

"Thereafter, Mr. Forsling was taken immediately to The Tombs?"

"Yes, and then was taken to your office located in the southern end of this building at 100 Centre Street."

"I requested this so that he could be interrogated about his possible involvement in the attack on the three women?"

"Yes."

"And you were present during this interrogation, as was Mrs. Carole Mason, a stenographer who works for the District Attorney's Office?"

"That's correct."

Karp left his place at the jury box and walked over to the prosecution table, where Assistant DA Kenny Katz handed him a photograph. Returning to the witness dais, he handed the photograph to Fulton. "Detective Fulton, I'm handing you People's Exhibit 21. Is this the man who was arrested, placed in the police car, and then brought to my office to be interrogated?"

"Yes, that's Lars Forsling." He handed the photograph back down to Karp, who walked it back over to the prosecution table, where he set it down and picked up a sheaf of papers.

"Prior to the interrogation, were you able to review the criminal history of Mr. Forsling?" Karp asked.

"Yes."

"What did you discover?"

"I did run a quick criminal background check," Fulton replied. "There was nothing major. A couple of citations for vandalism.

There was a notation that he was a suspect in attacks on Jewish businesses last November."

"That would have been the anniversary of Kristallnacht, an event in Nazi Germany and Austria in 1938 in which Nazis destroyed Jewish businesses, as well as assaulting and murdering Jewish citizens of those countries."

"That's correct."

"Were you able to learn anything else about Mr. Forsling?"

"He was considered to be one of the leaders of a group of neo-Nazis who gathered regularly at a bar called The Storm Trooper in Hell's Kitchen," Fulton said. "It's a small group, and not particularly notable, but active enough to have come to the attention of the NYPD Gang Unit."

"In reviewing what you could find about Mr. Forsling's activities, was there any record of him acting violently against other people?"

"Nothing specific," Fulton said. "These guys are always threatening to 'defend themselves' against minorities and ethnic groups by resorting to violence, and there were some members of this group associated with having records for violent crimes — one Jim Gerlach in particular. But

Forsling seemed to be all mouth . . . at least at that point."

Karp held up the sheaf of papers. "Detective Fulton, I am handing you the transcript of the interrogation of Mr. Forsling, marked as People's Exhibit 22. Would you take a moment to look it over and tell the jury whether you believe it to be a fair and accurate representation of that event?"

As Fulton quickly scanned the transcript, Karp again returned to the rail alongside the jury box. "This appears to be a fair and accurate representation of the interview with Mr. Forsling," the detective said.

"And this is an actual transcript of the conversation as it was taken down by a stenographer?"

"Yes, by Mrs. Mason, who I believe has been with the DA's office for more than twenty years."

"Detective Fulton, how would you describe Mr. Forsling's attitude during this interrogation?" Karp asked.

"Belligerent," Fulton said. "Paranoid."

"Did he use epithets and racist remarks when referring to you and me?"

"Frequently."

"If you'd refer to the second page of the transcript," Karp said, "what was the first question he asked?"

306

"He asked, 'Am I under arrest for the bomb?' "

"And my response was?"

"You said, 'You were arrested for disobeying the lawful command of a police officer.' And then you asked him if he was willing to answer your questions."

"Did he have a concern that something might happen to him if he didn't answer my questions? I'm referring to his response a few lines down from his question."

"Yes, he pointed at me and said, 'And if I'm not, you'll have your house nigger beat me up.' "

"Did you respond to this provocation?"

Fulton laughed. "If I had a nickel for every time some suspect referred to me as a nigger, I could have retired from the force a long time ago. No, I didn't respond."

"Did Mr. Forsling make any comments indicating he believed that he was being 'set up' by law enforcement to take the fall for the car bomb? I'm referring to his comments on pages three and four."

Turning to the pages, Fulton nodded. "Yes, first he said, 'You and your nig . . . your cop . . . think I did it and that's all that matters.' He then said, 'For all I know, you planted that bomb so you'd have a reason to go after us for murder.' "

"Did I indicate that Mr. Forsling was a suspect?"

"Yes, you pointed out that he and his friends had targeted the book signing and that he'd been arrested near the car that was bombed. You said, and I quote from page five: 'It makes you a person of interest; it doesn't make you guilty. I also know that you were sitting in the police car when the bomb went off and had a view of Mrs. Lubinsky's car. And that makes you a potential witness.' "

"What was Mr. Forsling's response to that?"

"He wanted to know if he could leave if he answered your questions."

"Was he worried about someone?"

"Yes," Fulton said. "He said his mother was an invalid and he wanted to get home in order to take care of her."

"What was my response?"

"You told him he was going to have to wait until the next morning to see a judge before he could post bail. You also offered to contact NYPD to do a welfare check on his mother, but he declined the offer."

"Why did he decline the offer?"

"He said that he was worried that a black or Hispanic officer would be sent and that would upset his mother."

"Did Forsling then agree to answer my questions?"

"Yes, though he initiated the next part of the conversation by alluding to a potential alternative suspect he claimed to have seen while sitting in the squad car."

"How did he describe this person?"

"As a 'funny-looking nigger' who he said was near the Lubinsky car. He said he saw him leaning over next to the car, and I quote, 'as though he was tying his shoe.' You then asked him to describe this person and he said — this is on page seven — 'You know, like his face was like half-black, half-white . . . like he had that thing that Michael Jackson had.' "

"Did you respond to that?"

"Yes, I said, 'Vitiligo, it causes a decrease in skin pigmentation.' "

"Did he answer my question asking if he recalled anything else about this individual?"

"Yes, he said this individual was with the group marked on the diagram as 'Locals' and that right before the bomb went off, he separated from that crowd. Quoting here from page nine, 'Then he took out his cell phone and punched in some numbers.' You asked him about the significance of that and he said that this individual didn't try to speak into the phone but was instead, this is page ten, 'looking at it when that Jew bitch and her friends got in the car. He was watching them and then boom.' "

"Was there a second observation he made about this individual?"

"Yes, his shoes. He said this individual was wearing 'cherry red canvas high tops.' He thought it was unusual because it was cold outside and there was snow on the ground."

Karp walked over to the witness stand and held up his hand for the transcript, which Fulton passed to him. "Did Mr. Forsling then terminate the interview?"

"Yes. He said he'd wait to see what we did with his information before he'd answer any more questions."

Karp walked back over to the prosecution table and picked up another set of papers, which he delivered to Fulton. "Mr. Fulton, approximately a week after the murders outside of Il Buon Pane, did you have occasion to be in an establishment known as the Jay Street Bar in Brooklyn?"

"Yes. I was there to monitor a conversation being recorded between Thomas Monroe and one Micah Gallo."

"I've handed you another transcript, People's Exhibit 23. Do you recognize it?"

Fulton made a show of looking the

transcript over although he'd reviewed it extensively during trial preparation. He looked up. "Yes, I recognize it."

"Without commenting on the contents, does it represent a fair and accurate transcription of this conversation you were monitoring between Mr. Monroe and Mr. Gallo?"

"It's word for word."

"Thank you," Karp said, walking up to retrieve the transcript from Fulton. "No further questions."

Rainsford turned to Mendelbaum, who was leaning over to listen to Stone, and asked if he wanted to cross-examine the witness.

"Yes, your honor," he said, standing and approaching the witness stand.

"Good morning, detective," Mendelbaum said, "though my stomach's telling me that it's almost lunchtime so I'll make this quick. Detective, during this interview with Mr. Forsling did he ever outright deny planting the bomb?"

"Not in so many words."

"Actually, not at all," Mendelbaum replied. "He accused my colleague, Mr. Karp, and yourself of jumping to that conclusion, but he never actually denied it either, did he?"

"You're correct, he didn't," Fulton responded.

"Nor was he asked. Isn't that correct?"

"We never got that far before he terminated the conversation."

"And before he terminated the conversation, he wasn't asked, was he?"

"No, he wasn't."

Mendelbaum walked right up to the witness stand, where he stood with his head craned to look up at the detective. "Mr. Forsling wasn't brought to the offices of the district attorney that night because he'd been arrested for disobeying a police officer, right?"

"No."

"In fact, he was brought to the offices of the district attorney because he was the prime suspect in the car bombing, isn't that true?"

"He was *a* suspect."

Mendelbaum looked surprised and turned to the jurors as if he'd heard some piece of stunning news. "Were there any other suspects I haven't heard about?"

"Not at that time, no."

"So he was *the* suspect, isn't that right?"

"At that time, he was the suspect, yes."

"However, Mr. Forsling alluded to a suspicious-looking character with some sort of marking on his face, wearing bright red canvas high-tops?"

"Yes."

"Were there a number of police cars on the scene that were equipped with dash cams?" Mendelbaum asked.

"Yes, there were."

"And did any of these dash cams reveal such an individual?"

"There was only one car with a camera pointed in the direction of the 'Locals' group."

"And did it show this individual?"

"Not that I could see."

"And wasn't there quite a bit of media presence at this demonstration, recording both sides of the event?"

"Yes, there were several television crews."

"And did any of their broadcasts depict such an individual?"

"Not in the amount of video I was able to view," Fulton responded. Although he couldn't say it, he was frustrated because the defense had won a pretrial motion that prevented him from saying that the television stations had refused to turn over their tapes of the events. He'd only been able to view what had been broadcast.

This time it was Mendelbaum who walked over to the jury box, smiling slightly at the jurors, most of whom smiled back at the grandfatherly figure. "Detective Fulton, one last question. You testified that Mr. Forsling didn't have a record for violence against other people. But I believe we're about to learn that he was quite capable of murder, aren't we?"

Fulton shrugged. "Yes, we'll learn he was capable of murder, but not these murders."

"Nice try, detective, but we'll see about that, won't we," Mendelbaum shot back.

"Oh yes, we will, you can make book on that one, Mr. Mendelbaum."

"No more questions, your honor," Mendelbaum dismissively replied.

"Mr. Karp, care to redirect?" Rainsford asked.

Karp rose and shook his head. "No, your honor."

"The witness may step down," the judge said, and looked at his watch. "It's a little early, but let's break for lunch and reconvene at one-thirty this afternoon. We're adjourned until then."

21

With the June sun shining invitingly through the window of his office, Karp decided he'd spend the lunch hour across the street eating something from one of the sidewalk vendors. He'd learned long ago that comprehensive preparation was the key to winning trials, as well as helping him stay relaxed and focused; as such, he was feeling good about how this one had been going and the groundwork he'd put in for what was ahead. *And that,* he thought, *earns me the right to relax a little and eat my lunch in the fresh air.*

Karp left his office through the side door and took the private elevator down to the secure entrance on the Leonard Street side of the building. He found Officer Ewin waiting for him outside the elevator when the door opened.

"I thought you might try to escape, Mr. Karp," the young officer said in his thick

New York Irish brogue. "If you're going out, I better go with you."

Karp frowned. "I was just going to grab a knish and eat it in the park," he said. "I think I'll be okay so long as I don't get run over by a yellow cab crossing the street or accosted by a deranged tourist."

"Have you taken a look out front lately?" Ewin asked.

"No, been a little busy, Eddie," Karp said. "What's up?"

"Well, this trial has folks a little stirred up," Ewin said. He began holding up fingers. "Security has kept the front of the building fairly clear, but then you got Nazis on one side of the barriers, and teachers union supporters on the other. Across the street are the charter school folks and next to them are the anti-Nazis. Judging by their signs and some of the things they're yelling, they don't much like each other . . . and none of them appear to like you. Except maybe the charter school folks; they seem to be the most rational."

"Oh, then," Karp said, smiling, "why didn't you say so? It's business as usual."

Ewin grinned. "Yeah, business as usual, but this time if you want to have lunch in the park, I'm going with you. I'm not about to have Detective Clay Fulton breathing fire down my neck because I let you wander among the crazies by yourself. And if something did happen, he'd pitch me off the Brooklyn Bridge as sure as every one of my uncles was named after a saint."

"They were, huh?" Karp responded.

"Yeah, we Irish Roman Catholics aren't real creative when it comes to names."

"Well, you can come with me, but only if you let me buy you a knish," Karp said.

"Never had one. Has it got any meat in it?" Ewin asked. "It's Friday and I'm not supposed to have meat. Another one of those fun Catholic traditions."

"Not to worry, I only eat the potato version. You'll love it; it's guaranteed to put hair on your chest," Karp said.

"Then you're on."

Karp and his bodyguard walked away from the crowds near the front of the courthouse and into the park just behind the court on Baxter Street. The protesters' attention was focused on each other and the media. On the far side of the park, Karp walked up to a cart advertising "the best knish in town."

"Why, if it isn't District Attorney Butch Karp," Herschel Finkelstein, the vendor, a tall, gaunt man wearing a yarmulke, said. "I'm surprised you made it through the gauntlet."

"No big deal. The protesters choose to stay at the front of the building. We chose the side door direct route and got here on the sly." Karp winked and smiled. "Let's just keep it our little secret."

"Hey, I'm not saying nuthin'." The vendor grinned. "You're my most regular customer."

"Good, then let me have two hot potato knishes with a little mustard, sliced down the middle," Karp said.

The vendor eyed the officer and extended his hand. "Herschel Finkelstein."

"Eddie Ewin."

"Let me guess, you're Irish Catholic, right?" he said.

"Practically raised by nuns," Ewin said. "How'd you know?"

"Well you got the map of Ireland written all over your face."

They both laughed. "You ever had this Jewish delicacy before? You're in for a treat."

"On that recommendation, I'll give it a whirl."

The conversation was interrupted by another voice behind Karp. "Hey Butch . . . motherfucker asswipe . . . what are you doing over . . . whoop whoop . . . here?"

"Afternoon, Warren," Karp said without

having to turn around to see who was standing behind him. "Another potato knish,
please, for our friend Warren Bennett. And
three sodas . . . make mine the usual . . ."

"Orange soda with ice in a cup."

"Thanks, Herschel, and whatever these
two gentlemen want."

"Why thanks . . . oh boy scum bag nuts
whoop whoop . . . Butch," Dirty Warren
said. "You didn't have to . . . whoop
whoop . . . do that."

"My pleasure, but I can ask you the same
thing: What are you doing over here? Isn't
lunchtime a busy part of your day?"

"Yeah, normally," Dirty Warren said with
disgust. "But nobody wants to fight their
way through the crazies for a newspaper . . .
tits damn . . . or a magazine. You really
messed me up with the mighty high-
profile . . . bastard bitch whoop whoop . . .
case this time, Butch."

Karp held out his hands. "Geez, I can't
get a break today. I guess the cause of justice
isn't very popular."

"Not today it . . . oh boy, ohhhhh boy . . .
ain't."

The three men took their knishes and
sodas and found a park bench. Even though
it was a safe place out of sight in back of
the courthouse, the sound of people yelling

319

into bullhorns drifted to Karp and his entourage.

"The Holocaust was a lie. Lubinsky deserved to die."

"Karp hates unions. Unions hate Karp."

"Down with racism. Karp's protecting Nazis."

"Wow, we're apparently the only friends you have left," Ewin joked.

Karp laughed. "And sometimes I wonder about you two."

"Very . . . fuck you . . . funny," Dirty Warren added.

The men ate quietly until Warren piped up with one of his movie trivia questions. "Okay, Karp, I got a good one . . . oh boy screw you asshole . . . for you," he said. "Name the movie and the character who . . . whoop whoop . . . said this: *Well, when I was an attorney, a long time ago, young man, I realized* . . . oh boy whoop . . . *after much trial and error that in a courtroom, whoever tells the best story wins. In unlawyer-like fashion, I give you that scrap of wisdom free of charge.*"

Karp patted his small friend on the shoulder. "That is a good one," he said, "but not because it was particularly hard. It's from *Amistad,* the story of a mutiny aboard a slave ship in 1839 and the subsequent trial

320

that was the beginning of the end of slaves being considered 'property' and not human beings. The quote is spoken by John Quincy Adams, the former president, played by Anthony Hopkins, giving advice to the free black abolitionist Theodore Joadson, played by Morgan Freeman. Eventually, Adams gives an impassioned speech — the story he's referring to — before the U.S. Supreme Court that wins the case in favor of the abolitionists and slaves. Thanks, Warren, sound advice then, and now."

Dirty Warren said nothing. He just smiled and closed his eyes as he turned his face up toward the sun.

Karp was still thinking about the *Amistad* quote when he and Ewin again crossed Baxter Street and approached the side entrance. They'd almost reached the door when someone yelled.

"There you are, you fucking Nazi lover!"

A large bearded man in a tattered Army coat emerged from behind a Dumpster and started walking toward them. "I've been waiting for you, Karp," the man shouted and raised a gun.

Karp felt himself shoved roughly to the side by Ewin, who stepped in front of him, gun drawn. "Drop the gun!" the officer yelled and aimed.

The bearded man stopped and let the gun fall. It made a sound as if it was made of plastic. "It's fake, just like you, Karp," the man said just before Ewin tackled him to the ground.

Karp watched as other officers rushed up and helped Ewin subdue the faux assassin. When the man was hauled off, he walked over to Ewin and held out his hand. "Good work, kiddo. You can keep the job, permanent," he said.

"No worries," Ewin replied, his face turning red. "It was a toy gun."

"You didn't know that when you stepped in front of me," Karp pointed out.

"As my dear old mum used to say, 'All's well that ends well.' I was just doing my job," the officer replied. "Now, I believe you have a trial to attend, unless you want me to call you in sick?"

Karp shook his head and laughed. "I guess if you can shrug off thinking you were about to take a bullet for me, I can find my way back up to the courtroom and do my job." He started to head for the door when Ewin spoke behind him.

"Hey, Mr. Karp, I appreciate what you do, too," Ewin said. "Somebody's got to hold the line for the community, and I'm glad it's you."

Something about the officer's comment seemed to return Karp's sense of calm. *Everybody in a healthy, functioning society has to do their job, and mine is to search for the truth and root out those who endanger the community,* he thought. *Time to refocus on this case.*

It wasn't that he would immediately forget about what just happened. But he had always been a first-class compartmentalizer, and the case, the courtroom, and the chase for justice beckoned him.

When Kenny Katz came rushing into the courtroom and found Karp calmly sitting at the prosecution table, going over his notes on his yellow legal pad, he exclaimed, "I just heard! Are you okay?"

Karp looked up. "Sure. Why wouldn't I be?"

Katz was a highly decorated former Army sergeant, but his jaw dropped. "I've been in combat," he said, "and know what it's like to have a gun pointed at you. I'd still be shaking if that had happened to me outside."

"Maybe it will catch up to me later," Karp conceded. "But I don't have time for it right now. Is there anything you want to ask me about what we're doing here before the judge returns?"

Apparently the entire courthouse had heard about the incident with the bearded man because when Judge Rainsford returned to the courtroom he, too, was concerned. "Would you like to recess for the day?" he asked. "We can pick this up again tomorrow if you'd like some time to decompress."

"Yes, boychick," Mendelbaum chimed in. "Take your time. That had to be traumatic, ach, such a world we live in, my friend."

At that moment, Karp happened to glance over Mendelbaum's shoulder and saw Olivia Stone looking at him. She alone seemed to be enjoying the news and sat with a smirk on her face. Their eyes met, and upon seeing her expression, his resolve hardened. "No, I'm good," he said, still looking at her, only now he was the one who smiled. "I don't want to slow this freight train down."

The smirk on Stone's face vanished, as did the anger and hatred that had been there throughout the trial. Instead, fear jumped into her eyes as the blood drained from her face. She turned away and pretended to be taking notes on a legal pad.

With that, the judge directed his chief clerk Farley to bring the jury in. Once they were seated, he told Karp to call his next witness.

"The People call Francis LaFontaine," Karp said. He and the rest of the people in the courtroom turned to look at the back of the room, where the two swinging doors were opened by a court security officer. A pasty-faced man in a wheelchair appeared. He was either in great pain, or so disgusted by what he saw that his face contorted into a grimace as another officer pushed him into the courtroom and to the front of the witness box.

"Raise your right hand and swear after me," Farley said.

Instead of raising his hand in the normal fashion, LaFontaine gave a Nazi salute. Seeing it, Karp's blood boiled. Earlier that morning, he'd met with the bar owner, who was none too happy about testifying. "I don't recognize the authority of the United Jews of America," he had said.

"Be that as it may," Karp had said, "I will remind you that you pleaded guilty to possessing a handgun and a sawed-off shotgun in New York City. If you testify truthfully, and don't give everyone a load of your Nazi crap, I'll tell the sentencing judge that you cooperated and that you told the truth. But if you want to play games, or you lie, and

I'll know it, I will do my best to make sure you get maximum time in state prison."

That put LaFontaine in his place at the time. Now he was acting up and Karp was angry. But Farley just gave LaFontaine a baleful look. "Do you promise to tell the truth, sir?"

For a moment, LaFontaine looked like he was going to spout off, but he half-glanced over his shoulder at Karp and seemed to think better of it. "Yeah, I'll tell the truth."

"He's all yours, Mr. Karp," Farley said, rolling his eyes.

"Thank you," Karp said as he positioned himself in front of the jury, facing LaFontaine. "Mr. LaFontaine, do you belong to the American Nazi Party?"

"Proud, card-carrying member for more than thirty years," LaFontaine said.

"As part of that group, do you look down on other races?"

"I believe in the separation of races and the inherent superiority of the white race."

"Does that include a dislike for those of the Jewish faith?" Karp asked.

"Why sure. Anybody with half a mind knows that Jews are behind most of the problems in the world," LaFontaine said. "Grasping, evil, half-human Jews are trying to establish a One World Order and

326

subjugate everyone else, especially the white race, which they despise."

"You are aware I am proud to be a Jew and that people like you I find to be repulsive."

"Oh, I know that."

"And therefore, you don't like me?"

LaFontaine's mouth twisted into a sardonic smile. "You're just another dirty Jew as far as I'm concerned."

"Mr. LaFontaine, would you explain to the jury the reason you're in a wheelchair?"

"Yeah, a son of a bitch named Lars Forsling shot me," LaFontaine said. "One bullet severed my spine so my legs don't work, and another tore up my guts so I have to wear a colostomy bag."

"We'll come back to that event in a minute. In the meantime, as a result of the police investigation into the shooting, were you also charged with crimes?"

"Yeah, some real penny-ante shit," LaFontaine replied. "Like some weapons charges?"

"You pleaded guilty to possession of a handgun and a sawed-off shotgun and agreed to testify today, didn't you?"

"That's right."

"Were you offered any sort of 'deal' for your testimony?"

"Hell no, 'cause I'm white," LaFontaine

said. "You'd have never even arrested a nigger for the same charges."

"Were you told anything about your testimony today by me?"

"Yeah, you said if I tell the truth, you'll tell the judge who sentences me."

"I believe you already told the jurors that you knew Lars Forsling?"

"Unfortunately, yes."

"How did you meet him?"

"He started showing up at some of our meetings."

"By 'our meetings,' you're talking about meetings of Nazi party members?"

"Our little local group, yes."

"And where did you have these meetings?"

"In my bar, The Storm Trooper, over in Hell's Kitchen."

"Approximately how long had you known Mr. Forsling before the events that put you in a wheelchair?"

LaFontaine thought for a moment, then shrugged. "Six months, maybe a little more."

"Could you describe for the jurors his personality and demeanor when you first met him?"

"What do you mean?"

"Well, was he loud or quiet, shy or

friendly?"

"At first he was kind of shy. But he warmed up pretty quick, especially when he started talking about how he hated niggers and Jews. That went over well with the rest of the boys."

"Did he tell you much about his private life?"

"Not really. I know he lived with his mother somewhere over on the Upper East Side and got a job shortly before all this shit happened as a night watchman at some construction site within walking distance of where he lived."

"Did his personality and demeanor change over time?"

"Yeah," said LaFontaine who shifted uncomfortably in his chair. "A lot of our members ain't the brightest bulbs in the pack, if you understand my meaning. They're kind of natural-born followers."

"But Forsling was different?"

"Well, he was smart, I'll give him that," LaFontaine said. "He started reading everything about the National Socialist Movement he could get his hands on, and could spout it all back out. That impressed a lot of the members, though I always thought there was something not quite right about him."

"Did he start to take on more of a leadership role?"

"Yeah, the guys started looking up to him, especially after he came up with the idea of joining other groups in the city for the American Kristallnacht," LaFontaine said. "Actually it was supposed to go on all over the country, but that sort of fizzled out. We had one of the better turnouts here in Manhattan."

"Can you explain to the jurors what Kristallnacht means?"

"Sure, the original Kristallnacht, or the Night of Broken Glass was a great uprising in 1938 in Germany and Austria. Good, hard-working Aryans who were tired of Jews ruining the economy and causing them hardships took to the streets and busted up a bunch of Jewish businesses. Some Jews tried to attack them, and a few people got themselves killed as a result. But mostly it was people saying, *Get out. You're not welcome in a Christian country or among decent human beings.*"

"And it was Mr. Forsling's idea to participate in this reenactment?"

"That's correct."

"Did that further his status among the members of your group?"

"Yeah, I'd say so. He was the big man on

campus after that."

"Did Mr. Forsling talk much about his future plans?"

"He was always talking about how he was going to move to Idaho," LaFontaine said. "He wanted to join up with some of the Aryan communities there. He said it was the place to be during the coming race war."

"Would you say that Mr. Forsling enjoyed his growing role among the members of your group?"

"Yeah, he was running around with his chest out, all puffed up," LaFontaine said. "You'd have thought he was the second coming of the Führer himself."

"Was it his idea to protest at Rose Lubinsky's book-signing event?"

"Yeah, he saw something about it in the newspaper."

"Let me backtrack a little here," Karp said. "What is your opinion of the Holocaust?"

"What Holocaust? Never happened," LaFontaine sneered. "It's just another lie perpetrated by the Jews so that everybody will feel sorry for them. They used it to steal Palestine — not that those sand-monkeys are any better; they stole it from its rightful owners, Aryan Christians."

"So you're saying that reports of Nazis

killing six million Jews and other minorities and political opponents, such as Gypsies, socialists, gays, and Slavic people, never happened?"

"Lies, all lies," LaFontaine scoffed. "If so many was killed, how come there's so many left now?"

"So what happened to all those people?"

LaFontaine shook his head as if debating with a not-so-bright kid. "I'm not denying that some people died. There was a war going on, you know," he said. "But mostly they ran off. And you might ask the Russians what happened to the rest."

"Would you say those views were commonly held by other members of your group, including Mr. Forsling?"

LaFontaine shrugged. "Sure, the truth is the truth, if you're not too blinded by Jewish propaganda to see."

"So, Mr. Forsling organized a protest because of Mrs. Lubinsky's book about her experiences during World War II?"

"You mean her work of fiction? Yeah, he organized the protest. He thought there was going to be a lot of media there, and even made a few anonymous calls to the television stations to let them know they should send camera crews."

"Did he talk about inciting any violence

at this protest?"

LaFontaine shifted in his seat again and grimaced in pain. "No. He wasn't much of a fighter. Now Jimmy Gerlach, God rest his soul, he'd have fought the devil if the devil was a Jew or a nigger. But Forsling was more about the publicity."

"He ever talk about doing physical harm to Rose Lubinsky or anyone else?"

"Nah, like I said, he wasn't into the rough stuff."

"Was there any mention of using a bomb?"

LaFontaine laughed. "I don't think he would have had the balls or the know-how to make a bomb."

Karp left his position on the jury box rail and slowly walked over toward LaFontaine. "At some point, did Mr. Forsling's attitude toward violence change?"

The smile disappeared from LaFontaine's face. He looked angry as he nodded. "Yeah. The afternoon after he was arrested, he came into my bar, all hot and bothered."

"Who else was present?"

"Just me, Bob Mencke, and Jimmy Gerlach, who worked for me as a bouncer."

"Did he say why he was all 'hot and bothered'?"

"Yeah, his mother had been killed in a fire."

"Did he also say who he felt was to blame?"

"He thought you did it, or had it done, you and that nigger cop sitting behind you."

Karp turned and pointed to Clay Fulton, who sat impassively. "This man?"

"Yes, the big nigger."

Karp looked at the judge. "Let the record reflect that the witness is referring to Detective Clay Fulton." He turned back to La-Fontaine. "Did he say why he believed we were responsible for his mother's death?"

"Yeah. He said you were blaming him for the car bombing."

"He was referencing the car bombing at Il Buon Pane that claimed the lives of Rose Lubinsky and two young women?"

"Yeah, that's the one," LaFontaine said dryly.

"Did you think he was responsible for the bombing?"

"At first," LaFontaine said. "I mean, when I heard about it I was like, 'Shit, the fucker growed some real nuts.' So when he first came in, I said something like, 'Well, here's the hero . . . good job.' Something like that."

"Did he admit that he was responsible for the bombing?"

LaFontaine shook his head. "No, as a matter of fact, he said he didn't do it."

334

Karp turned back toward the jurors, who were listening raptly. "Now, given your testimony about Forsling enjoying his growing leadership role and thinking he was 'the big man on campus' and the 'second coming' of Hitler, do you think he would have denied it if he'd had a role in the bombing?"

LaFontaine thought about the question. "Well, if he was smart, he'd have kept his mouth closed. If you want to get away with murder, only two people should know about it; one is the killer and the other should be six feet under. But Forsling liked to talk, and there was only the three of us in the bar, and we was all friends. Or at least we were. I think he would have at least hinted that he was responsible, and he would have probably wanted Gerlach for backup."

"But he denied it?"

"Yeah, in fact, he was kind of angry that we thought he did it," LaFontaine said. "And he was angry that you thought he did it and that's why you burned his mom out when he was locked up."

"Did he ask you for something?"

"He wanted my old Luger pistol, which I kept around the place in case anyone came looking for trouble."

"Did you also have another weapon for

such an eventuality?"

"Yeah, a sweet little side-by-side twelve gauge."

"Did you give the gun to Forsling?"

"Yeah."

"He say what he was going to do with it?"

LaFontaine shook his head. "He said it was better if I didn't know so that Johnny Law couldn't say I helped him. He did say he was going to Idaho after he did whatever he had in mind."

"What happened after you gave him the Luger?"

"He asked for my van."

Karp walked over to the prosecution table and picked up a photograph that he handed to LaFontaine. "Do you recognize this vehicle?"

"Yeah, that's my van."

"How do you know it's your van?"

"I bought it off a guy who did some welding for me, his name was Woodbury," LaFontaine said. "You can still see Eric Woodbury and Sons Metalworks on the side."

Karp retrieved the photograph, which he held up. "Your honor, I'd like to enter this photograph as People's Exhibit 24 in evidence."

Rainsford looked at Mendelbaum. "Any objections?"

"No, your honor."

Karp returned the photograph to the prosecution table and accepted another handed to him by Katz.

"Did you loan the van to Mr. Forsling?"

LaFontaine shook his head. "No, I told him that the cops could trace the van back to me and I didn't want to get tangled up in whatever he intended to do. I also said I needed it to get to work."

"What happened next?"

LaFontaine shifted in his chair as his face grew red and angry. "The son of a bitch pointed my own gun at me and said he was going to steal it. That's when Jimmy Gerlach tried to take him, but that bastard shot ol' Jimmy in the head and that was the end of him. I tried to go for my shotgun but he shot me, too."

"What about Robert Mencke?"

"Yeah, he put a hot one in Bob's chest."

"What happened next?"

"He robbed my till, took my van, and left me lying in my own blood."

Karp walked over to LaFontaine. "Do you remember talking to Assistant District Attorney Ray Guma?"

"I talked to some guy by that name."

"Do you remember when you first saw Mr. Guma?"

"Hard to forget," LaFontaine said. "I was lying on the floor of my bar, trying not to die, when that guy walked in from the back. He checked on me and my friends, and I heard him call 911."

"Did he ask you any questions?"

"Yeah, he was trying to help me by putting pressure on the bullet wounds and asked if I knew who shot me and the others."

"What did you tell him?"

"I said, 'Lars Forsling did it.' "

"What happened next?"

"The ambulance arrived, and as they were putting me in, he kept asking questions. I think he thought I was a goner and wanted to make sure he got his answers."

"Such as?"

"He wanted to know if I had any idea where Forsling might have gone. I told him the son of a bitch lived with his mom and was a night watchman at some nearby construction site on the East Side. I didn't know much more than that."

Karp nodded. "Thank you, Mr. LaFontaine. No further questions."

Rainsford looked at the defense table. "Cross, Mr. Mendelbaum?"

"Yes, your honor," Mendelbaum said. He rose from his seat but remained standing behind the table. "I believe your testimony is that Lars Forsling had assumed a leadership role with your group?"

"That's right," LaFontaine said.

"And as such, organized your group's attacks on Jewish businesses in November to celebrate the anniversary of Kristallnacht?"

"Yep."

"And it was his idea to protest the book signing for Rose Lubinsky?"

"Yes, that was him, too."

"And I believe your testimony was that you think it's a good idea if you kill someone to not talk about it. Is that right?"

"Only dead men tell no tales," LaFontaine said.

"Mr. LaFontaine, much has been made by my colleague, Mr. Karp, about Mr. Forsling having no previous history for violent crime. But he certainly exhibited quite a capacity for it when he shot you and your friends, didn't he?"

"Yes, he did."

"So would you say that a man who is capable of gunning down three friends in cold blood might also be capable of planting a bomb to kill someone he didn't like?"

"Yeah, I suppose if you put it that way," LaFontaine agreed, "you might say he was a cold-blooded killer."

"No further questions."

"Mr. Karp, do you have anything for redirect?" Rainsford asked.

Karp, who had been checking his legal pad, rose to his feet. "Just a few, your honor," he said, then looked at LaFontaine. "I just want to be clear. When Lars Forsling showed up at your bar after his release from jail, you thought that he was responsible for the car bombing the night before?"

"Yes, I did."

"And his response was, 'I didn't do it.' Is that correct?"

"That's right."

"And the reason he said he was agitated was that he blamed Detective Fulton and me for the death of his mother?"

"Yes, that's what he said."

"And that we unjustly suspected him of the car bombing?"

"That's about the size of it."

"And he wanted the gun and the van to exact some sort of revenge?"

"Objection," Mendelbaum said. "I don't believe that there's been any testimony regarding what Mr. Forsling intended to do with the gun or the van."

"Your honor, Mr. Mendelbaum is being disingenuous. He knows and very soon the jury will know exactly what the late Lars

Forsling did and said immediately after he left The Storm Trooper bar. For purposes of establishing an accurate evidentiary chain of events, I suggest the court permit the question to stand, hear the answer, and take it subject to connection."

"Very well, but you know the rules, Mr. Karp," Rainsford said. "I'll overrule the objection; you may answer."

LaFontaine smirked at Karp. "Yeah, yeah, he wanted to get even with you."

Karp turned from the witness. "Thank you, your honor, I have no further questions."

"Mr. Mendelbaum, do you have any further questions for Mr. LaFontaine?"

"No, your honor."

"Then the witness may leave the court," Rainsford said.

When he was gone, Rainsford addressed the jury. "Some of you may be wondering why I permitted this witness to utter those foul and upsetting, ugly racial epithets and vile religious references," he said. "I allowed it so that you could be able to decide the facts of this case understanding the sometimes harsh and oppressive realities of who some of these witnesses are. I believe you will be better able now to decide the credibility of this witness having heard his

341

testimonial utterances and observations without him being censored. Having said that, this will be a good time to take a break. We'll meet back here in fifteen minutes."

22

The next morning, Karp nodded to Fulton, who was standing by the door in the side of the courtroom leading to the witness waiting room. "Your honor," he said, "the People call Goldie Sobelman." The detective opened the door and poked his head inside to say something. He then stepped back, holding the door ajar.

Goldie Sobelman entered and for a moment stood transfixed and appeared to be frightened. Karp thought she looked a little like someone who had wandered into a Broadway theater from the street and found herself standing in a spotlight on a stage in front of a packed house. Her eyes searched the courtroom until they found whom she sought; she then relaxed and smiled.

Karp glanced back at the front row behind the prosecution table, even though he knew who she was looking for, her husband, Moishe. He was smiling at her and then nodded his head in encouragement. She raised her head, and began to walk confidently past him toward the middle aisle that would bring her to the well of the court.

She's going to do fine, Karp thought. He and Marlene had invited the Sobelmans over to their loft the night before, partly to talk to Goldie about her testimony the next day, but mostly for social reasons. They hadn't seen much of their old friends since the funeral for Rose Lubinsky nine months earlier. The rush of daily life, especially with two active teenage boys, an activist attorney wife, and the exigencies of being the chief law enforcement officer for New York County and its two-plus million souls, ate time like a starving dog eats a handout.

The funeral services had been held at the Third Avenue synagogue with standing room only, and thousands more mourners packing the lobby, the outside stairs leading into the building, and the sidewalks below. Those in attendance represented a wide variety of people from the Jewish community, the association of charter schools, many of Rose's former students and teaching colleagues, and a majority of the members of the temple's congregation.

At the services, Rabbi Michael Hamilburg praised Rose's book as "cathartic both to

Rose and to anyone who has dealt with the weight of their past — though in truth, I think Rose carried a far greater burden than she deserved — a testament to the power of forgiveness and love that will last on library shelves long after we have all passed." He also talked about how her work to champion charter schools had been interrupted, "but we, her friends and those who loved her, must see to it that it hasn't been destroyed. We must all pick up the mantle and carry her work forward."

The most moving eulogy was written by her husband, Simon, who asked Moishe to deliver it. As Goldie wept, huddled against Marlene, and Simon sat next to Karp, who kept his arm around the shaking shoulders of the old man, Moishe read:

"I was blessed to have met and married Rose Kuratowski. I thought that she was the most beautiful woman in the world the moment I first saw her, but I had no idea that the beauty on the outside paled in comparison to the beauty that resided within. My Rose was all about love; her love for books, her love of quiet walks along the beach or through Central Park; her love of people, especially her friends and children — when we lost our son she poured all of that motherly love into helping the children of other people. And I will always be grateful and humble that she loved me as well. I never felt that I deserved the love of such an angel, but I tried every day to earn it. I will miss having that challenge until the day we meet again. I love you my Rose, your Simon."

At the request of Simon, Giancarlo then sang "Va, pensiero." Listening, Karp thought his son's voice had gained power and depth and apparently others agreed as there was not a dry eye in the audience. But what had surprised and impressed him the most was when the rabbi asked anyone who wanted to say a word to come forward and Zak rose from his seat.

Taking the stage, Zak had at first experienced a case of stage fright and stood shifting from foot to foot, staring out at the congregation with a crumpled piece of paper in his hand. But then he'd looked down at his scribbled notes and cleared his throat.

"A couple of weeks ago I was having second thoughts about going through with my bar mitzvah. My brother and I were older than everybody else in our class, but it was more than that. I was struggling with what it meant to be Jewish. Like I told my dad, I didn't feel Jewish. I'd listen to what

Rabbi Hamilburg said about our upcoming bar mitzvah, but I just felt like a fraud. I'd hear a story about some heroic Jew in the past, but it didn't mean anything special to me."

Zak had looked then at his mother and father with a smile. "But I didn't want to disappoint my folks, so I kept at it even though I wasn't feeling it. No one was forcing me, and when I talked to Moishe about it he told me, 'If you don't feel Jewish in your heart and soul, then you should not go through with it.' But I felt bad. I'd heard about everything that happened to my fellow Jews in the Nazi death camps and felt like I should keep going because of that, but again it just seemed like something that happened a long time ago and didn't mean what I thought it should to me.

"But then I came here to listen to Mrs. Lubinsky talk about what had happened to her and how it affected her life. At first I thought it was going to be the same story about the Nazis and how she had suffered and then overcame it. But it wasn't like that, at least not all of it. The part that I identified with the most was how she struggled with the idea of being Jewish . . . that she didn't feel it in her heart. She didn't want to be a so-called 'dirty Jew,' as she said."

Zak paused and looked down at his feet. "I knew what she meant." He looked back up again. "My dad says I shouldn't say much about what happened to me and my brother and Goldie a few days ago so I'll just tell you what I learned from it. And that's this: being Jewish isn't supposed to be easy. We're not God's chosen people because God is going to give us an easier life and more stuff than other people. In fact, it's the opposite. Being God's chosen people means He chose us to be constantly tested and challenged, to be attacked and singled out . . . to see if we have the courage and faith to remain Jewish in spite of it all. And I think I understand it all now, that being Jewish is a test and how I do on the test will determine what sort of man I will become. Knowing that God is looking over us all, I will work tirelessly to be a moral man and like Mrs. Lubinsky reach out and help the vulnerable and defenseless. And I have Rose Lubinsky to thank for teaching me that."

Thinking about Zak's eulogy as he watched Goldie enter the well of the court and stand before Judge Rainsford to be sworn in, Karp allowed himself a moment of anger. Although death had been a constant companion for most of his career, her death had affected him as well. Seeing the impact her murder had had on so many people at her funeral left him incensed that such a good woman had died at the hands of those who worshipped at the altar of greed and power. That in order to accomplish their evil ends, Olivia Stone and Tommy Monroe employed an assassin to snuff out the life of Rose Lubinsky. In doing so, they had harmed not just Simon, or Rose's friends like Goldie and Moishe Sobelman. Their selfishness and amoral lust for power threatened the dream of a better education and better future for tens of thousands of children. He'd used that anger and disgust to help him focus on putting together the case to convict the defendant Stone.

After Monroe's arrest and subsequent interrogation in Karp's office with his attorney present, more vital information had come forward from an unexpected source. Having amassed sufficient evidence to convict the Brooklyn DA, Karp then sent Fulton to arrest her.

Flanked by two other detectives from the New York DAO unit, Fulton had marched into her office and announced to the receptionist that he was there to see Olivia Stone. When the flummoxed woman said he'd have to wait because Stone was in a meeting, he'd marched past her and into the Kings County district attorney's inner office and found her shredding documents.

"She told me to get the hell out of her office, or she'd call the police," Fulton reported to Karp. "I told her, 'I am the police and you're under arrest for murder in New York County.' She started yelling about getting even with you, but then started crying and begged me to leave."

Fulton did leave . . . with Stone in tow, as well as her computer. He'd left the two other detectives to start going through documents, including the box of papers she'd been in the process of shredding.

Stone had been brought to the conference room adjacent to Karp's office, where in the presence of Fulton he informed her that she'd been indicted for acting in concert with Thomas Monroe and Yusef Salaam to murder Rose Lubinsky, Mary Calebras, and Tawanna Mohammad. She'd stared at him like he was some sort of alien creature but didn't say a word.

Suddenly a crack appeared in Stone's façade. She began crying. "Please, you're making a big mistake. It was all Monroe's idea. Don't do this." Then she stopped, the tears dried up, and her face contorted into a mask of rage. "Everybody knows this is a political vendetta, Karp. I'll fry your ass and you'll be done in this town when I finish with you." Then she began sobbing and begging for mercy. He'd pointed to the telephone and said, "I think you should make that call," then he left the room, leaving her and Fulton.

A half hour later, a high-priced white-shoe lawyer from a Wall Street firm showed up and was directed where to find his client. Karp gave them a half hour, then knocked on the door.

The lawyer asked if there was a disposition to manslaughter doable as sort of "a gesture to a colleague in the prosecution business."

"Counselor, this is a 'no lesser plea case'; the only disposition will be to murder," Karp said.

The attorney, now incensed that his alleged civility was repudiated, held up a hand before Stone could respond. "We'll see you in court then, Karp. I hope you're ready for hell to break loose on this case."

"Is that a threat, counselor?" Karp asked mildly.

"No, it's a warning," the attorney sneered.

Later that day at Stone's arraignment, the attorney's attempt to have bail set for her was denied. She was remanded to Rikers Island pending trial and led away in tears. But the attorney then followed up on his threats by hitting the media circuit to depict Karp as a "loose-cannon conservative" and longtime advocate of a "racist" voucher system and "elitist" charter schools. "No one was more shocked by the death of Rose Lubinsky than my client," he frothed on the air and in the newspapers. "But for Karp to use this tragedy to go after a political opponent whose support for the public school system is one of the high marks of her career is below loathsome. And who's he protecting here? Who was the real killer? A Nazi, that's who . . . sort of makes you wonder about just how far to the right his politics are, doesn't it?"

Stone soon got rid of that lawyer and hired Irving Mendelbaum. It was the first smart thing she'd done since her arrest. *But it's not going to save her,* he thought as Goldie stepped up to the witness stand while James Farley poured her a cup of water.

Waiting for her to get settled, Karp thought about how the previous day ended with Ray Guma on the stand. His longtime colleague revealed how the day after Lubinsky's murder, he'd talked to a member of the NYPD Gang Unit, who suggested that he go to The Storm Trooper bar to locate Forsling's associates.

"Just as I was being dropped off, I heard what sounded like muffled gunshots from down the block," Guma testified. "But in New York it's hard to tell the difference between that and cars backfiring."

Guma said he'd proceeded to the bar. "A sign in the window said they were open, but the door was locked," he said. "I knocked but no one answered. So I decided to go around back to see if I could find someone that way. I'd just reached the alley when I was nearly hit by a white van; it didn't stop before taking off into traffic."

"Did you get a look at the driver?" Karp had asked.

Guma shook his head. "No, he kind of surprised me, and I had to jump back," he said. "I did note there was some writing on the side of the van, but I wasn't concentrating on the vehicle so I wasn't able to recall exactly what it was."

He'd found the back door of the pub open and walked in. "It was pretty dark inside, but after my eyes adjusted and I entered the front part of the bar, I saw a man lying on the floor in front of the bar — he'd been shot in the head — and another dead against the wall with a bullet wound in his chest. Then I heard a groan and found a victim who was still alive behind the bar. He said his name was Frank LaFontaine."

On cross-examination, Mendelbaum asked only a couple of questions, all of them to emphasize Forsling's violence.

Now it had come down to Goldie Sobelman to complete the first part of the People's case, which was to undermine the defendant's contention that Lars Forsling was Lubinsky's killer. After that the case against Olivia Stone would begin in earnest.

Before turning Goldie over to Karp, Judge Rainsford turned to the jury to explain the presence of the young woman who was seated next to the jury box. "This is Amber Doggett," he said, "and she is a board certified American Sign Language interpreter. The witness, Goldie Sobelman, can hear and comprehend, but she has difficulty speaking and communicates through sign language."

Listening to the explanation, Karp thought the judge handled it well. There'd been a bit of a dust-up over Goldie's use of sign language that required a pretrial hearing because the defense had objected on the grounds that she was capable of speech but chose not to talk.

Although not generally one to rely on

354

"experts," Karp had called in a psychologist who specialized in Post-Traumatic Stress Disorder. He testified at the hearing that "loss of speech" was not unusual for victims of sexual and physical violence.

"After hearing the details of this particular woman's treatment at the hands of the Nazis in the internment camps, it's a wonder she functions as well as she does," the psychologist said. "Declining to speak is one way of coping. She told me that she stopped speaking in the camp because she was afraid that if she tried, it would come out as a scream and she wouldn't be able to stop. She has since regained a limited ability to express herself through speech, but it's my recommendation that she be allowed to testify in the manner with which she is most comfortable."

The judge had ruled in favor of the People. After the hearing and away from his client, Mendelbaum pigeonholed Karp. "I hope you know, boychick, that this motion was not my idea," he said. "Perhaps, ethically, I should not say this, but sometimes this job wears on my soul."

"Irving, do yourself a mitzvah, and keep your soul intact," Karp said.

"Good afternoon, Mrs. Sobelman," Karp began.

Goldie's hands went into motion. "Good afternoon, Mr. Karp," the interpreter said for the jurors.

"I'd like to start by asking a few preliminary questions," Karp said. "Mrs. Sobelman, do we know each other on a personal basis? Are we friends?"

Goldie smiled and moved her hands. "Yes, dear friends for many years," the interpreter said.

"In preparing for this trial, what have I asked you to do?"

"Just tell the truth, the whole truth," the interpreter said. "You know I would never lie. Nor would you ask me to."

"Thank you. Our families are friends as well; you know my wife and children, I know your husband, Moishe."

"Yes." Goldie chuckled on the stand and signed with her hands. "You have a weakness for the cherry cheese coffeecake at our bakery."

The audience in the courtroom tittered at the humor, including the judge, the jurors, and Mendelbaum, though Stone sat impassively. "That I do," Karp said, "the best in the five boroughs. Now, let us move on. You knew Rose Lubinsky?"

The smile left Goldie's face and she nodded her head sadly. "Yes, she was my oldest and dearest friend," the interpreter said.

"When did you meet her?"

Goldie looked up as though adding the years. "I believe it must have been 1950 or '51," the interpreter said.

"And you and your husband were friends with her and her husband, Simon, who is sitting in the front row behind the prosecution table with your husband, Moishe, is that correct?" Karp asked, motioning over in their direction.

"Yes."

"The jurors have heard some testimony about Rose's experiences during World War II and that she wrote a book about it," Karp said. "But did Rose have something else that was just as, if not more, important to her? A cause?"

"Yes," the interpreter said. "She was very involved in the charter school movement."

"Did she ever say why she was so involved?"

"Yes," Goldie signed. "Although she taught in the public school system most of her career, she believed that, for a variety of reasons, the public school system was failing the children and that charter schools were the way to fix that."

"Did she ever express an opinion toward the teachers union?"

"Most of her career she belonged to the Greater New York Teachers Federation. She believed that the union had been necessary to achieve decent wages, pensions, health care, and better working conditions. However, she also felt that in the past twenty years or so, the union had lost its way, especially the union's leadership, which she felt was more interested in maintaining its power and perks than what was best for the children."

"Did she ever give you her opinion about union president Thomas Monroe?"

"For a variety of reasons, she believed that he was corrupt."

"Your honor," Mendelbaum interrupted, "I haven't objected to Mrs. Sobelman's testimony comprising hearsay statements because it hasn't concerned my client, but enough is enough."

"Mr. Karp," Rainsford directed, "please make your point and move on."

"I'll move on," Karp said. "Early in the evening on the night of the book signing at your bakery, Il Buon Pane, were you aware that neo-Nazis were gathering across the street?"

"Yes, my husband pointed them out," the interpreter said for Goldie. "He was concerned about the safety of our guests and wondered if we should cancel the event. But I told him, as he once told me, that if we let them dictate how we lived our lives, then they have won and we might as well throw in the towel."

Karp led Goldie quickly through the bombing and the scene at the hospital. When they reached the death of Rose Lubinsky, he waited a few minutes as she cried quietly until she could pull herself together.

"I'm sorry to put you through this," he said.

Goldie smiled. "I'm sorry it happened. But life goes on. Please ask me your next question."

"Would you tell us about the events of the next day concerning your encounter with Lars Forsling?" Karp said.

Goldie nodded and signed, "My husband had gone upstairs for his afternoon nap. Your sons, Zak and Giancarlo, were helping me clean up around the store when that young man accosted us with the gun. He said we had to leave with him."

"Were you able to leave some sort of signal for your husband that something wasn't right?"

Goldie nodded and held up her left hand before signing to the interpreter. "Yes, when the young man wasn't looking, I took off my wedding band and left it on the counter for Moishe to find."

"Why did you do that?"

"I had two reasons. If something happened to me, I wanted him to have it. But I was also letting him know that I was in trouble; he knows I have not taken it off since the day he put it on my finger."

"What happened after you left the bakery with Mr. Forsling?"

"He demanded that we drive to East Harlem."

"Did he say what this was about?"

"Yes, he was very angry. He said that his mother had died in a fire because he wasn't home to help her. He said he'd been kept in jail for something that wasn't his fault."

"Did he say anyone else was responsible for his mother's death?"

"Yes, he blamed you. He said that you were using him as a scapegoat for the bomb that killed my friend and those two other poor girls."

"Did you ask him if he killed your friend?"

Goldie nodded. "Yes. He said that you thought he did it because he was a Nazi and doesn't like Jews. So I asked him, 'Did you kill my friend?' "

"And what was his answer?"

"He said he was just there to protest. But

he said you wouldn't listen and put him in jail."

"Did he say what he planned to do with you and the boys?"

"Not exactly. I thought he might be taking us as hostages so that he could force the media to listen to him. But I was also worried — not for myself, I'm an old woman, but the boys — that he wanted revenge and might harm us."

"As best you can recall, where did he take you?"

"He took us to a building in East Harlem. It was under construction but he had the keys to the gate and to a side door."

"What happened there?"

"He made us walk up the stairs, but I only got part way before I fainted. Then one of the boys carried me. Afterward I learned that it was Zak, your son."

"Did he say anything more about the bombing during the time he held you hostage on the top floor of this building?"

"Only that you blamed him for it and that was why his mother was dead."

Leading her through the events that followed up until Forsling was shot by Marlene, Karp reached the point of Forsling's "dying declaration" that he was responsible for the bombing.

"Did you believe he was telling the truth?"

"Objection," Mendelbaum said, rising to his feet. "With all due respect, the witness is not a mind reader and shouldn't be allowed to offer an opinion on whether the defendant was telling the truth or not."

"Your honor," Karp responded, "this goes back to an earlier argument on this matter. The defense intends to use Forsling's 'dying dec' in an attempt to say that is the truth, despite all of the evidence to the contrary. Mrs. Sobelman was present at this man's death; she'd talked to him previously about this and heard statements from him that were contradictory to this one. I believe she is entitled to give her opinion as to its trustworthiness."

"Overruled, the witness may answer the question but let's keep it to the issue of trustworthiness."

Karp nodded to Goldie, who signed, "I don't think he was telling the truth. I think he was angry at you and wanted to get even. Maybe he wanted the notoriety as well . . ."

"Objection, your honor," Mendelbaum called out again. "Now she's speculating on the reasons she believes his statement was false. Again, she's playing mind reader."

"Sustained. I think this is enough of that, Mr. Karp."

"Thank you, your honor," Karp responded. "No further questions."

Mendelbaum traded places in front of the jury with Karp. "I'm sorry for the loss of your friend," he said. "And I apologize if any of this is hard on you."

"Thank you, Mr. Mendelbaum. And I understand you have a job to do, too."

"I appreciate that," Mendelbaum replied. "Now, Mrs. Sobelman, you've testified that Mr. Forsling was angry at Mr. Karp for accusing him of planting the bomb. But did he ever actually deny planting or detonating the bomb?"

"No, not in so many words. But he said he was just there to protest."

"So prior to being shot, he never said anything like, 'I did not plant the bomb.' Did he?"

"No, he did not say those words."

"But as he lay dying on the floor of the loft, he said, 'It was my bomb that blew up the car. I killed the Jew bitch.'"

"Yes, he said that."

"Thank you, Mrs. Sobelman," Mendelbaum said. "Your honor, no more questions for this witness."

23

Waiting patiently as the small, mousy black woman on the stand dabbed at the tears in her eyes, Karp reminded himself about what his one-time mentor Mel Glass told him when he first arrived at the New York DAO fresh out of law school at the University of California–Berkeley. *In a nutshell, to reconcile the difficult issues you'll have to resolve, and some will be tougher than others, our job is to search for truth and do justice. Wherever the facts and legally admissible evidence leads — whether to the guilt of the accused or to his exoneration — apply your sense of moral clarity to each and every case.*

Watching Goldie Sobelman cry on the stand when he asked her about the death of her friend was one of those "tougher aspects." And now yet another woman had been reduced to tears by the questions he needed to ask in that search for the truth.

Only this time the tears were tears of shame, remorse, and of a mother whose little boy had grown up to be a homicidal monster.

The witness, Alethea Burns, had first appeared in the reception room of the New York District Attorney's Office the day after Monroe's arrest. Karp had just opened the door of his inner office to give some papers to his receptionist when he caught the conversation she was having with Mrs. Milquetost. Or debate was closer to it as neither woman noticed him walk into the room and neither was giving in.

"Mr. Karp is a very busy man," Milquetost was saying in her best I'm-in-charge-here voice. "You can leave that and I'll give you a piece of paper to write a message on. I'll see to it that he gets it, but you can't just barge in on him."

The "that" Mrs. Milquetost was referring to appeared to be a laptop computer clutched in the hands of a light-skinned black woman in a tattered green wool coat and purple yarn cap. "No, I have to give it to him myself," the woman insisted. "I have to tell him something first. Let him know, please, that it has to do with my son, Yusef, and what happened last night in Brooklyn. Please, it's important."

At the mention of "Yusef" and "Brooklyn," Karp's radar had snapped into high alert. Under questioning, union president Monroe denied knowing the bomber's full identity. "Stone knew him back in the day from her work as a Legal Aid lawyer. He was some kind of firebug. I think she was shagging him, too. But I only know a first name, Yusef."

"May I help you?" Karp said to the woman with the computer.

"Oh," Milquetost said, disappointed and sensing a shift in who was actually in charge. "Mr. Karp, I told this woman you were busy and that she could leave that laptop with me, and that you'd get back to her if necessary. But . . ."

"That's okay, Darla," Karp said, walking forward and extending his hand to the other woman. "Hi, I'm District Attorney Roger Karp and you're . . . ?"

"Alethea Burns. I think my son might be the man the police are trying to identify . . . the man who was killed last night," she said sorrowfully.

Karp gestured toward the meeting room. "Let's go in here to talk."

Forty-five minutes later, Karp poked his head out. "Darla, would you call V. T. Newbury and ask if he can join me, please," he said then disappeared back inside. They spoke another hour after Newbury arrived before the door opened again and the three emerged.

Karp was holding the laptop in one hand and shaking the woman's hand with the other. "I know this is terribly difficult for you," he said. "But you've done the right thing here, and I can't thank you enough. We'll be in contact, and if anything changes as far as how to reach you, please keep my office updated. I gave you my card, and that's my direct number. If I can help you in any way, please call me."

As she was now on the witness stand, the woman had been crying, but she tried to smile and nodded at what he said. "I will, Mr. Karp. And thank you for hearing me out without judging. What he was doing was bad, but I'm still a mother wondering where she went wrong. So thank you. I'll stay in touch."

When she left the office, Karp turned to Newbury. His longtime friend and colleague was a New England blue blood, Harvard grad, and the DAO's resident geek assistant district attorney. In addition to being a walking talking law library who oversaw the DAO cases on appeal, he also did the tough, complicated white collar cases, and the more technology, gadgets, and computer lingo involved, the happier he was. In fact, he'd assembled a team that specialized in computer forensic and was salivating to get his hands on Mrs. Burns's son's laptop. "If this has what I hope it has on it, it's the key to nailing this case down," Karp said.

"We already saw some pretty damning material," Newbury said. "I agree that a deeper look could yield big returns; it's rare that the tip of the iceberg is all there is."

"Make it *the* priority," Karp said, handing over the laptop.

"Will do."

After talking to Monroe, Karp had believed that he had a strong case. With the computer, he referred to it as a "motion picture case," so overwhelming that a jury couldn't help but see the evidentiary impact of the prosecution's presentation. However, getting to it wasn't easy. Stone had not only been in the process of shredding incriminating documents when Fulton walked in on her, she'd deleted files and attempted to erase the history on her computer.

Newbury would soon be called to the stand to report the incriminating evidentiary findings from his team's examination of Stone's computer and the laptop delivered by Alethea Burns. Presently, Karp wanted her to establish the foundational basis for the investigation conducted by Newbury and his "geek" magicians.

So far with Burns on the stand, he'd established that Yusef Salaam had been born Henry Burns and only changed his name after he dropped out of high school. That alone was an invaluable piece of information he might never have found if the bomber's mother hadn't come to his office carrying his computer. The bomb squad had located enough of the bomber's hand to use for fingerprint identification, but there'd been no matches. As it turned out, "someone," and Karp had a good guess who, had purged the fingerprints of one Henry Burns from the system since he had been arrested as a juvenile for an arson case and represented by a young Legal Aid attorney named Olivia Stone, née Bekins.

Burns said her son had been a "good little boy, never any problem after my husband walked out on us. He was sweet and kind and took care of his momma." But then something had started to go wrong with his skin, like the color was draining out of him. When she finally got him into the free clinic, the doctors told her he had vitiligo. But they didn't seem to know much more than that, only that it might halt its progress or it could continue to spread. It had done the latter, and in such a way that half of his face looked white and the other half black.

Henry was only eleven years old when the disease appeared, and it was soon impossible to hide or cover up. The result was relentless teasing and bullying at school until he had no friends and became a recluse. He found solace in two things: an old computer his mom saved up to buy him, as well as access to the internet; that, and setting things on fire.

As she described the teasing her son suffered, Karp handed her two photographs. "Do you recognize the person depicted in these photographs, People's Exhibit 29a and 29b for identification?" he asked.

"Yes, the first one, that's my boy when he was only twelve," Burns said. "You can see the vitiligo on the side of his face and neck. The second one is Yusef, about a year ago." She handed them quickly back to Karp like bad memories.

"Your honor, I move that People's 29a and 29b be received into evidence," Karp said.

"No objections," Mendelbaum added.

"So moved."

It wasn't until the court steno marked the exhibits that Karp turned and noticed she was crying quietly. He walked up to the stand and offered her a box of tissues left there for that very purpose. He then lifted the water pitcher and filled her cup.

"Thank you, I'm sorry," she sniffled.

"It's okay," Karp said. "Take your time."

"I'm ready now."

"Okay, let me know if you need a break. . . . Prior to the events in this case, was your son involved in any criminal activity?"

"Yes. He started acting out. He liked burning things and would catch rats in cages and light them on fire. Then he lit a little girl's hair on fire. I tried to get him some help, but nothing seemed to get through to him. Then one night he threw a gasoline bomb into a building, injuring an elderly couple."

"Was he charged with a crime as a juvenile for that?" Karp asked.

"Yes, he was."

"And was he represented by a lawyer?"

"Objection," Mendelbaum said. "What's the relevance of this line of questioning?"

Karp sighed and shook his head. Mendelbaum knew he would lose this objection but had raised it for two ulterior motives. One was to make a point that he'd reiterate in his summation: that just because Stone had represented Henry Burns for the arson case did not mean they'd conspired to plant a bomb under Rose Lubinsky's car. *More matzo balls on the wall.* The second had been to interrupt the dramatic buildup Karp was working on.

"Your honor," Karp said, "may we approach the bench on the record?"

"Of course," Rainsford said and turned his microphone off so that the jury could not hear. When the attorneys were present, he turned to Karp. "Okay, you first."

At sidebar conferences, Karp always positioned himself facing the jury while he spoke softly for the record. He wanted to see how the jurors were reacting even if they couldn't hear. "In every relationship there is a beginning, middle, and end. The evidence will show chronologically its initial benign origins up to and including the defendant's complicity with Salaam in the fatal bombings."

Mendelbaum shrugged. "Look, it's not a secret that District Attorney Stone began her legal career as a Legal Aid attorney. I did so myself. She represented many different people. So what if one of them was this character, Yusef Salaam, what does that prove? Guilt by prior association?"

"Six months ago, she was shown a photograph and said she didn't know him," Karp countered.

"She was under duress," Mendelbaum argued. "She'd just been arrested and hauled out of her office by Detective Fulton, an imposing figure to say the least. Yusef Salaam had changed a lot physically, too — the disfigurement on his face — and he was using a different name when she represented him."

"I didn't tell her his name," Karp said.

"Okay, gentlemen, I've heard enough, I'm ready to rule," Rainsford said.

"Mr. Mendelbaum, your objection is overruled. Mr. Karp, you may proceed."

Karp turned back to the witness stand. He was going to have to regain the momentum he'd been building toward. "Mrs. Burns, you had just finished saying that after your son was charged with arson, he was represented by an attorney from the Legal Aid office."

"Yes, he was."

"And is that lawyer in this courtroom today?"

Burns's eyes darted over to the defense. "Yes, she is."

"Would you point to her?"

As she raised her arm and finger, she glared right at Stone. "That's her, right there."

"Let the record reflect that the witness

identified the defendant as the attorney who represented her son Henry Burns, also known as Yusef Salaam. Mrs. Burns, do you know approximately how long the defendant represented him?"

Burns thought about it before venturing an answer. "I'm not sure, but it went on for quite some time — months — and there were several court hearings during that time."

"Mrs. Burns, what brought you to my office approximately nine months ago?"

The woman bit her lip. "My son was killed the night before and I found something I thought you should have," she said.

"Where was your son killed?"

"In Brooklyn."

"How did he die?"

"He was killed by a bomb."

"Was this a bomb planted by someone else?"

"No. He . . . he was killed by a bomb he was carrying."

"How did you learn he'd been killed?"

"I saw it on the news," Burns said sadly. "I just got home from my job — I clean offices at night — and there *it* was on the screen clear as day."

"Please tell us exactly what was on the screen?"

"His shoe. The television showed his shoe in the middle of the street. They said that the police did not know the bomber's identity. I hoped it wasn't him, but I knew it was because of that damn shoe."

"What, if anything, was significant about that shoe?"

"It was one of his bright red sneakers . . . the canvas high-top kind they call Chuck Taylors."

"He had a pair of those shoes?"

"He had a whole collection of them and would wear them rain or shine."

"Or snow, Mrs. Burns?" Karp asked looking at the jury.

"That's right, even in snow."

"Did you contact the police right away?"

Burns shook her head. "No, like I said, I hoped it wasn't him."

"Did you find it was him?"

"Well, first I called 911 and asked if they had identified the person who'd been killed. But they said they hadn't. The operator asked me if I knew something but I said 'no' and hung up."

"Did you then try some other way?"

Burns stared down at her shoes and nodded. "Yes, I went into his room and looked at his computer."

"Were you in the habit of using your son's

computer?"

"No, never," she said. "That was his favorite thing in the world and he didn't want anybody else to touch it. I once accidentally bumped it when I was cleaning his room, and he pitched a fit. So I never went near it after that."

"But you did this time?"

"Yes," Burns said, "because I thought he was probably dead. I didn't want to believe that he was suspected of killing folks with bombs, but I had to be sure one way or the other." She began crying again. "You raise 'em up and they just children. They like Christmas and toys and puppies. They sweet to other people and love their mommas. But I have to accept that he changed." She sighed. "So I went into his room and looked at his computer."

"Did you need a password to get on it?"

"No, I guess he figured I wouldn't dare touch it after the fit."

"Mrs. Burns, do you have any experience with computers?"

"Some," she said. "I've been taking business courses at the community college to try to improve myself."

"And I take it that means you've learned to use the school's computers."

"Yes," she said, then smiled for the first

time. "Some of the younger girls even showed me how to Google stuff and get on Facebook. I like to look at animal photographs and videos."

"So you had some familiarity with computers when you looked at your son's computer?"

Burns glanced over at the defense table. "I saw some photographs."

Karp walked over to the prosecution table and picked up a set of 8 × 10 photographs. He looked through them, put one back down on the table, and then took the others over to the witness stand. "Mrs. Burns, I'm handing you five photographs, People's 30 A, B, C, D, and E for identification. Without describing the contents of these photographs, arc they some of the photographs you found on your son's computer?"

"Yes, these are some of them," Burns said. "And the reason I knew I should come talk to you. That and seeing the shoe on the television. But I decided to sleep on it. I laid awake all night hoping he would come home and it would be a big mistake . . ." She stopped talking and hung her head. "I don't even know if he loved me. He stopped saying so years ago though he was always polite as long as I didn't make him mad.

And he always came home . . . until this time."

"What happened after you got up that morning?"

"I watched the news and saw that teachers union president was arrested at the same place my boy died. They were saying that union guy was responsible for the women who died in that other car bombing in the city. I felt so sorrowful, like I brung a monster into the world. But I didn't know he would turn out that way. I didn't beat him or abuse him. I tried to love him best I could."

"It's okay, Mrs. Burns, nobody is blaming you. But I need to ask you a few more questions."

The woman looked up and nodded. "Sure, Mr. Karp, I can do this. So after I watched the morning news, I took a taxi to your office building."

"Did you bring something with you?"

"Yes, I brought Henry's computer."

"And did we talk about some of the same things we've been talking about today?"

"Yes."

"At some point were we joined by Assistant District Attorney Vincent Newbury?"

"Yes, he was a nice man. Well-spoken."

"Did you leave that computer with us to

be examined?"

"Yes, I did. I didn't want to see it anymore."

Karp leaned against the jury rail, knowing he had the jurors' full attention. "Mrs. Burns, did your son have a regular job?"

"Well, no, he was always looking for one but no one would hire him," she said. "But he did some work for some folks on his computer and got a little money that way."

"Did he ever go out of town?"

"Yes, from time to time he'd go visit a friend in Atlantic City. He'd take the bus and go up there for the day; I found some of his bus tickets in his pants pockets."

Karp walked back over to the prosecution table and picked up a clear bag containing what appeared to be a small slip of paper. "Can you identify the item in this bag?" he asked, handing it to her.

"Yes, it's one of those bus tickets I told you about. It says it was issued by the Port Authority in New York City and it's a round-trip ticket to Atlantic City."

"Mrs. Burns, I have two more questions at this time," Karp said. "Did your son ever talk about having a girlfriend or a lover?"

The murmuring began again in the gallery as Stone turned bright red and hunched over her legal pad, scribbling furiously. "Yes, he said he had a white girlfriend and that she was an important person. But he never told me her name. I didn't really believe him."

"Why not?"

"Because he lied a lot and I never saw anything that made me think it was true."

"Just one more question, Mrs. Burns," Karp said. "Were the police ever able to positively identify your son as the person killed by the bomb in Brooklyn?"

"Yes. They found one of his hands, and after you and I talked they were able to match the fingerprints to some things in his room."

"Thank you, Mrs. Burns. No further questions," Karp said, looking at Judge Rainsford.

Rainsford looked up at the clock. "It's time for our morning recess. We'll meet back here again in fifteen minutes."

The courtroom quickly cleared, including the defendant, who shot Karp a venomous look before being escorted out by the corrections officers. When they were gone, Mendelbaum walked over to where Karp was talking quietly against the gallery rail with ADA Katz and Clay Fulton.

"Could I have a private moment with you, my friend?" Mendelbaum asked.

Karp nodded to his two companions, who walked away. "Sure, Irving, what's up? I was just about to ask if you have any Snickers bars; I can use the energy boost."

"Ach, you're welcome to look, but you don't need it," Mendelbaum complained. "This is starting to remind me of the third fight between Muhammad Ali and Joe Frazier."

"The Thrilla in Manila," Karp said.

"Yeah, and I'm Joe Frazier taking shot after shot to the head," Mendelbaum said.

"He did take a lot of abuse but he was still standing after fourteen rounds."

"Yeah, but that's when the ref stopped the fight," Mendelbaum said. "And I don't think Rainsford is going to save me here. Anyway, what I wanted to talk to you about — and mind you I haven't broached this with my client yet, she thinks she can talk her way out of this one . . ."

"She going to take the stand?" Karp asked, raising his eyebrows.

Mendelbaum waggled a finger at Karp. "You'd love that, wouldn't you," he said. "If she does testify, it will be against my vehement objections. But these young lawyers think they can persuade anyone of anything. However, given the haymakers you've been throwing, I'd be remiss in my duties if I didn't explore the possibility of a plea deal. I'm thinking maybe Man 1, twelve years minimum. She'd be disbarred and ruined."

Karp listened politely but then shook his head. "I appreciate you doing what you can for your client, Irving," he said. "But I'm taking no lesser plea on this one. This wasn't some heat of the moment escalation dispute or shooting recklessly at a car in a road rage incident. This is someone in a position of trust, who abused that trust — murdered innocent people and was willing to murder more innocent people — for money and power. No, Irving, she's going the distance on this one; she's never going home again."

Mendelbaum regarded him coolly, then nodded. "Out for blood on this one, boy-chick. I'll let her know that's what we discussed." He left to go talk to Stone in the holding cell.

When court reconvened Karp looked at Mendelbaum, who shook his head no. The old man looked tired as he walked out to begin the cross-examination of Alethea Burns.

"Good morning," Mendelbaum began, "I know this has been hard on you, so I'll try to keep my questions few in number. I'll start by asking if you knew all of your son's friends."

Burns looked confused. "He didn't have many, he was a loner. But I don't remember him talking about any in a long time, except for his lady friend."

"So you don't know whether or not he knew Lars Forsling?"

"I never heard of him."

Mendelbaum walked over to the jury rail and put one hand on it as if to steady himself. "Mrs. Burns, I believe your testimony is that my client once, many years ago, represented your son in a juvenile case. Is that right?"

"Yes."

"And that they met a few times over the course of some months, including court hearings?"

"That's correct."

"And these photographs on your son's computer," Mendelbaum said, "there's no way of knowing for sure who took them or even if they were downloaded from another source?"

"I don't know enough about computers to answer that."

Mendelbaum pursed his lips. "There was nothing on the photographs that indicated who took them, correct?"

"Not that I saw."

Moving away from the rail, Mendelbaum

came to stand in the well of the court with his hands stuck in his pants pockets. "Mrs. Burns, you testified that you don't know what your son was doing or where he went when he wasn't home. Isn't it possible that he died because he was in the wrong place at the wrong time when a bomb intended for someone else went off?"

For a moment, Karp saw a glimmer of hope in the witness's eyes. A mother still wanting to believe that she hadn't given birth to a killer. But the hope faded as quickly as it appeared, she wasn't falling for it. "Mr. Karp told me that the detectives said my son was carrying the bomb when it went off."

"That's what you were told by the people who are trying to convict my client for murder," Mendelbaum pointed out.

"Yes, that's true." Burns was starting to look confused.

"But you don't know the circumstances, or what proof they have, that your son was carrying this bomb, do you?"

"Well, no, I haven't seen any proof."

"Did your son ever tell you who he was visiting in Atlantic City?"

"No, he said it was just a friend."

"Did he say it was his girlfriend?"

"No. He didn't."

"And did he ever identify this important white girlfriend of his?"

"No. He never told me her name."

"And as a matter of fact, until this trial, you thought he was making it all up, didn't you?"

"Yes, I thought he was lying. He lied a lot."

"Yes, he lied a lot, on that we agree. Thank you, Mrs. Burns, no further questions."

Rainsford looked over at Karp. "We're closing in on the lunch hour. Do you have any questions for redirect?"

"No, your honor, no redirect."

24

"Mr. Newbury, is it possible to determine the exact computer that is used to send an email?" Karp asked his question standing in the well of the courtroom with his arms crossed, looking up at his longtime friend and colleague, Assistant District Attorney Vincent Newbury.

Dressed immaculately, as always, in a dark blue Brooks Brothers suit, light blue button-down shirt, and a bright red silk tie with a diamond stickpin, Newbury was clearly enjoying his role as an expert witness for the People. The lines around his eyes and mouth had not eroded his boyish good looks, though the WASPy blond hair was thinning and there were hints of gray throughout. But his mind and wit were as razor sharp as they had been when he and Karp were both rookies finding their way around the New York DAO.

Although he was in the same generation

as Karp, Newbury gravitated toward the modern technology of the younger generation. The chief of the DAO's White Collar Crimes Bureau, he'd always been a meticulous prosecutor known for assembling the most intricate cases in such a way that a jury could easily see the big picture when he laid it out piece by piece. But he'd really found his niche when personal computers became a tool for prosecutorial investigations. As he'd explained to the jurors a few minutes earlier, he'd assembled quite a team — he called it the DAO Geek Squad — of forensic computer experts, accountants, and tech-savvy detectives. "Among our caseload are a lot of identity theft cases, and cases in which computers are used in the commission of crimes or to investigate and prosecute such crimes."

"Yes," Newbury answered. "Although there are some caveats and exceptions, the basic answer is that we can identify a specific computer as the sender or receiver of an email message, even if the message itself no longer exists."

"Without losing us in the internet jungle," Karp continued, "could you give the jurors a basic computer course?"

"I'll try," Newbury replied before turning

to look at the jurors like a professor preparing to lecture a class of freshman students. "I'm going to explain this as simply as I can, not because you're unintelligent — indeed, some of you may know more than I do — but just so we're all clear on the basics. You may have heard that computers using the internet have 'IP addresses,' or more specifically Internet Protocol addresses. An IP address is a number assigned to each device, such as a computer, printer, iPad or iPhone, that is part of a computer network. That number is the 'address,' sort of like 100 Centre Street is the address for this building. We good so far?"

Newbury looked from face to face, all of whom nodded. "Good. Now I won't bore you with all of the details — though it really is quite fascinating how the internet works — but essentially when someone sends or receives an email part of the information included in that email, though usually hidden from view, is the IP address where the message originated, and the IP address to which it was sent. Sometimes a message sent from one IP address may actually pass through other IP addresses before reaching the final destination, sort of an internet Pony Express, changing riders at each station along the way, but it can still be traced back to the originating device."

"And to reiterate, this IP address is specific to a device, such as a particular computer?" Karp asked.

"It can be, and most often is," Newbury said. "But say there is a large company office that has a number of computers all using the same network, they may have the same 'external' IP address, but they will also have an internal IP address for each computer that a message can also be traced back to."

As Newbury was talking, Karp glanced over at the defendant Olivia Stone. Her expression was one of mild boredom. He knew she was aware of it when he now turned to look directly at her instead of Newbury to ask his next question, though she kept her eyes on the jurors.

"Is it possible to use this to trace an IP address to a specific computer even if the emails have been erased, as well as the internet history, *and* the computer then 'wiped' to further expunge the record?"

Stone furrowed her brow, and her already pale complexion blanched further still. Her eyes fixated on Karp, she leaned over and said something to Mendelbaum, who shook his head.

"It's more difficult, but there are a few

tricks of the trade that make it possible, especially if the effort to remove the information was incomplete," Newbury replied. "We've all heard that nothing ever really disappears from the internet, and for the most part that's true. But the majority of casual computer users, even those who consider themselves to be security conscious and have all the latest removal apps, believe that by taking these steps, they can permanently remove information from their computers. However, if you know what you're doing and where to look, even some of these more sophisticated efforts to eliminate the information don't remove it all."

"So can you retrieve emails that have been deleted?"

"Usually not the email itself, though sometimes if we get to them right away before they've been permanently deleted and are cached somewhere," Newbury said. "But unless the user is really sophisticated and understands how it all works — and is worried about someone equally sophisticated — we can tell when and where an email was sent and where it was received."

Karp noticed that Stone's face had grown whiter still when he asked, "What is browsing history?"

"Browsing history on the web is a list of web pages the computer user has visited recently as well as such things as the page title and the date and time of the visit," Newbury said. "For instance, if someone searched the web for information on the New York County District Attorney's Office, they'd find a webpage — manhattanda.org — and that would be recorded by their web browser software as part of their browsing history. It makes it easier to locate the page again the next time, and is mostly for the benefit of repeat visitors."

"Can this web browsing history be removed from a computer?"

"Well, it can be deleted and then purged from easy discovery if the user wants, and there are a number of programs that can be downloaded to carry it a step further," Newbury said. "But once again, unless the user knows all of the different places and ways that computers store information, it can often be retrieved by someone with the expertise."

Karp moved over to the jury box and leaned against the rail. "Moving from the theoretical to the practical matters involved in this case, were you and your 'Geek Squad' asked to examine three computers?"

"Yes, we were."

"Would you identify for the jurors each computer you were asked to examine?"

"A Toshiba laptop belonging to Yusef Salaam," Newbury replied. "And two Hewlett-Packard desktop computers taken from the work offices of Thomas Monroe and Olivia Stone."

Karp noticed that Stone suddenly turned to her attorney and said something. Mendelbaum scrambled to his feet. "Your honor, may we approach the bench before this line of questioning goes any further?"

Rainsford nodded. "By all means."

Reaching the sidebar with Karp, Mendelbaum immediately voiced his objection. "My understanding, and granted I am an old man so all of this boggles my mind, is that given the lead-up to where we're at with this witness now is that the People will claim to have information related to these IP addresses that will connect my client to either of these gentlemen named."

"That's exactly what we're going to do," Karp replied. "And then some."

"Your point, Mr. Mendelbaum?" Rainsford interjected.

"We have no record of this information from the prosecution regarding these IP addresses or Google histories . . ."

"Browsing histories," Karp corrected.

"Yes, of course, browsing histories. So I'm objecting on the grounds that this is new information that should have been turned over to us. And since it wasn't, this line of questioning should be prohibited."

The judge turned to Karp. "And how do you plead to this accusation of withholding new information?"

"Not guilty, your honor," Karp replied. "The defense was given as much access to the computers as they requested, and they did have them examined by their own forensic computer experts. We didn't allow them out of the DA's office with the computers, and they had to work in the presence of Mr. Newbury and his associates, but they were given the opportunity to see everything our people saw."

Rainsford turned back to Mendelbaum. "Did you have someone examine the computers?"

"Yes, your honor, and the report I received was that there were no emails indicating any connection between these parties or incriminating browsing history. They did see some photographs on Mr. Salaam's computer that taken out of context might appear to be questionable, but I didn't hear anything about IP addresses or locating hidden material. And if the DA found such information, we should have been informed."

Rainsford looked disapprovingly and shook his head at Mendelbaum. "You know better, counselor. This isn't information that the prosecution was hiding from the defense, even if your experts didn't find it. In this case, both parties had access to the computers. I'm going to allow Mr. Karp to pursue this line of questioning. However, if you care to have your expert look at the machines again, I'm sure Mr. Karp will make them available to you."

Mendelbaum sighed. "I'll reserve my right to do that until after I've heard Mr. Newbury's testimony. I tell you what, though; I miss the days of typewriters and telephones you dial."

"Well, Mr. Mendelbaum, evidently computers do have some virtues," the judge replied.

Returning to his seat, Mendelbaum quickly conferred with Stone over the results of the conference with the judge. Karp was gratified to see her face tighten and fists clench; the chess pieces were moving exactly as he intended.

"Mr. Newbury, would you please give the jurors a synopsis of what the examination of the three computers revealed, such as it pertains to this case?"

"I can do that," Newbury said, and faced the jurors. "We'll begin with our examination of the laptop belonging to Yusef Salaam, also known as Henry Burns. Some of the information was easy to obtain as there'd been no attempt to delete or encrypt the material. That includes approximately twenty-five photographs we believed were of interest to the Rose Lubinsky homicide in New York County, as well as the attempted murder charge for the subsequent events outside the Jay Street Bar in Brooklyn."

As Newbury spoke, Karp walked over to the prosecution desk, where he retrieved the photographs he'd shown Burns. "Mr. Newbury, I'm handing you five photographs marked People's Exhibit 30 A through E. Were these among the photographs you just described as having been found on Salaam's laptop computer?"

Newbury quickly glanced through the photos and then looked up. "Yes."

"Would you please briefly describe the content of the photographs and what they represent?"

"Yes, these are photographs taken by an iPhone belonging to Mr. Salaam . . ."

"Excuse me for interrupting . . . how do you know that they were taken by that particular device?"

Newbury smiled. "Remember how I said IP addresses are assigned to different devices so that when something — such as a photograph — is sent from them to another device, we can trace the origination? Such devices also include iPhones. This particular iPhone and corresponding IP address belonged to Mr. Salaam and was found on his body following his death."

"Thank you. Please continue with your description of the photographs," Karp said.

"Of course. All of the photographs in People's Exhibit 30 A through E depict fires engulfing three buildings and two vehicles. With the aid of the New York police and fire department arson investigators we were able to determine that at least four of the photographs, and probably all five, depict acts of arson, and in one case, homicide."

"Were any of these cases resolved with the apprehension and conviction of the perpetrator?"

"Four of the cases remain open," Newbury said, "the fifth, the homicide, is what we're currently here to determine."

"Were these photographs Mr. Salaam could have picked up from media through the internet and downloaded onto this iPhone and later transferred to his computer?"

"No, we were able to determine that he, or whoever had possession of his iPhone, took the photographs."

"Mr. Newbury, would you please describe the contents of the photograph marked as People's Exhibit 30-E."

"The photograph shows a vehicle — actually a 2012 Ford Taurus — engulfed in flames. You can see two people lying on the sidewalk near the front passenger side of the car. And you can also see what appears to be someone in the backseat."

"Were you able to determine what this photograph represents?" Karp asked as he walked over to the diagram depicting the street crime scene People's 1 in evidence.

"Yes, it was taken from across the street . . ."

"I'm sorry, just a moment, Mr. Newbury," Karp said, and looked at Rainsford. "With the court's permission, may the witness be allowed to approach People's Exhibit 1, the diagram?"

"Granted."

"Thank you. Mr. Newbury, would you please come here and mark on this diagram of the crime scene the location of the photographer and direction of the camera when this photograph was taken?"

Newbury did as asked. "Here is the approximate place he stood and was facing this direction toward where the circle marked 'Lubinsky car' is on this diagram." He then returned to the witness stand.

"Were you able to identify the people you described as lying on the sidewalk, as well as the person we can see in the backseat of the car?"

"Yes, the two victims on the sidewalk are Rose Lubinsky and Alejandro Garcia. It is my understanding that Mr. Garcia had just pulled her from the car. The victim in the backseat was a young woman named Mary Calebras."

Karp walked over and accepted the photographs from Newbury, which he then passed to the jurors. As they were looking at the exhibits, he returned to the prosecution table and picked up two more photographs that he handed to Newbury. "Mr. Newbury, I'm handing you two more photographs. Can you identify them?"

"Yes, these were also found on Mr. Salaam's computer," Newbury said. "The first is a photograph of Rose Lubinsky taken from approximately thirty feet away. She appears to be speaking at a rally or meeting.

The second is of a young man we were able to identify as Micah Gallo. It appears to have been taken outside an apartment building from across the street."

"Mr. Newbury, was there anything else of interest in regard to this case on Mr. Salaam's computer?"

"Yes. We had to dig deeper as much of what I'm about to discuss had been deleted, and in some cases attempts to wipe the memory from the computer's hard drive were made. There was one other item he'd made no attempt to remove but is indicative of Mr. Salaam's character. He was what those who engage in social media outlets refer to as a 'troll.' He'd create false identities, including using photographs of other people he found on the internet, and would then engage other people, such as on Facebook, for the sole purpose of antagonizing and disrupting the lives of these people. He would make harmful remarks and sow dissension and then leave the conversation."

"What else?"

"We were able to discover several items from his deleted browsing history that was relevant to this case. This included looking up bomb-making instructions on the internet, including the use of C-4 explosives."

"Was any research reflected on the

computer regarding the method of detonating bombs?"

"Yes. He investigated several possibilities, such as using cell phones," Newbury said, looking down at his notepad. "He downloaded one title, 'A Quick Guide to Detonation Using the Vibrating Function on a Cell Phone.' The internet is full of such useful information."

"Please continue," Karp said.

"We also determined that Mr. Salaam used his computer to locate the Seahorse Motel in Atlantic City, as well as bus schedules and pricing for that destination."

Karp glanced over at Stone, who was bent over her legal pad writing, as her face turned bright red. "What else?"

"Quite a bit," Newbury said, looking at the jurors. "This goes back to our little chat regarding IP addresses and emails." He looked down at his notebook. "Mr. Salaam's laptop had an IP provider number of 172.16.254."

"And how does that pertain to this case?"

"Well, over the past two years or so, but particularly in the time directly preceding and following the murder of Mrs. Lubinsky, he received a number of emails from IP address 184.12.321."

"And the significance of that?"

"That is the IP address for the computer removed from the office of former district attorney Olivia Stone."

Up to that point, most of the media and others in the gallery had been following the discussion about computers and IP addresses with scrunched-up faces and looks of bewilderment. But suddenly, accompanied by a rising tide of murmurs and dropped jaws, it became clear where Karp was leading the witness, and he could tell it had for the jurors as well. Stone stopped writing and simply sat staring down at her legal pad.

"I want to be clear about something," Karp said. "Were you able to read the content of these emails?"

Newbury shook his head. "No, they'd been deleted and then wiped from the computer's memory."

"But you are able to determine that emails had been sent and received?"

Newbury nodded. "Yes," he said. "The hidden 'details' that accompany any email also include the date and time of the transmission and reception. That's how we were able to determine what I just said about the time directly preceding and subsequent to these attacks, including one sent a few minutes before the explosion of

Mrs. Lubinsky's vehicle that caused the death of three people."

Karp allowed Newbury's statement to sink in for a moment before continuing. "Was there any record of Mr. Salaam replying?"

"Only once. Most of the time he only received the transmissions and did not respond. However, on one occasion, the afternoon of the day following the car bombing at Il Buon Pane, he received a message from 184.12.321 and responded almost immediately."

"Was this the only evidence that he actually saw these emails?"

"Well, the fact that he received these messages over a period of two years and did nothing to prevent or block them would indicate that he was reading them," Newbury said, "but more than that, he seemed to respond in other ways through his actions. For instance, we were able to connect the reception of emails with the appearance within a day or two of a man matching the description of Yusef Salaam at the Seahorse Motel. This man would check in and then be joined by an unidentified white woman."

"You said a man matching the description. Did this man register under the name Yusef Salaam or Henry Burns?"

"No. As you know, the Patriot Act requires

that motels and hotels check the identification of guests when they check in," Newbury said. "According to the owner of the Seahorse Motel, which is something of a dive that rents rooms by the hour, the man who matched the physical description of Yusef Salaam presented a driver's license claiming he was one Charles Beamon of Cleveland, Ohio. However, we were able to determine that the real Charles Beamon — a forty-five-year-old Caucasian male standing five-foot-eight and weighing two hundred twenty pounds — lost his identification to a Coney Island pickpocket on New Year's Eve two years ago."

"Were you able to obtain photographs of the real Mr. Beamon and Mr. Salaam and subsequently show them to the owner of the Seahorse Motel?"

"Yes. The owner, a Mr. Islay Kennedy, formerly of County Cork, Ireland, could not identify the real photograph of Mr. Charles Beamon. However, he was able to identify the photograph of Mr. Salaam as the man known to him as Charles Beamon."

"Did you also show Mr. Kennedy a photograph of the defendant?"

"Yes. But he was unable to say for certain she was the woman who would join Mr. Salaam at the motel."

"Did he say why he could not identify her?"

"He said he never saw the woman without sunglasses and a heavy coat," Newbury said. "He also believed that she was wearing a brunette wig. He did say that she appeared to be in her late thirties to midforties."

"And would they arrive at the motel together?"

"No. Mr. Salaam would show up first on foot," Newbury said. "The unidentified woman would then arrive in a late-model silver BMW."

Karp walked over to the prosecution table and picked up a clear plastic bag that he handed to Newbury. "Mr. Newbury, would you please identify the contents of this bag?"

"Yes. It's the New York registration for a 2013 BMW F13, color silver, registered to the defendant, Olivia Stone."

"Do you know where the registration was located when taken into evidence by Detective Clay Fulton?"

"Yes, I believe it was in the glove box of the vehicle."

With the eyes of the jurors flitting over to the defense table where the blond defendant sat stone-faced and pale, Karp returned to the forensic examination of the computers. "Before we move on, were you able in your investigation to establish any sort of connection between Yusef Salaam and Lars Forsling?"

"There was nothing we found to indicate such a connection."

"What about between Mr. Salaam and Micah Gallo?"

"None."

"How about Thomas Monroe or the computer confiscated from his office at the Greater New York Teachers Federation?"

"None whatsoever."

"Two last questions regarding the browsing history of Yusef Salaam. Was there anything that pertained to the events in Brooklyn that claimed the life of Mr. Salaam?"

"Yes, on that day, a search was conducted on Google maps to locate the Jay Street Bar, and he also searched for the bus routes leading to that location."

"And did that coincide with any emails received from the computer associated with the office of the defendant?"

"Yes. This is the timing for the instance I mentioned in which he received an email from that computer and then responded."

As Newbury spoke, Karp looked at the jurors. They were paying attention but also looked as if they'd just been inundated with a lot of material to absorb. He turned to the judge. "Your honor, we'll probably be using the rest of the afternoon for Mr. Newbury's testimony and I was thinking that this might be a good time to take a break."

Rainsford glanced at the clock and nodded. "We'll meet back here in twenty minutes."

Karp left the courtroom to call Marlene but then returned as quickly as he could to go over his notes for the remainder of his questions for Newbury. He found Irving Mendelbaum sitting in his chair at the defense table, his chin on his chest and lightly snoring. The old man stirred and opened his eyes.

"Ah, boychick, caught me napping," Mendelbaum said with a tired smile.

"How you doing, Irving? You okay? You're looking a little beat."

"Am I? Well, I'm feeling beat . . . and old," he said. "All of this talk about IP addresses, and browsing histories, and iPhones . . . so much of it is going right over my head. This is the first time since I was a young and not-so-bright Legal Aid attorney fresh out of Columbia Law that I feel I am not adequately representing my client. I am simply not up on all of this computer stuff."

"You're being too hard on yourself, not to

mention you were never a 'not-so-bright' attorney," Karp said. "You're the dean of the New York defense bar and you're still on top of the program. And I have to confess, most of this computer stuff goes over my head, too. I don't even have a personal computer at home, I'm not sure what social media means, and I don't use email. I have to ask my boys or Marlene, who's pretty good at it, to explain any of it to me at home. And I'd be lost without Newbury at work."

Mendelbaum chuckled. "I've always liked Vincent. A good man and a trial attorney. I've battled with him several times in the past, and even won a couple."

"I know," Karp said, "because he takes every loss as a personal reflection on his abilities. But he doesn't lose many and dinosaurs like us have to rely on guys like him to lead us through the intricacies of the internet. You had your own experts."

"Yes, but apparently not as good as Newbury and his 'Geek Squad,' and I wasn't savvy enough to realize that. All I know is that they told me the computer memories had been wiped clean of any questionable material. Now I just feel old and not so smart."

Karp patted him on the shoulder.

"Sometimes there's no fighting the truth. But you'll live to battle another day, and you'd have to think I'm not so smart to believe that the old tiger is going to go down without a fight."

Mendelbaum nodded. "I promise to go out scratching and biting, but old, dull teeth and claws aren't much good when the hunter has a big new gun."

As Karp turned to go to his seat, Mendelbaum said, "Hey Butch, catch!"

Nabbing the Snickers bar out of the air, Karp laughed. "Thanks, Irving, they don't make 'em like you anymore."

"You still have good hands, you big lug," Mendelbaum shot back with a smile.

Ten minutes later, Newbury was back on the stand and Karp was pressing forward. "Let's move on to the computer seized from the office of Thomas Monroe at the Greater New York Teachers Federation building."

"Yes, Computer 193.41.523, as we like to call it," Newbury said with a twinkle, thoroughly enjoying himself. "That's its IP address."

"Would you tell the jurors about your examination of its contents?"

"Yes, actually we'd received some of that information earlier in the form of a flash drive given to you by Micah Gallo."

"What was Mr. Gallo's relationship to Mr. Monroe?"

"He was Monroe's assistant, sort of a second in command."

"Was the information on the flash drive identical to some of the information that was also on the computer?"

"It was the same information," Newbury said. "It had just been downloaded onto the flash drive."

"Was there anything particularly different about this information?"

"Yes, it had been encrypted, which is saying it was in code, which generally is done to keep the information secret from prying eyes."

"What, if anything, did you do to break the code?"

"Codes are made to be broken. We had to get a little help from a federal security agency, but we were able to break the code and decipher the information."

Karp picked up a thick, three-ring binder from the prosecution table. "Do you recognize this binder?"

"Yes, I created it."

"And what does it contain?"

"It contains printed copies of the information found on the computer after we broke the code."

Karp turned toward Rainsford and said, "I move to enter this binder and its material as People's Exhibit 32."

"Any objections?"

"None," said Mendelbaum.

"So moved."

"Mr. Newbury, the jury will be able to go through this material during their deliberations, but would you explain in general what they'll see?"

"Sure. The material is broken into three subsections, each of which are labeled. The first are records of bank accounts registered to various names and corporations. These banks are located in the United States, as well as the Cayman Islands. The second subsection contains a list of real estate holdings, the listed owners, and transactions, such as transfer of title and payments. The third subsection is the same information from the first two subsections, only now divided according to certain identifying marks found on the documents."

"Were you able to establish who the owners of these bank accounts, corporations, and real estate holdings were?"

"Actually, most of the accounts and corporations are not legitimate, as in, the people listed as the owners are either fictitious or people paid to use their names in order to disguise the identity of the true owners," Newbury said. "In other words, these were dummy corporations."

"Were you able to contact any of these people who were paid for the fraudulent use of their identities?"

"Some of them, but not all."

"Do you recall speaking to Monique De-Veres of Fort Lauderdale, Florida?"

"Yes, she appears as the 'owner' of one of the dummy corporations, as well as some real estate in the Florida Keys."

"Was her ownership legitimate?"

"No, Mrs. DeVeres is an older woman of Cuban descent who lives in a retirement village off her social security income, which she supplemented with several hundred dollars a month from the real owners of the corporation and real estate."

"Did Mrs. DeVeres plead guilty to fraud for this in Fort Lauderdale?"

"Yes," Newbury said. "A sad situation actually. She was having trouble making ends meet and has no family. She was placed on probation due to her age; she's eighty-three."

"You testified that in the third subsection of People's Exhibit 32, the information from the first two subsections was divided according to certain identifying marks found on the documents. What were these identifying marks?"

"They were letters written in pencil next to each of the documents, or next to the list of bank accounts," Newbury said. "Either a 'T,' an 'M,' or an 'O.' We were able to determine from our investigation that the 'T' was for Thomas, the 'M' was for Micah, and the 'O' for Olivia."

"Mr. Newbury, I believe your testimony is that there were no emails to or from IP address 193.41.523, identified as connected to the computer in Mr. Monroe's office, and IP address 172.16.254, identified as assigned to Mr. Salaam's laptop?"

"That's correct."

"What about between the Monroe IP address 193.41.523 and the Stone IP address 184.12.321?"

"Yes, there were quite a few emails going back and forth over a long period of time, including in the late afternoon prior to Mr. Monroe's arrest, at which point there were several more from the Stone IP address to the Monroe IP address, which were not returned until they, too, stopped."

"Were you able to read the emails from the Stone IP address to the Monroe IP address?"

"Yes, these were intercepted, and because

Mr. Monroe was incarcerated at the time, there was not an opportunity for him to delete them."

"What did they say?"

"Not a whole lot. Just several requests that he call her. The last one sounded quite desperate," Newbury said looking down at his notepad, "and I quote, 'Where are you? Call me, goddamn it.' "

"I'd like to turn now to Computer 184.12.321 seized from the office of then District Attorney Stone. First, was there something different about locating information on this computer?"

"Yes. This computer was linked to others within the Kings County criminal courts system, which included the office of the district attorney. As such it had an 'external' IP address associated with it and all of the other computers in the building, as well as an 'internal' number assigned solely to hers. Kings County refused to simply tell us the number, and we ended up having to subpoena their tech supervisor to get the number."

"I believe that you testified that except on one occasion, Mr. Salaam received messages from IP Number 184.12.321 assigned to the defendant's computer but did not respond?"

"That's correct. Except for the one response, it was all one-way."

"Can you tell me how many emails were sent from the Stone IP address to the Salaam IP address in the week, days, and hours prior to the car bombing that resulted in the deaths of Mrs. Lubinsky, Mary Calebras, and Tawanna Mohammad?"

"There was one about a week prior to the car bombing murder of Rose Lubinsky and the two other deceaseds."

"Were you able to note something that would lead you to believe that Mr. Salaam reacted to this email?"

"Yes, the following day he took a bus to the Seahorse Motel in Atlantic City, where he spent several hours in a room with the unidentified woman who arrived in the late-model BMW."

"Okay, let's proceed. After that, how many messages were there and when were they sent?"

"There were two more. One the day before the bombing."

"Was there any indication that Mr. Salaam reacted, such as another trip to the Seahorse Motel?"

"Not that we were able to discern."

"Okay, what about the third email?"

"It was sent several hours prior to the

bombing."

Karp positioned himself against the jury rail. "What about the following day?"

"That was when he received an email from someone in the afternoon and then responded."

"Was there something besides his email response that indicated a reaction to her email?"

"He appeared outside the Jay Street Bar where Thomas Monroe was arrested."

"Is that where he also died?"

"Yes."

"I believe that your testimony was that when you examined Computer 184.12.321, the IP address assigned to Mrs. Stone's computer, emails and browsing history had been deleted and attempts had been made to crase all evidence of them from the machine's hard drive."

"That's true."

"When was this done?"

"Approximately one hour before Mrs. Stone's arrest and the subsequent confiscation of the computer."

"Before I turn you over to Mr. Mendelbaum, was there one other computer you were asked to examine?"

"Yes," Newbury said, consulting his notepad. "Computer 312.55.435 belonging to

Micah Gallo."

"Do you know the circumstances under which this computer was turned over to the New York District Attorney's Office?"

"I believe Mr. Gallo brought it to your office."

"Were there any attempts to erase information on this computer prior to turning it over to the DAO?"

"No, other than the usual sort of housekeeping a computer user does. But nothing we could connect to anything regarding this case."

"Were you able to locate bank account information and real estate documents that incriminated Mr. Gallo in a conspiracy with Mr. Monroe and the defendant Stone to steal funds from the Greater New York Teachers Federation for their personal gain?"

"Yes."

"Was there any attempt to encrypt this information?"

"No. It was easy to access, and Mr. Gallo cooperated in showing us where to locate the information."

"Was there any evidence of contact between Mr. Gallo's IP address and the IP address assigned to Olivia Stone's computer?"

"None that we could find."

"What about between Mr. Gallo's IP address and Mr. Monroe's?"

"There were occasional emails between them, but it didn't appear to be a preferred method of communication, which is understandable considering they worked in the same office."

"Were you able to read emails on Mr. Gallo's computer between him and Mr. Monroe?"

"Yes, as I said, most were work related. However, there were some that caught our attention as being possibly linked to this case."

"Would you elaborate please?"

"Certainly," Newbury said, looking at his notepad. "One day prior to the bombing of Mrs. Lubinsky's car, Mr. Gallo received an email from Mr. Monroe that read: 'I want you to go with me to meet you know who tonight regarding what to do about the charter school bill. We're running out of time and options.'"

"Were there any others?"

"Yes, the afternoon of the bombing, Monroe instructed Gallo to meet him at the Jay Street Bar, and I quote, 'promptly at eight p.m. Don't be late,' unquote."

"Again, was there any contact between the

Gallo IP address and the Salaam IP address?"

"Not that we could determine."

"Was there anything in Gallo's computer to indicate that he knew or associated with friends of Lars Forsling?"

"Nothing we could find. You asked me to look into that but we couldn't locate any evidence that Mr. Forsling owned a computer or had access to one. We were also unable to locate an email address attributed to a Lars Forsling, except one registered to Lars Forsling in Cashton, Wisconsin, a sixty-five-year-old dairy farmer."

"This question is not in regard to the computers, but whether you were able to determine that Henry Burns, aka Yusef Salaam, was represented by the defendant, Olivia Stone, on a juvenile arson case when he was fourteen years old?"

"Yes."

"No further questions," Karp informed the judge and turned to Mendelbaum. For a moment, he felt compassion for the old man who rose slowly to his feet. But then he looked at Stone and returned his focus to the task at hand.

Following Newbury's persuasive testimony for the People, Mendelbaum had done his best to throw his matzo balls during his cross-examination of the assistant district attorney. All of his questions, however, had been anticipated, and very little, if anything, stuck. Karp could see it in the eyes of the jurors.

Mendelbaum tried to make a point that Newbury didn't know what the emails from the computer in Stone's office to Salaam's laptop actually said. "You have no idea what the subject matter was, do you?"

"No, but the timing of the emails and the efforts made to delete and hide them speaks volumes, don't you think?" Newbury parried.

Mendelbaum then attempted to portray the prosecution as the ones reaching for straws. "Without a shred of real evidence, you and my esteemed colleague, Mr. Karp, have been insinuating a romantic relationship between my client and this troubled young man, Yusef Salaam, while ignoring the possibility of something less scandalous. But, of course, that would not have fit the prosecution's scenario, would it?"

"From our investigation, you'd have to be in complete denial not to recognize it."

"Perhaps my old brain isn't comprehending correctly," Mendelbaum said at another point, scratching his head as if confused. "But on one hand you testified that your investigation of Gallo's computer did not indicate any sort of connection between him and Lars Forsling."

"That's correct."

"But then you told the jurors that Forsling didn't have a computer, or access to one, so how is that first statement even relevant?"

Newbury smiled and shrugged. "I was asked if the examination of the computer showed any evidence of an association. I was not asked if it was possible that Micah Gallo and Lars Forsling communicated in some other fashion, or could have known each other in a way that didn't involve computers."

"And how would you have answered that?"

"I would have said that I didn't know," Newbury replied. "That was not within the purview of my investigation. I would assume that others looked into that possibility."

Mendelbaum continued his cross-examination like a squirrel choosing only some nuts while ignoring the rest. "It's my understanding that when you showed the owner of the Seahorse Motel a photo lineup that included a picture of Mrs. Stone, he was unable to identify her as the mystery woman who met with Mr. Salaam. Am I right?"

And usually the simple answer was enough. "That's correct."

Mendelbaum did his best, but he didn't have much to work with and was up against a formidable People's witness in Vincent Newbury, who seemed to enjoy pulling his adversary into traps.

"Is it possible that someone else could have sent these mystery emails using my client's computer?" Mendelbaum asked.

"I suppose it's possible, but the computer and its email server are both password protected," Newbury said. "We did not find any evidence that someone 'hacked' into the computer in order to bypass the passwords, which leaves only the possibilities that the defendant gave someone her password and that person then sent these emails, and should have been reported as a possible suspect, or that the defendant sent them herself."

After Mendelbaum gave up getting any useful concessions from Newbury, Karp called Islay Kennedy to the stand. Once again to steal the defense's thunder, he asked the red-headed native of County Cork, Ireland, to look around the courtroom and see if he could "positively identify" the mystery woman who drove the late-model BMW. The motel owner had looked at

Olivia Stone for a long moment, but then shook his head and said, "I can't be sure."

Mendelbaum had, of course, made sure he reemphasized the point that the motel owner was unable to identify the mystery woman from the photo lineup and in the courtroom. But Kennedy had looked at Stone again when he said, "Who knows? The woman was wearing sunglasses and a bad brown wig."

"What makes you think it was a bad wig and not her real hair?" Mendelbaum asked.

Kennedy got an amused look on his face. "A lot of working girls bring their customers to my establishment," he said. "Believe you me, I have seen my share of bad wigs on the women *and* the men."

The courtroom erupted with laughter, which caused the witness to beam at his own cleverness. "I'm sure you have, Mr. Kennedy," Mendelbaum said, laughing himself despite the discomfiture of his client. "And a few other things as well. No further questions, your honor."

Rainsford nodded. "Mr. Karp, anything else?"

"No, your honor."

"Then on that note, we'll adjourn until morning."

25

The next morning, Karp walked to work an hour earlier than normal even for a trial day. He found that the exercise cleared his head and helped him focus, but this morning he knew he had visitors waiting for him.

Entering the reception area, Milquetost, who was always first in the office, nodded toward the meeting room. "They're waiting for you," she said.

Karp walked in and saw his visitors gathered in front of a laptop computer that had been set on the desk. One, Vince Newbury, stood watching behind the other two. The second, Islay Kennedy, touched his cheek and said, "Thinner here." The third visitor, a tall, striking red-headed woman in her forties, moved the computer mouse on the pad next to the computer, clicked, and then looked up. "Better, Mr. Kennedy?" she asked.

"Yes, very good," he replied.

Smiling, Karp walked over and extended his hand as the woman turned to greet him. "Agent Fitzgerald, good to see you," he said. "When I heard you were out of town, I thought I might have to forget about this. I wanted only the best forensic artist in the business. Where have you been?"

"Nice to see you, too, Butch," the FBI agent replied. She glanced at Kennedy. "I'm not at liberty to divulge much, but let's just say somewhere in North Africa getting witness descriptions of someone I believe you're familiar with . . . Nadya Malovo."

Karp grimaced and shook his head. "I can only imagine what that might have been about. Maybe you can fill me in some other day," he said as he looked at the computer screen, then at Kennedy. "Good morning, Islay. I appreciate you coming in again."

"Anything I can do to help," Kennedy replied.

"I think we're just about done with step one," Fitzgerald said. "What do you think, Mr. Kennedy?"

"Yes, most amazing!"

"What's next?" Karp asked.

"We're going to start adding the variables," Fitzgerald said. "Want to watch?"

Karp smiled and moved to stand next to Newbury. "Wouldn't miss it for the world."

■ ■ ■ ■

An hour later, Karp left his visitors and entered the courtroom. He smiled when he saw Irving Mendelbaum already inside and handing a candy bar to Chief Clerk James Farley.

"Ah, look what the cat dragged in," Mendelbaum said. He squinted at Karp and then shook a finger at him. "I take that back, more like the cat who ate the canary. What sinister plot are you hatching now, boychick? Whatever it is, I'm sure it's at my expense."

"Who, me?" Karp said, feigning innocence. Then he winked. "It will take more than a Snickers bar for that info."

"How about a Hershey's with nuts?" Mendelbaum laughed.

"Sorry, but, unlike certain people I could, and will, name, this is one district attorney who can't be bought," Karp said.

Mendelbaum clutched at his chest. "Oh, the slings and arrows," he moaned.

"I think you have a career in the theater after this," Karp joked.

Mendelbaum smirked. "I may need it."

A few minutes later, Farley called the court to order as Rainsford walked in. Then after the jury was seated, the judge nodded to Karp. "Are you ready to call your next witness?"

"Yes, your honor," Karp said. "The People call Thomas Monroe."

A collective gasp escaped from the spectators in Part 42 when Monroe walked in from the prisoner holding cell on one side of the courtroom. They were used to seeing the big, self-assured man at press conferences and union events dressed in his expensive suits and designer ties, holding forth in his booming New York Irish accent.

Now he was already sweating profusely, with dark, wet circles beneath the armpits and around the neck of the light blue sweat suit he wore, as he glanced furtively at the gallery. But what had elicited their surprise was the amount of weight he'd lost and the pallor of his skin after six months in The Tombs. His clothes hung on him like sheets lacking a breeze, and his once fat face sagged in loose folds and dark bags gathered beneath his eyes.

"Mr. Monroe, this way, please," Farley said, indicating the well of the court.

Monroe looked away from the stunned audience and cast his eyes down at the worn carpet as he shuffled past the first row. He hesitated as he started to step onto the witness stand as if the effort was too much; then he sighed, shook his head, and climbed up to be sworn in by Farley.

Watching the former union president as he sat down heavily on the seat, Karp wondered if, when he was a young man, Monroe had been able to see ahead to the eventual outcome as he took that first step toward corruption, would he have pulled back? Or was the die cast, the pull too strong, for someone with weak moral fiber?

As a new teacher and member of the union, surely he hadn't started off intending to betray students or work his way up the union ladder in order to wield power and steal millions of dollars from those who trusted him to represent them. Or was the dark seed already planted in his character, just waiting to sprout?

After Karp wrapped up their interview the night of Monroe's arrest, the union chief had expressed remorse. But at the time, it sounded like the sort of false contrition Karp had heard thousands of times from the guilty who hoped for leniency. Still, he wondered if, after all this time in jail surrounded by the violent and the evil dregs of society, and looking at a lifetime of more of the same, was he truly penitent?

It didn't matter. Karp could see the shame

in the man's fall from grace. He took no joy from it, but he felt no pity either. Except for the truly insane, human beings were creatures of free will who made their choices consciously and were aware of the possible consequences. Monroe had been fully cognizant that his actions were not only criminal, but morally wrong as well. He'd admitted that he was aware of the damage his malfeasance and theft had done to the union and those he was supposed to represent, the public school teachers and students. Yet, he'd wallowed in his ill-gotten gains. In order to protect his own self-interest, he'd fought accountability and progress, such as that represented by the charter school bill. Instead of trying to find a way to work with them to best serve all of those involved, he'd bought politicians, threatened, intimidated, and finally resorted to murder.

Karp leaned over the table and made a note on his legal pad. He then picked up a photograph and carried it with him as he took a position immediately in front of the witness stand staring at Monroe, whom he quickly led through the beginnings of his corruption, "initially just skimming off the top."

The more complicated dummy corporations, fake bank accounts, and real estate transactions didn't start until Stone came on board, Monroe testified. "She was smart and had it all figured out," he said. "Then after she became DA, we stepped it up even more. I guess we were feeling pretty bulletproof."

He described how they'd conspired to bring down Micah Gallo, a rising star in the charter school movement, "to make an example of what could happen if you crossed the union." But it had been Stone's idea to corrupt him, too, "so we could use him against the movement, and Lubinsky in particular. I thought it was a good idea to keep an eye on him."

Monroe shook his head and glared at Stone. "Instead, it turned around and bit us on the butt. If it wasn't for him, we probably wouldn't be here."

"What made you think that you could trust him?" Karp asked.

Monroe shrugged. "He wasn't involved in the murder stuff, but we knew that if we went down for the skimming, he'd go down with us. I guess when you're as corrupt as we were, you think everybody else is a thief at heart, too. I figured he liked the lifestyle too much to trade it in for a prison jumpsuit."

"When was the decision made to murder Rose Lubinsky, and by whom?" Karp asked.

"I think we got desperate. I'd hoped that she'd back off, or we'd find a way to back her off," Monroe said. "But she couldn't be bought, and we had nothing on her. So that's when she" — he nodded at Stone — "decided she had to go and brought her boy in."

"When you say 'she' decided that Mrs. Lubinsky had to die," Karp asked, "who are you talking about?"

"Her," Monroe said, pointing at the defendant. "Olivia Stone."

"And her boy?"

"I only met him a few times. His name was Yusef, or something like that. Looked like a circus freak with that face of his, and why she was banging that guy I'll never know. Wore bright red high-tops every time I saw him. I think she knew the bastard from her days as a Legal Aid lawyer. She used him when we were having trouble with people, like when we were after Micah."

Karp had Monroe describe the meetings that he would be asking Gallo about. "The first one, I asked Lubinsky to meet us at the Jay Street Bar and brought Micah along, hoping their past relationship might soften her up. The next time was at Stone's office;

I think he saw her guy. That's when we decided that if Micah couldn't come up with something to back Lubinsky off, she had to go. The third time was when I told Micah to be at the Jay Street Bar at eight sharp. He was late."

"Why did you tell him he had to be there at eight sharp?"

"Because I knew it was going down with Lubinsky. Stone told me to make sure we were someplace where other people would see us no later than eight."

"When was the last time you saw Micah Gallo?" Karp asked.

"It was at the Jay Street Bar again," Monroe said. "He'd downloaded some of my files, then called and said he wanted out — that the Lubinsky murder was over the top. But he wanted a hundred grand to keep quiet and disappear."

"And you believed him?"

"Like I said, right or wrong, I trust a guy with larceny in his soul," Monroe said. "That's something I understand."

"Was there some other reason you agreed to meet him at the Jay Street Bar?"

Monroe nodded. "Yeah. When he pulled up, Stone's lover boy was waiting across the street. He was supposed to plant a bomb and, BOOM, no more Micah Gallo.

Goodbye, witness."

"Didn't turn out that way, did it?" Karp asked. He knew the answer even better than Monroe did. When Alejandro Garcia left the bar, he'd walked in the direction of Gallo's car. Then he spotted Yusef Salaam kneeling near the back of the car on the driver's side.

"I saw the red Chuck Taylors," Garcia told Karp later that night after he'd dealt with Monroe. "The guy saw me coming and I guess freaked out and pressed the wrong button. Next thing I know, I'm knocked flat by an explosion. I still remember the fucking guy's shoe landing in the middle of the street, but there wasn't enough of him left to fill a bucket."

In the courtroom, Monroe conceded that the tables had been turned. "It was a setup," he said. "Gallo was working for you. The bar was crawling with cops. When Yusef set himself off to meet ol' Lucifer that big black detective arrested my ass, and the rest is history."

Karp looked over at Stone, but she was glaring at Monroe. *I guess that's what they mean by "if looks could kill,"* he thought. "A few last questions, Mr. Monroe. Were you charged with the murder of Rose Lubinsky?"

"Yes, I was."

"And did you plead guilty to that charge?"

"Yes, I did."

"Were you offered any sort of deal in exchange for your testimony here today?"

Monroe shook his head sadly. "No. You said if I testified and told the truth, you'd let the judge know that when I get sentenced."

"And have you told the truth here today?"

"Yeah, I've told the truth."

"And will you be going to prison for a long time no matter what?"

Monroe took a deep breath and let it out slowly before he nodded. "Yeah, I expect the only way I'll get out will be in a pine box. But maybe God will have mercy, and I'll get a few years at the end, to see my kids without bars between us again someday."

Karp looked at Rainsford. "No more questions, your honor."

26

Karp feigned uninterest in the quiet but heated discussion going on at the defense table between Irving Mendelbaum and Olivia Stone. Judge Rainsford had just asked if the defendant would be taking the stand to testify and, as Karp had anticipated, the former district attorney of Kings County was ignoring the advice of counsel.

"This is a mistake," Mendelbaum whispered as forcefully as he could without the jury hearing.

But Stone hissed right back pushing her legal pad at the old attorney. "It's my only chance. I can handle Karp. Just ask me the questions."

After Monroe's appearance and Mendelbaum's spirited but ineffectual cross-examination, Karp had concluded the People's case with two last witnesses. One was a security guard working the late shift at the building housing the Kings County District Attorney's Office. He testified that he'd let Monroe and Gallo, whom he identified on the stand through photographs, into the building after hours at the request of Stone a few days before the Lubinsky murder.

Admitting that he occasionally accepted monetary "tips," from Stone for "looking the other way," he'd also testified that Stone had another visitor that evening, "some freaky-looking guy in cherry red, old-school basketball shoes.

"He showed up before the other two and left after them," the guard recalled.

The last witness for the People's case had been Micah Gallo, who'd begun his testimony by telling the jurors that he'd pleaded guilty to grand larceny and had not received any sort of deal from Karp in exchange for his "truthful" testimony. He'd then poured his story out over the next two hours.

In a sense the People's case was over with Newbury's testimony; it was that damning. So Karp had used Monroe's and Gallo's testimony to drive the last few nails, like a fine carpenter putting the finishing touches on a well-built new home. The foundation had been poured; the frame erected; the walls and windows, plumbing, and electricity were all in place; and all that had remained was the trim and paint.

It was no surprise to him that Stone now felt compelled to testify in a desperate attempt to try to explain away or deny the evidence in the hope of finding one juror who might buy into her lies. He expected it because from the moment he sought to indict her for murder, from his trial preparation to the manner and order he'd presented the witnesses and the evidence, he'd planned for this outcome. Like a hunter setting a trap for a wary tiger, his purpose had been to lead her down a path to the witness stand. Even the testimony about her illicit affair with Salaam that had embarrassed and ridiculed her had been for that purpose.

Mendelbaum knew it and, like any good defense lawyer who didn't want his client to expose herself to cross-examination, he'd tried to talk her out of it. But in spite of her own law degree, which along with her experience as a Legal Aid attorney and the counsel of her more experienced peers, Stone's arrogance and humiliation worked against her. As Karp knew it would.

There were actually two reasons Karp had planned for this. The first was to go one step further to prove guilt beyond any and all doubt by letting Stone's own words expose her for what she was: a thief and a murderer. The second reason was more personal and went to his very core about how he felt regarding those entrusted by the public to protect and serve them, but instead would do anything to gain and preserve power and its attendant wealth. More than even the most base criminal who mindlessly stole or killed, someone like Stone, who lacked for nothing and had had every advantage, galled him. Their actions tore at the very fabric of society and everything he believed in. If there was a lesson to be learned in her downfall by others who might be considering a similar road, then he was all for giving it.

"Mr. Mendelbaum, has your client reached a decision on whether to testify?" Rainsford asked.

Mendelbaum looked one last time at his client, who nodded at the legal pad and then sighed. "Yes, your honor, the defense calls Olivia Stone."

Like a prizefighter answering the bell, Stone pushed away from the defense table and stood up. Walking purposefully toward the aisle between the defense and prosecution tables, she glanced venomously once at Karp and then made her way to the witness stand to be sworn in.

Mendelbaum moved more slowly as he picked up the legal pad. Most of his trial strategy had been to rely on the cross-examination of the People's witnesses, looking for small chinks in their testimony. His approach had been to forward the possibility of there being another, viable suspect, particularly Lars Forsling. Or, as his cross-examinations had suggested, that Monroe and possibly Gallo had arranged the murder and that Olivia Stone was an innocent dupe, guilty only by association.

When Monroe was on the stand, Mendelbaum had pointed out that he had the most to lose if the charter school bill was passed. But it only went so far.

"I guess that's true as far as my position as president of the union," Monroe replied. "However, Olivia relied on the union for its political support, and she had her hand as far in the till as I did both before and after she became DA. She had as much to lose if the union was audited."

Questioning Gallo, Mendelbaum noted that he was Monroe's "right-hand man and if anybody had the opportunity to act in concert, it was the two of you, isn't that correct?"

"Except," Gallo retorted, "I was the one

who turned all of us in. If I didn't, no one would have been the wiser. The charter school bill would be dead in the water without Rose, and we'd have had time to cover our tracks."

After Karp rested the People's case, Mendelbaum had called just two witnesses. One was a forensic computer expert who testified about "possibilities." The possibility that IP addresses could be manipulated. The possibility that someone had hacked Stone's computer, gaining access without her passwords. The possibility that the computers used by Monroe and Gallo had been more expertly "wiped" of information that might have led to exonerating Stone.

However, Karp had made quick work of the "possibility defense" on cross-examination. "You just testified about a list of what you call possible alternate scenarios to the evidence," Karp said, "but what about the 'probability' that these fantasies . . ."

"I object to the counsel's description of this expert's testimony as 'fantasies'," Mendelbaum had complained.

"Sustained."

"Let me rephrase: What about the probability that any of these 'possibilities' occurred, and do you have a single scintilla of evidence to back you up?" Karp demanded.

The witness had hemmed and hawed, had glanced at the defense table. He then conceded that "The probability is questionable given all that would have had to occur and the technical expertise it would have taken. I guess my testimony is more theoretical than proven."

With that witness going down in flames, Mendelbaum called Marlene to the stand. "You are the one who shot Mr. Forsling, is that correct?"

"Yes. He'd abducted my sons and Goldie Sobelman and was in the act of pointing his gun at one son's head."

"Then after shooting Mr. Forsling, you were present when he uttered a dying declaration, correct?"

"Yes. I was there."

"And did you hear him deny that he was involved in the murder of the deceased in this case?"

"No, I did not."

"However, you did hear him say — as he lay dying — that he was responsible for the bombing that killed the deceased?"

"Yes, that's what he said."

After Marlene stepped down, it was clear that Mendelbaum wanted to rest his case and rely on Rainsford's instructions to the jury after summations that the defendant declining to testify was not an admission of guilt. The standard wording would have been that it was the People's responsibility to prove guilt beyond a reasonable doubt and that the defendant was under no obligation to take the stand to defend herself or do anything else for that matter.

However, as Karp knew she would, Stone thought that she could talk her way out of a murder conviction. Thus the trap was sprung.

"Mrs. Stone, although it is against my advice and any obligation on your part that you do so, you've decided to take the stand to testify in your own defense today, is that correct?" Irving Mendelbaum began.

"Yes, that's true."

"And would you please explain to the jury why it is you're taking this step?"

Stone nodded and turned to the jurors. "I've been thinking about this for a long time now, and believe I need to set the record straight, as well as come clean."

The audience in the gallery buzzed with excitement. This was unexpected. However, Karp sat listening impassively.

Mendelbaum held up the legal pad. "And to set the record straight, you wrote down certain questions that you wanted me to include in your direct examination. Is that true?"

"That's right."

"So let me start with: 'Did you ever receive money and/or purchase property from funds that rightfully belonged to the Greater New York Teachers Federation?"

Stone took a deep breath then nodded her head. "Yes, I'm ashamed to admit it, but I'm guilty of theft."

The buzz in the gallery grew louder. Several reporters got up and ran from the courtroom to give the newsrooms a heads-up.

"When did this begin, and how did it come about?"

"Soon after I applied for the job with the union," Stone said. "I knew that Mr. Monroe had an interest in me that went beyond professional boundaries."

"His attentions were of a personal nature?"

"Yes, he started hitting on me."

"And yet you accepted the position?"

"Yes. I had huge student loans from law school and I just wasn't making any progress at paying those off, as well as keeping my other bills straight, on the pay they give a young attorney working for Legal Aid. I also thought I could do a good job on behalf of the teachers and students while making a decent wage. I believed I could handle Mr. Monroe's unwanted advances."

"Were you able to do that?"

"Yes, I was quite clear that I wasn't interested," Stone said. "But by the time he got the point, I guess I was doing a good enough job that he kept me on and for the most part stopped making advances."

"Did there come a point where you began accepting payments and gifts that were not part of your salary and were not from legitimate sources?"

Stone paused and wiped at an apparent tear, then nodded. "Yes. It began with extravagant trips that he called 'fact-finding missions' but were really just junkets, and 'bonuses.' I'm ashamed to say that I didn't turn them down, even though I knew they had to come from union funds."

Mendelbaum referred to the legal pad. "At some point did you indicate to Monroe that you were uncomfortable with these trips and monetary bonuses?"

"Yes," Stone said. "The gifts of money, in particular, were getting to be excessive. I was worried that we'd be caught, and that it would have a detrimental effect on the union. But he said it was too late, there was no backing out now so I might as well, and these were his words, 'jump in with both feet.' "

"And did you?"

Stone glanced down and shook her head before looking back at the jurors. "Yes. I jumped in with both feet. The money, the trips, the real estate investments, the whole nine yards."

"And how did you feel about it?"

Stone shrugged. "Guilty, at first. But then I began to justify it in my mind. I told myself that I worked long, hard hours — more than I'd anticipated when I took the job — and that I did good work. The union was strong and we'd made good investments with the funds on behalf of the union, not just ourselves. I convinced myself that no one was really being hurt; meanwhile, my college loans were paid off and I was enjoying life."

"Did you have other aspirations that you knew would require a lot of money?"

Stone nodded. "Working as a public defender straight out of law school, I believed in what I was doing," she said. "Everybody accused of a crime deserves good representation to protect their rights, including making the State prove its case, not just what some district attorney 'thinks' happened. Just like you're being asked to decide here."

Pausing to look meaningfully from one juror's face to the next, Stone then continued. "But I also saw the impact that crime has on our society and that sometimes good representation was keeping some truly dangerous individuals out of prison and on the streets. I decided when I took the job as union counsel that I'd work to pay my bills for a few years, but then I wanted to work on the other side of the aisle as a prosecutor and do more to protect my community. I know it was just this one girl's far-fetched dream, but I wanted to be the district attorney of Kings County, Brooklyn. However, I knew that I would be up against the 'old-boys network' of white males who weren't going to accept a female with fresh ideas. I was going to need a lot of money to bankroll my dream."

Mendelbaum gave the jurors his best puzzled look. "So how do you justify that admirable desire to protect the community with your admission of assisting Thomas Monroe with the theft of union funds?"

Again, Stone shook her head sadly. "I know it sounds foolish," she said. "But I separated the two in my head. I'd let myself be convinced by Monroe that the union was on such a sound financial footing that skimming a little off the top wasn't hurting anyone. And I had this wild idea of somehow paying it all back. I realize now that sounds disingenuous, but I thought that even if I kept the money, I'd do such a good job as district attorney, I'd be paying it back in another way."

Mendelbaum flipped one of the pages of the legal pad, then continued. "What is your opinion of charter schools?"

Stone looked thoughtful. "I think they're great for the students who have the privilege of being accepted to them," she said. "But I also believe in the public school system where every child is entitled to a free education and the same basic education as his peers. I think of all the brilliant people who have come out of the public school system, and I know that they far outnumber the brilliant people who attended private school, and let's face it, charter schools are just another name for private schools. Just look at the number of white children from urban areas who flock to them because they can; meanwhile, the children who are left behind — minorities, the poor, the disenfranchised — get the short end of the stick. And that stick gets even shorter when funds are siphoned away to support charter schools."

"Did you oppose charter schools even as

a district attorney?"

"Yes, I spoke out against them for the reasons I just mentioned."

"Was there a time when union opposition, with your participation, was turned against Micah Gallo, who at the time was the founder of a charter school in Brooklyn?"

"Yes. And I'm ashamed I didn't put a stop to it," Stone said. "Monroe was getting more concerned about the charter school movement and saw Gallo as one of its rising stars. He thought that if he made an example of Gallo, it would put a chilling effect on others. But I have to say I had no idea that Monroe and his associates were harassing him to the degree that they apparently were. I was too busy prosecuting crimes in Kings County."

"Yet you ended up prosecuting Micah Gallo?"

"I'm not going to pretend that I was a big fan of Gallo," Stone said. "Back when I was still with Legal Aid, I knew he was a gang member who'd committed violent crimes, though the cops hadn't been able to catch him. I saw him as just someone who was trying to capitalize off the charter school movement by starting his own school, with his own rules. But neither was I determined to do anything about him. However, when it was brought to my attention that he had broken the law — even if those making the allegations had ulterior motives — it was not my place to ignore the facts. I didn't make the laws, I just enforced them."

"What about afterward? When Gallo was forced to shut his school?"

"To be honest, I was done with him," Stone said. "He'd been tried and was found not guilty. I didn't agree with the jury's decision, but I respected it. However, Monroe wouldn't let it go; it was a personal thing with him, and as he told me, he was going to show that Gallo was as corrupt as anyone else, as well as keep his eye on him."

"How did he do that?"

"The same way he corrupted me," Stone said. "Gallo was broken. He had nothing. But Monroe acted like all was forgiven and that he wanted to help him get back on his feet. He started with small things, a good job, a nice salary, but it wasn't long before he brought Gallo into the fold. And by the time poor Micah started to balk, he was as caught up in Monroe's web as I was."

Mendelbaum looked down again at the legal pad. "Tell us about Yusef Salaam?"

Stone looked aggrieved. "Yes, or as he was called, Henry Burns. When I first met him, he'd been accused of arson. He was an angry, troubled young teenager not unlike so many others these days. But as I got to know him at the juvenile holding facility, I learned that he'd been bullied because of his skin condition, abandoned by his father, and that his anger was mostly for self-protection and his crimes were a way of acting out against a world he felt had betrayed him. Yet, beneath it all he was an intelligent young man who longed for friends, but had none; I know he was diagnosed with an antisocial personality disorder, but I saw a spark of his good side in the way he cared for his mother."

"How did your relationship with him change?"

Shaking her head sadly, Stone let out a sigh. "I guess this is one of those cases of 'no good deed goes unpunished' or," she said, looking at Karp, "it gets misinterpreted. Yes, I stayed in contact with Henry after I'd seen him through his court case. I even introduced him to Monroe. Whatever else he may be, Thomas Monroe once truly cared for children. I thought he might be able to talk to Henry about continuing with his education and even help him find a productive way to use his computer talents. Instead, Monroe used him for his own ends."

"I'd like to turn now to Rose Lubinsky," Mendelbaum said. "What were your feelings toward her?"

Stone shrugged. "Again, I'm not going to kid you. As much as I liked Rose on a personal level, I saw her as a threat — both to the union and public schools, but I confess, I was worried about her insistence that the charter school bill include provisions for an audit of the union. I know now that I deserve to be punished for stealing, but at the time I was badly frightened. I kept imagining what life would be like in prison for a former district attorney."

Putting the legal pad down on the defense table, Mendelbaum leaned against the table as if tired and crossed his arms. "So Mrs. Stone, you've heard all of this testimony about this conspiracy to murder Rose Lubinsky, these meetings and the flurry of emails. Is any of it true?"

"Not like it's been portrayed," Stone answered. "At least not from my perspective. For instance, the meeting at my office after hours with Monroe and Gallo did take place."

"And was Henry Burns, also known as Yusef Salaam, present?"

"Yes, and he arrived first. But I didn't invite him."

"Who did?"

"Tommy Monroe," Stone replied. "By this time, Henry knew who 'buttered his bread,' which as Gallo testified is one of Monroe's sayings."

"And what was the purpose of the meeting?"

"Well, it wasn't the way Mr. Karp is trying to portray it," Stone said. "It's true that we were talking about ways we might be able to get Rose Lubinsky to compromise about the bill, or at least delay its passage."

"Did that include a discussion about blackmailing her?"

Stone pursed her lips, then shrugged. "I admit that it might have seemed that way to Micah Gallo; Monroe was being pretty insistent on finding a way to stop her 'or else.' But my impression was that we were talking about finding a way to discredit her politically, as well as increasing our lobbying efforts. It wasn't like the charter school bill's passage was a done deal. The voting would have been close and it would have only taken a few votes."

"What about the notion that a decision was made at the meeting to 'remove' Rose Lubinsky by killing her?"

Stone scoffed. "Over a state assembly bill vote that wasn't even a sure thing? Yes, we were worried about the audit. But even if the charter school bill passed, we could have held it up with legal appeals; at least long enough to cover our trail. And to think that I'd condone resorting to murder is ludicrous."

"But what about the emails Yusef Salaam — Henry Burns — and the IP addresses we've heard so much about?" Mendelbaum asked.

"Just more of Monroe's cleverness," Stone said. "He thought that no one would ever look at my emails and my phone calls. So he insisted that I be the go-between whenever he wanted to set up a meeting with Henry. So he'd call me to set the time and place, then I'd email the information to Henry. But that's it. What they talked about or did at their meetings, I wasn't there."

"What were you doing on the night Rose Lubinsky was murdered?"

Stone acted as if the question caught her off guard and in a vulnerable state. Her eyes welled with tears and she struggled to speak. "I was having dinner with my husband . . . my ex-husband since all of this," she said, waving her hand at Karp. She stopped talking and it was a minute before she could go on. "I'm sorry, I'm sorry, I know I made my bed and have to lie in it, but I lost the most important person in my life, as well as all of my hopes and dreams. It doesn't help to know it was my own fault."

"Did anyone — Monroe — tell you to make sure you had an alibi at eight p.m.?"

"No, that was apparently something Monroe worked out with Gallo. I didn't know anything was going to happen."

"What was your reaction when you heard about the bombing?"

"Shock."

"How did you hear about it?"

"When I got home from dinner it was on the news."

"What was the first thing that came to your mind?"

"Well, they were saying on the television that there'd been a neo-Nazi demonstration and that one of them had been arrested," Stone said. "I thought that was connected to the bombing. In no way did I think even Monroe would arrange for something like that."

"Mrs. Stone, did you know Lars Forsling, or was he ever a former client or someone you prosecuted?"

"No, not to my knowledge."

"Did Monroe or Gallo ever mention him by name?"

"No, I don't remember ever hearing his

name until I learned he was a suspect in Lubinsky's murder and was then killed by Mr. Karp's wife," Stone said pointedly. "However, Tommy Monroe kept a lot of strange bedfellows beyond just Henry Burns."

Mendelbaum walked over to the defense table and dropped the legal pad. Slowly he strolled back over to the jury box, leaned against the rail, and paused as if he was troubled by his next question. "Mrs. Stone, I don't mean to be indelicate but I have to ask you potentially embarrassing questions about your relationship with Henry Burns."

Stone blushed but nodded. "I understand."

"Mrs. Stone, it has been insinuated that you were engaged in an extramarital sexual affair with Mr. Burns. Is it true?"

Stone covered her mouth with her hand and looked past him at the jurors. "I never . . . I mean, I couldn't." She stopped and caught her breath. "Since he was fourteen years old, I've been one of the only people who cared about him; I was able to look past his physical disfigurement, if that's what you want to call it. To be honest, I've cringed every time one of the prosecution witnesses referred to him as a 'freak' just because that's something that made him what he was in the end. But that's neither here nor there. Did I have an affair with him? Absolutely not. I was a friend and a mentor, nothing more. Even at that, the more he fell under Monroe's guidance, my influence grew less and less until basically I was just a conduit between the two of them. A messenger."

"But what about this mysterious woman who would meet him at the Seahorse Motel?"

Stone looked angry. "I have no idea who she is, but it wasn't me. To be honest, I think it was a setup to get to me. I'm not saying who was behind it, whether it was Monroe or . . ." She looked again at Karp. ". . . someone who had an issue with me as the district attorney of Kings County, or as an opponent of the charter school bill. But isn't it funny how the motel owner looked right at me here in court and didn't identify me as the mystery woman?"

"So you did not have a sexual relationship with Henry Burns, aka Yusef Salaam?"

"I did not. I never cheated on my husband with him or anybody else."

"Mrs. Stone, you've admitted here to having committed grand larceny, a serious felony, as well as official malfeasance, both of which are punishable by substantial time in prison. You're aware of that?"

"Yes, I'm guilty of those crimes and know I'll have to pay for them."

"Did you also in concert conspire, direct, or have anything to do with the actions that claimed the lives of Mrs. Lubinsky, Mary Calebras, and Tawanna Mohammad?"

"Mr. Mendelbaum," Stone said, "I am deeply ashamed of what I've done. I am a thief, and I brought dishonor to the position of district attorney of Kings County. But I am not a murderer!" She then burst into tears.

Mendelbaum nodded. "Thank you, Mrs. Stone. Your honor, I have no more questions at this time."

Rainsford looked at Karp. "Do you intend to cross-examine the witness?"

"Absolutely," Karp said, rising to his feet. He stuck his hands in his pockets and walked over to the jury box as if deep in thought. Then he looked over at Stone. "Who are the tears for, Mrs. Stone, the deceaseds or yourself?"

Stone looked up but didn't answer, so he went on. "Mrs. Stone, do you believe in free will?"

"What do you mean?"

"Well, you've painted yourself as this poor creature who had no will of her own to say no when the big bad wolf Tommy Monroe began plying you with ill-gotten gains. Were you unable to say no?"

"I was young and like I said I had these loans . . ."

"Like a million other kids in this country, but they don't steal, or abuse power, or murder people to pay them off and make a nice life for themselves."

"I didn't murder anybody."

"Didn't you testify that you believed that if you became the district attorney of Kings County, you'd be able to pull away from the evil clutches of Tommy Monroe? That you'd be the one with the power, and the full weight of the law, on your side," Karp said, "and that you'd be able to then right these wrongs you'd been involved in? How did that work for you?"

"I said, I took the money," Stone snapped.

"Yes. I believe you said that you didn't think anybody would be hurt with a little skimming off the top. So exactly what do you consider 'skimming a little off the top'? The mansion in Long Beach you purchased for three point five million?"

"It's more than a little."

"Indeed, and what about the property in Key West, which according to the last tax assessment was worth about two million?"

Stone just sat without speaking.

"More than a little? What about the beachfront home in Grand Cayman, or the bank accounts. It all adds up to another five or six million. Right?"

"Yes. Like I said, I'm not denying that I stole the money."

"No, not now you're not," Karp said. "Now you're hoping that admitting to a lesser crime will get you off the hook for murder. But until about an hour ago, you'd been telling the press, these jurors, and anybody else who'd listen that you were completely innocent of all of these crimes. So why should you be believed now?"

"Because now I'm telling the truth?"

"Really? And do you have any evidence to back you up?"

"I think the evidence can be interpreted in more than one way."

"Well, even the defense computer expert said that's not very probable. In fact, it was just a theory without any evidence."

Again Stone was silent, so Karp continued. "You know what I believe, Mrs. Stone?"

"Yes, that I'm involved in the murder."

"That's right. I think all of the evidence, the real evidence, says just that, and the only reason you're on the witness stand today is because you've decided that some time in prison is better than spending the rest of your life in prison, isn't that true?"

"No. I've told you what the truth is."

"Really? The whole truth and nothing but the truth?"

"Yes."

"Mrs. Stone, one of those 'truths' is that you deny having a sexual relationship with Yusef Salaam, and that your only contact with him was as the messenger between him and Monroe?"

"That's right."

"And is that as true as the rest of your testimony?"

"Definitely!"

Karp walked over to the prosecution table and picked up two photographs. "Mrs. Stone, do you have any tattoos on your body?"

Judge Rainsford looked at Karp and raised an eyebrow. "Mr. Karp, where are you going with this inquiry?"

"Your honor, I'm laying the foundation to impeach this witness," he said, pleased to see Stone blanch.

"Then proceed."

Karp stalked up to the witness stand and handed Stone one of the photographs. "I'm handing you People's Exhibit 33 to ask if you can identify the person in the photograph and where it was taken."

Stone frowned. "This is a photograph of me in the Cayman Islands a year ago with my husband. Where did you get it?"

Karp shrugged. "We found it on your Facebook page. The photograph shows you in a bikini, does it not?"

"It does."

"And is that a tattoo above your left breast?"

"Yes."

"What does it depict?"

"It's a mermaid."

"Thank you," Karp said. He held up his hand for the photograph and then handed her the other. "I'm now handing you People's Exhibit 34. For the record, your honor, this photo was taken from the computer of Yusef Salaam, and will be so authenticated by ADA V. T. Newbury in the People's rebuttal case if necessary. Mrs. Stone, would you describe what the photograph depicts for the jurors, please?"

Stone sat staring at the photograph. She didn't look up or speak.

"Mrs. Stone, I asked you to describe the photograph."

Instead, she shook her head. "No. I won't."

"No?" Karp asked. "This wasn't a yes or no answer. I asked you to describe what you see in the photograph."

Stone crumpled the photograph and flung it at the floor. She then sat glaring at Karp.

"Mrs. Stone," Judge Rainsford said. "You are under cross-examination and are required to answer Mr. Karp's questions. If you do not, your entire testimony may be stricken."

Stone sat mute. Finally she said, "I'm not mentally able to respond to that question or subject matter, your honor."

"Very well then, your honor," Karp said, bending over to pick the photograph up off the floor. "I'd like to show the blowup of the photo exhibit to the jury and describe it for the record."

"Go ahead, Mr. Karp."

Starting at one end of the jury box, Karp strolled along the rail holding the photograph up so that they could see it. Some looked away after a glance, others continued to watch in fascination. "The photograph is of a nude blond woman lying in what appears to be a motel room bed. If you look closely you can see an ashtray on the nightstand with the words 'Seahorse Motel' on it; there's also a pair of sunglasses on the stand and what appears to be a brunette wig. The woman's hands and wrists are bound above her head; her legs are spread-eagled and also bound to the bottom corners of the bed. Her head is turned away from the camera, but you can see she is wearing a blindfold over her eyes; she appears to be completely at rest. But you can clearly see the image of a tattoo above her left breast."

Karp stopped walking and turned toward Stone, holding up the photograph as he spoke. "Ladies and gentlemen of the jury, you will be able to view this photograph yourselves again during your deliberations. At that time, I think you'll be able to see for yourselves the tattoo of a mermaid above the left breast of the defendant, which you can then compare to the photograph the defendant identified herself in."

Looking at the witness, Karp said, "Mrs. Stone, I'm going to ask you again. Have you told us the whole truth today?"

Stone's lips pulled back as she snarled, "Go fuck yourself, Karp."

Judge Rainsford snapped, "Mrs. Stone, you're under oath in this courtroom and you will comport yourself with the dignity and respect it deserves."

Walking over to the prosecution table, Karp picked up a bag and returned to the witness stand. "Your honor, if you'd please direct the defendant to put these on for the purpose of engaging in an in-court identification," he said, and pulled out a brunette wig and sunglasses.

The final door of the trap was slamming shut. The day before when he met with FBI Special Agent Shannon Fitzgerald, Vincent Newbury, and Islay Kennedy in the meeting room adjacent to his office, the FBI agent had asked him if he wanted to watch while she added the "variables" to something she'd been working on with the motel owner. That something was a computer-assisted "sketch" of the mystery woman Islay Kennedy had seen with Yusef Salaam.

Fitzgerald was considered the best in the business when it came to computer-assisted forensic modeling. Her specialty was creating three-dimensional, lifelike images of people, particularly suspects, as well as missing persons.

Starting with a witness's basic description — man/woman, heavy-set/thin, dark-complected/light — she'd step by step add physical characteristics, including racial distinctions, the contour of the head, the size of the nose, the shape of the eyes and lips, the eyebrows and facial hair. Her computer held thousands of variations of faces that she could call up with a few clicks of the mouse.

She was such a technological whiz that Newbury was in awe, but what made her "the best" was the way she could pull information out of witnesses that they might not have even remembered at first. Kennedy's "amazing" assessment of the job she'd done creating a computer sketch of the mystery woman was par for the course.

However, she wasn't done. The variables she'd mentioned that morning in the DA's meeting room had been to add a wig and sunglasses to the image. Once again, she'd reached into her computer's files to locate short brunette wigs until Kennedy found the one he said was a perfect match. She'd then called up sunglasses — narrowing the choices to those similar to the description provided by Kennedy until, again, he spotted a pair he thought were the same the woman had worn.

She'd then applied them to the sketch and stood back smiling as Kennedy's jaw dropped. "That's her," he whispered. "That's the woman."

"Mrs. Stone, I'm ordering you to place the wig and sunglasses on your head," Rainsford said. "If you won't do it voluntarily, I'll ask court security to do it for you."

Stone's face contorted with rage, but she grabbed the wig and pulled it down onto her head, then shoved the glasses onto her face. "There," she snarled at Karp. "Are you happy?"

"Almost," said Karp, turning to Fulton, who was standing at the back of the courtroom. The detective pulled open one of the doors and nodded to someone standing outside. He then stepped back as Islay Kennedy entered and began walking down the aisle. However, the Irishman didn't get far before he looked at the witness stand and stopped.

"It's her," he shouted. "That's the woman! She's the one who came to my motel."

Karp raised his eyebrows as he turned back to Stone. "So, Mrs. Stone, are you sure you've been telling us the *whole* truth, as you have so self-righteously testified?"

Stone's face had turned white. Her jaw clenched as she stared at him full of anger and hatred. "I'm not answering any more questions, you chauvinist bastard."

Karp nodded and looked at Rainsford. "Your honor, you heard the lady, no further questions."

EPILOGUE

There was a moment of silence when the last notes of "Va, pensiero" faded into the recesses of the synagogue. Then the congregation was on its feet, clapping and voicing their appreciation for Giancarlo's contribution to the bar mitzvah ceremony.

Joining in the applause, Karp and Marlene turned to each other and smiled. "That's our boy," she whispered.

"Simply amazing," he replied.

Rabbi Hamilburg appeared, clapping along with the others until he made a motion for everyone to sit back down. "I think we all agree that was truly beautiful," he said. "Like listening to an angel. But we have one more presentation tonight, and so we must move on."

Karp glanced at the eight boys sitting in a row, the first six thirteen years old and then the two largest on the end, Giancarlo, and next to him, Zak. His "oldest" son looked nervous, but determined. His brother had offered to go last, only half kidding when he teased "so you don't have to follow me," but Zak had insisted on having the last word.

As the rabbi asked Zak to come forward, Karp thought about the change that had come over his son since their conversation not quite a year earlier when Zak wasn't sure about going through with his bar mitzvah. But a lot had changed since then.

After Stone's meltdown during his cross-examination, Mendelbaum had beseeched the judge to take an early lunch break so that she could pull herself together for redirect. "She's under a lot of stress," he told the judge as if it wasn't readily apparent.

Rainsford had looked at the witness, who was holding her head in both hands, and nodded. "We'll see everyone back here at one p.m."

The break served to calm Stone down. She now admitted that she'd carried on an affair with Salaam, but had been "too embarrassed to talk about my private life." She maintained that she didn't know about her lover's "other life."

The new attempt was so pathetic that Karp didn't bother to ask her any more questions. He'd point out the charade in his summation.

Mendelbaum had done his best during his summation, though it was something of a potpourri he asked the jury to consider. The possibility that Lars Forsling committed the murder. "After all, the district attorney thought he was a viable suspect." Or that Monroe and, possibly, Gallo, had conspired to kill Lubinsky. "It was the union that was being threatened by the charter school bill, not the Kings County District Attorney." And even that Salaam had been acting alone "knowing that his friends — Monroe and Stone — were concerned about the charter school bill and took it upon himself to kill its champion."

He noted that Stone had "laid herself bare" confessing to crimes, knowing it would cost her many years in prison and end her political aspirations. "But being a thief, an adulteress, and, quite frankly, a lousy district attorney who should have known better does not make her a murderer."

However, Karp had quickly dispatched the "other scenarios" by pointing out that there wasn't any evidence to back them up. "Only words, and words don't mean much when stacked up against the facts," he said. "Nor do the defendant's words that she was merely a thief mean much when all she's trying to do is avoid the full consequences of her actions."

Karp had then proceeded to build his case one last time, only now fitting each piece of the mosaic together where it belonged in the structure and showing how they inter-related. And he did so recalling Dirty Warren's movie trivia about John Quincy Adams's admonition to tell the better story. "It's a story," he told the jurors, "about the corrupting nature of power and the lust for what it can give someone who lacks the moral character to do the right thing when faced with temptation. It's a story with heroes like Rose Lubinsky, Goldie Sobelman, and even Micah Gallo, who turned back from the path he was on before it was too late. And there are villains — Lars Forsling, who showed us the dark side of hatred, and Yusef Salaam certainly. But also the people who used Salaam to their own ends."

Karp had walked slowly along the rail and looked each juror in the eyes. "But it will be up to you to write the final chapter. It's the chapter that you can go home and tell your friends, business colleagues, and family about when they ask you why you made the decision you did in this case. The chapter that says you examined the evidence and determined that the defendant was guilty of murder beyond any and all doubt. Only when you do that will this story come to a close. And that close occurs when the defendant understands that the trap she created for herself came about when she acted on the belief that she could steal, cheat, misappropriate, manipulate, and murder with impunity. By your verdict you will disabuse her of her delusional belief system."

Karp now turned to deal with the dying declaration issue. "You heard during the defense's summation, quite cleverly and ably explained by Mr. Mendelbaum, that his client is innocent and Lars Forsling is guilty because he said so as he lay dying. The trustworthiness of a dying declaration is based upon the notion of a shared value system of right and wrong, good and evil. The idea is that when facing death, God-fearing people will confess their sins. However, the more you heard about Mr. Lars Forsling from the witness Mr. LaFontaine, and what you heard and observed about Mr. LaFontaine, would it offend your common sense if I suggested to you that neither individual had a shared value system with us? And of course, given the context in which that statement by Mr. Forsling was made, the answer is they don't."

Karp then brought up what he called "the unholy alliance between the corrupt teachers federation administration and the public school system that it controlled. You heard the defendant in this case malign the charter schools by stating they are elitist and racist and basically private in nature. But like the rest of her testimony, of course, none of that is true. Rose Lubinsky on many occasions made it clear that charter schools are the salvation of children in inner cities, the minority neighborhoods of our town. Charter schools, she made clear, are public schools. They outperform substantially their failing and dangerous counterparts, the federation-controlled public schools. In order to ensure the expansion and continuation of the charter school movement, Rose Lubinsky had an important bill in the state assembly that this defendant and Monroe feared. And Rose Lubinsky was murdered because she was telling the truth about outstanding achievements of the charter schools, and threatened the power and the wealth of Monroe and Stone as well as the pathetically corrupt politicians they bought off to try and dissolve the charter school system at the expense of hundreds of thousands of children."

The jury had returned with its verdict after only three hours of deliberations. The defendant Olivia Stone saw the decision on their faces when they walked back into the courtroom for the last time and collapsed into her seat. She couldn't, or wouldn't, stand when Judge Rainsford asked the foreman how the jury found as to the charge of murder. "Guilty," he said over her sobs and pleas.

When it was over, the jury excused, the murderer led away to await sentencing, and the media had left the courtroom, Mendelbaum walked over to Karp and sighed. "I think it's time to take the shingle down."

"Why? You're still sharp as ever," Karp said. "The evidence was overwhelming, but you made us fight for it."

"Thank you, my friend," Mendelbaum said. "But it's not just losing the case, or even feeling like a dinosaur around all this computer talk. I don't know, the world has changed and I think not for the better. This one just left a bad taste in my mouth."

"Well, take some time to think it over," Karp said. "I'd miss doing battle with you."

"You'd miss my Snickers bars, you mean," the old man said, tossing one to Karp. "But

I'm going to go visit my daughter and grandchildren down in Florida. Maybe I'll just stay there. Either way I'll let you know."

In the fall, Karp had driven with Marlene and the boys to Albany for a session of the state assembly. There Micah Gallo revealed what Simon Lubinsky had passed to him from his wife. "It's the speech she was going to give," Gallo said, pulling the sheaf of papers from the manila envelope. "How she'd known I'd come around and give it for her, I don't know. I guess she had more faith in me than I had in myself."

"She was a great judge of character," Simon said.

Gallo gave the speech and closed with "those are the words of Rose Lubinsky. I am just the messenger she chose and a poor one at that. I'm also a convicted felon, allowed out of prison for this purpose, and I'll be returning for at least two more years. My sentence has been long and difficult, but it's not as long and difficult as the sentence we are handing down to the children if we don't seek every opportunity to improve the state of education. So I'm asking you to pass the Rose Lubinsky Charter School Fairness Act on their behalf."

Gallo had received a standing ovation

from the members of the state assembly. As he prepared to be driven back to a minimum security prison, he turned to shake Karp's hand. "Thanks for the letter you sent the judge," he said. "I think that's the reason I got the minimum."

"You did the right thing, Micah," Karp said. "I was happy to do it. So, what do you plan on doing when you get out?"

Gallo shrugged. "I won't be able to get back into teaching with a felony on my record. But maybe something with disadvantaged kids. Something that would make Rose proud."

"I think she already is . . ."

A month later, Karp had felt his own sense of pride watching his sons at long last chant the words from the Torah and take that symbolic step into Jewish manhood. There'd remained just one more task and that was the special presentations each boy had been asked to do.

As expected, Giancarlo had sung beautifully. But Karp wondered when the rabbi asked Zak to step forward and his son sat still for a moment.

Then his son rose and walked to the spot where Rose Lubinsky had stood when she told the congregation her story. His head was down and he seemed to be searching for the words Karp had heard him practicing the night before. He looked up and found his parents in the audience, then Moishe and Goldie Sobelman, and finally Simon Lubinsky.

"I am a Jew and proud of it," he said, and tapped his chest. "I feel it in here and I have my parents, my brother, and Rose Lubinsky to thank for it. Now let me tell you a story about two other Jewish heroes who made a difference in my life, Moishe and Goldie Sobelman . . ."

ABOUT THE AUTHOR

Robert K. Tanenbaum is one of the country's most respected and successful trial lawyers and has never lost a felony case. He has held such prestigious positions as Bureau Chief of the New York Criminal Courts and Chief of the Homicide Bureau for the New York District Attorney's Office. He was also Deputy Chief Counsel for the congressional committee investigations into the assassinations of President John F. Kennedy and Reverend Dr. Martin Luther King, Jr. For several years he taught Advanced Criminal Procedure at his alma mater, the University of California at Berkeley, Boalt Hall School of Law. His previous works include the novels *Tragic*, *Bad Faith*, *Outrage*, *Betrayed*, and the true crime book *Echoes of My Soul*.